THE HIGHEST

The *Vladimir Komarov's* groundtrack passed the crater Kopff on the wide floor of Mare Orientale, and they lost the signal from Earth. They had an hour to themselves on board until the orbit brought them round the eastern limb of the Moon over Near Side again north of Mare Smythii. An hour of silence.

"Just had a funny thought," Vitali Raisman said, letting go of the handgrip and floating free from the panel of the computer post. "We've really caught the Americans on the wrong foot this time, haven't we? And it's their presidential election next year, and the one who's in the office at the moment will be getting the blame for letting this happen, won't he? So do you realize what we've done, just we five Russians? *We* have just decided their election for them. Makes you think, doesn't it?"

It did.

The *Vladimir Komarov* fell effortlessly in a circle round the Moon, passing Maunder as it crossed the face of Mare Orientale. Ahead waited the terminator and the shadow side. No sun, no light of Earth, just stars and the dark bulk of the Moon turning sightless at your shoulder.

They circled into night.

About the Author

David Mace was born in Sheffield. He is the
author of three internationally published
novels: *Demon-4*, *Nightrider* and *Fire Lance*.
He and his wife live in Lancaster.

The Highest Ground

David Mace

CORONET BOOKS
Hodder and Stoughton

First published in Great Britain in 1988 by New English Library hardbacks

Coronet edition 1989

Printed and bound in Great Britain for Hodder and Stoughton paperbacks, a division of Hodder and Stoughton Ltd., Mill Road, Dunton Green, Sevenoaks, Kent TN13 2YA (Editorial Office: 47 Bedford Square, London WC1B 3DP) by Richard Clay Ltd., Bungay, Suffolk.

British Library C.I.P.

Mace, David, *1951–*
   The highest ground.
   I. Title
   823'.914[F]

ISBN 0-340-50704-7

For Wilf and Mary, my parents.

Acknowledgments

Two ideas mentioned several times in this novel are entirely the invention of Arthur C. Clarke. He proposed the use of communications satellites in geosynchronous orbits, nowadays a reality and sometimes known as Clarke orbits, in a paper "Extraterrestrial Relays" (*Wireless World*, October, 1945) and developed the concept of an electrically powered launcher in a paper "Electromagnetic Launching as a Major Contribution to Space Flight" (*Journal of the British Interplanetary Society*, November, 1950). The gross perversion of these ideas to become battle stations and railguns could not be further from Clarke's peaceful intentions.

I would like to thank the following people for their contributions towards the writing of this book: Wilfred K. Mace, for technical assistance in certain crucial matters; Paul and Julie Holmes, for supplying some essential details of the American way of life; Leslie Flood, for pointing out the ideal firearm for the airless environment of the Moon.

Departures from fact, either error or invention, are entirely my own responsibility.

David Mace
Freiburg im Breisgau

1 INAUGURATION

That was back in 1985, during the winter, the day the Arctic came to Washington. Maybe it came for the Inauguration Show.

The official day, Part One of the show, had fallen on a Sunday, when you can't parade in God-fearing Washington DC. But you can't inaugurate a triumphantly re-elected president without a parade, so they thought up Part Two and scheduled it for the Monday. There would be a giant procession through central Washington, and then a public re-run of the Sunday ceremony and the inaugural speech, this time on a huge podium before an actual audience of tens of thousands and a TV audience of tens of millions. All it cost was a vast outlay of public monies and private fortunes.

But then the cold came rolling down like an occupying army and took unchallenged possession of the streets. The giant open stand, complete with bullet-proof transparent walls, was heated like some overgrown turtle tank. Up there in a ring of cameras, the ceremony re-take would be staged complete with all the Sunday participants, plus a speech full of homilies and other perceptive promises of a permanent summer yet to come. But the heating would be no protection against that appalling iciness which had swept frail little human beings from sight. It was an utterly unusual cold of Arctic intensity, and literally lethal. Suddenly the boys and girls couldn't be allowed outside to parade in their costume colors, while the president's advisers feared something even worse than just the bad press of good wholesome teenage idolizers dying all along the route in their flimsy parade costumes and majorette tights. They feared that the acutely geriatric star of the production number at the focus of the whole extravaganza might himself not survive the performance, might collapse amid a cast of thousands. And that live, and coast-to-coast.

So Inauguration Two was canceled, and a pointlessly

minuscule reprise, edited down to the oath and speech and shorn of all the razzmatazz, was held indoors before the media's cameras and a selected audience of air-conditioned dignitaries. While in hotels, motels and barracks all over Washington city, good wholesome all-American teenagers, who'd studied, saved and prayed during a long warm year for this greatest of days, were weeping in despair and pounding their pillows in furious tantrums.

The barrier-lined avenues were empty, the rows of grandstands useless. It was even too cold to begin tearing them down. No one ventured out into that Arctic desert who didn't have to. A winter wind sovereign swept the streets.

The restaurant was quiet, just a susurrus of voices hovering softly in the air as lunchtime patrons talked, dined, did business discreet and subdued. The bar was half filled with lazier lunch-breakers taking their time before moving through to their reserved tables. The windows looked down on the center of a capital city laid waste by a thinly murderous wind. Such a pity about the show.

A waiter was leading Rosemary Maclaughlin across the bar to Hyland's table by the windows. Hyland rose to shake her hand. She tossed her hair in a little I-have-arrived gesture as the waiter seated her. Her hair was blonde, and she was wearing it in a long pageboy blow-dried generously out to the sides. She crossed her legs, right over left and lightly. Her skirt reached down over her knee to the rim of her boot. A career woman of thirty, attractive and not at all instantly steel hard. In her ears she wore tiny pearl studs on pink flower-petal surrounds.

She pulled a tissue out of her purse and dabbed at her nose.

"It's so *cold*. I only had to go from the cab to the door. All the way up in the elevator my nose was streaming. It isn't like this in Houston, let me tell you."

"It isn't like this in Washington in a regular January." Hyland's voice was summer warm to match the brown of his skin color. He glanced at the waiter, still waiting. "Rosemary, would you like a drink?"

"Ah – yes." She stuffed the folded up tissue into her purse. "A Grasshopper."

"Okay. And I'll have a martini. Dry."

The waiter went.

Hyland straightened his suit. Once you've made it so far in the white man's world that you can sit around expensive restaurants in perfect blue suits, you have to keep them straight. Nowadays it was turning into an automatic gesture – a wriggle into the back of the chair, a neat little pull on the bottoms of the long lapels, and everything just dandy.

"Joseph, isn't it?" Rosemary Maclaughlin was watching him with very steady eyes, bright blue-gray eyes. "State representative up in Seattle. Where Boeing builds its airplanes. I'm told you're getting well known in the aerospace lobby – out of state, even."

Joseph Hyland nodded. "I'm going to run for Congress. The timing's just exactly right, with the Star Wars contracts due to start rolling." He smiled. A very knowing smile.

"Aha." An entirely unexpected invitation to lunch had to have an ulterior motive, of course. But if he was playing lonely hotel rooms in Washington, he was wasting his time. She had her flight back to Houston booked for four-thirty, out of the cold and away from the inaugural fiasco. "Shouldn't you be entertaining someone from the Government? Or the Pentagon?"

"Oh, but they're all tied up with the indoor show right now. People like you and me get left out in the cold. We have to look out for ourselves. Right?"

"Right." He was still on her own side of forty and a handsome enough guy, though, if a little stiff and over-polished – as if his shoes and his suit and his body had all been pressed out of a single mold. "With the go-ahead on the space station safe now the president's back for his second term, my chief wanted our team strongly represented on the stands around the podium."

"Among the NASA extras."

"The NASA extras, exactly. It was okay with the White House to have another woman in the crowd of faces – they keep running into that anti-feminist image. So here I am." Across the bar, the waiter was coming with the drinks on a tray and with menus tucked under his arm. "And then here I'm not, because they moved inside with the genuine VIPs."

"My fate as well. Just another background black to keep the racial balance respectable. Rosemary, you're not only involved in design studies for the lead work on the space station. You were also at the symposium in the fall."

"The Symposium on Lunar Bases, yes." So it was going to be straight business, then. When a girl works for NASA and gets involved in studies for costly proposals in manned spaceflight, she soon gets used to the fact that dinner daters and lunchtime suitors are going to be angling for inside information and influence. It's reassuring and much more useful. It helps you strengthen yourself. "You're well informed, Joseph Hyland."

Hyland shrugged. "I pick my contacts carefully."

The drinks and the menus arrived. Hyland put his menu aside on the low table, in no hurry to order, so she closed her menu and did the same.

Instead she picked up her cocktail and sipped it. "And you want to turn me into a contact?" A little dab of lipstick had come off on the rim of the glass. Damn. She'd have to watch she didn't smear her image. Before the men will treat you as an equal you have to be twice as good and twice as well turned out. "Might I ask with what end in view?"

Joseph Hyland smiled expansively, a studied flash of teeth between pink-brown lips. "The promotion of common interest, Rosemary."

"The common interest being namely?"

"Space." He tipped his head and eyed her sort of sideways, a party-trick look to counter her own carefully steady gaze. "Space. The only unlimited room for expansion there is left."

Political expansion. Economic expansion. Big business for the aerospace industries. The never-ending pull of a perfect vacuum.

He sipped his drink, and then put on a serious face over his glass. The hand holding the stem wore a wedding ring, plain gold on brown skin. Men are allowed to marry and still keep their careers. "Rosemary, do you believe in space – in man in space – or is it just a job, a career?"

She shrugged. "It's a career, that's for sure. But not just a career. Let's say I didn't apply for a position with NASA because I really just wanted to engineer fancy new air systems or garbage incinerators. Sure, up there in space they have to be a new kind and they have to fit together in whole new ways, but it's what you get in the end that counts. And that's people up there seeing the most magical sight there is – the Earth from space. So yes, I believe in it. Do you?"

He nodded. "Ever since I was a kid. Ever since. Then it was a romantic dream. Now it's a goal I can actively promote. And being on the political side of the aerospace lobby gives me certain advantages, which I intend to use."

"To what end?"

"Rosemary, I want to introduce a concept and see how far we can take it. I want an exploitation of the coming situation. I want it right in from the start. I want maximum results."

He seemed to be keeping the lid on some genuine passion, some sublimation of a childhood lust for pioneering adventure. Something like that. "You want to form a company?"

Hyland flapped his hand, a hasty dismissal of a hopelessly distracting idea. "I want to introduce a *concept* for the utilization of space. Something that keeps the ball rolling and keeps the frame of reference opened out beyond just the military exploitation. I want something powerful to – something to balance up the Pentagon's concept of the SDI, the High Frontier." He frowned intensely, putting paler vertical furrows into the center of his forehead. "Something to keep the civil side, the peaceful side, alive. So we don't just go up there, point our guns down at the Earth, and stay with our backs turned on it all for ever."

Rosemary took her glass in both hands and turned it by the stem in her fingers, slowly round and round. Here was a man with a mission, maybe. Be careful, be cool, but be clever. "Well – I'd have to admit an awful lot of us at NASA aren't entirely happy with the military emphasis. We're working up for a space station. It's our baby, it's the obvious next step in space. But what's really going to carry it now is the Pentagon. Sure, the money will be mostly budgeted direct through NASA, and the station's primary activities timewise will be civil. Science, Earth applications, industrial. Things like that. But the Pentagon will always have first call on the entire space facility when and how they want it. That's the way the White House is working. That's the deal – in effect NASA works for the Department of Defense, or there's no money. It's even worse than the Shuttle program. It's not a bit like the motivation for Apollo way back then." Way back then. Not much more than a decade ago when the Apollo Program ended. You were still at high school. "A lot of people might be very pleased if you happened to know a way to pull funding for manned spaceflight on a purely civil basis. Do you happen to?"

Hyland pursed his lips. "We have to face facts. In space every goddam thing is so incredibly expensive. The only way to get funding for it in this world is by pulling the military handle. Civil spaceflight is really only still in the deal because the High Frontier, the SDI thing, is all automated technology all covered by defense secrecy. There'll be nothing all nice and shining to show on TV for all the taxpayers' money, so you have to put people up there, too. Politically, you need pictures of happy astronauts bouncing around in space. Right?"

"Well I guess so. It's a part of it."

"So if we wanted to get a space commitment that grows so big it takes on a momentum all of its own, what we really have to pull is that military handle. Because when you pull that handle, the jackpot comes pouring out into industry. *Then* the political feedback works and it keeps on pouring. The money doesn't stop."

"Political feedback like the aerospace lobby?"

"Aerospace and damn near all the defense-related frontier technologies. Ever since his Star Wars speech, they've been holding their breath on the president getting his second term. The word is that the Strategic Defense Initiative means contracts for thirty years. And what contracts! Billions! Industry wants it, and they're going to pull every political trick they know to get it. Billions and billions of dollars for thirty years. But then what happens after the bonanza? Nothing."

Rosemary shrugged. "There's always the Moon. Given the political commitment, we could see that underway in twenty to thirty years. Once a base is established up there, you have to maintain it. And the only cost-effective way to maintain it is to *expand* it, so they can start producing their own materials up there instead of shipping everything all the way from Earth. Gravitationally that's a long way uphill, you know. That's one awful lot of fuel and energy. That's the true cost of space."

"Not enough." Hyland shook his head emphatically. "Good sense once you're there, but to go for the Moon you've got to have a *reason* to go there. National prestige won't do, that's for sure. It took us there with Apollo Eleven in sixty-nine, but we didn't stay. You have to pull that military handle."

"I thought you were against the military emphasis?"

"Oh I am. But like I said, we have to face facts. We have to figure out where the money's going to come from, then we let that serve our own intentions. We need a huge space commitment that pulls our side of things along in its wake. That's the way you're going to get your space station, that's also the way we're going to get the bigger thing. Even the Moon. And once we're *there*, and once our presence on the Moon is expanding halfway towards a colony to back up the *strategic* job we fooled them into going there for, Rosemary –" He was leaning forward now, glass back on the little table, both hands clasped tightly together. "*Then* we have something that's going to run for ever because the investment's been so high. We've built something that's going to go on independent of any temporary strategic fashion for putting fancy weapons into space. We got it made."

She looked away from the man for a moment, letting her gaze sweep across the bar area and out into the lunchtime restaurant. The swell of voices was rising gently in there, time was passing, her appetite was rising. She looked at the leather-bound menu lying beside her cocktail glass. She looked at the little lipstick stain on the rim of the glass. He was waiting for her to join his conspiracy. She was expected to count herself in before he would tell her what it was. "This – ah – concept to get the whole ball rolling. Maybe get us to the Moon after all. What would that be?"

"Easy," he said, sitting back again. He smiled, he tugged his jacket straight. He planted both brown hands on the arms of his chair. "What's the idea behind Star Wars, the Strategic Defense Initiative? Not that fiction about an impenetrable roof to make nuclear weapons down here redundant. Everyone but the president knows you can't build a roof that would keep out all the Soviet warheads. Right? So what's the strategic concept?"

"Partial defense? If the Soviets would attack, they'd lose too many of their weapons on the way over to be able to destroy our missiles and our command structure. So we could guarantee to hit them back so hard after they'd already thrown all their weapons at us, that they'd never dare to try it."

"Exactly. A sword and a shield, instead of just a sword. The problem, though, is that if we build ourselves a shield, all that's going to happen is that they build themselves one as well. And then we're back to the same old balance of terror."

"Sure – if Moscow could afford it. We don't even know if *we* can afford it. But if we can and they can –" She rummaged through her memory in search of an expression for what she meant. "There was some general already called space the strategic high ground of the future, wasn't there? Well then, if we and the Soviets can *both* afford it, at least we'll be up there with them on the high ground."

"We will. True. But it isn't the highest ground. I don't know whether the Soviet economy could stretch itself to match an anti-missile screen in space. But they don't have to. And now *this* is the point. If you can destroy a significant number of missiles from orbiting battle stations, what's happening? Several thousand warheads, attacking in low paths from one point to the other on Earth, are being taken out by several hundred weapons orbiting on higher paths where they can get enough of a view to see what's going on right below them. Now how do you stop that defense working against those missiles? What do you do, so you can launch an attack that gets through?"

"What do I know? Harden the missiles or something?"

"No need. You put up several dozen of your own weapons in higher orbits. They can take out the several hundred battle stations in lower orbits, that would otherwise take out several thousand of your missiles on their way from launch to target down on the Earth. That's the high-tech *cheap* option."

Hyland looked at her in quiet triumph. "That's a matter of obvious logic and the simplest practicality."

"But —" But what, exactly? Surely the task of knocking out a few hundred battle stations circling in perfectly predictable and highly visible orbits just had to be easier. Orders of magnitude easier than trying to thin out thousands of missiles all skimming at once along short and unique trajectories from the Soviet Union to the United States. It would be child's play by comparison. "And no one's thought of this before?"

"I'm sure they have. But they're sure as hell not saying a word. They don't exactly want to get their SDI declared a total illusion before the Government starts flinging the money around."

"I guess they wouldn't. And the whole time you can keep on going higher and higher, putting one countermeasures screen out behind another, step by step for ever. I mean, any orbit you are, there's always some higher ground. There's no *highest* ground."

"Oh, but in practice there is. Isn't there?" Hyland reached for his menu, stood up and extended his hand to help a lady rise. A warm, brown hand. "Rosemary, let's get planning over our meal."

Outside, the white and icy Arctic wind held on to Washington.

2 ACROSS THE SKY

1 Tyuratam

Outside the sun dazzled the Cosmodrome at Tyuratam. A shimmering breeze rolled slowly in from the steppe, a dry and steady prairie breeze that teased up dust from empty expanses between the eighty launch pads, a hot and lazy furnace breath that bowled along the baking roadways and sun-struck railtracks. Outside and far away, tiny cars and trucks and service vehicles crawled the vast web that laced together the towers and pads and sheds and bunkers. Outside, just outside, the breeze caught the boiling vapor emissions from the insulated tanks and pulled their vanishing condensation streams into inconstant fluttering banners. It came from the northeast, that breeze, leaving the sun-scorched heart of Kazakhstan and heading thirstily for the Aral Sea. On the way it drank oxygen and hydrogen. Through the docking window above his head he could see the evaporation plume from the oxygen tank licking across the roof of the lander, gasping and dispersing, a perpetual disappearance into nothing at all.

Not nothing at all. It was air out there, hot, parched, summer-stunned air going all the way up to that perfect blue sighted by the crosswire range markings on the docking window. No daring space mission this, out beyond the secure envelope of the atmosphere. Just two Earth-bound cosmonauts on the ground.

"Bloody wind," Vladimir Ivanov said again. "Suddenly there's a bloody wind."

"Breeze," said Tsherbakov's voice over their earphones. He was sitting with Raisman and the monitor team six hundred metres away in the bunker. "Gusting up to twenty kilometres an hour."

They had an anemometer over there on the roof of the bunker. They had anemometers all over the expanse of the

Tyuratam field, twirling round and measuring the windspeed. All they didn't have was the breathlessly stifling morning the forecast had promised them. And for the takeoff, only for the takeoff in this risky machine, you needed stagnant air. Not a movement to shake or tip it.

"Bloody breeze, then," Vladimir said, turning his head in search of sympathy.

Leonid shrugged, and tipped his head back again to look through the cross-sights of the little window and up into the fathomless sky. Leonid Steffanovich Shalyapin, aged forty-two and married with two children, a civilian and a senior cosmonaut, Soviet shuttle pilot and mission commander, a Soyuz veteran who has since flown shuttles clean through the sky a dozen times and is now on the training shortlist for Mars – grounded by a breeze. It was a little frustrating. And with every second, more of the incredibly cold liquid hydrogen fuel and more of the almost as cold liquid oxygen oxidant boiled away through the vents from the insulated tanks, and soon there wouldn't be enough left on board to sustain the lander through its short familiarization flight, and they'd have to cancel, and the whole complicated and weary business of preparation since first light would be for nothing, would have gone up in smoke. Gone up in vapor, conjured away by a hot little wind that had breezed in from nowhere. "How much longer have we got?"

"At this evaporation rate?" Vladimir studied the readouts on the copilot's panel. "About three minutes."

And then they would have to call it off, shut down the vehicle's flight systems, and let the ground crew siphon off what was left of the oxidant and fuel before even that was lost to the morning air. And the rim of the seat was digging into his back, so he lowered his head and stared instead out through the forward window at the bunker with its roof full of instruments across the far side of the concrete apron. They just had frame seats with nylon strapping in the lander, a comfortable way to take your ease in the one-third surface gravity on Mars. They didn't need the seats for lander flight – the main engine pulled exactly one gee at one hundred per cent power, giving you your Earth normal weight. That would be enough to get down to and back up from the surface of Mars. To lift off here they would have to throttle through to one hundred and ten per cent. At one hundred per cent they would merely hover.

"Still air on the eastern perimeter," Tsherbakov's voice reported in their ears.

"We might be lucky after all," Raisman's voice added. "Stand by for ignition."

They'd been standing by for almost fifteen minutes. All they had to do was press the buttons. There was no count-down on this exercise, not even computer guidance, not even a flight path to follow. All the lander's computer had to do was control the actuators that gimbaled the main engine in its mounting, sending a stream of instructions to vector the direction of thrust slightly off vertical in any direction to counteract any tendency of the machine to tip out of a precisely horizontal attitude. The lander was inherently un-stable, balancing on a point of flame under its belly, and any small tipping tendency had to be caught and corrected instantly before the thing flipped over and drove itself head down into the ground. That was why they had to have still air for takeoff. Air moving along the ground is turbulent, and if an air movement tipped the vehicle slightly the com-puter would vector thrust to correct, sending it traveling sideways and losing height, risking a collision with the ground that might be hard enough to wreck it. And you didn't want that to happen, because it was one of the only two production models they had beyond the prototypes, and writing it off or even damaging it seriously enough might delay the Mars launch for a year, waiting for the next available start window. And of course it had two lives inside, plus several thousand litres of propellant that was horrendously explosive once mixed.

They had no ejector seats. Those were too heavy for the stripped down machine in full Earth gravity and besides, when they'd been tried out on a flying test bed, the kick of the first one had tipped the thing so steeply that the second had gone off horizontally and slammed straight into the ground. They had no parachutes. There was the round dock-ing hatch in the ceiling and the metre-high access door in the side wall behind Vladimir's seat, and you couldn't get out through either of those quickly. Nor could you use a parachute at all of fifty metres.

It wasn't a test flight, after all. Vitali Raisman and Pyotr Grishin had test-flown the Mars lander all of a month ago. The idea this morning was to take the thing up to fifty metres and hold it there, to get used to hovering it and to moving it backwards and forwards and sideways, to get used to rotating it, all by using the little clusters of attitude motors mounted on the four corners of the machine. That was all. But you had to know what you were doing before you could land on Mars. They would have three hundred seconds of fuel so that each of them could play with the lander in the air.

"Windspeed five and falling," said Tsherbakov's voice.

Leonid Shalyapin was the only civilian cosmonaut playing with the lander today, although there were five on the shortlist of pilots, engineers and scientists training for the mission. Vladimir Ivanov was a lieutenant colonel, as was Andrei Tsherbakov. Vitali Raisman was a full colonel. Tsherbakov was also on the cosmonaut strength of the State Committee on Space Defense. But they all looked the same at work at Tyuratam in their flight overalls. Leonid and Vladimir wore white caps fastened under their chins, with built-in headphones and little microphone booms. Both strapped into their frame-and-webbing seats and ready to go.

"Windspeed two and falling."

"We'll try it," said Raisman's voice. "If we miss this we'll stand down."

"We're ready," Leonid said. He put his hand on the right control stick, the main engine throttle. The left control was the four-way snap stick and trigger for the attitude motors. "Start the pump."

Vladimir pressed the starter switch. In the space below and behind the cramped little crew cabin, the electric motor driven by the batteries started to spin the fuel pump. The batteries were designed to maintain the vehicle for fifteen days on the surface of Mars – they could run the pump for almost a minute.

The lander was an ugly thing. Its main body was rectangular and contained the two spherical hydrogen tanks with the main engine between them. On each side were mountings for a payload pallet, one to carry a four-wheel rover and one to carry instruments for use on the surface. The upper level had the oxygen sphere housing in the middle, the battery and systems housing at the rear, and the crew space at the front – room for three people to sleep in hammocks, to eat, and to avoid each others' elbows. The lander stood on four legs splayed out from its corners. It would take three people – half the mission crew – down to the surface to work at one site, bring them up again, refuel from the mother ship in orbit, and take the other three down to a second site and bring them back, too. Then it would be left parked in Mars orbit. The whole mission was due to go next summer. It would last a total of fifteen months, there and back, two and a half spent at Mars. By the time it returned the second mother ship would have been built and would be ready to go. And the Americans didn't even have a concept for a Mars mission.

"Windspeed zero."

"Go if you want to," Raisman said.

"We'll go." The fuel and oxidant levels were right down to the red line. "Open the pump feed valve."

"Open," Vladimir said. The two-line valve let the pump's secondary rotor suck fuel mix through into the turbochamber.

"Ignite."

"Ignited." The mix burned, the exhaust gas drove the turbine that turned the pump, and the starter motor was no longer necessary. "Turbo on. Starter out."

"Open main valve." And then the pump's main rotor could suck litres of propellant mix every second out of the tanks and force it into the combustion chamber.

"Open. Locked to throttle."

Leonid pushed the throttle gently to keep the propellant coming. It was all like the ancient pioneer days, the books he read as a boy, doing it manually instead of having a computer run it. "Ignition."

"Ignition."

The hydrogen flame roared at them, scorching the concrete beneath the lander. He pushed the throttle out to fifty per cent. A glance out of the side window at the flickering geyser of furnace-hot air. No smoke, barely even light from a hydrogen flame. "How's windspeed?"

"Windspeed zero," said Tsherbakov's voice.

Leonid pushed the throttle through to one hundred per cent, and there was nothing but inertia holding the lander on the ground. A single breath would push it sideways. The thrust meter was perfectly steady, not even flickering. "Going through to one hundred and five." He tipped the throttle further.

Thrust came smoothly up to one hundred and five per cent. Very gently, very gently indeed, the lander began to come up off the ground.

"Contact lights out," Vladimir reported. "Landing pads clear."

"Going through to one hundred and ten." That was all the power they had. In free fall it would have accelerated the lander at a rate of eleven metres per second every second.

She came up a little faster, leaving the scorched ground, her clumsy shadow sliding out in front of her. Lifting into the air.

The three-way attitude axes in the center screen on his panel were steady, no rotation, pitch or roll. The view through the window above the screen didn't matter. They had clear airspace for kilometres around. Just those attitude axes. If the computer got it wrong and let the lander tip more than fifteen degrees, there was no way the attitude control thrusters could level it again against the combined leverage of the main engine thrust and the gravitational pull of the Earth. They would flip over and power into the ground.

"Ten metres," Vladimir said. "One per second up. Radar altimeter now on. Twenty metres. Three per second up. Twenty-five metres. Four per second up."

Accelerating slowly. Exactly level. Main engine thrust at exactly one hundred and ten per cent.

"Thirty-five metres. Six per second up."

Lateral drift. The ground was slipping sideways out there,

the lander's detached shadow migrating southwest. They'd risen into wind but were high enough for it not to matter.

"Fifty metres. Eight per second up."

Leonid pulled the throttle back to eighty per cent to take off their upward velocity. Fifty metres was their hover altitude.

But the thrust readout stayed at one hundred and ten per cent.

"Sixty metres. Sixty-five metres. Ten per second up. Throttle back."

"I have."

Raisman's voice: "Leonid, throttle back. You're going too high."

"I have throttled back. To eighty. Reading is still one hundred and ten."

"Ninety metres," Vladimir said. "Twelve per second up. I read thrust at one hundred and ten, main valve fully open."

"The throttle's locked." Leonid took it down to fifty per cent. The thrust readout stayed at one hundred and ten. "The control isn't jammed but the setting's locked. Try manual. Close the valve one tenth."

Vladimir turned the control on his panel that activated the valve directly, edged it round one tenth of its free turn.

Thrust stayed at one hundred and ten.

"Main valve jammed," Vladimir said flatly. He went on turning the manual control quickly back and forth. "Jammed fully open."

They were climbing into the sky. Perfectly level, the lander was stubbornly ascending under maximum thrust. The valve wouldn't close so the propellant feed to the main engine couldn't be reduced, so the thrust couldn't be cut back below maximum. It would go on up and up until the propellant gave out after a full three hundred seconds of burn. Then the lander would plummet to the ground and destroy itself. And them.

How can you stop it?

Raisman's voice: "You're seven hundred and fifty high. We have your ascent rate at sixteen per second."

The bunker was so far away down there, just visible over the window rim and sinking. Tyuratam was opening up, a vista of roadways and railtracks, launch pads and support complexes. Twenty kilometres away – that was this week's shuttle on the pad. He wasn't going to fly one of those any more.

"Nine hundred metres," Vladimir said. "Seventeen per second up. Valve still jammed open."

How can you stop it? The turbo-pump is a constant speed mechanism, powered by exhaust gases from the pump feed line. You can't throttle the power to the turbo-chamber, just switch it on or off with the tiny valve. The only control of thrust is the main valve, the amount of propellant it lets the pump sluice through to the main engine's combustion chamber. Combustion is self-sustaining as long as fresh pro- pellant keeps coming. You can only stop the burn by closing the main valve or by stopping the pump and so cutting off the propellant supply. But the valve is jammed at full and the lander hurtling into the sky.

"Eleven hundred metres. Seventeen per second up. Valve still jammed. Seventeen per second? Is thrust coming off? Still reads a hundred and ten."

"Air resistance," said Raisman's voice. "Drag balancing your one metre per second net acceleration."

"Thrust still one hundred and ten," Leonid said, not listening to himself. This is death. This one is going to kill you. There is no way to cut back the thrust, to make the lander hover and then let it sink slowly under control. It will go on up until the propellant is exhausted, then fall. All you can do is stop the pump, kill the engine, and let it happen straight away.

How can you *stop* it?

"Fourteen hundred metres. Seventeen up. Valve still jammed. Leonid? What do we do? There's still two hundred seconds of propellant. That'll take us to – about five thousand metres."

"Four thousand eight hundred." All just mental arithme- tic. And at four thousand eight hundred metres the engine will cut and the lander will fall. Fall for how long? For thirty-one seconds – can do that in your head. Hit the ground how fast? At three hundred and ten metres a second, about the speed of sound. No, there's air resistance. The lander's as aerodynamic as a brick. Terminal velocity will be way under that, stretching the time of the fall by half as much again. But it will still kill you.

How can you stop it?

Just stop the pump and cut the engine and get it over with. Stop the pump?

"Seventeen hundred metres. Seventeen up. What do we do, Leonid?" Vladimir's voice was flat. But his face was bloodless.

Raisman: "We're working on it. Some of the designers are right here, don't forget. Try working the throttle and the manual together."

"All right. Leonid – push to full open."

He pushed the throttle to full.

"Hard back to zero – now!"

He snapped it back.

Thrust one hundred and ten.

"No good. Nineteen hundred metres. Seventeen up. One hundred and seventy seconds propellant."

Tsherbakov: "They're drifting over the perimeter."

Raisman: "You're drifting out over the south perimeter."

Tiny down there, the multiple fence-line stretched away in front of them. On its south side were wheat fields, still summer green. Through them ran a grid of irrigation channels taking water from the Syrdarya river. Far away south, towards the river, was the rail link from Kzyl-Orda to Novo-kazalinsk, cutting out the lazy meanders, taking the quick way. Like straight down.

They would die in a scatter of multi-million-rouble scrap in a wheatfield on a collective. Fitting end for heroes.

"Two thousand one hundred. Seventeen up. One hundred and fifty seconds propellant. Leonid? Is there anything we can *do*?"

Stop the pump and fall. Can you start it again *fast* enough?

"Leonid? Is there anything?"

Leonid took hold of the left control, the snap-stick directing the attitude thrusters, the tiny jets that tipped the machine around its own axis.

Raisman: "We're still working on it."

Leonid pushed the throttle back to full, just to be sure. "Close the pump feed valve."

"What?"

"Close the pump feed valve. Stop the pump."

"We're at two thousand two-fifty. If –"

"Close the valve at two thousand three hundred. Makes the calculation easier."

"But –"

"Do it! Do it, man!"

"All right! At two thousand three. All right. Coming up. Coming up. Coming up. Now!"

The roar of the hydrogen flame stopped.

His stomach came up into his chest, the hip belt held him to the seat. Weightless and falling. They were falling.

"Main engine out." Vladimir almost whispered it.

The lander, the aerodynamic brick with legs and with things on its back, was falling. Wobbling. The three axes in the center screen started to tip. He snapped the left-hand control around, firing tiny bursts from the attitude thrusters. Had to keep it level. Whatever else, it *had* to stay level enough for the next burn. "Open the pump feed valve."

Vladimir was staring down out of the forward window. The ground still seemed so far away. But the altitude readout was rippling down.

He had enough with the stability and with the calculation checking over and over in his head. "We're restarting the pump. Open the pump feed valve!"

Vladimir jerked his head. Then turned the switch.

"Start the pump."

Vladimir pressed the starter motor switch. No sound of the motor over the windrush. The lander was bucking and wobbling.

"Ignite." And the ground was coming.

"Ignited. Turbo on. Starter out. Main ignition?"

"At one thousand four hundred. Call the altitude." The ground was growing. All those wheat fields. No chance to check it through again. And the pump is sucking cold propellant through the engine.

"Altitude one thousand six. Ignition at one-four? Now one thousand five. One-four-fifty. Ignition!"

The hydrogen flame roared. They had weight. The thrust reading jumped right to one hundred and ten. So the valve was still jammed wide open. Just like it had to be.

And she's level. The computer is gimbaling the main engine and holding her level as she falls, as she fights at full power to brake that fall. As the ground comes closer.

"One thousand metres. Nine-fifty. Nine hundred."

Without control over thrust you have to juggle with control over burn duration, distance and velocity. That's a horrible thing to do instantly in your head. You use intuition, not calculus or a computer's incrementals. And in eight or nine seconds you'll find out if you were right.

"Six hundred. I think we'll still hit. Five hundred."

Raisman's voice: "You look good. You might make it."

The wheat fields are coming up. A sea of pallid green stalks in the breeze. Here comes the lander's shadow to meet them. "Get a rescue helicopter out to us. Fire tenders. Anything."

Raisman: "We're doing that."

"Two hundred. One-fifty at sixty down." Vladimir grabbed the corners of his control panel.

Leonid fired the attitude jets vertically down. Too little thrust and far too late, but try. The shadow comes sweeping over the green to meet them.

"Ninety at fifty down."

The dusty green wheat waves welcome. The shadow sharpens on it, ripples over it.

"Forty at thirty down."

Soil between the stalks.

"Ten metres. We —"

The seat slammed his spine. His hands ripped from the control levers and smashed into the seat frame. His chin hit his chest.

Nothing else.

Vladimir was better off. Vladimir was reaching over and unfastening the hip belt for him. "No." Blood came out of his mouth. "The pump. Stop the pump. Close the feed valve. We'll explode."

"Already closed." Vladimir was tugging him out of the seat. "Main's out. But the wheat's burning. When it cooks the fuel we'll still explode. So get on your feet!" Vladimir pulled the cap and its communication wires from Leonid's head, then grabbed handfuls of his overall at his shoulders and *hauled*.

And there he was sliding between Vladimir's seat and the rear wall. His hand flapped all by itself at the locking wheel on the access door.

╱ Vladimir pushed past him, dropped on his knees and wrenched the handle round. The door hinged inwards, and smoke came in.

Vladimir ducked his head and looked out, then pulled his head back in. "Don't use the ladder. It's burning down there. Jump. Jump as far out as you can." And he grabbed him by the arm, pulled him down and pushed him at the open door. "Go on, man!"

He was choking in the smoke. He was crouching like an idiot in the tiny doorway and saw only angry orange flames below him. Flames that crackled. But otherwise just smoke. Where was the clear ground?

"Come on! I want to get out of this as well!"

He was starting to jump when Vladimir pushed him.

Then there was another nothing pause.

Then there was ears of wheat slapping his face. And Vladimir's face was there by his hip, upside down, with blue sky beyond it. The jolting was horrible.

Then there was a catastrophic noise and that awful falling again.

Then he was trying to get up to see over a pallisade of wheat stalks, but Vladimir pulled him down again and pushed him into the ground. His fingers scrabbled between flattened wheat stalks and pushed into soil. Into earth, the wonderful wonderful earth. And there was hot sun on his face, but when he opened his eyes a black cloud was surging up to cover it.

Vladimir's face appeared, filthy with smoke and dirt. "That was the bloody lander. Bloody blown up. They'll never let us poor bloody bastards anywhere near Mars. Bloody hell."

"Sorry." And still blood in his mouth. And a *pain* starting in his tongue. "Sorry about that."

"What? Sorry? Leonid, you bloody fool – *you* got us down alive!"

2   Orbit 1

These days Columbus went from west to east, and went an awful lot faster. Columbus girdled the world in an hour and a half.

Columbus was starting to grow. Extending clean across its twin keels was the lattice beam which supported the huge solar panel arrays. Suspended between the keel booms, it now had a satellite servicing hangar, and a completed H-plan raft made of pressurized modules linked together by tunnel connectors and equipped with a main docking hub. All the pressurized modules were cylinders forty-five feet long and fifteen feet in diameter, some fitted internally to serve as microgravity laboratories, others equipped as living accommodation or control and service areas. The space station was finally becoming reasonably spacious inside.

Outside it bristled with communications antennas and monitoring instruments. There was a lot of science, and still more defense intelligence work, to be done above the atmosphere. There was also the bread-and-butter business of servicing and refuelling free-flying platforms carrying contract payloads, and maintaining the orbital transfer vehicles that lofted satellites into higher orbits and then brought them back down again to the station for routine overhaul. With service engineers and a respectable workshop available on station, you finally got a reasonable life expectancy and a decent return on investment for satellite technology. You also had the competitive edge over the Europeans once more by only agreeing to service long-stay satellites that launched on your own carriers. ESA would have to get its act together with its own space station, or it would eventually have to withdraw from the launch contracting business. In the meantime, America had its revamped Shuttle fleet with more than a decade of service, the Pentagon was already operating the first of its fully reusable TAVs that flew on spaceplane wings powered by air-breathing engines, and NASA was chasing funding for its much bigger transatmospheric launcher. The only real rivals were the Russians, as always.

The brain of Columbus was the command deck section at the center of the H-plan raft. Arrayed round the cylindrical walls were instrumentation modules for the maneuver station, life support systems, communications, external operations, data management for industrial and science activities, satellite control stations, and Pentagon Corner.

Browning was busy at Pentagon Corner, the work station controling Space Force's specialized functions. Reeber was floating beside him, watching one of the screens. A cleanly crew-cut pair, those two live-in soldiers, Lieutenant Colonel Dick Reeber and Major Alan Browning, all of the resident military among the present crew of eight. The new service, the United States Space Force, was getting confident about asserting itself these days. So it should, with space filling up with its private satellites and the first battle stations due up any time now. It had gotten as far as standardizing its ranks on the Army and Air Force model. That hadn't meant a title change for Reeber seeing as he was an ex-Air Force man, but being formerly with the Navy's own NavSpaceCom, Browning had metamorphosed overnight from a lieutenant commander to a major. But that was all so many dumb games.

Roger Marshall was station commander, a civilian, and a NASA career astronaut. He was one of those people who had ceased to be happy with the accelerating militarization of space. Nowadays NASA's budget had reached an all-time high, but the Defense Department was the bigger budget big brother, and it was starting to throw its weight around in the shape of its Frankensteinian Space Force creation, using muscles of security considerations and access priorities. Roger Marshall was bitter as hell, because someone had quietly let him know that the Defense Department's liaison office inside NASA had been channeling unhappy questions about him to the space agency's managers, querying whether his observed attitudes showed adequate awareness of national security requirements, whether he was really the right stuff as the Pentagon defined it. Marshall was just waiting for the compliant managers to let the axe fall, to take him off the space station list and give him a desk instead. That obedience to the Pentagon caused the most acid part of his bitterness.

Reeber and Browning had commandeered time on the Columbus telescope, and never mind the dislocation of the sky-mapping program it was supposed to be running for a bunch of astronomers down in Arizona. Through the telescope they were shooting away whole rolls of seventy-millimetre format film. Marshall hung finger light from a hand grip next to the communications monitor station. Together with Merryn Swanton and Charles Watkins, he watched the repeat of the telescopic image they'd called up on the high resolution screen.

Tipped up there in black nothing hung the Grid Iron, the newest and biggest Soviet space station. It was a flat array of multiple squares built by linking together single cylindrical elements. It was so big it had nine complete squares made up of twenty-four elements, nice square holes you could play ticktacktoe on. Grid Iron was what Tass and Novosti press releases called the Orbital Park. At present a shuttle was parked there, along with a variety of free-flying platforms and orbital transfer vehicle stages. And, of course, the Handle.

Grid Iron, along with its Handle, traveled in an orbit inclined at forty-six degrees to the equator. Columbus circled in an orbit sixty-three miles lower and at an inclination of twenty-eight point five degrees to the equator. The altitude separation meant that there was no possible risk of collision, of course, but on every single mutual circuit those two orbits crossed each other twice. Grid Iron and Columbus rarely came anywhere near each other because orbits at different heights had different periods, the time it took to fall right around the Earth and come back to the point where you started measuring from, so the two space stations were forever strung out at different points along their respective orbits. But this one was a very close pass. They were over the Indian Ocean and crossing the equator, Grid Iron heading out northeastwards while Columbus slid underneath in a direction nearer east-northeast. In the lower orbit, Columbus was gradually overhauling Grid Iron, catching up from behind and passing out in front, sixty-three miles lower and almost two hundred south. At closest approach they'd been less than one hundred and fifty miles apart. So Reeber and Browning shot their magazines of film, military intelligence being a never ending task.

Grid Iron and its Handle, swimming in vacuum.

The Handle had been growing for ten months now. At first just a twin boom framework, it had taken shape as modules and components were shipped up and welded into place. Only after the terminal unit, with its foil-shrouded but clearly discernible rocket exhausts, had been nursed into position at the end of the frame was it finally confirmed. The Handle was a true *space* ship, a vessel that would set sail from Earth orbit and never descend into any atmosphere. And the Handle was big, designed for large loads and deep space missions. A mission to one of the inner planets, was all that Tass announced. Well, that was obvious enough. You had to carry one hell of a load of propellant to go to another planet: propellant to boost out of Earth orbit and into an interplanetary trajectory, propellant to lose speed and enter orbit around the target planet, more propellant to leave that orbit and enter a path falling back to Earth, still more propellant to decelerate and enter a parking orbit around the Earth once again. For all of that you needed a big ship.

The clinch came with those satellite photographs of test versions and then finally a complete looking prototype of a lander outside a shed at the Tyuratam Cosmodrome near Baikonur. There was only one inner planet worth a visit that had surface conditions you could put human beings into – Mars.

"Aside from the Moon," Charles Watkins said, "they get everywhere before we do."

"Do they?" Merryn Swanton hung arm in arm with Charles Watkins. Together they were working dedicatedly at understanding across ethnic barriers, she being white and he black. Off duty they were having a near continuous party, going through all the positions already proved by other pioneers of free-fall sex, and by now adding some new techniques to the Space Station Sutra. The way the two of them were going at it, one day it would all end in marriage.

"First man in space. First woman. First permanently manned space station. Now the first Mars mission." Watkins turned to Roger Marshall. "Right?"

Marshall nodded. "And the first satellite. All we managed was the first atom bomb. Useful things like that." And he could see by their expressions that they knew the remark was meant to needle Reeber.

"Constant funding," Reeber said, twisting in the air and turning his back on Pentagon Corner. "None of this stop-go budgeting that's messed up every United States program as presidents come and go. Right now we're on another downturn. Democrat in the White House, bleeding hearts in Congress. So Moscow's ahead again. I hope they have the sense to do telecasts from the surface of Mars and release them world wide. Then we'll get some sense in Washington and get the funding running."

"Funding for who? Space Force already gets everything."

"But we need more. There's one big job to do up here. And right now there's a down-turn coming. That's the Democrat way of trying to win the next election – cut defense and raise entitlements. What use is a society full of people with their self-reliance crippled by government handouts, when you can't defend it and it gets wiped out one day? No use." Reeber turned back to Browning and the Pentagon's monitors.

The terminator was coming up ahead, down on the dazzling Earth. The evening sunset line, the beginning of night, it reached from the ocean across India and the Himalayas, across Tibet and China and Mongolia and into Siberia. The day would be coming to an end at Tyuratam. It had been a bad day for the Soviet Mars program. Reeber had let that much out from the secure exchanges he had with CSOC, the Consolidated Space Operations Center, in Colorado. The string of surveillance satellites that routinely overflew Tyuratam had picked up a lander vehicle test that obviously ended with a crash and a fire.

"Maybe Mars is going to be delayed," Merryn Swanton said. "If they wrote off a lander and maybe killed the people in it. That would be a blow. That kind of thing's awful."

It was sobering. It reminded you that in the space business, routine safety was just a system failure away from death.

On the standard monitor screens, on the groundtrack program eyes, the terminator passed under them on the cloud-wrapped magical dome of the Earth. The Earth turned west to east, once around every twenty-four hours, but they wound themselves around it many times faster, west to east as well and overtaking it forever.

They were catching up on Grid Iron, too. And then there it went into the shadow, and the telescope view dimmed right down. From Grid Iron, Columbus would still be glittering in light.

The tally board for camera operations showed that Reeber and Browning had already switched to infrared film to pick up differential heat sources on the Soviet space station. Hundreds of pictures of the same old Grid Iron – the work was never done.

Then Columbus went into the terminator. The power load switched automatically from the solar panels to batteries. They would be getting their sunlight-independent nuclear power generator with the next programed extension – unless Congress cut the money at the last moment. The only money they wouldn't cut was damn weapon money.

Merryn Swanton switched on one of the ten-inch screens and fed in the NBC channel carrying East Coast networked breakfast television, a channel bounced to Houston and then through two satellites before it arrived at Columbus. High-tech overkill for a little entertainment, maybe, but living up here you couldn't afford to feel cut off from home. And besides, Merryn had a special interest. This would be the first transmission of the pre-recorded weekly Space Station Bulletin, and Merryn was the one who'd delivered it this time around. Once the networks had recorded it direct from Columbus, the only chance to see it and find out how well you'd done was to catch one of the transmission slots.

Merryn hooked the little stethoscope phones in her ears like someone typing up a dictation, and got the sound that went with the snappy succession of advertisement spots right after the newscast.

The telescope monitor went blank. Major Alan Browning was shutting the instrument down. They had all the shots they wanted of Grid Iron and the Handle.

"Hey! What are they doing?" Merryn Swanton was pointing at her soundless screen. On it was a talking head. It was replaced by a map of Southern Africa. Animated arrows stabbed over the border from Namibia into South Africa. "They've canceled me!" She pulled the earphones free and let them twist in the air on their lead. "Canceled me for some dumb special report."

"Special report?" Marshall asked.

"The dumb South African war. The South African army's gone back into Namibia again to hit the ANC bases." On the screen a fat arrow was laid across the mutual border, pointing back from South African territory into recently independent Namibia. Then the map was replaced by news camera shots of trucks rolling and distant smoke rising over scrub desert. "Why should that be important enough to replace us, tell me?"

"They've gone back into Namibia?" Charles Watkins, by color and perhaps also by political persuasion, tended to see the South African conflict in more or less clear terms. The ANC guerrillas might by now be exclusively Moscow supported, but the white regime in Pretoria was grossly racist, and that was about that.

"That's a mistake. That's a bad move." Reeber shook his head in professional disapproval. "They have guerrillas active right through their own country. Going back into Namibia could stretch them too far. They could start losing everywhere."

"What about my bulletin? I spent *hours* putting that together. What about my fucking bulletin?"

Roger Marshall let go of his hand grip and pushed off across to the exit tunnel. "Guess we'll all just have to get back to work. Okay?" He got hold of the rim rail and pulled himself through into the tunnel connector on his way to the next module, a man adrift and leaving the scene.

3 *Star City*

Leonid Steffanovich Shalyapin had a degree in mechanical and electronic engineering. He also happened to have made his pilot's license while still at school so that he could help out with crop-spraying on the collective back home near Shepetovka in the western Ukraine. So during his military service they taught him jets and helicopters. He was quite simply a born flier. His professional life began with transport jobs in support of oil and mineral extraction projects in northern Siberia, flying between pocket-sized prefabricated strips laid on a tundra that was pure ice in winter and a swamp all summer. Then he had spent three tours flying engineers and scientists around Antarctica and picking people out of impossible blizzards every time another emergency rescue was mounted. Ten years ago, at the age of thirty-two, he had started his cosmonaut training. Tatyana had simply said that if he *really* wanted to do it – well he should try. Besides, think how proud the children would be. So now he was a veteran of fourteen space missions. He had flown twice to Mir on Soyuz-T craft at the turn of the nineties, and in the past four years he had flown twelve shuttle missions, the last six as commander, before he transferred onto the training shortlist for Mars. And in all that time he hadn't had a single crash landing, had never even damaged an aircraft or spacecraft, and had never sustained a single injury.

Until two months ago.

Well, he was walking without a stick again, and he hadn't needed a bandage around his wrist for almost three weeks. Even at forty-two, your bones heal eventually.

"Come in, Leonid Steffanovich! How are you? How's the old ankle? Sit down. Sit down. How was the vacation? Family forgiven you for frightening them like that?"

Lieutenant General Viktor Brusin was crew director of the manned spaceflight program, with an office in the new administration complex at the Gagarin Cosmonaut Training Center. The Center was the focus of Star City, barely an hour's drive northeast of Moscow. Brusin had trained as a cosmonaut in the seventies but had never made it into space. He was far too tall for the Soyuz vehicle used at the time, with something of a weight problem as well. He had long ago resigned himself to the fact that he would never fly a mission or experience space at first hand. He made a perfect crew director, because he cherished his tiny army of space-going cosmonauts as his surrogate adventurers, but he was still envious enough to accept no shortfall in their perform-ance. He had relaxed somewhat about his weight gain over the years, and with his combination of height and solid bulk now made an imposing figure – especially in the company of the shorter people who still tended to get selected as cosmonauts.

Leonid had a traditional spaceman's build – a little below average height, and compact. Only his proven performance as a top rate pilot prevented him from feeling dominated and even intimidated by Brusin's presence. Added to that was the old insecurity – a civilian pilot cosmonaut competing with all those military people. Of course, things had improved with time and the expansion of the program to include so many engineers and scientists, so that civilians were about equally represented overall. But among the top grades of vehicle pilots and mission commanders, a non-military man or woman was still a rarity.

In Brusin's presence everything was really much more comfortable sitting down. He relaxed in the chair, or tried to. "My wife says from now on I should believe her about the car when she claims that every washer counts."

"You should. Oh yes. That was one of the most damned expensive washers the space program has ever heard of."

The washer had been tiny, a mere three tenths of a milli-metre thick. Someone servicing one of the inspection cameras must have left it loose inside the casing. When the camera was used to check the interior welds of the liquid oxygen tank before fueling the lander, the washer had fallen out into the tank. When the main valve was opened it had been swept down the feed line, must have lodged on the half-open valve, and then slipped between the valve and the flange of its casing when Leonid had throttled through to fully open. It had jammed the double valve solid. When the investigation team had sorted out the bits and pieces that were left of the lander, there was the washer still inside the valve housing, welded in place by the heat of the explosion.

"Now what did you want to see me about?" Brusin asked, not one to delay matters with indirect approaches. "How you stand personally, perhaps?"

"Yes." Exactly that. The neutral atmosphere of the accident debriefings and the positive enthusiasm of Raisman and even that icy bastard Tsherbakov, and above all of Vladimir Ivanov, were all very well. But the official verdict is what counts.

"Well now, if you had a military rank you'd probably be getting a promotion. As a civilian you'll be getting an equivalent rating anyway. Quite frankly, I feel your action was brilliant. How on earth did you calculate it so quickly? Above all, the drag on the thing as it fell. You've seen the figures. We all know how close it was. If you'd restarted the main engine a second later, you'd have hit so hard you'd have killed yourselves on impact. If you'd restarted it just two and a half seconds earlier, you'd have come out at a hover at fifteen metres, with the choice of cutting the engine again, falling the rest of the way and killing yourselves, or else climbing slowly back up into the sky. *How* did you do it?"

"I think I must have guessed." Leonid shrugged. "Didn't get it quite right, after all, did I? That's what I'm worried about. Am I still on the shortlist for the Mars mission?"

"Ah." Brusin hesitated. Then he shook his head. "I'm afraid – no, you won't be on the shortlist for Mars now." He looked somewhere over the top of Leonid's head. "No one's on that list."

"What?" Leonid didn't understand. "*What*?"

"No one's going to Mars." Brusin looked directly at him again. "It isn't a reflection on you, has nothing to do with your abilities or performance. The final order came through a few days ago. It's on the basis of a decision of the Central Committee. The Kremlin is changing priorities. They have other goals now and are in a hurry about them. You can forget all that Martian geography and atmospheric physics you've been learning. Mars is canceled."

"But –" That was idiotic. Every element of the program was assembled. They were ready for launch in less than a year. "But the investment. The planning. The money!"

Brusin shook his head. "Mars is canceled."

4 Caucasus

The summer was about to end. You could see it by the way the snow had crept down from the peaks. Isolated patches of whiteness lurked in the shadows down there in the pass. And the wind was bitter cold and thin, cheating all the warmth out of the hard, clear light of the sun. It had been much more hospitable in the rock-walled tunnels and caverns inside the mountain.

The road down there was busy with trucks and construction vehicles. The road wound over the pass, coming from Ordzhonikidze in the north and heading south for the Tbilisi down on the plain that stretched in haze below the sudden southern ramparts of the Caucasus. Up here the cold sun was brilliant, the air perfectly dry. Southwards, the low level haze of late summer shimmered silver across Gruzinskaya and Armanskaya. On the edge of it all was a dark little line of faraway mountain peaks with white snowcaps. Those mountains were two hundred kilometres distant, in Turkey. Southeast, it all ended in dazzling haze – even in this perfect air you couldn't see all the way to the mountains of Iran. But it felt like one of the roofs of the world, perched up here on this mighty wall stretched between the Black Sea and the Caspian. Very high ground indeed.

"That's the projection tower up there." Vladimir Boschok pointed up the rock-ribbed mountainside. "Thing that looks like an observatory dome." His varilite glasses had dimmed since they emerged from the mountain, and he could easily stare into the dark blue glare of the sky. Those glasses were a luxury import and as expensive as his lined leather coat. He was site manager and magnificently paid. "Hardly notice it once we've finished here. That tower is the one and only eye of this cyclops. Can't have your enemy coming along and just putting it out."

"Let's go down to the office." Svetlana Glagoleva was the engineer supervising the gradual installation of the free electron laser. She wore a belted nylon parka, padded and with a fur-trimmed hood. Her sunglasses were slightly less high-salaried chic. "It's cold enough, and I don't think these two will have adjusted to the thin air yet. You need more than a one-day visit for that."

Tsherbakov and Alova stood on the path in their long uniform greatcoats with collars and lapels flapping in the wind, with their gloved hands stuck in their pockets. Their broad-crowned officer's caps weren't keeping their ears or faces warm, either. For a day-long orientation visit at this time of year you didn't bring winter issue. They were both from the State Committee on Space Defense. Andrei Tsherbakov was thirty-five, a lieutenant colonel and a space veteran, lean and taller than usual for a cosmonaut. Maria Alova was blonde and was younger, a captain and a trainee cosmonaut with the State Committee.

And this monster they were building here inside Mount Kazbek was one of the State Committee's biggest projects.

The path led down the bleak mountainside to where the site office cowered against the slope, a long and low-roofed structure supported on stilts along its forward side and hunched into excavated rock against the ice winds of winter. It was a prefabricated building with a wooden board floor and a dim corridor running through it from one end to the other. And it was warm.

Boschok's office had two walls lined with shelves and pigeonholes. Box files, binders and folders crowded the shelves, blueprints and drawings in loose rolls and in closed tubes choked the pigeonholes. More tubes stood stacked on end in the corners. The big central table was awash with files, folders, papers and plans, the desk under the double-glazed window supported stacks of files and floppy disk holders which all but buried a computer screen and keyboard. The Kazbek Space Defense Laser was a huge and complicated installation, after all.

They hung their coats and parkas, their greatcoats and military hats, on pegs on the wooden wall next to the door, and then seated themselves around the overloaded table. Ah, to be sitting down! As a newcomer you were oxygen starved up here – the tour of the endless tunnels had been a strain.

Svetlana Glagoleva packed her sunglasses away in their case and relaxed decorously in her chair. "Really we're in a friendly race with the other sites. We should be the first to complete. Up there in the Pamirs they're above the permanent snowline, and at Aborigen Peak in the Cherskogo Range they might be at a lower altitude than here, but they have all the problems of working in Siberia. Supplies can get stuck even on priority projects like these things."

"All three will be free electron lasers?" Maria Alova asked.

"Yes. The laser we're building will ultimately be frequency tunable, but initially it will be fixed on one single infrared window where there's low absorption in the atmosphere. The special advantage of a mountain is the low water vapor and low dust content of the air – that soaks up laser energy like a sponge. The maximum designed output on the initial installation is five hundred megawatts in pulses one hundredth of a second long – five million joules of energy in each pulse. It will fire one pulse every five seconds. To achieve that peak energy, we need a two gigawatt electron beam. And to drive *that* you have to have pulse accumulators and storage rings fed by nuclear reactors capable of providing a steady two gigawatts of power. The whole thing's an absolutely enormous machine, but it's also enormously useful."

. "It's incredibly potent." Boschok's varilite lenses had lightened at last and the condensation on them had cleared, so that he could see clearly once more. "That five hundred megawatt output is concentrated into a beam only two metres across where it leaves the top of the projection tower up there. The optics are *huge* – weigh *tonnes*. It goes up to a relay mirror which orbits exactly thirty-five thousand six hundred and eighty kilometres above the equator. That's a Clarke orbit – takes twenty-four hours to go round once, so it's geosynchronous, stays over the same spot on the Earth."

"Now Vladimir," Glagoleva said, "I hardly think you need to explain a geosynchronous orbit to a couple of cosmonauts."

"Cosmonaut and trainee," Alova said quickly. Andrei Tsherbakov was correct, even reasonably friendly, but he seemed to her to be particularly aware of the hierarchical prestige that went with his four years' space experience.

Boschok steamed on out of his embarrassment. "The relay mirror is steerable. It refocuses the beam and either directs it straight at the target, or bounces it back down to a battle mirror moving in a lower orbit, which then in turn reflects the beam to a target. The ground optics here are also steerable so that we can switch the beam to other relay mirrors in Clarke orbits if the main mirror is lost. The idea is to be able to take out in mere minutes – using a rapid series of hundreds of shots from each laser installation – *all* American military satellites. Spy satellites, communications and navigation satellites, early warning satellites, orbital missile and laser platforms, orbital railguns – *everything*. When the fourth site at Narodnaya in the North Urals is added – it will use a series of relay mirrors on polar orbits so that it can shoot right over the pole – when that's operational, we'll be in a position to destroy *simultaneously* all American orbital weapons wherever they happen to be strung out around the Earth."

"The Americans harden their systems," Tsherbakov said.

"Not against the kind of energy we'll be able to deliver here," Glagoleva answered. "No mirror or mirror alignment can be absolutely perfect, but the beam would only have a ten-metre spread if it was bounced straight back down here. In a hundredth of a second pulse, that means an *enormous* amount of energy delivered to every square metre so fast it can't possibly dissipate away harmlessly. One pulse, and this hut and us and everything else in it would just explode into flames instantly."

"The whole thing," Boschok said expansively, forgetting once again that his visitors were from the State Committee on Space Defense and therefore perfectly familiar with the aims of the project, "has to be seen as our answer to the American SDI. To build a Space Shield like they're doing is hideously expensive and also hideously dangerous, because even if you believe them when they say it's purely defensive, what does it defend?"

"It defends their offensive weapons against our offensive weapons," Maria Alova said, politely. "It protects their ability to attack us because it prevents us from using our weapons to damage their ability. We can't defend ourselves against them."

"Exactly." Boschok clearly thought she was a bright girl, while Glagoleva was trying to hide her opinion of her colleague's out-of-date chauvinism. "With their Space Shield they can threaten us, blackmail us – even attack us and get away with it, if a president even madder than usual gets into power. One of those brainstormed fundamentalists, say. So – our answer is to direct our efforts at the most vulnerable aspect of their strategy, namely their Space Shield itself. All its orbital components circle in perfectly predictable paths, which makes our targeting task *much* easier than trying to knock out a sudden swarm of attacking missiles. In a time of crisis when it's got right to the brink, we just annihilate their Shield and leave them as vulnerable to a nuclear attack as we are, no more and no less. They'd still have their ground-based lasers, just like the ones we're building, but that's all. So they'd have to climb down off their warhorse and start talking again instead of threatening us."

"Unless," Glagoleva said, "they panicked and launched an all-out attack the minute their space defenses started to go. It isn't a magic solution, this. It has to be used cautiously."

"You said bounce the beam back down here," Tsherbakov said to her, "and it would destroy this hut in an instant. Could the laser hit a target on the surface of the Earth? Could it be used against a ground target?"

"Yes," she said thoughtfully. "That would be possible. If we knew the location of the target – the *precise* location. Of course, the beam energy would be reduced by a second passage through the atmosphere, but it would certainly work. Enormously destructive, too. It could put down a complete pattern of hits in a matter of minutes. If the area where it hit included *my* house or car or tank or ammunition dump – or field of wheat for that matter – I wouldn't want to be anywhere near when everything went up in flames."

"I don't think we need –" Boschok was interrupted by the ringing of his telephone, the single ring of a call put through by his secretary from the next office. He turned his chair to face the jumbled desk, lifted the telephone out from behind a pile of files, and raised the receiver. "Boschok, site manager." Then his eyebrows went up slightly. He hauled out more of the phone's extension cable and then handed the apparatus across the heaped up table towards Tsherbakov. "For you. A Comrade General Volkov of the State Committee on Space Defense."

Tsherbakov took the receiver while the rest of the machine was balanced on a heap of computer printouts by Boschok. Now what was so important that someone as senior as Volkov was chasing him with phone calls? "Tsherbakov."

"Glad I caught you first try, Colonel," said Volkov's voice. "News for you. The crew selection. Confirmation just came through from Star City. Congratulations. You've been selected as lander pilot for the new mission. You're on it."

"I am?" *That* was a piece of news worth waiting for, that was for sure. "Who else is on?"

"Grishin will be commanding the lander. Good that two of our own people are on the mission, or there'd have been complaints, I can tell you. Overall mission commander will be Raisman, and Shalyapin will be main ship pilot. Blochina will be flight engineer. Shalyapin and Blochina didn't make it just because they're civilians so it will look good in the world press, by the way. They're damn good people, too."

"Yes, I'm aware they are." Andrei Tsherbakov was also aware that his face had done an unheard of thing and cracked into a grin. But just for once he didn't mind.

5 *Washington*

She always seemed to get to see Washington in the winter. Did the city really have green foliage on its trees in summer, or were they all hiding something? At least it was nowhere near as cold as she'd known it to be in Washington in winter, although there were snowflakes drifting out of a dark January sky when she checked into the hotel.

And the committee. The House Appropriations Subcommittee on Space Utilization had gotten around to doing its combined Sherlock Holmes and thrifty housekeeping bit on the stage-three programs fundings. As coordinating manager in the Stage-Three Programs Development Office, Rosemary Maclaughlin had to attend at the subcommittee's whim so that it could decide where to cut carefully and surgically, and where to simply slaughter. There were four congressmen on the subcommittee, including Joseph Hyland, but he was the only space lobbyist. The other three, one Republican and two Democrats, were strongly anti-space. This year the run-up was starting to election year at the White House, and the subcommittee members were concerned to pull out evidence of – if you were Republican – the way the current Administration was wasting money, or else – if you were Democrat – of the way the Party was anxious to help the president by finding out the areas that could be cut to save money. It was a hanging committee, and Hyland was outnumbered and couldn't really help her. Well, at least she was tough.

Rosemary Maclaughlin was forty. She wore her blonde hair cut in a pageboy once again, not too long, and done in a tangle of curls that were swept back at the left. She'd started dyeing her hair to keep the blonde tone smooth and even. She wore plain gold hoop earrings. Altogether it made her very attractive but very serious, very confident, fit even to face a very unfriendly committee.

"Think they're really going to be that unfriendly? I got my training with basically sympathetic Congressional committees."

Joseph Hyland just shrugged. His jacket was over the back of a chair but he still kept his tie on for work, even deep into the evening – the mark of a man versed in public respectability and responsibility, the mark of a conservative member of the House of Representatives.

"Can you guess what the verdict's going to be on stage three?"

"Rosemary, I can already tell you." His voice was getting even warmer with the years. At forty-seven he wore glasses to work – they lay upturned on the papers on the table. "They'll go for a suspension of the Earth-Moon transportation system. They'll negotiate the Pentagon down to a miniature version of a second space station, and they'll exclude NASA involvement. They'll go along with the Transav prototypes on the basis of justifying the development costs. The climate is so bad that the full Appropriations Committee will probably adopt the subcommittee recommendations, and when the whole thing gets put to the House, the House will most likely vote it through without restoring a single cut. The Pentagon's going to lose all funding for its polar-orbit station proposal. And they're going to dissolve your Lunar Facility Studies Office with just enough of a holding allocation to prevent the work you've done so far from simply being thrown away. So that's the end of going for the Moon. No more highest ground. The only major continuations with nothing more serious than cosmetic cuts will be the ongoing SDI expenditures, but even there the new starts are going to be in trouble. About the only thing that would keep the Moon option open and running would be if the Pentagon came clean on the vulnerability of their entire space defense apparatus. But they aren't going to do that for free, and they'd exterminate any mere politician or NASA employee who tried it. They are just never going to admit that such an astronomical investment of taxpayers' money is, in its present state, a ready made at-a-stroke total write-off the minute the Russians have built a system to counter it. Which is exactly what the Russians are doing as fast as they can."

"In short – shit?"

"In short, shit indeed."

Rosemary's document case had defecated – neatly and cleanly – over most of the hotel room. Papers, files, data presentations and information sheets were spread around on the table and over half of the bed and even some of the carpet, all of it paper ammunition to fling at the subcommittee tigers. But witness and one subcommittee member, they could present it how they liked – the tigers would strike. It was dark, late evening outside, with wet snow slithering down the windows and falling for another twelve stories into the cold streets. Snow, thermometers and hopes all descending. Only the television in the corner seemed unaffected, signing pictures happily to itself with the sound turned out. And those pictures were all about the latest steps in the accelerating fall of South Africa.

"When the Soviet ship launches," she said. "Maybe that'll bring a turn-around. Competition and all that."

Hyland shook his head. "Mecklen – he's our little subcommittee chairman. I guess you didn't catch his news interview earlier today. You'd still be traveling. He said let them go to Mars if they want. He said – get this – that there are no inhabitants there they can ally with and turn against us, so they can't make the Red Planet any redder than it already is. It's a good joke. Wish I liked his motives. And him a fellow Republican at that. Ah – I guess they really are going to Mars?"

Rosemary nodded. "Must be. We have clear pictures of the latest module they bolted into the Handle. A large lander complete with legs. No doubt of it. Their launch window opens in around three months and goes for another three. Depends on what kind of transfer configuration they intend to use. The higher the energy the later they can afford to go."

On the television screen a voiceless White House spokesman was mouthing evasive answers. You had to be careful what you said about South Africa or you might turn out to have prepared the way for it to become an election issue the following year. And that you really didn't want as the incumbent Administration, because it was starting to look as though white South Africa might really be starting on its lamentable way down the tube. Pretoria had suffered three major setbacks in rapid succession, and together they attained the proportion of a modest catastrophe. The re-deployment of troops into Namibia to erase guerrilla bases there hadn't worked, had caused heavy losses to the units sent in and to the follow-up units sent to get them out again. Air power and armor just don't amount to everything when fighting a counter-insurgency war. The dilution of their forces through the Namibia extension, coupled with the imperative need to protect the white cities, the industrial and mining areas, and the major agriculturally producing regions, meant that the Pretoria government had been obliged to loosen its grip inside the independent black homelands of Swaziland and Lesotho – which was exactly what the ANC had been waiting for. Now the pro-Pretoria black leadership in both quasi-countries had been toppled and the ANC guerrillas had won two enormous chunks of territory. Pretoria had got itself into trouble and was looking for help. After all, it was defending the Southern Cape from predacious communism, wasn't it? All that the United States was prepared to offer at present was a major increase in the availability of satellite surveillance facilities for South African forces. Politicians in general and presidents in particular tend to be middle-aged and elderly. They tend to remember Vietnam.

"Is that the same kind of lander they wrote off last summer at Tyuratam?"

"What? Oh. Yes, seems to be. They obviously had a spare, and they're confident enough to fly it on a real mission." Rosemary turned back to the TV and glared at it. "South Africa all the time. Reminds me of that day last summer when for the very first time NBC dropped our Space Station Bulletin. Then CBS did it. Now even ABC are going to axe it. Do you know what their executive said? He said space just isn't interesting any more. It's routine." Now where was the remote control? Nowhere in sight. "We're defeated by our own success." The thing must still be there in its slot on the side of the TV. She stood up and headed for the shimmer-ing screen in the corner. "We have to let them tag our manned space presence to the Defense Department's fucking spending spree up there. *Our* development produces vehicles like the Shuttle and now the TAV to run it for them. Everything goes in a *big* way and it goes safely and smoothly. No deaths, no crashes or other significant accidents since eighty-six. And so? So it isn't interesting!" She switched off the television with enough force to have squeezed the heart of the chief executive of ABC.

She marched over and planted herself on the edge of the bed, getting ready to call room service for something to eat just as soon as she'd calmed down. She shouldn't get angry at anything or anyone any more, dammit. She was a fully committed professional. That was her life. So talk gentle subjects. You have to be cool for the committee tomorrow morning. "Joseph, you haven't told me yet. How's Gloria?"

Joseph Hyland beamed. It's nice when a man of forty-seven can beam at the mention of his wife. Some marriages work well, even these days. "She's just fine. Her only complaint is my apartment here. She likes our house in Seattle much better."

"Ah well, a home of your own is always better. And the kids?"

"Oh, Denise is going through that difficult phase of teenage self-assertion, but we're all being very civilized about it. John escaped to college last year and is having a glorious time. He likes the study, believe it or not. He likes the social life and the *girls*, now he has a place of his own. Gloria's worried he's going to turn macho. And how about you, Rosemary? Any excitement on the personal front?"

"No." She flapped her hand vaguely. "I'm still between, taking it easy. Guess I'm getting choosy as I get older. And the single guys in their forties and fifties are the half of them carefree divorcees trying to make like they're having their youth over again. Men just don't seem to mature. They regress, don't adapt to a different pace of living. And with my job there's the salary problem. Now I don't want to start demanding that a guy absolutely has to earn as much as or more than me, but that asshole Bruce was just too much by far. I need a lover and a friend, not some kind of latter-day gigolo. Hey now." She caught herself up. "That's going to get depressing. Let's change to something to enthuse about.

I have this unladylike desire for a real roast beef sandwich. I'm starving." She reached out and picked up the telephone receiver. "Should I have them send you up something?"

Joseph shrugged. "Why not. But just one full sandwich, because I really have to be getting back soon. I have to keep up on reports from back home – when you have Boeing in your constituency you're busy. And I have an eight o'clock start in the office tomorrow, what with these damn hearings eating up half the working day."

"Okay, one for me and one for you, too. And a beer! I want a beer. How about a Budweiser?"

Outside it was a bright morning wet with snow that melted in the sunshine. Rosemary put on her charcoal gray skirt and jacket with a white blouse and a white satin necktie to outbid the subcommittee in correctness, discretion, sobriety, precision, and style. Professional elegance, a smooth voice, a steady gaze and a cool and calm demeanour – those are the weapons that a successful career woman must master if she wants to be given any kind of a chance on the basis of being good at her job.

The House Appropriations Subcommittee on Space Utilization didn't reside in the old committee suites in the Capitol Building, but met instead in one of the functional rooms in the new extension across the avenue. There was just one usher supervising the recording equipment and another on hand at the door. The witness table had only four places for witnesses, with or without lawyers in tow, and behind were only two short rows for press and public. Not even the full committees were such media shows any more now that the measures induced by the continuous outgrowth of security consciousness by the Government, by its agencies and by private corporations had begun to take effect. There was more and more work in closed session, and you couldn't even imagine something on the scale of the Watergate Committee happening nowadays – the imperatives of national security could no longer for any reason tolerate the public demolition of a president.

She gave them information sheets stacked with data comparing the performances of the modified Shuttle, the Pentagon's TAV and NASA's proposed Transav series vehicle. Give them something complicated to keep them under control. She gave everything the easy way on the sheets, proper MKS units that allow you to compare and equate quantities together directly with minimal mental effort, but always with the everyday American equivalents in brackets: rocket motor thrusts in pounds as well as kilogrammes, orbital altitudes in miles as well as kilometres, masses in pounds and short tons as well as in kilogrammes and metric tonnes, dimensions in feet as well as in metres. She drew the line at converting millimetres to inches. Who in hell wanted to multiply things in their heads by twelves and sixteens and five-thousand-two-hundred-and-eighties, anyway? She didn't train as an engineer in the last quarter of the twentieth century just to sink back into a cryptic bog of medieval measurement.

Stage one had been the Shuttle and the other extant systems and capabilities up until 1989. Stage two was the Columbus space station and the whole SDI commitment. Stage three would be the final superstructure on the concept, the big scheme for NASA and for Space Force, with shared interests in transport and facilities and sites, even if the aims they were pursuing might be very different.

The Shuttle was getting old, was no longer capable of absorbing any increase in payload deliveries, was in urgent need of supplementation and eventual need of replacement. It was also still too expensive to run and had never recovered a cent of the indefinitely deferred development costs. With the TAV it was different, and with the Transav it would be different yet again.

The TAV, the first transatmospheric vehicle in the world, was child of a joint development by NASA and the Department of Defense. It was the original space airplane, taking off horizontally, and gaining lift efficiently with wings instead of standing on its tail belching fire. It burned hydrogen fuel, but its engines breathed air – they took their oxygen from the atmosphere instead of carrying it along with them. The consequent saving in weight meant that an acutely stream-lined vehicle, with stub wings and no bigger than the Shuttle, could deliver a good quarter of the Shuttle payload into orbit without any massive external tank or takeoff boosters and without throwing *anything* away. The TAV accelerated up into the stratosphere and then coasted on into orbit. It carried small pure rocket motors for orbital maneuvers and for the final deorbit burn, and it made a glide re-entry and landing just like the Shuttle. Its operating costs were so much lower that it could undercut the Shuttle per pound of payload and still guarantee to recover its entire development costs.

The TAV was the Defense Department's machine, operated by Space Force. It had been in successful service for twelve months. It was a small payload vehicle, inadequate for some of the delivery jobs the DOD had on its schedule and completely unsuitable for NASA's requirements. What was needed was a bigger version, an efficient heavy lifter. What was needed was the Transav.

The service version of the Transav would be twice the size of the Shuttle orbiter and would take two thirds the payload up to higher orbits for less than half the cost per kilogramme. The design and development phase was complete, and now it was time to build two prototypes.

"Why," Robert Mecklen, the chairman, wanted to know, "do we in fact need to continue with the program? What do we need it for? We already have the Shuttle, and we're firmly ahead of the Soviets in that department, since their own shuttle has only been in service for a little over four years."

"We need it because of the substantial cost saving it will provide on running the already established stage-two programs, and for minimizing the running costs of the proposed stage-three programs. Stage three is a package that doesn't make sense with the Shuttle. Without the Transav it doesn't have its base. Going ahead with the Transav is the only alternative to throwing away the substantial investment represented by the development to date on all stage-three programs."

"I think," said Ruth Buchannan, Democrat and the toughest opponent of space investment on the subcommittee, "that you can take it we're fully familiar with the momentum argument. It can be used to justify just about any spending escalation."

They were hostile as hell, and there was just nothing that Joseph Hyland could do to redress the balance.

Mecklen, Buchannan and Richard Waxman, the other Democrat, attacked her outright on the proposal for a second space station. It would be larger than Colombus and would be built in a five hundred kilometre – three hundred ten mile – orbit inclined at twenty degrees to the equator. Both the Defense Department and NASA wanted it, and they needed the Transav to build it. The facility would serve NASA with science and manufacturing applications, with better satellite maintenance, and as a base terminal for launching future unmanned interplanetary missions. The DOD, in the person of Space Force, wanted it for bigger and better defense-related activities as their space defense systems expanded. And of course, both of them needed it as a staging post to the Moon. But for the subcommittee majority it was just an utterly useless luxury.

"If the Soviets are going to go for Mars," Mecklen said, "if they put all their off-Earth efforts into that, then the urgency of beating them to the Moon – which incidentally we already did in 1969 – seems, to say the least, more imagined than real."

"Let's not talk of racing the Russians," Joseph Hyland said. "It's embarrassing. We beat them to the Moon but didn't stay there. They beat us to a satellite, to a man in space, to long duration flights, to a permanent space station – and they keep on in there, which is the essential point at issue. Miss Maclaughlin, maybe you'd better have patience with us and explain something of gravitational wells and related energy costs."

Well that was an excellent cue at least to get the primary justification of going for the Moon on the record once again.

"You can easily visualize the gravitational field set up by a planet as a well with the planet sitting in the bottom. The more massive the planet, the deeper the well. For any object to escape from a planet, it has to be thrown hard enough up that well so it has sufficient energy to go all the way to the rim at the top before it falls back down again. There's a minimum speed you have to throw it so it just reaches the top of the well, and that is the escape velocity for the planet concerned. Now the Earth is around eighty-three times more massive than the Moon, so its gravity well is far deeper. For the Moon, the depth of the well you have to jump out of, and so the escape velocity you have to jump up with, is correspondingly much less. The escape velocity from the Earth is almost eleven point two kilometres a second, or twenty-five thousand miles per hour – but the escape velocity from the Moon is less than two point four kilometres per second, say five thousand three hundred miles per hour. That means to get any given mass away from the Earth, you have to give it around four and three quarters the velocity that you would to get it away from the Moon. That means expending twenty-two and one half times as much energy. Put in energy terms, it's twenty-two and one half times cheaper to go anywhere from the Moon than it is to go from the Earth."

Hyland planted a further clue. "And how does this energy advantage affect space activities in the vicinity of Earth?"

"Simply that until you get right down to low orbits, it actually takes *less* energy to get all the way there from the Moon and to stabilize orbit than it does to hop up from the Earth. The Earth is gravitationally downhill, the Moon is gravitationally uphill, and Earth orbits are somewhere in the middle. The Earth is low ground, Earth orbits are higher ground, and the Moon is the highest ground of all. When you take into account that all the hardware and supplies we use in space, and all the fuel needed to move it around up there, has to be lofted into place from the Earth – which means expending energy, which means expending money on an equivalent scale – it would be far preferable to be working from the Moon than from the Earth."

"Would it be at all feasible to work from the Moon?" And there was Waxman getting at least momentarily carried away by the argument. "Are the necessary materials available there?"

"It's all there, Mr Waxman. Apollo demonstrated that. There are ores lying around on the surface from which it's possible to extract both hydrogen and oxygen with basic chemistry. We can also recover iron, titanium, aluminum and so on, together with an endless supply of silicon. Taken together, that means building materials, and also the means to make both water to support human life, rocket propellant

to transport materials and fuel to service space activities
There's also a limitless supply of industrial energy in the form
of unattenuated sunlight. The scenario is most eminently
feasible. Once we can manufacture materials on the Moon
and ship them to where we need them, we'll be saving on
energy and therefore on cost on all space activities being
supported by the operation. And space activities are already
proceeding on a major scale right now, permitting major
savings. The logic for going to the Moon is impeccable. The
Moon is gravitationally uphill, and to overcome gravity you
need energy, and energy is the true cost of space."

"But," Mecklen objected, "it would require a massive
investment to go to the Moon in the first place – going uphill
and against the grade, in your terms. We've seen NASA's
costing estimates before on this. Just to get there and establish a self-supporting facility represents an extraordinary
investment."

"But it's a one-time investment. The minute the lunar
facility is self-supporting, it doesn't cost a single cent to
expand it further and to develop a materials return into
near-Earth space. The facility can do that itself. I have all
the relevant information with me right here. We can go into
just as much detail on the costing breakdowns as you like."

"A moment ago," said Buchannan, "you mentioned the
true cost of space." She rested her elbows on the bench and
leaned her chin on her folded hands like a school teacher
preparing to take her victim apart. "Costs have to be cost-
effective. The true cost-effective use of space is using it to
achieve *relevant* results. For example, using our established
remote sensing and surveillance capabilities to assist in com-
bating the communist insurgents in South Africa. And that
we already are doing, Miss Maclaughlin."

So after all, the friendly lecture on a cold and sunny morning
didn't go down so well. The majority trio went on to shred
the Earth-Moon Transport System proposal, and then announced the lunchtime recess. She packed her papers
together and headed down the corridor feeling altogether
defeated. The spend attitude of the technology fixing mid-
eighties had flipped over into a save attitude and that was

that. She crossed the marbled lobby and headed for the front doors and the sun-dazzled melting winter day outside. A small army of cabs were waiting out there on the approach.

"Rosemary!"

She turned, right at the doors. Joseph Hyland came running out of the long corridor and across the lobby. The security guards recognized a Congressman, and went back from alarm to routine.

He skidded to a halt on the polished floor. "Rosemary! My secretary just called through to the committee office. Called from my office. Had to catch you with the news."

"What news?"

"The Soviet spaceship. The thing they've been building up there. It's moved out of orbit."

"It's *what*?"

"It's undocked, fired its engines, and boosted out of orbit."

The Handle had launched? "But that isn't right. They can't go for Mars right now. The planets are in the wrong place. The configuration won't be good for three months yet."

"Well they don't seem to care. Where are they going then with a lander? Has to be one of the planets."

"I don't know. Jupiter? The moons of Jupiter? That would be one hell of a coup if they could already do that."

Joseph Hyland just spread his hands.

Rosemary took a cab to NASA's Washington office and made a nuisance of herself. If someone could get information on the Handle's trajectory passed through she might be able to figure out where it was going. It could be a political godsend.

They had the data for her within an hour. It was worth missing lunch.

Below flowed bright and enormously broken upland terrain. The smoother and darker maria of the equatorial Near Side had been left behind. The maria were vast craters caused by the impacts of enormous asteroid-sized hunks of rock, huge plains walled by mountain ranges thrown up by the cataclysmic event. The maria had then flooded with molten rock from the interior, rock which had cooled and set and turned them into frozen lava seas. The later phases of random bombardment with lesser debris from space had cratered the maria and the highlands around their rims to produce the mapper's chaos that turned steadily outside the ship. That jumbled landscape was so old. There was nothing new here except the little human visitors and their spaceship artefact. The maria and most of the craters had been formed between four and three thousand million years ago when the solar system was a much younger place and the human race not even a mere twinkle in some anaerobic microbe's eye.

Crüger was just disappearing over the bright horizon behind, Rocca was sliding directly below, its south wall a sharp ridge reaching out towards them. The Cordillera Mountains had risen against infinite black on the western horizon ahead of track.

"The antenna's aligned and tracking." The computer was pointing the high gain S-band number two direct at the site on the ridge of the Cordillera Mountains. Number one was pointing constantly back at Earth. Leonid Steffanovich Shalyapin waited for the carrier frequency telltale to light on the board of the communications post. They knew the lander was safe, of course – mission control was in constant contact with the two of them down there. But the *Vladimir Komarov* had retained direct contact with the lander only until it had attained hover over the landing site and then gone ahead for touchdown and engine out. Then the ship had lost contact with both the lander and with Earth as it swept on along an orbit that carried it westwards over the Mare Orientale, and the Moon had interposed its bulk across the line-of-sight signal paths. Ah – there was the telltale with the frequency identification. "Signal acquisition."

"Good." Vitali Raisman was the mission commander, but he had work to do on the flight deck of the *Vladimir Komarov*. On the next orbit they had to launch the Moon's first communications satellite. Selenos-1 would separate from the mother ship's carrier frame, and then its propulsion motor would fire to boost it up into a higher mutual orbit around both Earth and Moon. The satellite was bound for a ledge in the slow gravitational whirlpool around the Earth-Moon system, the Trojan point which led the Moon by sixty degrees around its orbit. The leading Trojan point was one of the five Lagrange positions where the gravitational pull of both Earth and Moon, coupled with the velocity of the satellite, would combine in perfect balance to keep it fixed at a single point in the sky with respect to both planetary bodies, falling round in front of the Moon forever. Once Selenos-1 was in place the *Vladimir Komarov* would be able to relay signals both to the lander and back to Earth for almost half of its hidden orbital path across the Far Side of the Moon.

"Telescope aligned and photography run commencing." Yelena Blochina, their flight engineer, was suspended in free fall at the ground monitoring post. Her task on this pass was to take yet more photographs of the landing site and the surrounding terrain with the sixty centimetre telescope on board. The lander was down at fourteen degrees south seventy-nine degrees west, right out on the western limb of the Moon as seen from Earth. Photographic surveys from orbiting satellites had covered the area, of course, but only the telescope could provide the extreme of high resolution that the planners back on Earth required. That telescope would have searched for safe and smooth landing sites on the surface of Mars according to the scheduling of the original mission. Adaptations of the hardware to go for the Moon had been less than minimal. It was the navigation data and the crew training that had been changed.

"*Komarov* calling," Leonid said over his headset microphone. "Do you read me? Over."

"We read you, Leonid." That was Pyotr Grishin's voice. "Here's your first report from Moon Base, one hour and fifty minutes after touchdown. Systems are fine, we're fine, the Moon is fine and the weather's fine. Nothing but sunshine, and not a cloud to be seen."

"Tell him that *proves* the Moon has no atmosphere," Yelena said. "The Americans must have been telling the truth after all."

"Yelena thinks you're talking nonsense, but she says so very nicely. Over."

"Does she? Can mission control hear us? Over."

"No." But he checked the instrument readouts just the same. "This is a private channel. Over."

"Then tell her to watch out when I get back on board. She's ravishing and her sense of humor is the cream on the cake."

"Pyotr's getting disgustingly basic about you again."

Yelena tossed her head, sending a whiplash along her ponytail in free fall. "Nicely or nastily?"

"Oh very nicely."

"Then I might just still speak to him about it. Ask him to put his lights on for the photographic pass."

"Pyotr? Please put the navigation lights on for our telescope. We'll be passing over in – when?"

"Seventy-eight seconds," Yelena said.

"In seventy-eight seconds. Over."

"Lights on." That was Andrei Tsherbakov's voice.

Vitali Raisman turned from his computer post. "Ask them how it looks down there."

"Vitali asks how does it look down there?"

"Beautiful," answered Pyotr Grishin's voice. "We have the ridge running left and right of us and this incredible landscape of hills and crater walls falling away to the east in front of us. It's all shadows and highlights. Apart from the black sky it's like looking across – I don't know – rough ground covered in snow, just after sunrise when you look into the sun. And the Earth. Above the horizon is the Earth. Its just a crescent bent like a bow or an arch, perhaps, and the sun's right up above it. It's a wonderful sight."

"Sounds it. Remember that description for the news conference."

"Description? We'll be pointing the camera at it the moment everyone back home has had enough of our handsome faces. Nothing less than Yelena could compete with this. I ask you honestly, Leonid. Do you really think either Andrei or me are lovely to look at?"

"Don't answer that." Andrei Tsherbakov actually injecting some humor into his voice. The view down there must be splendid indeed. "Lights out?"

"Yelena, did you get your pictures?"

"The computer got them."

"Yes, you can put the lights out. We'll be losing you behind the ridge in – fifty seconds. Any messages?"

"Tell Vitali to get it right with the satellite first time, please. Can't go on like this. I need my long soothing chats with Yelena."

"Vitali," Yelena said. "Next orbit we have to patch mission control into the channel to keep him under control."

"Yelena says she's going to censor you next time round."

"She can't do that – I'm in the Party."

"Before we lose them," Vitali said, "don't forget to congratulate them on a safe landing."

"Vitali sends our congratulations on a perfect landing. Was it perfect?"

"Of course it was perfect. Andrei and me make a marvelous team."

"Yelena will get jealous."

"Leonid, if you encourage him I'll murder you."

"Loss of signal in ten," said Tsherbakov's voice.

"All right, Leonid, kiss the others goodbye for us. See you all in two hours. We'll still be here."

"Where were you thinking of going?"

But the ridge of the Cordillera Mountains cut off any answer. He closed the channel.

"You know," Yelena said, still watching the telescope run as the instrument began to photograph the west flank of the mountain range that was always hidden from Earth, "for a colonel from the State Committee on Space Defense, our Pyotr's a jolly fellow."

"If you'd just landed the first Soviet expedition on the Moon," Vitali said, "you'd be jolly, too."

The *Vladimir Komarov* crossed the wide valley between the Cordillera range and the Rook Mountains, heading into the Mare Orientale, heading paradoxically westward into the Eastern Sea. The Mare Orientale was a huge bullseye formation, more on Far Side than on Near Side. Only the massive mountain rings of the outer and inner walls, the Cordillera and Rook ranges, were visible at their eastern extent from the Earth. The lander was down on the high ground on a small plateau right beneath the ridge of the Cordillera range. In the coming days Grishin and Tsherbakov would be making camera surveys of the plateau in changing sun angles so that the planners on Earth could estimate the size and location of every rock and hollow on the ground and then decide exactly how to site the buildings of the future base. On a later orbit the *Vladimir Komarov* would launch an automatic one-way lander platform to go down and to be guided to a landing in the terminal phase of the descent by the two men in the lander. The platform would carry more equipment to deploy around the site, stored supplies for future visits, and a ground vehicle. When the sun had risen higher and the shadow angle was less acute, they would be making two longer survey trips with the ground rover, one to check the nature of the terrain eastwards towards the Earth, and one to take an initial look at a possible route across the crest of the Cordillera and down the western slopes into the first ring of the Mare Orientale. They would make no attempt to drive down from the ridge. Exploration in that direction, the main purpose of the base, would have to wait until the base had been established with its own lander parked permanently on site and with several rovers available. No one was going to blaze a trail down the hidden side of the Cordillera Mountains until a rescue option had been established. To do that you needed a permanently inhabited base, and to permit that you needed a second ship in addition to the *Vladimir Komarov* so that one would always be available to rescue people from the base in an emergency, even if the other was being serviced at the time.

There would be a second ship within six months and a third within another year. Each of them, designed originally to haul an expedition payload all the way to Mars and back, would be able to deliver up to four one-way lander platforms. The Moon Base Program was a crash program making use of the payload and lander capacity designed for Mars and so generous on the short trip to the Moon. It was designed to exploit to the fullest the time advantage they had over the Americans. Because everything that the Americans would need to use to get to the Moon and begin building their own base still existed only on paper.

The *Vladimir Komarov's* groundtrack passed the crater Kopff on the wide floor of Mare Orientale, and they lost the signal from Earth. They had an hour to themselves on board until the orbit brought them round the eastern limb of the Moon over Near Side again north of Mare Smythii. An hour of silence.

"Just had a funny thought," Vitali Raisman said, letting go of the handgrip and floating free from the panel of the computer post. "We've really caught the Americans on the wrong foot this time, haven't we? And it's their presidential election next year, and the one who's in office at the moment will be getting the blame for letting this happen, won't he? So do you realize what we've done, just we five Russians? *We* have just decided their election for them. Makes you think, doesn't it?"

It did.

The *Vladimir Komarov* fell effortlessly in a circle round the Moon, passing Maunder as it crossed the face of Mare Orientale. Ahead waited the terminator and the shadow side. No sun, no light of Earth, just stars and the dark bulk of the Moon turning sightless at your shoulder.

They circled into night.

Rosemary wouldn't hear of him staying in a hotel – he was going to be her guest, and no argument. It made a good excuse for her to cook a real dinner. She could make up the bed for him in the spare room. No trouble whatsoever. When such a very friendly Congressman came to visit the Johnson Space Center, well he was going to be treated more than just well. But not even the best hotel in Houston was good enough for this occasion. There were ten years of personal ties, ten years of pursuing a common goal, and this was a celebration for a victory finally in sight.

It was dark outside the windows, dim in the shadowy corners of the big room. It was a big house for a woman living alone. She'd put a tape of some sort of jazz on the stereo, and left him with a martini and a sheaf of prints of the Soviet spaceship. The *Vladimir Komarov*, the former Handle on the Grid Iron, looked like a real ship of space should – skeletal, bolted together, and blunt.

"Rosemary? Who's it named after?"

"What? The ship?" She came back in from the kitchen and headed over to the table at the lighted end of the room. "After the cosmonaut Vladimir Komarov, the first human being killed in space. Well, on a space mission. He was flying Soyuz-1 in nineteen sixty-seven. The parachute snarled after re-entry and he was killed when the capsule hit the ground."

Joseph Hyland nodded. "I guess I remember. Has the lander returned to the ship safely?"

"Yep. Moscow has just announced the successful rendezvous and docking. Eight days down on the surface up there. Longer than any Apollo visit – as long as the Apollo Eleven mission right from launch until splashdown. Splashdown! My, those were the days, when we threw *everything* but the astronauts away."

Hyland laughed. "Someone once said the Saturn-5 was like a transatlantic liner that could carry only three passengers and sank at the end of its maiden voyage. Expensive."

"Expensive indeed. Where'd I put my drink? Oh, thanks. Yes, and they've been *busy*. A softlander package and all."

"They're really going to start and build a base?"

"No doubt of it. Those telecasts from the ship have been explicit enough. Have you gotten to see the English transcripts yet? And the latest *Pravda* piece announces they're going to build a second vehicle to alternate with the *Komarov*. They don't say when, but I guess it could be kind of fast if they just happen to have the parts all ready and waiting to be lifted into orbit and fitted together. The carrying capacity of that ship is enormous – I'd guess up to twice the payload of the transit vehicle we're planning to build. They're way ahead of us. The *Komarov* must surely have been intended for Mars like they always said – for the Moon they'll just be carrying more payload instead of fuel mass, I guess. I mean the crew module's so big. There are just five of them on this mission, but it could maybe hold twice that. It must have been designed spacious for the haul to Mars."

"Could we scale up our transit vehicle?"

"No. Not without throwing away the design we've got up to now. It all fits together – the transiter modular size, the Transav's lifting capacity, the size and mass of the lander vehicle that the transiter would carry. We'll just have to up our delivery capacity by building three transiters straight out. Russians on the Moon! We have to milk this thing for every dollar we can get."

"We'll get the dollars."

"You really reckon? No, look – these are fuzzy little things taken by ground telescopes. Yes, that one's better. That one's from the Space Telescope. But this last set – they're really sharp. See? The side frames, engines, tanks, the softlander pallet in place, the lander vehicle docked to the crew module. That lander's huge compared to the thing we're going to build. These good ones were all snapped from a TAV right after the *Komarov* started to move away from Grid Iron. You reckon we're really going to get the dollars?"

"We'll get them. You people, the DOD, the aerospace

companies – you're going to trample each other in the rush.
Did you catch the news? 'After so many years, human
footsteps are once again disturbing the ancient dust of the
Moon – and this time they are Russian.' Real stirring stuff –
our fire-eater is going to be in after the next election. The
Democrats are *never* going to pull themselves out of this
mess. No one's ever going to forgive them for cutting back
the space investment. It's going to be Apollo fever all over
again, but on a scale like never before. Russians with a base!
Russians looking down on us every night from the Moon!
They're a perfect demonstration of *exactly* what our stage
three proposals are all about. Now things are really going to
happen!"

"Not before time! After so many years, I was thinking the
whole thing was going to fail. Come the election – well! Have
you decided yet about standing again?"

"I've decided. If we return the next president, I won't be
standing for the House. There's going to be a little job for
me at the State Department. Bureau of Space Affairs, no
less."

"Sounds good. You at the State Department, me at
NASA, and Russians up on the highest ground. With a lobby
like that, it's really got to roll."

3 TURNING POINT

8 *Veldt 1*

Frank Simons, Valsfontein, Cape Province

This tiny town in the veldt has finally seen too much war. Ten years ago this broad valley south of the high Nuweveld Mountains had no experience of the troubles of the black townships and the white cities. Cape Town, Port Elizabeth, Durban, and above all the sprawling district around Johannesburg and Pretoria, were far away. Guns and terror and death were no concern of the white farmers and their black laborers in this open grassland of scattered trees, wheat fields and pasture.

It took a long time for the guerrilla war to reach Valsfontein. The guerrillas operated at first in the north of the Republic, and in the beginning they paid heavily: lightly armed troops facing a mechanized army always do. Gradually the African National Congress forces acquired more and better weapons and equipment. Above all they gained recruits from the black population and support from black African countries, despite the unease felt by some at the ANC's closening ties with Moscow. Soon the guerrilla war was being carried across the Republic's entire northern border. The South African army tried to re-invade Namibia, but became over-stretched and was forced to withdraw to meet the worsening pressure in the north and east. With the overthrow of the pro-Pretoria leaderships in Swaziland and Lesotho the ANC gained new safe enclaves for its forces. The ANC moved from making raids to taking control of the countryside.

The war came to central Cape Province last of all. It came because of the roads and the railway. Both the main road and the rail line from Cape Town to Kimberley and Bloemfontein, and on to Johannesburg and Pretoria, cross this broad grassland valley, passing through the town of Beaufort West and running on north-eastward on their way towards the mighty Orange

River. They represent South Africa's single most important artery. Valsfontein is only fifty miles from Beaufort West and from the road and rail link.

Once the ANC had overrun the countryside and the forces of the Pretoria government were confined to the killing grounds around the cities, the battle to sever the Republic's arteries could begin. The routes between the urban centers became so dangerous that not even armed convoys could travel them in safety. The rural towns were subjected to ever heavier attack. The only safe way to move was by air. The Republic of South Africa began to dissolve into a patchwork of small white-held city enclaves. South Africa's cities have always lived on the backs of their black laborers: now these same urban poor became the hiding place for terrorists operating inside the city areas.

Valsfontein lies on the narrow road between Beaufort West and Aberdeen, another little town near the important road and rail link between Port Elizabeth on the coast and Bloemfontein in the north. The war closed in from both sides. The last white residents left Valsfontein over two years ago, and the ANC overran the place a few months later. Air attacks failed to dislodge the guerrillas but destroyed most of the houses and huts and killed a few score of the black inhabitants, mostly women and children and old men. A guerrilla war kills more civilians than any other form of conflict devised by man.

The rescue effort began eighteen months ago, fueled by Western fears of an imminent communist takeover on the Cape. Money and war materials poured in. Already enjoying intelligence gathered by US spy satellites, Pretoria now received a massive influx of weapons, aircraft and above all helicopters. The United States also provided a fleet of transport aircraft, together with aircrew and maintenance troops, to take on the burden of transporting men and supplies between the white-held cities. This new and bloodiest phase of the war had begun.

The perimeters around the cities have expanded, pushing the guerrillas aside. Major attacks have cost the ANC in Lesotho and Swaziland their main bases. The roads from Pretoria and Johannesburg are open again as far south as Kimberley and Bloemfontein. South African forces hold the open country from Britstown to Colesberg. The long road from Port Elizabeth to Colesberg is in government hands. In the last few weeks, volunteer units have fought their way east along the road from Cape Town, and South African regulars have pushed west across country from the Port Elizabeth highway as far as Aberdeen. Yesterday the leading army battalion established itself in Valsfontein and is now bringing up reserves. A ranger battalion took Beaufort West by air and is holding the focus where the arms of the pincer movement will meet. When the final push is made and the join-up completed at Beaufort West, several thousand guerrillas will be trapped in the south of the central Cape. The Republic of South Africa is winning again for the first time since its debacle in Namibia five years ago, and the war is at a turning point.

It is quiet in Valsfontein. The last inhabitants have fled and the ruined streets and houses belong to the army. Since this morning no more mortar rounds have landed and the harassment by snipers has ceased. Helicopters have been flying in men and materials all day, or thundering overhead on their way to Beaufort West. The only casualties have been among the trucks rolling in from Aberdeen along a road still worried by rocket and mortar attacks. It is hot and dry and the rains have almost failed this year. Out in the deepening night the ANC are regrouping to prevent the final push forward. It is the calm before the storm.

Shari Laurin put the handwritten sheets back on the dusty table. "That's a classy piece of copy you've got there, Frank. One way to make a story out of a day when nothing happened."

Frank Simons shrugged, a shortish bloke as hot and dusty as the air in the ruined bar. "Thought I'd do a piece to remind people how this war got to where it is today. Even the readers of the liberal British press have less than perfect memories, you know." He sighed. "My editor is bound to take half of it out."

"Put something exciting in." Shari tipped back her damaged chair until it threatened to collapse. "Tell them what happened to me and Jim yesterday."

Shari Laurin and Jim Walters, her cameraman, had been moving up into Valsfontein the day before with the leading troops. The armored buffalo in front of their car had taken a mortar round which killed half the men inside and set the vehicle burning. Its tanks went up and engulfed their car. Both of them got out in time, and even managed to rescue their videocamera, its batteries and the bags of cassettes. The car and the rest of its contents went up in flames, including the picture monitor, the thirty-inch dish aerial and the satellite transmitter. As a result they couldn't file reports until they found someone to rush their tapes back to the company office in Port Elizabeth, two hundred miles away.

The big three American networks had rented a communications satellite and moved it over a suitable meridian to receive from South Africa and feed pictures back to the States. Not only could the local offices put reports together and send them over ready for screening, teams in the field were also able to rough edit their own reports and beam them straight through to the home studios. It was a good instant news system, but useless of course without your dish antenna to point at the satellite.

Frank folded the sheets together and slipped them into his shirt pocket. "Yesterday there was a firefight here to report. Today it's eve of the big battle, as it were. We reporters aren't the news."

"We're just here to record the show." Shari reached for her can of beer on the table, and her chair stamped forward on the bare cement floor. "Sent today's out already?"

"Yes." The army had set up a telex at the battalion's signals tent. In recent years the South African authorities had been eager to help reporters explain their plight in facing an apparently unstoppable communist insurgency, and now that the tide had turned they wanted the whole world to know of the brave fight. At the moment they positively loved foreign reporters, even if they would persist in showing pictures of the native civilians caught in the crossfire. They loved all reporters but for Shari. With Shari they had problems.

Shari Laurin was black.

She wasn't even brown – halfway acceptably colored. She was uncompromisingly, glossily black. Shari had her hair permed into long loose curls in the American image of a successful career girl, she wore Adidas shoes and a backpacker's jacket and shirt, with jeans as authentic as dollars could buy, but she was black. Everywhere she went in South Africa the whites had to do a double-take, swallow hard, shake her hand, give her briefings and answer her questions. She was the color of the enemy, the communist bandits, the ANC terrorists, the natives, the niggers, the kaffirs. They took it as a deliberate provocation by her bosses, but they talked to her just the same to show what tolerant multiracial anti-communists they really were.

It was a provocation – on Shari's part.

They were in the dusty and damaged remains of a bar on the south side of the single main street of Valsfontein. It had once been the center of white society in town. Now it was a partial ruin. The roof was still in place over the bar room itself, and the door was still on its hinges and even opened and closed, but the roof was missing from the back rooms where the owner used to live. At the rear of the building even the walls were down, and the back yard was a knee-high jungle of dry grass and parched rose bushes. They'd turned the place into the headquarters of the Valsfontein press corps – Shari and Jim, Frank Simons, and Umberto Giglioli from *Corriere della Sera*.

The beer wasn't from the ruined bar. It was all that was left of some packs of cans Umberto had used to purchase his ride in Frank's battered car, and which the two of them had handed out in a fit of camaraderie it was now too late to regret. There hadn't been all that many cans.

The press corps would sleep in the bar. They could spend the night in the open, of course – it wasn't going to rain tonight any more than it had rained for over two months – but there was always that little risk of getting shot by ANC raiders or jumpy South African soldiers. The grassland outside was tinder dry, the reporters were dry, and the beer was as warm as the evening. They had battery-powered camping lamps burning on the bar and slung from the rafters to brighten the place, and night-patrolling insects were beginning to stray in through the broken windows, prisoners in a dim dungeon of bright-eyed bulbs.

Jim Walters came in from the hot and darkening night. He gave Shari a torn-off telex strip, pulled up one of the more stable looking chairs, and joined them at the bleak little table. "The boss's answer."

"Huh," Shari said. "'Nearest spare satsender in Jo'burg. Stay where at if looks good. Make fucking pictures.'"

Jim shrugged. "Guess it was a bad day back in old New York."

"What did you send out?" Frank asked.

"'Satsender fucked,'" Shari recited. "'Car fucked. What do with fucking pictures?'"

Jim Walters looked around for evidence of unopened cans of beer. "Umberto?" he asked hopefully. "Any more beer?"

At the table on the other side of the room, Umberto Giglioli spread his hands in regret. In one hand he held a turned up card. He was playing patience by some arcane rules, just a senseless routine to pass the time. He was playing against the deck and using rows of spent cartridge cases to keep count of the points. The cards appeared to be winning.

Jim produced a packet of cigarettes from his shirt pocket, took out a cigarette and lit it, then tossed the pack across to the rickety patience table. It skidded through the downed cards. Giglioli took a cigarette, nodded thank you, and tossed the pack back again. It slapped onto the dusty table between the beer cans.

"Anything new on the radio?" Jim pocketed the cigarettes.

Shari shook her head. "We voted to listen to the night."

"In case a raid comes in," Frank amplified. "With the army poised to plug the last gap, the ANC have to do something. They can't just let a defeat like this happen."

"If they do," Shari said, "then we bet on the wrong place."

Jim flicked cigarette ash on the floor. "Message still the same?"

The Voice of Free Africa, broadcasting from Gaborone in Botswana, put out a continuous fare of news, propaganda and straight lies, laced with coded messages for ANC units. The messages were addressed either to families or friends – field forces or urban commandos. The only message broadcast the entire day had been *pay attention families and friends, it burns at midnight*.

"Exactly the same," Shari said. "Just the one message.

Maybe they're not planning much of a war in the near future. Hear of anything on the army's net?"

"Nothing. It's all quiet right here. The rangers in Beaufort West are taking rockets and pretty heavy harassing fire, but that's what you'd expect. They're the pivot for closing the gap."

"Maybe they're right not to plan too much more of a war." She raised her voice to include Umberto Giglioli. "What do we all think? Has Pretoria gone and done it after all? Turned the tide and won the war against numerical odds, the political momentum, the sympathies of the majority of the population?"

A general pause for thoughtful correspondents.

"Four million whites against twenty million blacks?" Frank shook his head. "I'd have said it was impossible, but now I'm not so sure. If the ANC collapses here in the south – then I expect Pretoria really might win the war. *This* war, that is. But after all the bloodshed and the hatred generated, they're going to have to be even more repressive than before to keep order. Which means that one day there'll be a new and even nastier war."

"Rosy prognosis, Frank. How about you, Umberto? What do you think of the war so far?"

"You can't support racism, fascism. But the minute you start the war the moral issue is destroyed." Umberto Giglioli waved his cigarette to indicate the scope of the problem. "A war has its own momentum, just two sides existing to kill each other. At least you know who the enemy is – everyone black or everyone white. That makes it easy, white and black. Pretoria has always played on that association of good and evil. Now that the ANC have become communist, the issue is completely the other way round. This is the end of a century that's been about nothing but fighting the good fight – for freedom defined this way, or for freedom defined that way. For capitalism or communism, for two different ways of keeping power over the masses – bribery or beatings. And we make it all simple in white and black. Here it's become capitalism versus communism, West versus East, literally white against black."

"So," Jim said, "which side are you on?"

"I want to see the blacks win their human rights – but I don't want to see the communist dictatorship that will trample on their political rights. I want to see white South Africa destroyed – but I wouldn't kill a single human being to make it happen." Giglioli shrugged his shoulders in a huge apology. "I am a confusion of liberal values. I take no sides."

"What about you, Shari?" Frank said. "You're American, so you should be anti-communist. You're black, so you should be anti-racist. What do you think?"

Shari frowned, caught out by her ambivalent birthright. "I don't know. I guess this is all like Vietnam was, one way or another – except that we don't have our own troops involved. It's all just like Vietnam. Except this time the enemy isn't slant-eyed little gooks who speak a funny language you can't understand. This time the enemy looks exactly like me." She shook her head. "So I guess I don't know."

The door to the outside world opened and Rutters came in and out of the darkness, a pistol strapped to his hip. Captain Rutters was the unit's adjutant and the nearest thing at battalion level to a press relations officer. It was a very peripheral duty in a front line unit.

"You all here?" he said, with all the self-evident superiority a commissioned rank can supply. "Good. Stay in here for the night. It's a front line position and the soldiers are very jumpy. The blacks can easily get through our perimeter in the dark."

"They're the right color for night attacks," Frank said.

Captain Rutters ignored the witticism. "Coming up on them by surprise would get you shot just as certain as if you were a black. And there might be something big happening somewhere tonight."

"We heard it," Jim said. "Radio Free Moscow, Gaborone branch."

"So do something about these bloody *lights*, for God's sake. Put them out. Go to sleep or something." Rutters eyed the handful of beer cans, Umberto's cards and the cartridge cases. "Get drunk. You can do that in the dark."

"Can't." Umberto shook his head. "No more beer."

"Well at least put some blankets over the windows."

Jim fanned his own cigarette smoke. "But then we won't get any air."

Rutters tried to control himself. "You stupid buggers. They know we're here whether they can see us or not. But if they think they need an aiming point they'll pick any lights they can see. So put them out or cover the bloody windows! For your own good!"

Umberto Giglioli abandoned his game and started looking around the room for something suitable to put over the windows.

Rutters followed the haphazard search for a few moments with his unimpressable officer's eyes, then shook his head. "Colonel Tromp would like you to know there's a courier going out on one of the copters tomorrow morning. If you have any films you want to despatch, get them to the signals post before o-seven-hundred." He turned to Jim Walters. "Do you have any films?"

In a two-person team of reporter and cameraman, the reporter is the boss, and Rutters knew it perfectly well. Jim looked round at Shari for her reaction to the studied insult.

Shari looked up at Rutters with black coal eyes. Then her face snapped into a ridiculous smile. "We got some pictures massah. Yassuh. But not dat one we wants. No suh." She pointed at the end of the room nearer her table. "Massah Rutters over *here*." Then she pointed at the far end of the room. "And massah Rutters' bent little motherfucker on the ground over *there*."

Rutters stomped out. The door was still capable of slamming without coming off its hinges.

Frank shook his head at Shari. "You're theoretically immune, being American, but you're not bulletproof. Go on like that and he'll accidentally catch you in some crossfire or something."

Shari just shrugged.

Moonlight at midnight, in the midst of dark and lightless grassland, nothing but the warm wind whispering romantic motifs under the cloak of colorless night.

Actually the moon was only halfway through its first

quarter and giving little enough light from a cloudless sky – away from its silver-yellow luminance on the black velvet dome overhead he could see fields of stars. And there was no grassland closer than two hundred yards. There was nothing around him but the silhouette shapes of shallow roofed houses and shacks and of splintered ruins of bombed and blown up buildings, timber and brick and shards of corrugated iron. It was silent except for the breeze.

Frank stood in the ruined rear of the bar room building, where the roof was open to the sky and the walls tumbled and smashed to nothing. He might have already been technically in the back garden, but it was difficult to tell. He had come out to see and to hear the outside night without venturing into the exposed street, and now he was caught in inadequate moonlight in a tangle of fallen roof timbers and wooden tiles and all the rubble underneath. How he was going to get back into the even deeper shadow under the broken edge of the roof on the way to the lightless interior of the building he didn't quite know. He wouldn't see anything at all underfoot in there. This had been a mistake, it seemed.

He heard the door go, invisible in the shadow under the roof. Then someone stumbled on something heavy and unstable, and hissed some sort of curse.

"Shari? Is that you there?"

"Hey! Is someone out there?" More rattling of rubble. "Huh. A girl goes quietly out back, and what does she get? Sightseers."

"Is it urgent? I can't get out of the way quickly. I think I'm stuck."

"Stuck? No, it isn't urgent. Just something to do seeing as I can't sleep." Shari's shadowy figure emerged slowly into the thin moonlight. "Stuck?"

"All this bloody stuff." Frank waved his hand at the sightless debris around him that his legs disappeared into. "Won't let go of me."

"Maybe the building's hungry for a little human company." Shari's shadow teetered suddenly and almost toppled over. Pieces of rubble rolled hollowly. "Ow! Fuck it. You don't think this place is booby trapped?"

"Course not. Why booby trap a pile of debris? Now the *bar* could have been booby trapped."

"Now he tells us." Shari was a clear figure in the moonlight, her jacket and shirt and jeans reflecting at least some of the weak light. But her face and hair made a black apparition with gleaming eyes and a flash of teeth as she spoke. "And what are you doing out here?"

"It's about midnight. I was just interested to see if anything starts up anywhere."

"You really have been spooked by the message. Burns at midnight."

"Haven't you? Anything spooks me. A war gives me the shits."

"I try to think of it as facts. Insofar as you can sort them out." She came to a slow halt with only a shredded roof timber between them. "And pictures, insofar as you can get them without getting your head blown off. This is my first war. Been here nearly two years, off and on. Seems my bosses like what I put together. Don't know, but I do something right. You've been here for five years, I recall."

"Yes. Ever since it got properly started after the Namibia defeat. I suppose I've seen everything."

Shari was silent for a moment, looking round at the night. Then she shifted her feet on sliding rubble again. "It's quiet. Let's get back inside."

"I've been thinking about that. It's probably better not to go back the way we came. It looks easier this way. Less rubble. That looks like a gate in the wall over there."

"Good idea. There's a back alley runs parallel to the street."

They stumbled and clattered into the rubble-strewn space of the back yard, kicking and cursing their way over tiles and broken bricks, all bits and pieces of someone's past. Parchment-dry and paper-sharp grass rustled around their knees in the moonlight.

"When I was a little girl I thought this kind of thing would just have to be romantic. No offense, Frank."

"No offense, Shari. A beautiful woman by moonlight. But in this mess, in the middle of a battlefield in the middle of a war?"

They were halfway towards the gateway gap in the back wall. Shari stopped and looked up at the broad crescent moon. It shone faint highlights on her face, gleams on an ebony sculpture.

"Things don't change much, do they, Frank? Human beings are weird. The Russians have their base up there now, and so do we. Permanent buildings permanently occupied, spaceship visits every month and all that. We've been there a year and they've been there over four years – four and a half. And down here we're still killing each other. I guess four and a half years isn't such a long time to have any kind of an effect."

"What kind of effect?"

"Oh – pointing out the world's one small place and we're all in it together and that."

"Now you're getting philosophical."

"Me?" She looked at him, dark eyes hiding in moon shadows. "Guess I am. Waste of time, isn't it? The Russians are supposed to be building some kind of super-laser up there, if you can believe what the Pentagon says. Something so they can take our space defenses out all in one go if they want. Maybe they've built it already and are going to use it tonight, tomorrow, day after tomorrow. Then we'll get frightened and launch our strike before they launch theirs, and they'll launch theirs before ours lands, and that'll be the end of everything. No more little side issues to worry about like capitalism versus communism down on the Cape of Good Hope. Some hope." She scanned the close nightscape of crushed black husks of one-time buildings, then squinted at the moon again. "Clear night like this – a big enough laser up there could reach the ground, couldn't it? Be effective at least against unprotected targets."

"Suppose so." He'd read something about the idea somewhere. "Set anything alight unless it was soaking wet."

"Everything around here is dry enough, that's for sure."

They picked their way around moonlit tangles of rose bushes run to brambles. The gate was still in its place in the gap in the wall, but it fell outwards from its hinges when they tried to force it open. They stepped over it into the rubble-littered alley. Now all they had to do was to find a way around to the front of the building again.

"Frank? I think there's a way through this side."

"You fucking stupid buggers!" a voice yelled at them out of the ruined darkness across the alley. "You want to get shot?" The voice went on in Afrikaans, with a quiet Afrikaans answer from the shadows.

They started picking their way through the absolute darkness of a narrow passageway, running their hands along the walls, brick on the left and rough wooden boards on the right.

"Just once," Shari muttered behind him, "I'd like one of these Afrikaner soldier boys *not* to call me a stupid bugger."

They felt their way through the tactile cleft, hoping they wouldn't tread on anything nasty and dead, or anything dangerous – anything at all from a rusty nail to an unexploded mortar bomb from the fighting of the previous day. Mud they could forget. It hadn't rained in so long that the entirety of southern Africa was experiencing the worst drought it had known for twenty years. The grass of the surrounding veldt was palest yellow and the texture of dry straw.

They emerged into the dim moonlight of the street. Pulled up at the verandahed front of the former bar was Frank's sorry car, hiding its battered shame from miles of mistreatment in the anonymity of night. Shari and Jim's car was missing, of course – a burned-out wreck shoved off the road halfway back east towards the next little township of Kiewietskuil.

There was a sharp concussion off to the north. The *whump* of a mortar shell landing. And then a second.

"That way somewhere." Shari pointed across the street. "See the flash?"

"No." It was hidden by the buildings. "Couple of hundred yards away?"

Whump.

"Think so? Those are big ones."

Whump, in the same direction.

"One-twenty-twos," Frank said. After a while you get expert at telling the crashes and flashes of one weapon from another.

Then a brief flash, and a *whump* away at the end of the street.

"Hey! That was different. They going to mortar the whole place, Frank?"

He was looking at the glowing figures of his watch – ten minutes after midnight. Another crash off to the north or northeast.

"Shari!" That was Jim's voice from the veranda. He came out of the shadow, his videocamera and battery pack under his arm. "Get our stuff before we lose it!"

"Frank! Come on. All the cassettes are in your car."

They started hurrying past the veranda to his half-wrecked Renault. More mortars came in down the street on the west side of Valsfontein.

"What's that?" Shari stopped and pointed at a darkness crossing the western sky. "Cloud?"

"Smoke," Jim said, slinging the battery pack properly.

"But there's nothing out there but a few old farmsteads and miles of grass. Wiegnaarspoort's ten miles further, and our side shelled it flat yesterday. Why should that be burning?"

More 122mm mortars came in, north and back east.

Frank unlocked the hatchback so that they could get at their supply of cassettes and batteries, then went round to the driver's door. There was the sudden *tak-tak-tak-tak* of small arms fire away on the northern perimeter. He pulled open the door and started fumbling around inside where the courtesy light merely marked out the shadows. A flash and a *whump* just down the street.

"Why aren't our side answering?" Shari was almost jumping up and down out there. "They're not so dumb they can't get their act together. Hell, they have a mortar-spotting radar."

The battalion had a mobile radar capable of measuring the trajectories of incoming mortars and computing the exact position of the launchers. That was the kind of material and technology fix that had helped turn the tide in Pretoria's favor. Normally the ANC would have to strike their 122s after firing only a couple of rounds, or they'd find an answering mortar barrage coming right down on top of them.

He found his camera bag with its camera, films and recorder batteries. Where the hell was the recorder? The small arms fire rattled on in bursts, G3s for the army and Kalashnikovs for the guerrillas. Easy to tell who's who. There was the strap. He hauled the recorder out and started to back out of the car with his trophies. There was the sharp *womp womp* of lighter mortars striking in, good old Soviet-made 82s. He straightened up and slammed the door. The northern night in Valsfontein was a flicker of flashes, a clatter of gunfire and the stomping of mortar shells.

Whop-whop-whop went the army's light mortars, company and platoon squads firing back at last. The sheen of phosphor grenades lit up the smoke rising over the northern side of the township as South African troops among the ruins and dug into foxholes created burning islands of light out in the darkness. The firefight there was getting denser. Officers' whistles were piping – the best way ever devised to communicate with trained and experienced troops in a night action in close proximity. Silhouetted armored cars with roaring engines rolled across the street back east, heading for the action. A pair of tracked personnel carriers followed, dark bulky boxes slewing onto the street and then slewing off again with squealing tracks.

"Where's Umberto?" Shari wanted to know. "Where?"

"He went off somewhere earlier." Jim was sighting through his shouldered camera, trying to make something out of the dark confusion. "Think he went along to the signals post. Maybe ten minutes ago."

"That's the place for information," Frank said.

"Well okay!" She really was jumping up and down. "So let's go!"

They headed west along the street. A continuous barrage of mortars was coming in. The Afrikaners were firing back with their light weapons, but nothing was silencing the ANC tubes. The firefight on the north side was flaring madly, an endless percussion of machine gun and rifle fire. The staccato of the 20mm cannon on the personnel carriers and the sharp barks of the 85mm guns on the armored cars joined in. The armored cars had nightsights and could probably even see what they were shooting at.

A stick of mortars marched right across the street in front of them – fractional flashes and instant columns of dark soil and banshee fragments whining.

They hit the shuddering ground and clawed into it. Handfuls of splintered tarmac and broken earth, firm and fragmentary as life. Dirt and stones spattered down on their backs.

The sharp shudders stopped. The ground just went on jarring faintly from faraway shocks. On his knees and filthy, he couldn't hear anything and couldn't see anything but after-imaged mortar bombs exploding everywhere soundlessly as he blinked at the night. Then a broken cascade of battle sounds pushed back into his ears – G3s and Kalashnikovs, mortars, 85mm guns and the iron-bar staccato of 20mm cannon, the pop of grenade launchers and the crack of grenades, the breathless whoosh of rockets firing at South African positions. He wasn't just blinded by the flashes – it was really darker. Smoke was veiling the moon.

Umberto Giglioli stumbled right over them in the darkness.

Jim pulled him down onto the ground. No one was standing up again until their nerves had come back. "What," he said over the din, "is going on?"

"They threw me out. They're too busy." Giglioli hunched there, looking round at the crackling night. "The ANC have got through the outer perimeter on the north side and are carving it up. But they're being held by the inner perimeter."

"How come –" Shari was stopped by a heavy mortar exploding on the street forty yards away. "How come their fucking mortars are still coming in?"

"The mortar-spotting radar got hit. Good targeting by the guerrillas. The Afrikaners should have moved it again after nightfall. One of the first rounds landed right on top of it. The battalion's heavy mortar squad is a mess as well. The company squads are firing back, and the attack's being contained at the moment –"

There was a flash of flame and then a huge concussion to the northeast. The ground shook. A column of filthy smoke went up, lit from below, eerie and evil in the night. One of the armored vehicles hit.

"The big news is from Beaufort West. The rangers are in

serious trouble. Incendiaries or something. The whole place is alight. All the country around them is burning."

"Anything else going on?" Drowned in a string of mortars.

"Pardon?"

"Anything!" Shari yelled. "Else! Going on!"

"Don't know!"

Still on his knees, Jim Walters had his camera at his shoulder and was pointing it towards the column of boiling smoke that went up into the dark. If he could get a usable shot of that he'd be making prize-winning television, and no mistake. And then over all the erratic din of battle came the sudden thundering and thumping sounds of the battalion helicopters taking off into the night sky and the obscuring smoke, getting off the ground before any mortars could find them.

Gray grassland fenced by a palisade of fire. It was after sunrise, but the sun couldn't penetrate the clouds choking the sky. A smoke pall poured over them, lifting reluctantly from the ground in front of the orange flames and then riding on the fire-fed breeze into the south, a blackness of another kind attacking Valsfontein.

They'd driven in Frank's Renault along a farm track to the northwest of the township and out past the positions re-established by the army after the guerrillas had withdrawn into the night. When they came to a farmstead reduced to rubble years ago in some other wave of the war, they stopped the car. The veldt ended just beyond there, where the slanting smoke roof and the undulating straw-yellow grassland met in a seam of dancing flames. The dried-out trees dotted across the open pastureland made elaborate pillars joining grass and sinking sky. The smoke wrapped the pillars tighter, the fire swallowed them one by one.

Shari perched on a piece of tumbled down wall and talked to the camera, while Jim filmed her with the fire wall in the background. She talked into a microphone connected to the camera by a stretched out extension lead. She looked over her shoulder at the fire line crossing the veldt, and then back at the lens.

"The night action lasted barely two hours. The battalion's helicopters were forced by ground fire to fly at a height where they could perform no more than a spotting function. Half of them were brought down by missiles. There was no air or artillery support available at any time. What air strikes could be flown were fully committed closer to the distant cities, while all artillery positions within range were under direct attack. Even the one-o-five battery with the rest of the regiment only ten miles away in Kiewietskuil was too busy fighting ANC on its own perimeter."

A tree trunk somewhere inside the wall of flames exploded, and sparks and burning pieces of wood showered down out of the smoke in front of the fire, setting premature light to the brittle grass.

"When the ANC forces withdrew under cover of darkness, the South African companies regrouped and moved to re-occupy their outer perimeter on the north side. At that stage the battalion had taken only moderately heavy losses."

In the night Frank had watched the living remnants of those moderately heavy losses being carried into the lights of the headquarters surgical tent – mangled messes of flesh and blood and bone. There were too many casualties to cope with, because this war was geared to patching the messes together in the field and then lifting them straight out by helicopter. But suddenly there were no medvac helicopters anywhere to be had.

"In the meantime spotting helicopters here and with other units had identified the fire lines – long straight lines of grassland fires out to the north and the west, overlapping and crossing the whole area and moving with the wind. The rangers in Beaufort West are completely ringed by a fire which is reported to be engulfing their positions. Fires are also being blown by the wind into Kiewietskuil where the other half of this regiment is encamped, and have been reported by brigade HQ in the town of Aberdeen further to the east. Since dawn it's become clear that fires have not only been laid around every concentration of South African troops, but also across the open land in between. The ANC guerrillas have laid a net of fire to catch their enemy. And this is the part of it the wind is driving down on Valsfontein."

She looked over her shoulder. The flames were roaring eagerly to themselves and swallowing their victims one by one. A tree with smoke combing through its flattened crown suddenly became a torch, then a tangled flaming candelabra. Then the grass fire slid in front of it, and the flaming spectre disappeared behind the smoke. On the ground the grass smouldered, and then just melted into flickering orange heat.

"The ANC mean it this time. The fire line is exactly square across the wind and is running right down on the South African positions in the town. The vegetation is so dry that it burns like a torch. There's no water here. The only thing that could stop the advance of the flames would be firebreaks. But to build firebreaks you need bulldozers, and time. There are no bulldozers around here, and there's no time because the fires seem to be everywhere. The position has already gone from serious to critical."

A tree came toppling back out of the fire wall, a splintering skeleton of flames that fell apart and ignited the grass in front of the main fire. Streamers of choking smoke were drifting past them across the ground. You could feel the heat on your face as you stared towards the fire.

"That'll do, I guess." Shari coiled up the microphone lead as she walked towards Jim and his camera. She unplugged the lead and stuffed it together with the microphone into the cassette bag slung from her shoulder. Jim went on taking pans along the wall of flames.

Another tree exploded inside the fire, sharper than a grenade.

"It isn't a hundred yards away," Frank said. "Let's get back before – before we get cut off or something."

Shari nodded. "Jim! We're leaving." She crossed with Frank to his beat up car, still parked with its front to the approaching flames. Umberto Giglioli leaned against the open passenger door, an unused camera dangling from his hand. "How *do* we leave, anyway?"

"Drive back into town." Stupid question, stupid answer. Frank felt the heat of the flames creeping up on his back.

"Sure. And then? There's no road south, and that's ANC country anyway. Even if we could go west we'd just run right into big trouble, because that's where they're concentrated. Back east the fires are coming down right along the road. So?"

"Christ knows." Frank opened the driver's door.

Umberto, dirty and stained and as tired as the rest of them, started to get out of the way for Shari. "Follow the army. Where they go, we can go."

Bouncing back along the track, where they should have encountered a squad of Afrikaners they found only empty foxholes. They didn't find the army until they got back among the ruins of Valsfontein. Half the battalion was driving off down the main street and the rest were loading up as fast as they could. Battalion HQ was disintegrating into ordered chaos as equipment was rushed out of the ruins they'd been using, as tenting was removed, folded and loaded onto trucks, as cables were reeled in and stowed aboard the radio trucks and Land Rovers.

Captain Rutters obviously couldn't believe his eyes. "Still *here*? Where've you stupid buggers been? We're pulling out!"

"What's the situation?" Frank said. "Can we talk to the CO?"

"Not *now*. What do you think? He goes for a quiet beer while all this is happening?" And Rutters stared balefully at Jim Walters, diligently capturing the organized rout with his camera.

"*What's* happening? That's what we want to know."

"Everything, dammit. Everything's happening. The fire's coming right into the town and the blacks are marching up behind it. We can't stay here. Anyone can see that."

"Well at least," Shari said to the confusion around her, "call an air or artillery strike on the ANC."

"Hah! I said *everything's* happening. It's like this *everywhere*, the whole Cape Province. Even the cities! They made night attacks to keep us busy and then laid the fires. Even the *cities* are burning, I tell you. Cape Town, Port Elizabeth, East London. I don't know what the rest of the country's like."

"What's that got to do with –"

"The airfields, all the air bases. *All of them*. They're burning! We've no aircraft, no helicopters, nothing. Our artillery positions are all in the same mess as we are. Nobody can stay put to give fire support. First battalion and our own battery are getting ready to leave Kiewietskuil. We'll follow them right through to Brigade HQ in Aberdeen. We regroup there. You think we'd run away from a few fucking kaffirs if we had the stuff to fight them with? It's the fires. The bloody fires!"

"But if we go east – the fire's coming down right along the road. How do we get out that way? We need copters."

Contempt won over the captain's mounting fury. A reporter, a bloody woman, a bloody coal-black woman at that, trying to better him at his own business. "Of course we need fucking copters, but there aren't any. So we go along the road. Where else? We can't just go off at a run across open country. The fire would still be coming behind us and the blacks will be waiting for us. If we went charging into them in no formation at all, what do you think they'd do to us? Mincemeat. The road east is the only way out of this fucking mess."

"Well how did they do it? The ANC can't be everywhere and start fires *everywhere* all at once. How'd they do it?"

"God knows. God only fucking knows."

It took Frank another ten minutes to get Umberto back into his car and to convince Shari that Jim had got enough shots of the battalion bowling out of Valsfontein as fast as it could go. He stamped on the accelerator, slewed out in front of an armored vehicle, and overtook a tall-sided buffalo overflowing with troops. The soldiers on board were too anxious to jeer as the international press left Valsfontein as fast as its wheels would carry it. The irony was that Frank's eve-of-major-victory report was probably hitting the streets in morning Britain right at the moment, and at the same time the breakfast news bulletins would be carrying the first confused reports of a disastrous reversal for the army of the Republic of South Africa.

They drove through smoke clouds that rolled across the east road. Progress was slowed by wrecked and burning vehicles caught by mines or hit by one of the mortar rounds that kept coming over from the safe side of the fire. The guerrillas had nothing to worry about as they moved in the open north of the flames, free for once of both air attack and artillery barrages. By the time they reached Kiewietskuil the fire had reached the road and was burning its way through the town. There were abandoned artillery pieces among the blazing buildings. Ammunition boxes kept exploding in the flames.

Army vehicles shying further south across the tree-strewn grassland were running into trouble from squads of guerrillas waiting for them out there. The big and noisy vehicles, in no formation and in a hurry, made easy targets. Frank stayed with the units trying to get back along the road line eastwards. But the fire was already rolling right over the road. Any vehicle that succeeded in charging through the flame wall without exploding right in the middle found itself suddenly out on an open field of ashes and the target of concentrated ANC fire. It was a more manageable nightmare in the heat of the downwind side. So no one was going anywhere and the confusion was getting worse. Frank drove his Renault round in circles in the middle of a growing gaggle of army vehicles milling about and looking for a way through the flames that wouldn't take them into a killing ground on the other side. After a full quarter of an hour, with no useful suggestion coming from his passengers, he struck off slowly across the open grassland to the south of the fire front, diagonally away from the road.

After a while they were on their own, three reporters scared shitless, bouncing about in a battered old smoke-blackened Renault between scattered trees and through tall grass on parched veldt that was waiting for the fire to arrive. After only two hours, the car's suspension was disintegrating under them. Just ahead was a dried-up river line, and on its further side a raised bank topped by stunted skeletal trees.

"Stop!" Shari was pointing past Frank's ear. She almost arrived between the front seats as he hit the brake. Jim, in the passenger seat, tried to help her unjam herself. But she was only interested in pointing up ahead. "Sweet Jesus."

On the low skyline, under the stunted trees, were little head-and-shoulder silhouettes grouped around a dug-in machine gun. The weapon's barrel swung round as they watched, and disappeared against one of the hunkered silhouettes.

"Sweet Jesus! They think we're army boys."

They were going to shoot up the Renault. Frank would

see the bullets coming, for a fraction of an instant. No time to shout and explain. No time to do anything at all.

"Your camera!" Umberto yelled from the back. "*Jim!* Your beautiful big camera! Hold it out the window! *Show* them!"

Jim suddenly shook himself. He hauled the big video camera off his lap and shoved it out of the open window at arm's length. He waved it slowly up and down. Couldn't they see it?

Couldn't they *see* it?

"Now drive slowly," Umberto said. "*Slowly*. Drive slowly and go past them."

Frank pushed the gear in. Crashed it. He shut his eyes at the screech and waited for answering bullets.

"Frank! Do as he fucking says! Jesus."

Frank opened his eyes. He tried the gear again, and got the car lurching forward.

The barrel of the machine gun stayed down and ready to fire. Kalashnikovs were pushed over the rims of foxholes and pointed at them.

"Don't they know we're on their side?" Frank was pumping pounds of camera up and down on the end of a quivering arm. "We show the world how clever they are. They gotta love us."

The Renault bounced down into the stony dirt of the dry river. The weapons pointed down at them. The front wheels sawed grooves into the opposite bank. Then the car hauled itself forward and slithered half crabwise up the slope. It wasn't grass. It was ash. The stunted trees above were charred bones of wood. The fire had already burned here and then passed on along the wind.

The guerrillas, silent and crouched in their ash-rimmed foxholes, let them pass.

They found themselves driving over smoking black-ash ground where one of the overlapping fire walls had already seared the veldt. They'd escaped through a seam in the surrounding conflagration. They veered northeast and aimed for Aberdeen. They found the little town still burning, with corpses and smoldering army vehicles littered all around it. Over the next half day less than a third of the two battalions trying to pull back to Aberdeen managed to get through. The catastrophe was little short of a complete massacre. They took the road northeast across scorched country recovered by the ANC, trusting to luck and good eyesight to avoid any mines or ambushes. What eventually wrecked the car was a mortar crater in the dark. When they finally limped into Graaff-Reinet in the middle of the night, all they found were dying fires and the remnants of a regiment from another division.

Chinooks from the US logistics unit in Port Elizabeth came in under cover of darkness, and they caught a ride back to the city on the coast. The American aircrew were high on exhaustion, excitement, and fear. Flying in with the smoldering dawn, they saw the burned out suburbs and the devastated central district where the fires had been stalled by the sea, and finally got an idea of what had happened on the night the blacks set fire to South Africa. The Boer Republic had been burned to the ground.

10 *Autopsies*

Frank Simons, Johannesburg

Smoke still hangs over much of Johannesburg, three days after the fireraising attack that, in the course of one night, devastated all of South Africa's major cities and most of the open country in government hands. In Johannesburg and the dormitory towns that make up this almost fortress-like enclave, the fires are only going out as they run out of material to burn. The task of extinguishing the blazes was impossible. Throughout the Witwatersrand enclave, from Pretoria to Vereeniging, from Krugersdorp to Springs, fires sprang up simultaneously and enveloped whole streets and districts almost immediately. With literally thousands of buildings alight at once there was nothing that could be done. Streams of people fled their homes and choked the arterial roads that crisscross between the urban centers. The panic caused such dreadful congestion that many then died, trapped in their cars as the flames arrived.

Most of the whites in Johannesburg and the surrounding towns are now homeless refugees camping in the ruins of their own streets. Thousands suffer from burns or smoke poisoning. The battered medical services are stretched to the point of total collapse, and still they cannot cope. The plight of the white civilians is miserable. They have no shelter, they are short of water, conditions are dangerously insanitary, and the food supply is on the verge of collapse. Nothing at all is being done for the blacks penned in their ruined ghetto townships. During the night following the fireraising, vengeful mobs of whites carried their own version of fire and death to the fenced-off ghettos that still remain within Witwatersrand, and thousands among the trapped residents are thought to have died.

No work goes on in any of South Africa's gold or diamond mines. No factory is operating, no farm in the white-run areas has survived intact. There is nothing left with which to support the war effort, and the majority of the Republic's white population is destitute. As an economy, South Africa has been destroyed overnight. No single corner exists unharmed to assist other areas in the process of recovery. The army of the Republic now seems doomed to defeat. It has suffered devastating losses in some areas as whole regiments were trapped by the bushfires and virtually eliminated. More than half its aircraft have been destroyed on the ground along with the bases from which they flew. In contrast, the ANC forces will have prepared for the effects of the bushfires that they laid with such devastating effect, and will have survived virtually without loss.

It now seems only a matter of time before fullscale war comes into the white cities. Indeed they have already experienced a catastrophic example of total war. The wholesale destruction of a country, causing the total collapse of its economic structure, is known among the American military as environmental modification, or "enmod" warfare. What happened to this country three days ago was the first true application of "enmod" warfare, and it was the beginning of the end for white South Africa.

The mystery of the moment is, how did the ANC do it? How did they light fires from one end of the country to the other, and above all, how did they succeed in starting thousands of simultaneous blazes in houses and factories such that entire urban areas were engulfed in the spreading flames. How did they enter the cities?

The fires laid around camps and bases of the South African army are easily explained: the ANC's own guerrillas were thick on the ground around such targets. The endless rows of fires laid in series across wide stretches of open country are a different matter altogether: air and satellite pictures confirm that they were in places tens and even hundreds of miles long. How coordinated and simultaneous fire-bomb attacks should be possible against thousands of houses spread throughout hundreds of closely protected suburban estates remains totally unexplained. The theory gaining ground today is that Moscow interfered directly in a spectacular action to support the ANC. The amazing notion that Moscow might have turned its space lasers on South Africa is instantly popular and serves to save the face of the South African army: not even they could be expected to take on a superpower and win. Whether or not Moscow would really engage in an act of open war against a regime quite so dear to the Western world, and whether or not space defense lasers could be used to do it, are two as yet unresolved questions.

Excerpt of press briefing with Barbara-Ann Schwaetzer, White House spokeswoman, March 12th

LENNERT, *NBC*: What's the thinking here on the possibility of the South African turn-around becoming an election issue?

SCHWAETZER: Well, I doubt anyone will pull it into the election between now and the fall. Not at this late stage. After all, it wouldn't have been necessary for *this* Administration to rescue Pretoria two years ago, if the previous Democrat Administration had offered more effective help before the situation developed into a fullscale war. No one would have anything to gain by making an election issue out of it, the way I look at it.

BROGLI, *Washington Post*: Is consideration being taken as to mounting a counter-ANC infiltration, a military campaign, to perpetuate the war even after the Pretoria government has been defeated? Somewhat on the Nicaraguan or Angolan model?

SCHWAETZER: Not that I'm aware of, Mr Brogli. I think it's rather early to discuss the defeat of the Pretoria government while it still has control of the cities. I guess the White House – and Congress, too, let me add – would certainly be prepared to give a sympathetic reaction to any democratic resistance movement on the ground there, should such a movement come into being. I can imagine medical and educational aid being considered. However, with only Moscow-oriented regimes in the neighboring countries, I fail quite to see what could be done to prevent the entirety of Southern Africa falling to Moscow. Beyond that, I really can't answer your question. It's getting too far into speculative future events, which we cannot predict.

WILLIAMS, *Time*: Returning to events of a few days ago in the South African war, do we not detect some degree of disharmony between statements issuing from the State Department and the Pentagon with respect to the implementation of environmental warfare on the Cape?

SCHWAETZER: I perceive no disharmony, Mrs Williams. That enmod has been carried out in South Africa is totally beyond dispute. That's everyone's assessment.

WILLIAMS, *Time*: I was referring to the mechanism employed. Specifically, the South African government now states firmly that it has no explanation for the extent and severity of the fires, other than that support was provided for the ANC by Soviet anti-missile lasers redirected at ground targets. Here in Washington, the secretary of state claims there is no evidence that we have to suggest a use of lasers by the Soviets, and at the same time the Pentagon asserts there is strong evidence for just such a use of space defense lasers. What is the position at the White House?

SCHWAETZER: Our position is essentially one of caution on making judgements that involve a categorical accusation against Moscow. Before you do that kind of thing, you should be pretty sure that you're right. Let's say that the evidence presently available is at best what you might describe as circumstantial. I believe right at this moment the Pentagon is waiting for a detailed report from the South African authorities, which should give their interim findings on ground-based mechanisms – ANC terrorists throwing firebombs, and that kind of thing. It's understandable, of course, that the South African authorities are having some trouble putting together a comprehensive report in the circumstances currently obtaining down there. Our own intelligence findings will be made public as soon as they're in and collated. We'll all just have to be patient on that one.

CAGE, *Transworld-Telenews-2*: What is the current White House position on the moon laser theory? The Pentagon can surely monitor the pointing alignment of Soviet mirrors arranged in orbit, and so determine whether space defense lasers in the Soviet Union could have been focusing their beams on the fire areas at the time in question. Since no one has seen fit to assert that the mirrors were pointing like that at the time, does this rule out lasers in the Soviet Union, and does the notion that the Soviets used a laser built up there at their Moon base stand as the front-running theory? I point out that only yesterday, Under-Secretary Hyland at the State Department came right out and said the Soviets have no laser up there.

SCHWAETZER: Well, a Moon laser is certainly a possible explanation we feel we have to take seriously. Let's be clear on this. The Soviet laser installation believed to be on the Moon may not have been used to execute this enmod in South Africa. Its location right on the limb of the Moon at Mare Orientale makes it particularly difficult for us to observe, and thus to establish in how far the installation is already operational. There are still a whole lot of checks to be made on that one. However, it most certainly could have done it. The capability is there. Which unfortunately also means that the capability is there to do the same kind of damage anywhere else on Earth – even to United States territory in time of war. It poses a major threat to us right here on the ground, as well as to our space defense systems, and that threat is of a severity which cannot be ignored. We're going to have to extend our own capabilities in this area.

CAGE, *Transworld-Telenews-2*: By extending our capabilities, do you mean taking some form of action – that is, if the laser installation proves real?

SCHWAETZER: Well yes, something might indeed have to be done about that laser, I'd say.

Internal Memorandum USSF March 13.
From: Special Operations Div, S. A. Enmod Response Group.
For: Chief of Staff Office, United States Space Force.
Subject: Skyrock Option.

1 RECOMMENDATION ONE. Immediate despatch to S. A. of intelligence task force team. Purpose: cooperate on ground with S. A. Bureau of State Security to establish detailed information on provable ground-laying of fires and precise identification of fire areas not explainable through ground-laying. Goal: determination of possible Soviet laser enmod capabilities and performance.

2 RECOMMENDATION TWO. Data collection and assessment from all-sources search to determine readiness state of suspected Soviet laser installation at Mare Orientale.

3 RECOMMENDATION THREE. Discussion with Joint Chiefs of Staff to alert other services on scale of potential threat from Soviet Mare Orientale installation and already established ground lasers both to US Space Defense System and to US air, sea and ground forces, in particular in light of actual impact on S. A. ground formations and air bases, and predicted enmod impact on US forces. Intention of joint consultation: establish supportive climate for eventual adoption of point 4 below.

4 RECOMMENDATION FOUR. Familiarization with Skyrock Option Study (attached) with assessment target decisions:
   1 Yes/no to contingency deployment of Skyrock Option.
   2 Yes/no to pre-emptive enactment of Skyrock Option.

5 RECOMMENDATION FIVE. Skyrock Option to be discussed on rigorous need-to-know basis and not outside USSF departments.

4 NEAR SIDE

11 *Transit*

ELTS-16 MISSION / LUNAR SURFACE
PERSONNEL ROTATION
    UPGOING: KENNEDY SC to PILGRIM
    OD-Mission 1597 / Vehicle: Transav-OV-5
    ELTS-16 / Vehicle: ELTS-Transiter-3
TO PLSF-1 ARMSTRONG, DURATION 177
DAYS:
    1 Morris Elwood Gates, Maj USSF, 33,
negroid
        ADV Pilot, Base LSS Specialist
    2 Julia Piclert, Maj USSF, 29, negroid
        DOD Earth/Space Surveillance
    3 Richard Sullivan O'Carra, M.D., 39,
caucasian
        Medical, Bioscience
    4 Beverly Diane Ryle, PhD, 28, caucasian
        Geology, Seismology
TO PLSF-2 ALDRIN, DURATION
(WITHHELD):
    5 Alan Miles Browning, Col USSF, 42,
caucasian
        ADV Pilot
    6 Greg Bleazard, Maj USSF, 31 negroid
        ADV Pilot

The Transav shuttle, as long and sleek as a Concorde, hard-docked at four seconds over the time line. Once rendezvous had been achieved with Pilgrim there was time enough, of course. A space station isn't going anywhere, just falling freely and forever around the Earth in its own little circuit amid the great cosmic dance of balanced masses. Anything falling exactly alongside it kept it company in a companion orbit until someone fired a reaction motor and destroyed the velocity match. So there was no need for such time-line precision. But the Transav pilots took a pride in precision, and four seconds was good.

They towed their free-fall baggage through the docking tunnel into Pilgrim and dispersed to pass the time. The delay was caused by the wait while two final softlander supply pallets were maneuvered out of the Transav's payload bay and slotted into place on the remaining payload points in the Transiter's mid-structure. And then the Transiter would be ready to fly Mission 16 of the Earth-Lunar Transit System, would be ready to take them on their tour of duty on the Moon.

With her bulky spacesuit pack and her effects bag tethered to a hold point, Beverly Ryle floated in front of a viewing port in Pilgrim's side and watched the sliding miracle of Earth. During her one and only previous experience of space she'd never tired of that magnificence, brilliantly bright or night-city speckled, slipping round and endlessly round just a window, a vacuum and a couple of hundred miles away. It had convinced her, completely and for ever, that it was worth all the pressures that came with pursuing the dream career.

Those pressures were real enough. She was a qualified geologist and geophysicist. She had been on NASA's astronaut payroll for three years, and during that time had completed her doctoral dissertation in the brand new subdiscipline of lunar geophysics. The title was *Perigee-related Seismic Events in the Lower Mantle and Asthenospheric Transition: Alternative Core Models of Lunar Structure.* Like all scientific endeavors, it was doomed to eventual oblivion. In this particular case oblivion might come soon, because as of fifteen months ago America was back on the face of the Moon, and sometime there would finally be enough data to sort out which of those core models was the one and only real lunar structure. Well, at least Beverly herself would be one of the people doing the finding out.

Completing the dissertation while going through astronaut training hadn't been easy. But a tour on Columbus had clinched her determination to survive both sets of hurdles. Then had come the moonbase training, the long wait before scheduling for her first rotation, and finally the twenty-one day semi-isolation of the health optimization procedure, designed to avoid astronauts taking diseases with them to the Moon. Now she was on her way for her first six-month tour at Armstrong Base, the adventure she'd been working up to for years. First she'd discovered an interest in geology and geophysics. Then came the specializing interest in lunar geophysics, and the determination to make her doctorate so that she could get into NASA and onto the Agency's Moon Program. James, her husband, had always encouraged her with her studies, and had built up her self-confidence. He had encouraged her with her NASA application and with fighting a way through the first selectional hurdles. He had helped her cope with the frustration of waiting for any kind of mission scheduling, and with the stress that went with the defense of her dissertation. James had been so wonderful.

It was such a pity that over the past year he seemed to have been almost resenting her success and her commitment. There he was, a city hall analytical chemist, and there she was, a highly paid scientist astronaut, one of an elite, with a huge future career advantage, adventurous work and a generous touch of glamor. Americans on the Moon, no less! That was the nation's newest frontier, the highest ground it had ever scaled. Space was big interest news again, and the United States was wonderfully proud of its pioneering boys and girls. Hi, I'm James Heaton from New Orleans, I'm black and very proud of it, although I'm just another junior analytical chemist who pokes his nose into the toxic mess our industries keep on making. Yeah, but your wife now, she's got a PhD and she's an *astronaut* and she's been to the *Moon*, and she's *white*, isn't she? Bet that really makes you feel like you're somebody, married to *her*.

Beverly's hair was dark and cut as short as she could bear it. There wasn't a trained hairdresser anywhere this side of the atmosphere, and she would be away for six months. She floated in front of the circular window and watched the breathless rolling spectacle of the rotating Earth. Pilgrim was crossing Africa at around fifteen degrees south, crossing the skies of Zambia, Malawi and the north of Mozambique. That was Lake Nyasa out there to the north, a gleaming expanse glimpsed through cloud speckles that crowded together under the rim of the planet's space horizon. Out of sight to the south was South Africa and its vicious war. The sensational news had happened just as she was leaving for the tour. That morning she'd made love with James for the last time for – fully seven months it would be, before she finally returned to their home in Covington – and then he'd driven her into New Orleans on his way to the lab, and she'd taken a flight to Houston to enter the three week semi-quarantine before launch. Then she was flown with the others to Kennedy, and they had boarded the Transav, ready to go.

The Transav undocked and moved away from Pilgrim through her field of view, firing flash bursts from its clusters of reaction motors. That was the way back to Earth that was leaving.

The Transiters were jointly operated by NASA and the Department of Defense. They plied regularly back and forth between Earth orbit and Moon orbit, one on a mission, one servicing back at Columbus or Pilgrim, and one ready to fly an immediate rescue in an emergency. The schedule was as regular as clockwork, one transit mission every synodic month, arriving just after sunrise at Armstrong and just before sunset at Aldrin. The Russians also had three transit vehicles nowadays, which also made one trip every month. Those were all built to the same outsized Mars mission design – each time one of them went to the Moon it delivered twice as much payload as the American craft could carry. There was a lot of catching up to do.

A Transiter was essentially two cylinders lined up end to end, but held apart by a pair of long lattice girders spanned between the cylinders' side walls. The rear module contained the main propulsion motor and propellant tanks, and it had attitude motor pods and platforms for communications antennas mounted on its outsides. The forward flat-ended module contained the pressurized facilities for the two pilots and their transiting passengers. It also housed the life-support systems, the flight control electronics, and had more reaction motor pods and platforms for antennas and cameras. Slung one above the other in a long stack between the two girders of the mid-structure were one-way SLMs – softlander modules usually known as Slams – loaded with supply pallets for the bases. This trip the Transiter was carrying two Slams for each base, plus a reserviced ADV lander for Aldrin that was docked at the crew module's forward axial hatch.

Life was crowded for eight human beings for three days in the compartmented cylinder of the Transiter. Without the optimization of space made possible by free fall, where people can tuck themselves comfortably into any convenient corner, it would have been impossible. There are facts of life about space. One was the free fall toilet, which left a thin jewelled scatter of frozen droplets and freeze-dried fragments along their route, adding to the dispersed nebula of tiny particles filling out space between the Earth and its natural satellite. Ultraviolet and vacuum sterilized, US and Soviet nature mingled most intimately, most infinitely thinly, now that everyone was going to the Moon. And sleeping on the way, which was the second fact of life. Beverly slept in a sleep restraint, a zippered bag held in place by elasticated cords top and bottom, a perfect sleeping cocoon. Free fall is *comfortable*, it is the most luxurious bed ever devised. And also the most expensive.

Two nights in free fall. Sex in free fall? There wasn't enough time or privacy to form liaisons on the Transiter. Beverly hadn't tried sex in the weightless world of her Columbus tour, either. There had been factors like a distinct unease at the lack of acoustic privacy, coupled with fidelity to her husband, not wanting to make the most of her first astronaut mission in quite *every* respect while leaving James standing down there in New Orleans.

Fidelity wasn't a requirement, now. She and James had decided on an open marriage right back then when they were both newly graduated at college. But Columbus had been a closed world and therefore so close, and a relationship might so very easily have become an affair. James had made rather more use of their open marriage. Twice he'd even taken a regular girlfriend – once while she was on Columbus and once while she was away at Ames where the lunar seismology and mineralogy work went on these days. That had been the same girlfriend both times – Karen, a research assistant in French at Loyola University. Well now, this time Karen was going to France as an exchange lecturer for the new semester, so there could be no risky affair developing there. Meanwhile, James Heaton, that gorgeous guy she'd landed herself, wouldn't be too lonely for the next half year.

Beverly spent as much of her time as possible on the eventless voyage looking out of the tiny observation windows. The pilots held the Transiter oriented tail-on to the sun to simplify the solar heating problems. She had a constant view out one side of the slowly dwindling half-disk of Earth, and out the other of the slowly growing half-disk of the Moon. The Transiter was on an elongated figure-eight trajectory, starting out from a west-to-east orbit around the Earth and crossing over to an east-to-west orbit around the Moon, falling across the sky between the two bodies. The Transiter fell crabwise and effortlessly from one to the other through infinite blackness, through a perpetual dream of splendor in a hard, sharp and brilliant heaven.

Of the four passengers bound for Armstrong Base, Beverly, Richard O'Carra and Julia Pickert were new to the Moon. Only Morris Gates, the black USSF major who would be their ADV pilot for the trip down to the surface, had been there before, once on a shorter tour at Armstrong and once at Aldrin on Far Side. Of the two DOD astronauts bound for Aldrin this trip, Alan Browning was a Moon veteran but Greg Bleazard was on his first time to the surface. Those two were not unfriendly, but they were thoroughly untalkative as if they had some secret business to hide for themselves, something they kept checking through on computer screens fed by slot-in microprocessor memories, something they discussed in quiet and cryptic terms. Browning had a kind of encapsulated aloofness that set him apart. He treated his fellow Space Force astronauts as colleagues – he even accepted Beverly and Richard O'Carra, in a reserved kind of way – but Browning was the first astronaut from the Department of Defense Beverly had ever met who made you aware the whole time of his military rank. It was first names all the time, but he was a colonel and you certainly weren't.

But time on board the Transiter was too easy to pass. The transit was a beautiful, coasting, crowded dream journey.

The Transiter fell into the shadow cast by the three-and-a-half-thousand kilometre bulk of the Moon. With eyes adjusted, you could still clearly see the surface features in reflected earthlight sliding below. But then they fell on around the limb of the Moon into complete darkness without sunlight or earthlight. Nothing but a black presence filling half the sky, plus a hard tapestry of stars.

With the Transiter tail on to its path direction as it crossed over the lightless center of Far Side, the pilots fired the predetermined retrograde burn from the main engine, the orbit injection burn which precisely canceled enough of the vehicle's velocity for the Moon's gravitational pull to capture them in a one hundred kilometre high orbit inclined at nineteen and one half degrees to its equator. That was the standard delivery orbit for routine missions. The monthly delivery was timed to arrive with the Moon just past half-full as seen from Earth, perfectly arranged so that the sun had risen above twenty degrees in the eastern sky at Armstrong on Near Side but had still not sunk as low as twenty degrees in the western sky at Aldrin on Far Side. That gave bright sunlight at a shallow angle at both sites, ideal for seeing the ground topography for landing maneuvers.

In sunlight again and with the surface of the Moon rolling past one hundred kilometres away, they came round the eastern limb and saw the splendid half-Earth rising, humanity's home ground seen from humanity's highest ground. Browning and Bleazard transferred to the Ascent-Descent Vehicle to ready it for departure later on the orbit.

Fifteen minutes after they began traversing Near Side, the Transiter crossed up over the equator at thirty-eight degrees east and circled onwards above Mare Tranquillitatis, where Apollo 11 set down all those years ago in 1969. They overflew the marker craters Sosigenes then Julius Caesar and Boscovich, and the pilots acquired PLSF-1 Armstrong by line-of-sight telemetry. They crossed over the small hills on the south side of Mare Vaporum and then on into Sinus Aestuum, with Eratosthenes to the northwest and the even bigger crater of Copernicus coming down from the horizon beyond. To the right of track the vast range of the Apennines,

the Montes Apenninus, curved away over the northern rim of
space and separated the receding flatness of Mare Serenitatis
from the approaching flatness of Mare Imbrium.

There was a brief television screened telescope glimpse of
the tiny base facility tipping through a changing perspective
on the moving Moon below them. For half a year, that was
going to be home.

They circled out beyond Montes Carpatus over Oceanus
Procellarum, losing direct contact with Armstrong and diving
into the earthlit night.

Browning and Bleazard undocked in the ADV while they
still had earthlight for the maneuver. A squat and four-legged
spider shape, its protective outer film gleaming darkly in
dull gold, the Ascent-Descent Vehicle retreated to coast
alongside a thousand metres away. Together, ADV and
Transiter headed towards the western limb, starting to lose
the Earth. Shallow earthlight picked out jagged contrasts on
the walls of Vasco da Gama, Bohr and double-ringed
Einstein below them. Looking south with the aid of the
telescope they could see the mountain-wall ramparts of Mare
Orientale disappearing into the darkness of Far Side beyond
the reach of the Earth's reflected light. Further south over
the horizon, where the ridge of the Cordillera Mountains
was bathed in silver-white earthlight, was the Soviet base.

They circled out over the Far Side night again, the formations of Hertzsprung and Korolev only guessed in starlight.

The glittering jewel-line of the sunset terminator stretched
north-to-south across the ramparts and floor of Gagarin. As
they crossed into blinding sunlight the ADV fired its deorbit
burn and started to drop behind and slowly down towards
the chaos of the Far Side highlands. At the southernmost
extent of the inclined orbit, at nineteen point five degrees
south, the Transiter flew over Tsiolkovsky.

They looked out of the windows at the huge walled crater
and its pyramidal central peak, splendidly sculptured in
shallow and iron-hard sunlight. They looked at the tiny little
facility of Aldrin Base on the telescope screen, sitting there
on the darker basalt floor between the central peak and the
north wall. They listened to Aldrin talking the ADV down
all the way. Two of the crew down there were due to rotate

back to Earth, ascending a few orbits later with the on-station ADV that was to be taken back to Pilgrim for reservicing. The crew of Aldrin regularly comprised four men on overlapping three-month tours. It was the two civilian science astronauts who were rotating down to Earth, leaving an all-military team for the lonely life at the base in the middle of Far Side. Aldrin had the awesomeness of Tsiolkovsky, but it had no Earth in its sky.

The Transiter circled onward, swinging gradually north again. Crossing between Gibbs and the crater Brunner on the border of Mare Smythii, they had another earthrise.

The ADV with four outgoing personnel started up from Armstrong ahead of them. It approached slowly for rendezvous, a brilliant glittering thing coated in broken gold which fenced the sun. It achieved hard dock while still in earthlight over Near Side. Three of the spacesuited occupants came through the tunnel, then Morris Gates went into the ADV to take over from the pilot who had watched over its flight computer on the way up. The returning ADV pilot came through. The four people rotating back home again stripped off their spacesuits in free-fall acrobatics and declared themselves free of the Moon. They were the first group to have done a full six-month tour at Armstrong. Their arrival half a year before had followed the expansion of the base to accommodate twelve people, exactly nine months after the first American landing at Sinus Aestuum that had marked the return of the United States to the Moon.

Beverly Ryle, Julia Pickert and Richard O'Carra got into their own suits and took their helmets and their personal effects bags through to stow in cramped corners of the crowded ADV interior. It was so crowded that there would have been no room for seats even if they had been necessary on the Moon. But you didn't need seats – not when pulling a maximum of one gee on the descent and not in the gentle one-sixth gee of the lunar surface. The Ascent-Descent Vehicle was developed from the old Lunar Module of the Apollo Program, but bigger and broader and consisting of only one stage. It was based on the ground and designed to go up to orbit and back down again repeatedly. It could just cope with four people and their baggage. The Soviet lander, originally designed for Mars, was bigger and could carry far more payload. Moscow was altogether still one hell of a jump ahead up here.

They crossed over Far Side again, crossed the terminator into the sun. Morris Gates undocked the ADV and separated, and they were floating independently in front of the skeletal Transiter, a technological life all of their own.

Over Near Side again, both the Transiter and Earth talked with them. Coming up north of the equator over Mare Tranquillitatis, the Sea of Tranquility, the on-board computer fired the deorbit burn and the Transiter began to pull ahead of them while the surface of the Moon came very gradually closer. This time as they passed Boscovich and then Rima Hyginus, the sunken crater chain of Hyginus Rill, and began to cross the plain of Mare Vaporum, the surface features were twice as close. When the ADV automatically began to pitch head up the sun struck blinding through the forward windows. Morris Gates rolled them with their backs to the Moon, and for minutes they had only the Earth to look at.

When he had voice and data telemetry with the base he pitched the ADV upright and they could see the Moon's surface coming up at a shallow angle towards them. The flat, thinly cratered and puckered plain of Sinus Aestuum, the blinding sunlit rampart wall of Eratosthenes on the horizon ahead with the stark and sun-struck south end peaks of the Apennines marching away to the right. Up came the base, visible as a little row of interconnected circular buildings with solar panels on the flat roofs, sliding closer and closer to the right, to the north of track. The wall of Eratosthenes and the mountain peaks started to sink below the shrinking forward horizon. At the base they could make out the other two on-station ADVs parked on the landing area to the south together with a disorderly scatter of unloaded SLMs. They could even see tiny four-wheeled buggies parked by the base. Someone was out there in a suit beside one of the buggies.

The descent engine fired and the rushing ground slowed to a slide, came closer and closer, gradually stopped sliding. They hovered. Gates moved the ADV over the optimum target marker and then set it down gently, throttling back the engine and letting the shock absorbers on the landing legs accept the weight. He shut down the engine and began the close-down routine for the ADV's flight systems. They stood around him, shoulder to shoulder in their suits, their Snoopy caps pushed back off their heads so they could talk to each other directly without the headphones built into the caps getting in the way. They stood around him while he worked, and shuffled to get as much of and as wide a view as possible out of the forward windows. An open buggy with a single figure on one of its seats was driving towards them, coming to pick them up in pairs so that they could connect their suit umbilicals to its life-support packs for the drive across to the pressurized interior of the base. On the far northwestern horizon, Eratosthenes was just a long and uneven dazzling line of electrum under perfect black. The ground was blinding sunlight on concrete gray.

Morris Gates found a natural break in his shutdown routine and turned his head. Beverly was peering entranced past his shoulder. He grinned at her. "Well, here we are. This is it. This is the Moon!"

12 *Sinus Aestuum*

Excerpted from *The Conquest of the Moon*, NASA/DOD Joint Informational Publications:

PLSF denotes Permanent Lunar Surface Facility and refers to the lunar bases. PLSF-1 Armstrong is located at 14°N 8.5°W in Sinus Aestuum, the Bay of Fires, 55 km (34 miles) southeast of the major crater Eratosthenes.

The basic structural module is a flat-roofed cylinder 6 metres (19.7 feet) in diameter and two stories high, which stands off the ground on eight jacked supports. The module is delivered on a bare SLM ("Slam") nested in the payload struts of a Transiter and then softlanded on the surface. Access to the module is through doors in the lower level, which are either sealed, connected to adjacent modules, or fitted with an external airlock. The upper level is reached by a vertical ladder in the center. The module can be partitioned at both levels. The individual sleeping cabins are grouped around the central ladder on the upper levels. At the time of publication Armstrong comprises seven modules interconnected in a north-south line, with a module M1 at the south end and facing the landing area, and M7 at the north end.

The main power supply is from a 100 kW Nuclear Energy System (adapted from the proven SP-100 orbital NES) and from a 500 kW scaled up Nuclear Energy System. In order to achieve radiation safety, both NES units are placed individually in small craters some distance to the northwest of the base, well clear of activities in the immediate area of the complex. The power and control cables to the base are shallowly buried under half-conduit covers and the cable lines are marked by flag sticks. Supplementary power is supplied from steerable photovoltaic arrays ("solar panels") on the roofs of M2 through M7, the roof of M1 being reserved for communication antennas. The solar arrays are backed up by battery stacks which can maintain the base on saving routines right through the long lunar night.

Due west of the base is the parabolic dish used for radio-astronomy and for DOD Earth/Space surveillance tasks, its main activity. Due east are the five telescopes of the sliding-cross Experimental Optical Interferometry Facility. Both these installations are controlled over buried cables in preference to radio telemetry in order to ease eventual frequency crowding in the base vicinity.

The base is regularly staffed at present by twelve personnel, resident for six months and rotated at the rate of one group of four every two months. These personnel are of mixed sex, and include: the base commander; a doctor; a power systems specialist; a life-support systems specialist; a communications systems specialist; a suits/buggies/remotes (SBR) specialist; two Space Force officers engaged on specific DOD duties; an astronomer; two geology and geochemistry specialists; and a supplementary scientist or engineer from either NASA or the DOD. There are at all times at least three ADV pilots among those resident at the base. The personnel always include from four to six DOD Space Force astronauts, of whom one is also the deputy commander. The base commander at Armstrong is always a NASA astronaut.

Beverly got a cabin in the upper level of M7, the north end module, with a little round-cornered window that looked out northwest towards the burning wall of Eratosthenes. She stowed her suit in its constituent bits in a wall locker near the airlock in the geology lab downstairs, and just about had time to take possession of the cabin by flinging her effects bag onto the single bunk, before she had to attend the arrival briefing in the control center in the upper level of M1 right at the other end of the base.

The circular control center had the regular quota of windows, but otherwise the circuit of its interior wall was an unbroken array of consoles and instrumentation. There was a display board with a control console and a seat in front of it for every function at the base, together with the stacked cabinets of the multiple main computers. In the center of the floor was a hole with the ladder going down and with four slender roof support struts going up from the corners of the hole to mate with the ceiling. In the ceiling were air grills and recessed lights set above rows of translucent baffles. The control center was bright, fresh, cool, and also crowded.

Lelia Wenders, the SBR specialist and an ADV pilot, was sitting at the flight control console and guiding down the first of the Slams that had been launched from the Transiter on the follow-on orbit, tracking it visually and on radar and waiting to take remote steering control for hover and touchdown. Charles Watkins, the base commander, and Colonel Andy Bakum, his deputy, were doing the formal greetings to the Moon for Julia Pickert, Morris Gates and Beverly. Richard O'Carra was already in the medical lab and busy picking up the workload of the constant medical monitoring right away. Doctors are busy people.

Six people in the control center, one seated at a console and the others standing Moon-easy in a bunch around the other side of the ladder hole, but otherwise a perfectly balanced group – three women and three men, three civilians and three military. Even the ethnic mix was perfectly matched – Julia, Morris and Watkins for black America and Lelia, Bakum and Beverly for the whites. A perfect little microcosm of harmony.

"The name's Charles, but call me Chas," Watkins was saying. He was a picture of summer, forty years old but not spreading yet, lounging brownly around his base in shorts and sandals and a button-necked teeshirt. He looked around the six-metre center. "I guess we don't have to waste time going over anything here – you've all trained on the simulator in Houston. Same for each specialty area. But what you don't get down there is a mock-up of the entire base – just plans and pictures – so let's recap the internal layout. Some of it's even new to you, Morris. The place has expanded since you were last here."

"Two modules," Morris said. "The last time I was here, there was room for only eight people."

Chas Watkins grinned. "Previous time I was here we had four people, but there wasn't exactly the room for them. Okay now, what do we have? Down below us right here we have the south airlock, stores, and Andy's surveillance center."

"Closet," Andy Bakum said. "It's kind of small."

"Then in all the other six modules we have two cabins on each upper level, plus stores spaces, the astronomy lab and the medical lab. Downstairs it's more differentiated. M2 has the recreation space, M3 has the kitchen and canteen. In M4 are two airlocks, the toilets and showers, the waste processor, the water cycler and so on, and there's the main air system extending into the upper level. M5 has the heavy stores area as well as the little fitness gym, which by common consent is regarded as a torture chamber. M6 has our materials and maintenance workshops and the main consumables stores. M7 has the geology lab together with its chemicals store, and the north end airlock. And then right through the base, in every corner there are more stores, battery stacks, and more stores. We have so much stuff stashed away in so many places, that if anyone ever draws an item and fails to update the inventory on the computer – even if they do it just the one time – well as a punishment for the *chaos* that would cause in here, they get to EVA from the north airlock to the south airlock without a spacesuit. And that's no empty threat, is it Andy?"

Andy shook his head emphatically.

"So, this is Armstrong. Seven modules in a straight line, each one six metres across and with a one-metre connecting sleeve at each junction. That's forty-eight metres of base, and that's your home for the next half year. It's cosy and friendly, and most of it runs smoothly. We keep having trouble with the number two NES – last time it took Tania Sheldon fourteen hours to coax it back onto full load, and nowadays we need those five hundred kilowatts right through the local night if we're going to keep up with our programs here. Our load-toter handyman still can't be fixed so it can open the trap under the waste compactor itself, so we always have to send someone outside to help with the regular garbage detail. And the new shower they gave us last delivery is just too fancy to work right four times in a row. That's a maintenance problem you'll get very familiar with, Morris."

"Chas." Lelia Wenders had risen from the flight console

seat. "The Slam's down okay and I'm letting the residual propellant vent. Be back in around half an hour to check the level. Okay?"

Chas nodded, and Lelia crossed to the ladder hole and let herself just drop downstairs, almost *drifting* out of sight in the low weight of the Moon.

"Okay, now," Chas said. "What else do we need to cover? We all share the general work load and I try to keep the roster weighted fairly, but if there's any discontent with that, if anyone feels they're getting a bad deal, come right to me and talk it through. Don't let anything like that stew first – we can't afford tensions, locked up in here. One absolutely rigid point is the night duty systems watch. Everyone takes a turn every twelfth day, regular as clockwork. It's mostly just a case of watching over the base systems monitors and the automatic pre-set programs and the comm. links. There's always a bunch of people down at Houston and CSOC running things remotely up here. If any specialty-related work has to be run in real time during the night, the right people will be in here to do it themselves. Right at the moment, though, you have the rest of today and all of tomorrow to settle in. Organize your cabins, get to know the place and the scenery outside, get acclimatized to life here. Right, Andy?"

"Right," Andy Bakum said. "See how long it takes you to learn how to get up out of a chair without bouncing right up and hitting your head on the ceiling. That kind of thing."

"First thing you do, though, is go to our new doc and let him take a blood sample for establishing a datum on each of you. If you can manage that without getting concussed on the way he's sure to be grateful, considering he's already had to start work. Any questions as of right away?"

Julia, Morris and Beverly looked at each other. Not a question among them. Morris let his eyes linger on Beverly, looking straight past Julia at her as she looked back at him.

"Well then, that's about it for now. I'd just like to stress one last point, although you know it already. Sex." And Chas nodded his head in heavy seriousness. "Sex is an inevitable hazard of space. A group of people locked up in a cramped little area for months and with only enough work

to do to keep them occupied around twelve hours a day –
and privacy isn't even an illusion. Sure, the cabins and toilets
and showers all have doors. But the interior walls and floors
are just plastic and honeycomb aluminum, and the doors
don't all count for much, either. To dry yourself after a
shower you have to come out of the cubicle and stand in the
open corridor. So – as a result we all get to know ourselves
very well in here. Well with sex there are the NASA/DOD
regulations we all know so well, plus the informal rules which
you'll all have learned by now. Stick to the regulations and
the rules and everything's going to work out just fine. For
example, I met my wife that way during a tour on Columbus
five years ago. Anyhow, I'll reiterate the two most important
informals – no one has to do it if they don't want, and there
is no disallowed way to do it so long as you don't try it out
in the public or work areas. And I'll add that under my
command, anyone trying to set up or play with sexual jealous-
ies will get stamped on good and hard. The same applies to
anyone who tries playing politics and the like among the rest
of the personnel. We have to be a harmonious crew, all
respecting each other as persons and getting along just as
well as we can work it." Chas Watkins smiled, a big broad
smile. "And so far, in just two months of my commander
tour here, that's the only order I've had to give, and I'd like
it to stay that way for my next four months."

Morris Gates was still looking at her, smiling slightly in
that way men sometimes have when entertaining predatory
thoughts. Was he after her and not Julia Pickert, his ethnic
nearest? Did he maybe have residual racial hangups, a compensatory need to make white women? With men you never
can tell – the nicest of them sometimes turn out to have the
weirdest motives. Well she had her own handsome negro
already, James Heaton, her husband waiting for her back
there on Earth.

Routine on the Moon.

The time skeleton on which all work was hung was made
up from two cycles. The primary cycle was the local dark-light
period, the synodic month of twenty-nine and a half Earth
days, of seven hundred and eight hours and forty-three

minutes, the time that it took the sun to go once around and reach the same elevation in the sky again, for the shadows to reach the same length and direction as the Moon revolved around the Earth and the Earth progressed along its orbit around the Sun. Half of the twenty-nine and a half days was spent in dazzlingly harsh constant sunlight. The shadows shifted and shortened, they disappeared at the lingering lunar noon to leave a blinding and featureless landscape around the base, then crept out again and lengthened towards the snail's pace local sunset. But there was no change in the brightness or the color of the sunlight. There was no atmosphere that it had to shine through at changing angles, nothing that could conjure infinities of dawn or evening rainbow reds. There was just the burning and pure light, which took no hue at all from the dusty surface where it struck. The Moon is the color of concrete, achromatic.

Then would come the lunar night. Then you would get earthlight.

The Earth is fixed in the sky and is almost directly overhead at Sinus Aestuum. At midday, at high noon, it is a bare thread of crescent next to the sun. But at Sinus Aestuum sunset the Earth is a half disc that from then on takes a week to grow to full at the slow-time midnight and then shrinks back to half at sunrise another week later. From the Moon, the planet Earth is a brilliant thing to behold. It is four times as wide as the Moon when seen from the Earth, it has thirteen times the area and most of that area on the sunlit portion is covered with dazzling white cloud tops. At full, the Earth pours a flood of silver-white illumination down upon the stony grayness of the Moon.

The primary cycle determined the timings of the Transiter visits. Every month one of the vehicles brought pallets loaded with supply and equipment payloads, every second month it brought with it a partial crew rotation.

The secondary cycle was arbitrary on the Moon. It was the twenty-four hour turn of terrestrial days, keeping pace with life in the United States three hundred and eighty-four thousand kilometres, almost a quarter of a million miles away.

The days were punctuated by mealtimes. The food was good, wholesome, American. It was also freeze dried,

thermally stabilized and then irradiated to protect against
bacteria. It was reconstituted and then heated or cooled as
necessary in the walk-in – just walk-in – kitchen. There was
nothing home grown yet at Armstrong. For that you needed
a garden, for a garden you needed water, and to get water
you needed the results of the geochemistry endeavours and
the planned-for products of a small-scale materials recovery
factory. That was one of the things that Beverly and Peter
Elms, the senior geologist, were working towards.

The evening was a rest period, and there was also a
mandatory exercise period every morning in the torture
chamber. You had to wear weights strapped around your
ankles and above the knee, around wrists and above the
elbows, a hip girdle, a shoulder yoke and a headband filled
with lead powder. There were two sets of leaded weights,
one for the average female and one for the average male and
between them worth the masses of almost ten astronauts to
bring them to the Moon. They brought your body weight up
to more or less Earth normal for the workout, and you had
to work on out for a solid half hour, running on the treadmill,
doing pressups and situps and stretch-bends. Doc Richard
watched the observance of the ritual like a hawk. You
couldn't have American heroes returning home after half a
year on the frontier, wobbling and emaciated and catching
instant heart conditions under the restored regime of Earth's
heavy surface – that would be very bad public relations, and
really not so very good for the returning heroes either. But
it was Chas Watkins who fiendishly arranged the workout
timetable. The torture chamber had just enough room for
two people at one time, and the touch of evil genius Chas
had devised was to put a man and a woman in together to
maximize the competition – a man had more initial attack
and a woman had more stamina, and neither was going to
be put down by the opposite sex. The workouts worked out
tough.

The day work was varied enough. Beverly got to go outside
in a suit twice in the first three days. One time was for the
daily shit-bin detail when no other EVA was scheduled that
could take care of it along the way. Every day a container
of compacted and dehydrated non-reclaimable waste had to

be disconnected from underneath the base of M4 and taken across to the garbage trench to be emptied. They should have used one of the remotely steered handymen and saved all the hassle of suiting up for an EVA, but unfortunately the handyman couldn't open the latches on the trap under the garbage compacter because its claws didn't reach in far enough to get at them. The whole mess was a basic design error that couldn't be alleviated without replacing the entire manipulator superstructure of the handyman. Extension claws sent up to solve the problem just broke off, and so it was a whole lot easier to let a dexterous set of human fingers on the end of an arm attached to a crawling astronaut do the job. At least there was no smell when you were inside a suit and surrounded by hard vacuum. You took the container to the trench and emptied it, raked out the contents nice and thin so that the flood of ultraviolet light could kill off every last bacterium and virus, and then carried the container back and fixed it into place. The garbage trench wasn't just a dump, of course. It was full of invaluable materials that would be exhumed to make the Moon's first horticultural soil in around a decade or so.

Her second EVA was to assist Mike Calder, a major and a DOD Space Force engineer. In preparation for future expansion work, he was testing out how to make concrete on the Moon. The key idea, of course, was to minimize the amount of mass you had to lift all the way from Earth. There was an awful lot of rock ready and waiting on the Moon, and you could grind it up to make aggregate and mill it right down to a powder to make a particle matrix for the resin adhesive. Mike was testing the quality and reliability of different casting methods, and he was tussling with the mysterious consequences of dry mixing and dry setting in a vacuum. The results were working out fine for beam structures stressed in tension or with bending moments, but compression structures kept on crumbling.

Most of Beverly's work was in the geology lab downstairs in M7, coordinating with Peter Elms to get through routine tests assaying a whole backlog of rock samples. It all went towards building up a detailed picture of the geology and cratering history of the whole region around Armstrong,

right from Copernicus in the west to the far eastern rim of
Mare Vaporum, and from the borders of Sinus Medii in the
south to the extreme northern end of the Montes Apenninus.
It was a huge enough area, but then it had been formed by
huge enough events in the distant past as asteroids and
mini-planets crashed to form the giant craters and the vast
maria. All the samples from further afield than a there-and-
back buggy drive had been gathered by hopping a geologist
and a pilot out in an ADV to inspect the ground.

In the geology lab they also crushed and ground selected
rock, and then put it through a magnetic separator to recover
the fragments of ilmenite from the rest of the pyroxene and
plagioclase in the raw material of basalt rubble. The ilmenite
then went through a benchtop process of refinement – you
heated it and reduced it with hydrogen, and in the end you
recovered oxygen, iron and titanium. They also had control
runs to do on an experimental vacuum pyrolysis plant outside. You loaded it with rubble and soil scraped off the
surface of the ground, heated it to between three and five
hundred degrees, and presto – you collected hydrogen gas.
With oxygen to breathe, with hydrogen to burn it with in
order to power spacecraft or to generate heat and electricity,
with water as the byproduct of that combustion, with iron
and titanium to make into machines, with concrete to build
foundations and larger structures – one day they would be
self-supporting here on the Moon. But for the moment the
bench rig was tiny and the pyrolysis plant toy sized. The
plant sat out there on the blank ground under an aluminum
foil sunscreen strung between four poles – a glittering awning
that didn't twinkle, didn't rustle, didn't move in any breeze.

Evenings she had time for her own professional passion –
getting to grips with the control center console that monitored
the seismology packages. Those seismic stations in line-of-
sight of the base were monitored by automatic telemetry.
The other packages, whether just over the nearby horizon
or spread far away across the Near Side of the Moon, were
sampled either by routine interrogation from Houston on
Earth, or from Armstrong by way of any of the satellites
now orbiting the Moon that weren't exclusively dedicated
to Defense Department work. The most important relay

satellite was Troy-1. It orbited in a fixed position with respect both to the Earth and the Moon at one of the Trojan points. The Trojan points were a pair of so-called Lagrange points that flanked the Moon along in its orbit, one leading the Moon by a constant sixty degrees and the other following sixty degrees behind. The Russians at Mare Orientale occupied the leading position with one of their Selenos series satellites, the United States maintained parity with Troy-1 at the trailing position. Over Troy-1 you could interrogate any of the distant soft-landed seismology stations on Near Side from the control room at Armstrong, and it was also over Troy-1 that both Armstrong and Earth could talk to Aldrin at Tsiolkovsky on the invisible Far Side of the Moon.

Nights Beverly spent in her little cabin, a quarter segment of the upper floor of M7, up above the geology lab, with its little window looking northwest towards the raised rim of Eratosthenes. Softly so that it filled the cabin, or over headphones so she could play it loud, she listened to music from the collection she'd brought along or from the base's modest library. Bach or Beethoven or Brahms, Haydn or Mozart or Stravinsky – which one had the music for the Moon, for its slow cycle as your private world tumbled with thoughts and songs of distant Earth? She played them all. She played the Brandenburg Concertos round and round. She always had.

The harsh, incessant sunlight reflected off the ground and came in through the window and bounced around the wedge-shaped room. Nights she drew the black blind, and lay listening to the constant hiss of the air system, to Peter Elms and Cindi Patterson in Peter's cabin next door. Looking straight up at the dark ceiling she was looking straight up towards the Earth transfixed in the sky, looking at its night-side now at lunar noon. James was a quarter of a million miles away up there. So very far. Was he alone and lonely, too? With all of America to play with, and all of it half full of women, he might be getting something out of his side of this open marriage. Frustrations and potential envies. Go to sleep.

The new number two shower, the new high technology one with a push button and a microprocessor to dose the water, broke down five times in the first seven days there.

Major Morris Gates was the life-support systems specialist on the base, and he got quite adept at repairing the shower, although the repairs didn't hold any better for him than they had for his immediate predecessor. You could always tell the shower unit had failed again when you saw the pair of soapy footprints left in the corridor of M4 by the latest victim while changing to the other cubicle to rinse down.

Then one of the two toilets showed Morris its clogging trick. Everyone was coincidentally far too busy to assist the resident plumber, so Morris got his hands real dirty and was in a bitch of a mood all the rest of the day. This was high tech in the raw, and would someone just give him the *names* of the goddam fools at NASA and the Department of Defense who designed this thing?

During high noon on the Moon Beverly got to go on her first field trip EVA, Lelia Wenders accompanying her in one of the buggies. The ground vehicle had four wheels with electric drive, a steering joystick, and built-in life-support units under each of the frame seats so that you could plug in your suit umbilical while riding and so save up the six hours time of the PLSS, the personal life-support system, on your back for actually walking around. It was an open-frame car and had two roll bars adorned with antennas. It had equipment racks, batteries, high and low gain omni antennas and a dish antenna, it had an inertial computer to navigate with and even a radio squealer alarm rocket that could shoot up to over a thousand metres and squawk at a sixty kilometre radius horizon ring. Once you were over the horizon of Armstrong's shortwave radio mast, if you wanted to talk with anyone you had all of two choices. You could aim the dish antenna at Earth to talk to mission control or to get a relay back to the base, or you could aim it at Troy-1 to get a relay with twice the signal path and so with twice the return signal delay.

They drove out twenty kilometres southeast, alone on the face of Sinus Aestuum. It was one of the last sampling trips due in a closer ring right around the base, part of a grid of sample points that still had to be filled in. Beverly photographed and collected pieces of mare basalt and of anorthositic gabbro, a deep crystal rock type probably originally ejected onto the surface by the huge meteorite impact that had made the crater of Eratosthenes. She selected some vesiculated basalt rocks, scarred by ancient pockmarks caused as bubbles of gas burst that had been trapped in the cooling lava billions of years ago, and picked out some fragments of breccia turned up when she scraped over the ground. She also took scoopfuls of the fine surface dust of the regolith to test for hydrogen adsorption and recoverability. Lelia Wenders was a good companion to have along. She was competent at recognizing the rock types and she could take care of the borer probe to measure a two-metre deep temperature profile of the local regolith, the granular lunar topsoil fractured and churned over by an endless history of meteorite impacts large and small.

On the drive back they rolled over a blindingly lit empty and utterly barren plain, throwing up constant parabolic plumes of concrete-colored dust from each of the four wheels. What do you talk about together for a private hour? The Moon. And lovers, and life on Earth. She looked at the moonscape sliding past her, gilded by the gold-coated sunvisor pulled down over her faceplate. On the flat plain of Sinus Aestuum the horizon was so very close, only two kilometres away. Without any air to obscure details, little humps and craterlets in the distance were as sharp and clear as those close at hand. Here she was, not walking but driving on the Moon at its endless high noon, the furnace point of the sun lined up behind the darkened Earth directly overhead. The heat of the sun would fry her without the protection of the white and insulated suit, just as surely as the vacuum would kill her instantly if the suit perforated and let her air escape. The telescope bound astronomers of centuries ago, romancing about seas and scenery on the Moon, had called this place Sinus Aestuum. There was no romance here but the name was right for this static desolation – Bay of Fires.

Another field trip EVA, with the sun halfway down the western sky, this time with Morris Gates teamed up to drive her.

They headed northwest towards the rim of Eratosthenes.

The drive would take all day, and you couldn't eat a meal in a suit. You were stuck inside there hitched up to the urine bag, you had your insuit drink bag filled with glucose enriched fruit juice, and you had to stay hungry. They drove straight for two hours until they were forty kilometres from the base, and then they got onto gently rising and uneven ground that was ridged more or less radially out from the slowly looming crater wall that crossed the world ahead of them. The rampart of Eratosthenes was no longer blinding under the sinking sun angle – there were shadows up there on the broad slope under the ridge. They began to have to divert out of the way not just of little craters and of big and aeons-ancient boulders, but around inconvenient slopes and breaks in the climbing ground.

Morris wasn't talkative. He was a military astronaut, after all, and she was only a junior scientist astronaut on only her second tour in space, her very first on the Moon. He was as untalkative on the drive as those four military types around the other side of the Moon at Aldrin. Chas Watkins had told her that this time around there was an astonishing lack of chatter back and forth. The people on Far Side were so unmistakably isolated without even a sight of the Earth in their sky, and usually took every slightest excuse to talk over Troy-1 with Armstrong or mission control at Houston, and to hell with the otherwise irritating five-second delay on the return signal. The present foursome at Aldrin was actively discouraging conversation beyond the needs of functional information exchanges. Maybe they were less tongue-tied with their own people at Space Force's Consolidated Space Operations Center in Colorado. CSOC and the DOD was a different world from NASA.

Maybe Morris wasn't talking to her because she was the one who nominally broke the shower this morning, which meant an extra job waiting for him this evening when he would be already good and tired. Or because being stuck with this drive to shepherd a geologist took him away from work on assisting Tania Sheldon, their power systems specialist, with the remote controlled unloading of a Slam delivery of spares and replacement fuel elements for the two nuclear energy system generators. That would be more useful and

sociable work than bouncing around all day in the driving
seat of a buggy cruising across the vacuum-packed desert of
the Moon. He seemed to be getting very close to Tania, so
after all he had no special kick about only making white
women. And he remained silent for the next two and a half
hours as they gradually wound their way up the outer slope
of the wall of Eratosthenes. Once in a while they crossed a
line of buggy tracks. They were utterly alone in that empti-
ness, but they weren't the first people ever to go there.

They eventually halted only a couple of hundred metres
under the ridge at a point where the slope suddenly got too
sharp to risk with the buggy. They disconnected themselves
from the vehicle's life-support units and lived on the sub-
systems strapped on their own backs. They had climbed high
enough to be able to see right back southeast over Sinus
Aestuum towards the base. The sun was half behind them
and all the little slopes and undulations of the plain caught
the western sunlight and flung it back at them. It looked like
a great transfixed burning sea of once-liquid flame, like the
incandescent skin on a vast brimful cauldron of molten silver.
She raised her sunvisor and was blinded by the backwash
light. She lifted a camera with a telephoto lens and pressed
its eyepiece to her faceplate – stopped right down to control
the light, she could make out the base as a tiny line of white
beads stitched onto the horizon under the ultimate black of
the sky.

They tuned their suit radios to each other and to the buggy
relay channel, rotated the buggy's high gain dish to aim it at
the base, and checked in. Then Morris Gates turned away
and started up the last slope on the featherlight Moon.

This was a seismic expedition to investigate the crater-rim
mountain structure. They didn't need to climb to the ridge,
and they had equipment to deploy.

The sunvisored spacesuit that was Morris turned around
and looked back at her. His voice spoke straight into her
ears. "We have a flexible time line. Since you're here you
might as well see the view from the top. Come on."

They clambered up the last two hundred metres or so. The
steepening surface of the regolith was in places so tricky and
slithery that it slipped away under her boots. It got steeper

like some old schoolbook illustration of what a crater on the Moon might turn out to be like. She needed both feet and both hands, one sixth gravity or no one sixth gravity. She was scrabbling with her fingers combing the dirt, clinging on and scooping handfuls of soil, fistfuls of moondust that wouldn't hold her. Morris stuck his hand down into her field of view, took her weight, and hauled her up over the last piece of breaking ground onto the convex crest. She was breathing heavily with her breath bouncing back at her from the faceplate in front of her nose, the suit's cooling system was trickling like an overworked fridge as it worked to remove her excess body heat produced by the exertion. Glove in glove, his suit clasped her hand. She couldn't see his face behind his darkened visor, just her own spacesuit reflection with a miniature convex panorama of moonscape behind. In her ears he was breathing heavily, too, but his breath was calming down.

He let go of her hand. Beverly dusted off her suit and brushed clean the little windows on the chest console of life instruments. They walked up the last rounded slope towards the sun.

They stood where the crest suddenly dropped away down the first steep terrace of the inner slope. It was breathtaking! They were only a thousand metres higher than the plain behind them, but the broad sunken floor of the huge crater was almost four thousand metres below the rim, twelve and a half thousand feet down. The opposite wall, flooded with terraces of black shadow, was all of sixty kilometres away. In the middle of the broken expanse of the floor, its summit lower than the ring of mountain wall, was a shattered peak with flanks of ink shadows turned towards them. With no air to make the ground far below hazy, or to blur the opposite wall with deep distance, there was no impression of scale. Just an overwhelming sense of hugeness.

"This is about the best light to see it in because the shadows are just right for the shape of the slopes." His voice was transformed. What must his face be like behind that golden sun-visor? "Here is the best place on the whole rim because it falls so steep and sharp on the inside. It's splendid. It's a *splendid* sight."

It was an utterly magnificent sight as she looked across Eratosthenes into the half-high sun.

"Sure – it isn't like Tsiolkovsky. That's *really* something. There are a whole lot of places at Tsiolkovsky you have to really *climb* up to. Can't drive a buggy up to them because it's too steep, and can't set an ADV down on them because it's too rugged. Tsiolkovsky is the ultimate sight. But this crater is magnificent just the same. It's absolutely the best sight you can see anywhere in buggy range of Armstrong."

"It's magnificent." Beverly turned in a full circle, slowly. There was the dizzying fall across scarps and terraces to the floor of Eratosthenes, there was the molten Bay of Fires, there were the hard peaks of the Apennines marching off in an abrupt line over the northeastern horizon. "We're so high. It's such high ground."

"Oh it sure is. This here is the highest ground."

They stood for long suspended minutes, transfixed by the empty splendor of Eratosthenes. That was strange, to stand next to someone sharing his moment of peace, but separated by two spacesuits, by two armored skins and by hard and hostile vacuum in between. She couldn't even see his face for the sunvisor. There was just the intimacy of his voice like lips against her ears.

There was work to do. They climbed and slithered back to the buggy, they drove along the outer slope to the target site on the wall, they buried their seismic charge and spread out the seismographs across the slope. They fired the charge from two thousand metres away and watched the perfect parabolic plume of ejecta – human beings making their own wheelbarrow-sized crater on the flank of that natural wonder, utterly outdone but determined to pretend they weren't overawed. They got the readings which she would feed into the computers in Armstrong and forward down to Ames where the real number crunchers were available. The results would tell them the depth of the regolith on the wall and something of the deeper structures of the rim mountains, whether they were created from folded over ejecta or from a molten set of waves thrown up by the impact of the huge meteorite that had excavated Eratosthenes three thousand million years ago.

It took hours to double check the exact locations of the seismographs and to pack up the entire array. Then they plugged themselves into the buggy and started for home, picking up and retracing their own tire tracks. Morris let her drive down on the flat plain. He was silent again, had hardly a word to say, and this time she knew the reason. Morris Gates was communing with the awesome silent magnificence of the Moon.

13 *Earthlight*

The director of Lunar Surface Operations, Rosemary Maclaughlin, aged forty-five and with immaculately short-cut hair, was on the screen and talking with a two-and-one-half second time lag from Houston. The director rated a two-way, full-color visual linkup – one of the privileges of rank is limitless bandwidth. She wore one of NASA's miniature earphones clipped over her ear, with a tiny microphone boom angled forward beside her cheek. "What we'd like you to do is just a short talk from Armstrong for National Educational Television – as covered by the publicity obligation in your contract. We just want a NASA tape that NET can use in schools and so on. Feel you can cope with that, Beverly?"

"I guess so. If I'm not going out live or anything, maybe. And if you tell me what to say. I mean a talk on what, exactly?" And outside the control center the slow sun was sinking magnificently below the western horizon, and the night line of the terminator was slithering across the plain around the base. She wanted to watch her first endless sunset and her first transition to earthlight on the Moon.

"Just describe your own specialty. The structure of the Moon and how it's elicited, the surface morphology and cratering history, the nature of the rock and the regolith, the chemistry, the potential for materials manufacture, self-sufficiency and materials export. All of that, but superficially and at an introductory level. You don't have to give a university grade lecture or even a class report. This is strictly basic and for school use. You don't have to worry what grade you're aiming at because the educationalists will select where they can best use it. You might add the career opportunity. The career angle never does any harm, but don't labor it.

The whole thing should be around ten to fifteen minutes long. Sound feasible?"

"I guess so. When should I have to be ready?" Sinus Aestuum, the Bay of Fires, was extinguishing in a swelling tide of stretching shadows, and she couldn't see it. She was stuck here in a chair in front of the communications monitor and camera, instead of standing transfixed at a window.

"In around fourteen days. You'd have to sit up there in front of the camera and talk direct into it. That way we get a schools tape and at the same time a public relations package – an attractive and young and female scientist astronaut talking right up there on the Moon with the base control center in the background. Don't worry about how to do it. You can consult with our specialists here any time about how to put it together and even for rehearsing it through if you want. You have my personal guarantee there'll be someone at your disposal here if you decide to take it on. But you'll have to put it together in your free time. That's why I'm asking you personally – it's a favor on top of your work load."

"Oh, I guess I don't mind, if it's a short talk. And so long as I get help with what and how and so on." The sun only moves at half a degree every hour across the lunar sky, the sinking of its disc of fire below the horizon is an endless pause in cosmic time. But before the call started it was already three quarters down and slipping steadily away.

"You can specify pictures to be patched in later just about as you like. Our people here will tape it, and then you and they work on the playback. You can edit out pauses and fluffs, put in the pictures and stock footage or whatever to cover abrupt edits. The procedure makes it a piece of cake. I know because I've done it enough times myself. How about it?"

"I guess – I guess I'll try it. Why not? If it just doesn't come off you can always just throw it away." Outside there had been brilliant swathes of burning light to the west, all speckled with long rock shadows aimed by the sun. To the east there had been nothing but pools of shadow spilling into each other, overwhelming the brilliant upsun rims that still dammed them in.

"Exactly. No one can come to any harm. On the other hand, if your face goes a little bit public it can do you nothing but good in the long run. Okay, then, Beverly – we'll call that fixed. Wait three or four days until you've got your ideas together, then ask for someone to consult on it down here. Okay?"

"Okay. Ah – do you want to speak with anyone else up here?" The sun would be gone, already vanished. There were no more level floods of light across the control center ceiling.

"No, my business was with you. I guess we're finished, so close the channel if there's nothing more you want."

"No, there's nothing more I want to ask. Guess I'll close the channel."

She did it just slow enough, at least, for her words to cross the long divide to Earth and for Maclaughlin's farewell nod and smile to cross back again.

But the sun had already gone. Sinus Aestuum had drowned in darkness.

Chas Watkins was sitting at the other communications desk with an earphone clipped in place, an audio channel only. He unhitched the earphone and laid it down on the desk console. He looked at least as frustrated as Beverly did as she turned away from the blank window on the triumphant night. "That's some talkative guy, I'll tell you." He sighed.

"Problems?" Andy Bakum was emerging like a slow motion pantomime demon through the ladder hole, easing himself up effortlessly hand over hand.

"I just tried that guy Browning. I just called Aldrin. Got to be a tradition, hasn't it? They're sitting around there after most of two weeks of darkness without even the Earth to look at, and so we send them best wishes with the sun when it leaves here and heads off around to brighten their lives." Chas shook his head. "That guy just won't talk. He won't be drawn. I ask him how things are, and they're all either optimal or just plain nominal. I don't remember him being like that."

"You know Browning?" Andy had his feet firmly on the floor beside the hole. He smiled at Beverly. "See the sun go down? Great sight."

"I missed it. Maclaughlin wanted to talk to me."

"Oh, too bad. Chas? You know him?"

"Who?" Chas asked. "Browning? Hardly. I coincided with him on a tour on Columbus five years ago. I mean he didn't have much to say then, but he was friendly. Well he's friendly enough now, I guess. But he just won't talk. None of them will. We might just as well try calling up the Russians at Mare Orientale."

"Want to? I could patch you into their Lagrange satellite." Andy grinned. "I haven't been monitoring the traffic over their sat this long without being able to pull off a little trick like that. How's your Russian? You speak any Russian, Beverly?"

Beverly shook her head.

Chas shook his head, too. "Four DOD astronauts at one time at Aldrin. They're so secretive. Whatever it is they're busy at, apart from keeping the place running, it sure isn't science."

"Military science," Andy, a Space Force colonel, suggested. "There is such a thing, you know. But Browning, now. He's a real serious kind of guy, Chas. Real sober – although I don't know him so well. Those Special Operations people keep close."

Chas shrugged. "How would anyone get to know an archetypal taciturn soldier like him?"

"Browning would keep his mouth shut to anyone about his work unless he was ordered to talk about it, whether it's secret or not. That's the kind of dedicated guy he is. So if he's running Aldrin, the people at Aldrin are going to be quiet."

"Any idea what they're up to?"

"Nope. No idea. Space Force has a whole bunch of things it wants to test out up here, but I'd only be told about anything that affects my job."

"Ah yes, security," Chas said, almost uncomfortably. "The big disadvantage of the defense business."

"Oh, we learn to live with it. Say!" Andy Bakum turned to Beverly again, still luckless beside her night-black window. "It just surfaced out of my dull little mind. This is your very first time up here, and you got to miss the sunset transition.

That's shit. I mean, I sent Julia back to her cabin just so she should watch it."

"You missed the sunset transition?" Chas said. "Andy, we can't let that happen, can we?" He turned his seat slightly and reached across to the base systems board. "Take another look outside now, Beverly. Go on."

As she was turning away from their grins and back to the blank window, Chas killed the control center lights.

And it wasn't the triumph of darkness, now that the blazing eye of heaven had gone. Her eyes had no overpowering contrasts to deal with, and they saw a different world. A quarter of a million miles above the base, the half-Earth was pouring a silver-white radiance almost directly down from the zenith and casting no shadows on the concrete gray plain of Sinus Aestuum. Outside and all around Armstrong was a pale expanse far brighter than the stars. Outside and all around the base was a plain of pale milk.

Seventeen hours and eleven minutes after lunar sunset, the number two Nuclear Energy System, the five hundred kilowatt unit, shut itself down.

It happened in the dark, as usual, when there was no sun available to supplement their power through the solar cell arrays. With still thirteen more days of darkness to go and not wanting to start draining the battery stacks sooner than necessary, Chas Watkins put the base on first-stage conservation routines to keep their power consumption within the one hundred kilowatt limit of the perfectly functioning number one NES. The failure of the number two unit proved to be the trickiest to alleviate since the big scenes it had pulled when it was first installed and put on line. It took Tania Sheldon, along with the full time assistance of Morris Gates both at the remote steering desk and outside on EVA, all of two and a half days to coax the prima donna of a nuclear machine back into life and apparently contented function. There was swearing and cursing at Armstrong, and more of the perpetual and hopeless breaking of heads at Houston, at Jet Propulsion Laboratory and at the US Energy Department. JPL and the Energy Department were busy trying to develop an alternative uprated model of the hundred kilowatt NES that also produced five hundred kilowatts – and that worked. Everyone else was waiting.

She made her first call, voice only, back home to James at their house near Covington, across Lake Pontchartrain on the other side from New Orleans. The calls were limited to fifteen minutes and their number strictly rationed. After all, NASA was paying for the whole thing, even the telephone charges from Johnson Space Center to the recipient's home – evenings, of course, at reduced rate of charge. Beverly talked from the control center. It was neat the way everyone else managed not to be there when the call was booked. The participants were just herself, her husband, and the nameless communications engineers who monitored every link between Armstrong and Earth.

The call itself was not so neat, somehow. James seemed to her impatient, almost in a hurry. Awkward, anyhow. And he didn't cope at all well with the time delay that she'd learned to plan in to all conversations with Earth in the previous three weeks. James kept starting up again in the gaps instead of waiting, kept talking over the beginning of her answers, got confused and irritated. At least they avoided a fight, but it was not at all a skilled and loving call. It was plain clumsy of them – James not adjusting to the oddities of the channel and also managing to convey the impression that it was all an intrusion, as if he really had something else to do and somewhere else to be right then, and Beverly not managing to find a way to mend up the mess as the over-cool and over-edgy conversation proceeded. Sure, at the end he said he loved her. But he sounded every single one of those quarter million miles away.

There was another EVA to do. She had to return to the sample point twenty kilometres southeast of the base where she had been on her first EVA with Lelia Wenders, because she'd more or less managed a bull's eye. The samples she'd brought back had turned up a higher than usual proportion of ilmenite, and ilmenite was one of the things that the future was all about. It was to be a one hour journey out, with an intended four hours driving around on a grid collecting basalt samples. A resource that good had to be mapped out accurately. Morris Gates volunteered for the support job on the trip. He actually *liked* EVAs and he liked the Moon. That would be the only motive behind the intense smile he'd thrown at her along with the announcement that he couldn't resist her company alone in romantic earthlight.

Morris wasn't such a competent recognizer of rocks as Lelia Wenders, but he knew his limitations and so didn't mess things up by overreaching his abilities. He was a gadgets and machinery man, and above all an ADV pilot. He originally joined the Air Force because he just *had* to fly. Then he transferred to Space Force four years ago when the hullabaloo about the Soviet hands-down win to the Moon was still fresh and the joint NASA/DOD Moon Program was just getting into high gear. Well now here he was, he said, his second and deeper dream fulfilled and holding fresh, not tarnishing with time. This was his third visit up on the Moon.

He managed such a rapid sequence of duty tours by being a good enough ADV pilot to stay top of the list. Beverly knew from Chas that Morris was one of the best, if not indeed the very best. At Far Side during his tour at Aldrin, Morris had made the first landing ever attempted on the fearfully rugged peak of the mountain sticking up in the middle of Tsiolkovsky, hopping up from the base and hovering over the selected site for a long, a very long time before risking a touchdown. It had been a tight little one-man mission to roll boulders down off an only halfway flat site, no bigger than the span of the ADV's legs, so that any subsequent landing would be less risky, and to secure a rope at the top of Thousand Foot Cliff so that in future work parties would be able to scale the long and near vertical rock face. It had been the most daring flying exploit yet undertaken on the Moon, and it was all in the service of the Department of Defense, who one day wanted antennas and a radar scanner and who knew what else operating up there to protect and seal off Tsiolkovsky.

They collected Beverly's rocks by bright earthlight, sometimes shining halogen flashlights at potential samples before grabbing or discarding them. Morris drove her everywhere, charted the locations and cataloged the sample bags, overturned the big rocks for her and documented everything she told him to with the camera. He was a patient and perfect helper. Tania Sheldon was lucky that he managed to work with her so often.

They headed back on the slow one-hour return journey. The plain of Sinus Aestuum, slightly undulating, lightly cratered and sparsely strewn with rocks, rolled endlessly past them in a horizon to horizon circle of visual blankness. The Earth was at full overhead, and its soft and silver-white light made no angled shadows, picked out no features at all on the ground. A boulder would come down off the horizon two kilometres ahead, and then just disappear in the blend of smooth illumination. When Beverly was driving, Morris had to keep on warning her of craterlets in front that she was heading for at full speed. His eyes were better schooled for the job, so she let him drive.

They were silent, though they could hear each other's relaxed breathing transmitted to their ears. That was a curiously close companionship, surrounded by a pale and milky featureless sea. It induced a kind of dream. She bent up her knees, she shuffled down with the PLSS pack on her back nestled into the seat, and tipped her head back inside her helmet. She gazed at the overhead Earth, trapped under the top rim of her faceplate. It was full and brilliant and it washed the stars out of the black sky. It was so beautiful in some sort of way that she couldn't say to herself. She relaxed in the featherlight dream of the Moon, gazing up at planet Earth. It was day there in America, too, getting late. What was James doing at the lab, what was he planning for the evening? Who was he planning, maybe, in which case what did she look like and what was her name? Open marriage doesn't always feel as good as it sounds to be in theory.

Morris was driving steadily with one hand on the central joystick control, but he was twisted towards her in his seat, just a little way. His visor was raised because there was no need to protect his eyes against the ferocity of the sun. Behind his faceplate, his dark brown features were shaded from earthlight, but the backwash light was strong enough to see that his head was turned back sideways so that he could watch the way ahead. Why was he sitting like that – a cramp or something? She watched him for a while. She kept her eyes closed and enjoyed the faint pink glow of Earth through her eyelids, but she opened those eyelids a little way now and then, just a little way to see. He was watching her. He was watching her face, repeatedly turning away from the pale whitewashed ground ahead and looking at her for moments on end, long steady-eyed gazes. The sound of his breath transmitted into her ears was soft and subdued.

They got back in the late afternoon of Armstrong's day cycle, parked the buggy under its aluminum foil shield that would protect it against both solar ultraviolet and the invisible rain of particles and micrometeorites, and coupled it up to have its batteries recharged. Loaded up with sample bags, they cycled one at a time through number two airlock in the mid-position M4 module. They dumped the samples in the corridor beside the water purification plant, ready to carry through to the geology lab later. Then came the laborious business of extricating themselves from the spacesuits which had served as intimate second skins for the past six hours. It was an awkward procedure at the best of times. In the narrow corridor space between the pair of airlocks and the opposed doors through into M3 and M5, fitting themselves around the four vertical support struts and the ladder in the center going up to the level above, it was worse.

They cracked the snap-rings of the helmets and lifted them off, then unplugged the built-in headphones and microphones of the Snoopy caps and pulled those off their heads. They helped each other to disconnect and dismount the PLSSs, the Portable Life-Support System backpacks. It got hot in the suits immediately the coolant system was out of action, the suits being made of excellent insulating material. They pulled off the dusty outer Moon boots and gloves, cracked the snap-rings at their wrists and pulled off the pressure-skin inner gloves. From then on it was easier with bare fingers. They helped each other with cracking the waist snap-rings and then hauling the rigid torso complete with its flexible arms off over their heads. They removed the partially depleted drink bags from inside the torsos, and then stood the half-suits upright on what was left of the clear floor. The decapitated things stood there like the truncated middle sections of some pure white suits of fabric-covered armor – Japanese, or something. They struggled out of the trousers and integral boots.

They stood clad from neck to wrists and toes in the white tube-mesh of the inner coolant-carrying garment, with the clinically transparent urine bag dangling between their thighs so that anyone who happened by could see how much they made during the day. It was just something you got used to. Even if you somehow never realized it before, at the very latest when you were fitted for a spacesuit you learned the truth – the human body is a functional mechanism, and nothing more. They disconnected themselves from the oh-so-friendly catheters of the urine collection devices and put the loaded things out of the way for emptying and cleaning. They unzipped and stripped off the inner garment. They stood there barefoot and naked but for Morris' underpants and her own briefs. Visual privacy on the base just didn't exist, so nobody minded.

Cindi Patterson came through on her way from M3 to M5. She had to more or less clamber over the stuff they'd spread around the available floor. "Hi. Had a nice trip? See you got lots of rocks there." She paused in front of the door to M5. "Mike's getting dinner out of the fridge today, so if you have any requests, get them to him in another half hour at the latest. And be sure and take a couple of showers each before you join us all for dinner. You must have been in those suits for *hours*. Pooh!"

Cindi disappeared before Morris found anything to throw.

As he straightened up she looked at his deep brown body, lightly muscled and slightly lean. When she got to his eyes he was looking thoughtfully back at her.

Priority one, into the two toilet cubicles, after which the showers. When she emerged from the toilet, Morris was already in the number one shower and running its thin trickle of water behind the opaque door. Beverly kicked off her briefs, checked the towel she got from the drawer was really fresh, hung the towel on the hook beside number two, slipped inside and folded the door closed. She got herself wet and soaped up with the dual purpose shampoo and body soap, pressed the switch pad again to rinse – and nothing. Number two had gone on strike again. Goddam it.

She stepped soapy-footed out into the corridor. Morris was just coming out of number one, wet and darkly glistening. He realized the trouble she was in and made room so she could squeeze in right past him, turning his back. Her elbow slid momentarily across the small of his back, her hip brushed his buttocks. She closed the door from the inside, tingling. She turned on the water and rinsed down quickly. She opened the door again to reach out for the towel.

She thought it was Morris going to hand the towel inside for her. Then realized Morris was stepping naked through the gap and closing the door behind him. He was still as wet as she was herself. She touched his chest with her fingertips. And then she had one arm around him and had hold of his penis in her other hand so that it grew immediately hard. They were pressed together pushing, and his hands were sweeping up and down her back from shoulders to buttocks and sowing fires. Her face was in his neck, she was pulling on him and his fingers were stroking in deep between her buttocks. Then he reached right through and touched her.

And that was it. So simple. It would have happened right there in the shower cubicle, but they had all of their junk littered around outside and it had to be removed and stowed away. She removed her share in a dither, the touch of the skin of his neck and shoulder still fresh on her cheek and mouth. The evening communal meal went by in a daze. She hoped a hidden daze. The decorous hour of do-nothing leisure time in the recreation area was spent with her pulse stuttering in her throat.

Sometimes you just can't pretend that your body is all your own. It isn't. And sometimes you actually want it that way.

Through one partition wall was storage space, through the other was Peter Elms's cabin, through the door which cut off the apex between the walls was the ladder down to the geology lab, and outside, through the quarter circle outer wall and up through the ceiling, was cold vacuum and earthlight. But the little cabin was warm. The bunk ran along one side, head to the outside and foot up by the door. Against the other partition wall were clothes lockers and drawers, and around the curve and under the window was the private work area and desk. The free floor area came out triangular, and tiny. The blind was up from the window and gentle earthlight filled the cabin, a soft pale sheen shining onto walls and ceiling from the illuminated ground of Sinus Aestuum. The tape had moved on to Brahms's Number One. The second movement began, beautiful and uniquely lyrical.

"What's that now?"

"Still Brahms. The second movement."

"Oh. Don't know my way around classical stuff."

"Spend a little time with me and you'll soon learn."

They lay naked on the bunk, Beverly half on her back with the pillow and the pushed aside sheet to lean against the wall, Morris on his stomach beside her, propped on his elbows and smiling close. She stroked her fingers over his long brown back, over his buttocks and onto his thigh, idly up and down.

"You were looking at me the whole time in the buggy on the way back, weren't you? I saw you."

"Earthlight becomes you." A grin. "The light on your face. Made you so beautiful. But fragile, I guess. Captivating."

"Really? I didn't realize you were going for me at all. Didn't think I had a chance."

"Thought the military weren't allowed to fraternize with the local civilian population, huh?"

"No. But the whole time I was thinking you were getting, or maybe had already got together with Tania."

"Someone my own color, huh?"

"No." And there she was, smooth dark hair and white skin in pale earthlight. "My husband, let me tell you, is a pure blood negro from New Orleans – he studied out of state but he works there again now – and he's distinctly darker than you, and he's got real *curly* hair."

"Well me, too. This is just the joint military and space tour cut. What's your hair like when it's longer? Soft and kind of wavy? Or is it straight?"

"But I thought, I was sure, you were getting together with Tania."

"No I wasn't. Besides, Tania already has something going with good old Doc Richard."

"She has? They have? I didn't know that."

"See? We're all of us more private in here than you might think."

"Except between neighboring cabins. I can tell you exactly when and for how long Peter and Cindi do it. And half of what they said before, during and after if I wasn't able not to listen."

"That's the way it is. I figure I'll try asking Peter if he might like to swap around cabins, so I'd be right next door to you. If you don't mind?"

"Oh, no." Please James, forgive her, as he always promised he would. "I don't mind."

"Because you can't *sleep* two at a time in these things." He turned towards her, sliding onto his edge of the bunk and seeming at risk of a slow-motion but unstoppable fall to the floor.

She slipped her arm through under his neck to hold him, and they nestled up close. Stroking him, she touched his penis and watched his eyes close and smile. She touched a sticky droplet of fresh semen. My new man, my man of the moment, also has his supply in order. Not a ladylike and quite a basic thought. "And the whole time I was just sure you were after making Tania."

"No, I wasn't. Beverly, I wanted you since the first minute I saw you. Back at Houston, before they even flew us to Kennedy for launch."

"Right back then? And all the time, you didn't let on?"

"Well – I didn't know but you might not be interested in me, or interested at all. And anyway, you have to be cautious about these things – we have to live peacefully together here for months. Besides, you're married."

Was that supposed to make her pause for thought, or just do duty as an explanation of him holding back?

He pressed even closer. He slid his hand up from her stomach and stroked her breast, squeezed it to a cone and did that certain something that opened her throat as she breathed. With finger and thumb he teased the nipple. She took hold of his penis and hardened it. She cupped his testicles, wound up tight.

Softly, talking against her temple. "We do it the same way round again. Okay?"

"But I want to try the other ways. In this weight."

"We have five months, Beverly. Let's get it together easy. Tricks can wait, huh?"

"Sure. Sure sure sure."

"But this time be sure and take a good hold of my ass. In this weight you can bounce more than you think, and we might part company just when we don't want to."

"I'll keep you. Oh, I'll keep you." She took his hand down.

Beverly sat in the control center in front of the camera and recorded her publicity talk for Houston.

She told how the maria, the so-called seas, were formed by giant impacts billions of years ago that scooped out huge basins and threw up rings of broken highlands around them. The basins had then filled with lava pouring from the interior of the Moon, turning them into the flat plains of basalt rock that had persisted up to the present. She explained how the regolith, the so-called soil, was formed by the slow but constant churning over of the top few metres of rock by a gradual rain of small meteorites during the billions of years since the violent early period of the Moon's history. She explained that the basalt of the plains, of the maria, included the mineral ore ilmenite from which they could mine the precious materials iron, titanium and oxygen. She told how you could recover hydrogen from the surface rocks, the hydrogen having streamed imperceptibly down onto the Moon as part of the tenuous wind that came from the sun.

And with oxygen and hydrogen you had a source of power, you had water, and you had rocket propellant.

The lunar base would first become self-sufficient, and then it would begin producing in excess of its own needs. So what did you do with the excess? You exported it, eventually using an electromagnetic launching track known as a Clarke launcher, something like a giant railgun but used for entirely peaceful purposes. A Clarke launcher would be the cheapest possible way to fire off exports directly down to orbits around the Earth, where those exports would enormously reduce the cost of all space activities. And that idea, mounting the huge investment involved in going for the Moon so as to reap a far vaster return, was the heart of the concept called the highest ground.

Peter Elms needed no persuasion about changing cabins with Morris. After five months he was delighted to get a different view.

The Transiter on the ELTS-17 Mission arrived on schedule one and one half days after local sunrise. It brought two SLMs loaded with supply pallets, and a third which delivered a new base module to the surface. The Transiter carried two Slams for Aldrin, too, but no one was going to be told what was on those.

The Slam delivery meant work. First of all someone had to pump out the residual propellant from the SLMs and transfer it to the sunshaded storage tanks outside the base. Then the pallets had to be unloaded and the stores stacked at the outside dumps or brought through the airlocks for interior storage. And then they had to tackle the new M8 module.

The wheel assemblies had to be locked into place so that M8 could be hauled up to the north end of the line of base modules. The airlock was sealed and removed from M7, the new M8 was jacked into exact position and mated with M7's north end door, and then the airlock was re-attached on the north side of M8. It required precision welding, two full days of work for Cindi Patterson and Chas Watkins. Pressuring up M8 was a slow procedure with hour-long pauses to check that the seals were holding. When there was still no measurable loss of pressure after twenty-four hours at full, Chas let them reopen the doors between M7 and M8 and commission the new module. That was lead work for Morris, connecting up the air, water and electricity supplies.

Once M8 was finally integrated into the base, Peter Elms and Beverly started installing the equipment delivered along with the module. The lower level of M8 was to house a larger lab-sized extraction plant for purifying and processing ilmenite from basalt slurry. Its planned oxygen production capacity, coupled with the maximum output from the vacuum pyrolysis plant, was enough to generate a splendid ten litres of water every week. That didn't sound much, but it covered the net weekly loss at the base and represented the first ever saving on Earth-to-Moon transportation costs. That was an important start.

The number two shower failed one last time. Its oh-so-clever valve control was no longer repairable – patched up and re-machined to the point of disintegration. Replacement parts were ordered from Houston. There was a communications circuit failure, one of the black box units in the K-band downlink to Earth crapping out. Cindi Patterson fitted a replacement and spent half a day trying to diagnose the fault in the failed unit. After a consultation with Houston she elected to throw it away.

And there was no more putting it off any longer – Beverly had to submit herself to an amateur barber. She preferred risking Tania Sheldon's efforts than the skills on show from Andy Bakum or Peter Elms. The result was one you could live with.

Nights, the Earth cycle nights, she spent with Morris in a featherweight Moon-bound dream.

The second lunar dawn brought its flood of fire to Sinus Aestuum. Mike Calder, Lelia Wenders, Cindi Patterson and Peter Elms packed up to leave. Two days later the ELTS-18 Transiter arrived and the four of them went up to rendezvous in an ADV piloted by Lelia. One orbit later the ADV returned with the new personnel, Cherryl Donahue, a Space Force major and the pilot, Tony Randers, a Space Force captain, and two of NASA's geochemical engineers, Ed Wiseman and Lucille Abrams. The unusual thing about ELTS-18 was that it carried no rotation personnel for Aldrin. Browning and Bleazard had been there on Far Side for two months, and the other pair of DOD astronauts had been there for three, the full tour length at the isolated and cramped little base. But they were obviously staying a while longer. The Transiter had two fully loaded Slams for Aldrin along – the place was getting more supplies than people these days. The new arrivals had no idea what that might mean, and Andy Bakum couldn't even guess. The Far Side of the Moon remained cloaked in silence.

The replacement valve control for number two shower arrived that delivery. Morris fitted it, and the shower worked. It worked without a hitch for five whole days.

Then he had to give the mechanism its first remedial repair.

Ed Wiseman and Lucille Abrams, with Beverly in the role of assistant, got on with organizing the new materials production process. Once things were running smoothly in M7's geology lab and in the mini-factory inside M8, Beverly started catching up on the seismology traces recorded during the previous weeks. There was nothing big, of course, no really energetic event produced by either a moonquake or the impact of a large enough meteorite. She would have looked at something special like that as a first priority as soon as the computers registered it – after all, she was the one who had published the most up to date refinement and comparison of those competing models of the deep structure of the Moon, so why shouldn't she be the one to solve them, too? In taking the time to run the individual events on the computers she was paralleling work done by the people on Earth, that was true, but then for lunar seismology she really was something of an expert. The collection of data comprised only a handful of very minor quakes and their hour-long echoing signals, but the checking out took her right through the local slow motion sunset and into a third lunar night.

Earthlight again over the Bay of Fires, beautiful but cold. After the glaring surges of radiance that swept back and forth with the sun, the soft and static and stationary earthlight was like the slack between tides, the quiet time before something happens. Before her passions really rose in the sex games with Morris? They weren't cooling down together as the thrill of a new adventure faded, they were heating up. Sinus Aestuum was a bay of passionate fires, it seemed. And of confusions, because she loved James, waiting for her back home. But she was also acutely aware that there was not much more than three months left for herself and Morris before their tour was over. So Bay of Fires, but Bay of Troubles, too.

15 *Seismology 1*

The Earth was a half disc again, and the lunar dawn was due in thirty-four Earthly hours. Outside the windows, Sinus Aestuum was a ghost landscape bathed in a pale pearl sheen. Inside, the circle of consoles whispered away to themselves in electronic communion with each other, with the instruments and functions they controlled, or with partnered computers and monitoring facilities back on Earth. Armstrong ran itself.

She had all the lights burning to keep her awake through the silent watches of the night. She only had to be there so that someone was awake, just in case. All alone all night in the control center and waiting for nothing to happen. She could surround herself with music in the circular space, played not too loud so that it didn't disturb the lucky sleepers in M2 and beyond. The Schubert sonatas were over, and in the long silence she'd come down again from the winding spirals of the piano works. Now it was time for Bach again. She put on the Brandenburg concertos, One through Six. Bach composed like a novelist, bound by convention and necessity to short little sounds much like words and sentences, but binding them together into patterns within patterns, into long and flowing passages of experiences. Bach enveloped her. There wasn't much to talk about, after all. There was no interruption. It was Annette Sing running the communication desk during the skeleton science and monitor watch at Houston tonight, and Beverly left her in peace to her companions down there and her thoughts. Beverly pursued her own thoughts, and hoped Bach would forgive her inattention just this once. They kept coming back to Morris sleeping brown and naked in his bed in the tiny earthlit cabin back in M7 above the geology lab. Gaudy, gorgeous thoughts.

The first and the second movement of the First slipped by, *allegro* and *adagio* half heard. The third movement began.

A discreetly intrusive beeping from the astronomy console, a change in the pattern of lights. Beverly wandered sleepily over and seated herself to see whatever was happening. The Experimental Optical Interferometry Facility was changing director functions. It was situated due east of the base on a portion of dead flat ground, and comprised a single one hundred-centimetre telescope at the center of a cross made by four tracks, along each of which a sixty-centimetre telescope could move in and out from the center. The entire array, backed up by tiers of computation, could simulate all of the resolving power and some of the light-collecting capacity of a single telescope mirror one hundred metres across. It was the forerunner of a generation of immensely powerful optical instruments. It was also very useful to the military.

On the monitor screen was a readout giving the programed observation that had just completed, and also the one that was now running. The four trackable units were involved together in some observation run entirely from Houston for some lucky astronomer somewhere. The target was coded merely as a piece of the sky in coordinates she couldn't decipher and which wouldn't have told her anything anyway. Her specialty was deeper and darker, interior and earthier. Oh yes! Morris and James were getting mixed up in her head, brown blended with brown, and beautiful.

Number five, the fixed position center unit, was shut down, was not involved in the observation. She watched for several minutes as the four sixty-centimetre units stared parallel into space, tracking fractionally to compensate for the gradual rotational movement of the Moon, just one arc second in every two seconds of time. The third movement of the concerto ended, the fourth began.

The four telescopes stopped gathering light. Their panel indicators showed them sliding out along the tracks of the array to a new separation. Then they commenced the slow parallel track again, following the target star. All four were observing with CCDs, extremely sensitive charge-coupled devices, on their instrument tables, so it must be a very faint source indeed. Maybe it was one of the experimental planetary system searches – looking for the faintest of all objects, planets shining dimly by the reflected light of the star they circled. There were no silent watches of the night for the astronomers responsible for the run, it was all pre-programed and steered automatically. They were tucked up snug in bed like normal people everywhere. It was 02:30, the First was beautiful and she was tired.

The Second Brandenburg was playing, the second movement *andante*. The beeps and the function lights brought her back from the music.

The slow and incremental observation by the sixty-centimetres was going ahead at gradually increasing separations as they sought to simulate the resolution of a giant single mirror. But now the hundred-centimetre number five was in action, too, pointing with a different orientation at a different target. There was a new readout on the monitor screen. Number five was running an observation coded for the Defense Department.

Of what? The telescope was using the visual camera on its instrument table, was watching something bright enough to see very easily, something either in the vicinity of the Earth or in the space between Earth and Moon. Beverly tried to call up the picture on the second monitor to get a real-time view of whatever they were looking at. The screen stayed blank. On the program monitor a blocking instruction blinked a request for the clearance access code. Which of course she didn't know. The military's typical security paranoia. Who was she going to go tell, anyway?

The second movement ended and the third began, *allegro assai*. The four sixty-centimetre units shifted again in their own sedate little dance. Number five was making a fast track, five degrees of arc per minute, elevating and swinging from northeast through north. It had to be tracking some satellite orbiting the Moon, something in a high-inclination orbit and probably something altogether military, possibly even Russian. Something that the DOD was keeping secret. She watched the pointing data from the automatic eye out there east of the base, as it responded to remote instructions sent from Earth and followed some unknown thing as it crossed the lunar sky. Long live the military machine. Maybe she should be playing Holst's "Mars", five beats to the bar of thundering war.

The Second ended. Now came the wonderful Third. 02:50.

The Fifth concerto began with extempore beeps astronomical at 03:20. Number five had stopped tracking and had shut down, pointing fifteen degrees up from the horizon around west-northwest. Presumably the object it was following had gone into the shadow of the Moon and was no longer visible. The DOD's observation had deleted itself from the monitor screen. They'd got their moving pictures down there in CSOC, in the Consolidated Space Operations Center in Colorado, and didn't even say thank you. They just disappeared without a secretive trace. The other four units were still running the same long and patient program observation on the same object.

Beverly yawned. That was the excitement over for this night watch, nothing now but boredom until breakfast. She yawned again and stood up. Wander to the toilet, just for something to do. Bye-bye control center consoles for a couple of minutes, automatically working away without me. Excuse me, dearest Bach, for having to walk out on you.

She dropped free-handed down the ladder.

Almost a quarter hour later, with the Sixth already begun, she was all but dozing in her seat in front of the communication console. Standing up wouldn't help – in one-sixth Earth normal you really can sleep on your feet.

Little beeps and bleeps again from halfway around the control center circle. From the seismology panel. Telltales were glowing, alert little eyes of red and blue. A fault in one of the seismographs? She crossed over to see.

It was a response from the seismology station thirty kilometres away from the base. It was the first seismic event she'd ever *seen*, the first one she'd ever watched with her own eyes as it came in, despite years of working with such data, despite all the theorizing she'd done on terrestrial and lunar quakes for her doctoral dissertation. This was her first natural quake or meteorite impact in real time. A seismologist at last!

She called up the trace on the screen. A thin line ran in from the lefthand margin, absolutely straight, and then broke into a narrow little wiggle. The trace was already extended and wiggling silently and tinily onwards. P waves, primary waves, compressional waves, the reverberations from some distant shock passing the seismometer, passing the base. Nothing to feel, of course, no shake or tremor from a wave of such low amplitude. But a real seismic event. She checked the computer was recording it, which it was doing, of course. She watched the tiny little wiggling line, fascinated, watched the vibrations of P waves from an energy release as they passed through the body of the Moon. She called up the onset time at the seismic station. 03:44.

With data from more stations she could get a triangulation on the source. She selected the automatic station three hundred and seventy kilometres north in the Apennine Mountains, pulling the trace out of the computer since the station sent a constant telemetry stream to the base in real time over Troy-1. There was the trace again, apparently identical at the maximum resolution the screen would allow, with an onset time of 03:44.32. For a triangulation she needed a third station. The one east around the Moon in the eastern Mare Tranquillitatis would be far enough away. And there was exactly the same trace from the Sea of Tranquility, onset time 03:45.54, and with those three times and locations the computer would be able to do something. She brought it on line, accessed the subprogram and told it to compute the epicenter. The first movement of the Sixth ended and the second, *adagio ma non tanto*, began its infinite yet restrained sadness.

Beverly crossed back to the communication console, picked up the plugged-in earphone and spoke to Houston. "Anyone still awake down there? I've got a neat little seismic up here."

Two and a half seconds, then the voice of Annette Sing coming up out of the Texan night. "Really?"

"Yep. Sure have. It isn't much of an amplitude, but it's real neat. Ah – but I guess it's only exciting to a seismologist.

Do you want to maybe take a look at it on direct telemetry instead of waiting for the regular data package from us?" She didn't have to do anything. They could call for direct telemetry from Houston.

A pause, and then something a bit like the end of a yawn. "Sure. Why not? Give us something to look at. Nothing else is happening tonight." A long pause in one ear, Bach at his most lyrical and sorrowful in the other. The music knew that time runs out for mortals, that everything glides to an end. She wanted to get off the line and go look at the triangulation result. "Still there, Beverly?"

"I'm still here."

Two and a half seconds. "We're looking at it from number one station. Little thing is right, sure enough. Is that a quake or an impact?"

"Hold on. I'll go take a look at the traces." She unhitched the earphone and crossed to the seismology board.

The answer on the location was waiting patiently for her on the screen. COORD 14°S 79°W, ERROR RAD 75KM, DEPTH 000.0KM. Depth zero, at or within a hundred metres of the surface. She looked at the traces again, inspected them. There were P waves but no follow on S waves, shear waves that you got from the rock slippage in a quake. There were no Love or Rayleigh waves, surface-propagated waves that would have given a strong signature if it was a quake. And the first motion, the first kick of the sensor at each of the three stations, was upwards instead of some up and some down. A coherent front of primary compressional waves had burst out from the source, just as if it had been an explosion. So she skipped back to the communication desk and picked up the earphone.

"It's an impact. No doubt about it. The traces have all the classical explosion-type features, and the localization puts it at or near the surface. It's a meteorite."

Two and a half seconds. "Anywhere near you, maybe? Go pick it up sometime?"

"No chance. It's a quarter of the way around the Moon, almost. Fourteen south and seventy-nine west, somewhere on the northwest margin of Mare Orientale."

Two and a half seconds.

Two and a half seconds more. And more. The music wept at the loss of time. "Beverly, did you say fourteen south, seventy-nine west? That's the location of the Soviet base."

"Oh my God."

"You haven't fed the data in scrambled, maybe?"

"No, I haven't fed the data in scrambled. I guess – I guess – I'll call up another station to tighten the triangulation. Just hold on a moment."

She crossed to the seismology panel again and called up the single seismometer at Aldrin on Far Side. That spread should really tighten up the result. She could call telemetry from the instrument there without waking anyone at the base – being just four, they didn't have to keep a night watch. With a five second instruction delay over Troy-1, she accessed the seismometer and interrogated it for data gathered over the past ten minutes. Up came the trace, exactly the same trace, with 03:46.35 as its onset time. She fed the station code and the time into the computer and the screen rewrote the result. COORD 14°S 79°W, ERROR RAD 5KM, DEPTH 000.0KM.

She got to the earphone again. "Confirmed. Fourteen south, seventy-nine west, error radius only five kilometres. That's on four stations. That's got to be reliable."

Two and a half seconds of sorrowing music. "Oh shit. Error just five kilometres? That puts it just about right on top of the base. Hell. I mean, our estimates are that they have at least sixteen people there. Oh shit. And I guess we have to get some people out of bed down here."

"I guess so. I'll go wake Chas."

Silence, and then the final movement of the Sixth began, with its simple refrain and its magical inversion speaking of hope, of a certainty of things yet to come. In counterpoint Bach was quietly telling his own story – it goes on, it does go on. Somehow it goes on.

Unless, maybe, you were caught at the Soviet base.

The time was 03:55.

Andrei Tsherbakov, forty years old and now a full colonel, was enjoying himself. This wasn't just one of Moscow's better restaurants, it was one of Moscow's best, with crystal chandeliers, velvet wallpaper and astrakhan covers on the upholstered chairs. And the food! The soup had been excellent, his salad with fresh Black Sea prawns had been perfect, and the champagne for the first courses was one of the best Krimsekts you could order anywhere. He had insisted that Aleksandra should have the delicate caviar salad, and on this special day he hadn't even blinked when little Georgi Andreievich chose the sturgeon, which of course came in a portion big enough to fill him up before the meal had even reached the main course. Zoe had chosen the prawn salad, just like her father. She was shooting up as if she wanted to be as tall as Andrei, and was going through that brief age when she positively admired her father and everything he did. And why not, indeed – Andrei Tsherbakov was one of the first two Soviet citizens ever to land on the Moon. After Pyotr Grishin, now a lieutenant general, he was the second to set foot on its surface.

Together they had founded Luna Base over five years ago, and since then Andrei had been back there four times and had spent a grand total of nineteen months of his life on the mountain ramparts of Mare Orientale. It had made him and maintained him as a famous figure – well, famous for anyone who was neither a politburo member, a chess grand master nor a top ice hockey player, anyway. Of course, the solid prestige and the slight mystique of a Red Army officer, combined with his own careful aloofness and an instinctive distrust of open-hearted camaraderie, kept the mild nightmare of any kind of personality status successfully at bay. He maintained a strictly private life, which for him was very important – a man must have the confidence, consent and self-contained support of his own wife and children. No question of Aleksandra taking a job again now that Georgi was at school all day. No no, he needed her to keep alive that vital still center of home and family. And the money would have been immaterial. He had a colonel's salary and Red Army privileges, plus all the hefty financial supplements that went with also being a senior cosmonaut pilot, and on top of that a cosmonaut's very special privileges, too. And Aleksandra had no use for work comrades to whom she could show off her husband's famous name. That was a school game for the children, a supreme advantage they had over all their classmates. A father who was the second man in the Moon and a Hero of the Soviet Union – not very socialist and egalitarian, true, but damn good fun. No, Andrei alone was the family's self-sufficiency, and Aleksandra's role was to polish and dust and breath private life into that family and marriage, without which his self-sufficiency was neither possible nor purposeful. He earned more than enough, and they could afford to splash out now and again without thinking twice. Like eating in *this* restaurant today – his birthday! He was forty today, and there was no point in crying about it, so let's make a real treat for the family instead. He'd simply taken the day off, and that was that. The Soviet Union's Manned Spaceflight Control Center in Kaliningrad could do perfectly well without him for a day. The single focus of today was this sumptuous celebratory lunch for the four of them in Moscow.

A waiter came and removed the dishes from the fish course, the wine waiter arrived and poured out the last of the champagne for Aleksandra and Andrei. Zoe declined, her hand held politely over her glass the way her mother had taught her. At thirteen she had to ration herself under her father's eye so that she could enjoy a share of the wine with the main course and the desserts. Georgi had to be content with the half glass of sparkling champagne he'd been allowed in honor of the occasion, and was eking it out with a methodical solemness. The wine waiter twisted the bottle perfectly to catch the last drop before it dripped from the rim. Andrei

Tsherbakov beamed at his wife, so beautiful today. He was starting to feel *good*.

The restaurant was almost full – hardly surprising, when it offered such excellent food in the sweet cool shade on this blazing and baking summer day in Moscow. When he was a boy, his father had to *pay* to get into a restaurant in Leningrad. Restaurant full, was it? All the tables booked? How would the reception desk like one of these? Ten roubles, twenty roubles, sometimes even fifty roubles. A good thing his father had money, being an electrical supply engineer, and a senior one at that. And when you got inside the restaurant was invariably empty, and everything on the menu was invariably off until another banknote appeared, and then when the food finally came it was cold. No banknote in any of the Soviet Socialist Republics could warm it up again. But his father had simply liked going to restaurants. On trips to Moscow, too. The bribe on the door had cost twice as much in Moscow. And to get in while a politburo member was eating there, and to cause a risk that disapproval might descend upon the manager for allowing a politician's privacy to be disturbed – well for that you had to pay with one hundred, two hundred roubles, that much for sure. Did politburo members get cold food, too, in those days?

Things were different nowadays. The state had only a minor share in the ownership of this restaurant, and some of the best were wholly private businesses, if taxed up to their eyeballs for the privilege. The setup wasn't exactly pure socialism, but it made them run for profit and compete for custom, and that made them *good*. It was one of the purely beneficial aspects of all the reforms that had been introduced over the past fifteen years – reforms which, among other things, had produced the unfortunate effect of reducing the absolute value of a Red Army officer's perks and diluting the social mystique of military service a little. And Afghanistan hadn't helped that, of course. But on the whole those reforms were probably good things. After all, they had produced a revived economy that was able to shock the shit out of the Americans with things like the Moon landing. It had taken Washington four hectic years to get its own people up there, and the Americans might have established two separate bases in the eighteen months since they took up residence on the Moon, but the two together were still smaller than Luna Base, and even at the Sinus Aestuum site the development was way behind.

And the reforms *had* discovered excellent restaurants.

The wine waiter removed the tall champagne glasses – all except Georgi's – and replaced them with tulip glasses for the wine. And there came two waiters wheeling the covered trolley with the main course between the intervening tables.

And behind them, the crystal paneled doors to the foyer burst open and in strode a man followed by a receptionist in a hurry. The man wore a teeshirt and good western jeans and had his leather jacket slung over his shoulder and sunglasses in his free hand. It was hot outside, with brilliant sunshine. He scanned the populous tables while the receptionist pulled at his arm. He couldn't come in here in casual clothes, could he, even if those were genuine imported jeans. They didn't go with the chandeliers.

The man in the casual civilian clothes was Lieutenant Colonel Alex Stechlin of the State Committee on Space Defense. What was he doing running around in the sun at late lunchtime?

Stechlin shrugged off the receptionist, dodged an intercepting waiter, and hurried after the food trolley across the restaurant floor. He arrived simultaneously with the trolley and its attendants, and he looked terribly anxious.

"Knew you'd be here. Knew you'd be." The wine waiter, the food waiters and half the people at the neighboring tables wanted to know why. "Hello, Aleksandra. Sorry about this." And that was it for friendly formalities. "Andrei, there's been some sort of explosion at Luna Base."

"*What*?" And nobody else understood either.

"Some sort of explosion. A bit more than an hour ago."

"Bloody hell."

"Oh no!" Aleksandra said, looking at him.

"There's no information – what it was, casualties, nothing. All we know. *Knew* – I've been hunting you for half an hour. All we know is that there was a large explosion at the base and an immediate loss of all signals traffic."

"Andrei? What do they have there that can *explode*?"

"A lander's propellant tanks, Alex? A depressurization of the whole base?" His wife, his daughter, even his little son, the restaurant staff and the diners – they were all caught in the sudden surrogate drama.

Alex Stechlin just shook his head. "No idea. Come on. They want you right away in Kaliningrad. They're pulling in absolutely everyone who might be able to help, until they have a better idea of what's happened and what to do. So come *on*."

Andrei stood up, dropped his napkin on the tablecloth, fished out his wallet and handed it over to his wife. "Finish the meal. Enjoy yourselves for the rest of the day. Be good and help your mother have fun, won't you? Zoe? Georgi? I'll telephone you at home late afternoon or whenever I can later. Enjoy the day just as we planned. Someone has to celebrate my fortieth birthday, after all."

Aleksandra nodded, clasping his wallet in one hand and touching his wrist with the other. Then she found her brave face to dispel the worries of the children.

He smiled. "There's no danger to me, after all. So – make the most of the day so that you've all got lots to tell me when I get home again."

He left Aleksandra with her charges and her table and her tacked on smile.

They weaved between the tables. "Shalyapin's commandant at the base on this rotation?"

"That's right." Stechlin threw a glance over his shoulder. "A civilian. Is he really as good as they say?"

"He is. What are the chances of a rescue mission? The next ship is scheduled to leave for the Moon in eight days. How much sooner can it start?"

"Don't know. I've been looking for you for half an hour. I'm not up to date." Stechlin pushed open the crystal-paned doors to the brighter foyer.

"The Americans. Are they running to schedule?"

"There's a Transiter on its way. Started on schedule yesterday. Two and a half days and it's there." Stechlin stopped, halfway down the marble steps to the main doors. "An early rescue is probably impossible, isn't it? The Earth's already in its last quarter over the base. Total darkness before anyone could get there, and sunrise only in seven days. If their lights and guidance radar are out of action, no one could land there before sunrise."

"True." Andrei Tsherbakov stared for a moment at the brilliant summer on the other side of the glass entrance doors, his mind chasing disaster and deepening darkness on the Moon.

Nine in the morning, five hours since whatever it was had happened at the Soviet base. A breakfast of coffee and eggs had helped, but now the circular space of the recreation room was starting to distance itself once again on the other side of a veil of mental slowness. By rights she should be wrapped up in her bunk and catching three or four hours' sleep. Morris sat beside her on the couch, supporting her with an arm around her shoulders. Having someone to lean against almost made the enforced wakefulness even worse, but the leaning was lovely. Morris wasn't that alert himself – like all the rest of them, he'd had something like three hours less sleep than usual.

Sandals and ankle socks and bare brown legs following, Chas Watkins dropped slowly down through the hole in the center of the ceiling, ignoring the ladder. In view of the irregular start and anticipated busy progress of the day, Doc Richard had graciously allowed him a shortened exercise period, after which he'd showered and then been up to his cabin to change into a fresh teeshirt and shorts. He landed on the floor as easily as someone who'd just dropped down a couple of rungs of a ladder on Earth. The Moon is a very gentle place.

"Beverly, did you get an answer yet on the size of the event?"

"I did," she said. "I estimate it somewhere between one and two-point-five times ten to the eighth joules. That's really not so big. The error's wide because the amplitude on the trace is so small."

"And you're still happy it's an explosive event, not a quake?"

She nodded. "All the first movements on every station we have are in the same sense, there's no apparent shear wave, no Love wave, and the amplitude of the Rayleigh wave compared to the P wave is negligible. Plus it was right at the surface, near as you can distinguish."

"Any way to tell if it was a meteorite impact or some kind of explosion?"

"Not that I know of." Oh, and shaking her head really didn't do her any good. She was *tired*. "And before you ask, I don't have a figure for the second event because it isn't relevant so I saved myself the effort."

Chas just looked at her. "What second event?"

"Didn't I tell you yet? Thought I did." And Morris was squeezing her gently, comfortingly, to stop her getting irritated. "Okay. I didn't notice it at first until I realized the traces are too long for a single event, even with the long reverberation time of the Moon. So I searched the traces to look for a break or anything, and I found an obvious overlap, a point where a second event was picked up. The onset time is twenty-five to thirty minutes later than the first, depending on the station."

"Was it also at the Soviet base? A follow-on explosion or something like that?"

"If it had come from the same location the delay would have been the same at each station, wouldn't it?"

Chas didn't react. Morris squeezed her again.

You shouldn't snap like that. "Um – sorry, Chas. Guess I'm tired."

Chas dismissed it with a little flap of the hand. "Did you run a location?"

"Yep. Sixty-nine-point-seven south, one-thirty east. That's around fifteen hundred kilometres almost due south of Aldrin."

"Somewhere down near the south pole on Far Side." Chas shrugged. "No way that could be connected. Just a time coincidence. Was that a surface event?"

"Yes. Must have been a meteorite."

"Nothing way down there to explode," Morris said.

Cherryl Donahue looked through the connecting door from M1. "The director's on the line from Houston again, Chas."

Chas nodded. What they were waiting for was a decision

on going ahead and at least setting up a rescue mission ready to go, the three resident pilots flying the three ADVs to the Soviet base to pull out as many survivors as they could find. With just one pilot in each ADV and with the ADV from Aldrin joining in, they could bring out up to twelve people on the long two-liftoff and two-touchdown trip. But if they were going to try it they had to get started, because fueling up and flight programing the ADVs would take hours, and the pilots had to make a familiarization study of the place they were flying to.

Chas followed Cherryl into M1 and up the ladder to the control center. Beverly and Morris followed after. Beverly started up the ladder – how can you be so weary in one sixth gee? Morris gave her a lift under her hips that sent her sailing effortlessly up to floor height.

Head and shoulders in the field, Rosemary Maclaughlin was on the communications console screen, rating a visual linkup again. Cherryl switched on the console microphone and angled the pickup camera a little upwards. Andy Bakum came up through the ladder hole, too, abandoning the secrecy of his tiny DOD specialist office downstairs. They bunched up inside the field of view of the camera.

Maclaughlin had found some precious minutes to make up and to perfect her directorial composure since she had rushed into town and arrived at Johnson Space Center four hours ago. Now you could believe she got up in the middle of the night as a matter of routine. "I see all three pilots are gathered," she said, meaning Andy, Morris and Cherryl. "We now have a firm decision on the rescue suggestion. It's no go."

"Crazy," Chas said.

Two and a half seconds, then a slight shrug. "You don't know the terrain. We don't know if the Russians there are still in a position to help with a landing talkdown – or even if anyone there speaks English. There's no sunlight and minimal earthlight, and that's at eleven degrees elevation above the horizon, which is way below optimal."

"But we have three pilots here, and they all just happen to be Space Force whizz-kids as well. They can handle it."

"We can," Andy said. "We already discussed it. I fly first, then I talk in Morris and Cherryl."

Two and a half seconds, and then a set of the face. "The answer is no."

"God dammit, they might be Russians over there –" Chas was actually angry at his program chief. "But they're *people*, too. They're cosmonauts – our kind of people. We should give them any help they can use."

Maclaughlin's expression stayed set. "Personally I agree. I tend to your way of thinking, and I've represented your suggestion appropriately. The answer from the consultation stays no. CSOC say no. They couldn't okay risking the ADVs and they won't allow any of their people on any such mission – which takes care of you three pilots and also both of those at Aldrin right now. I checked with NASA headquarters, and they say no and that the Pentagon and CSOC and effectively the entire Defense Department says no. I don't know if it went to the president but it might have. The president's been at the Oval Office desk for a couple of hours already over in Washington. But the option is no longer even on the table. Besides, it could be that it isn't too much of an emergency after all."

"How do we suppose to know that? We don't have any satellite due to overfly the site, and before sunrise it couldn't see much if it did. Does the Pentagon have clairvoyants on its payroll?"

Two and a half seconds for the infuriation behind the question to linger loud.

"Maybe they do have clairvoyants. Some people down here are already dismissing the meteorite theory on the basis of statistical improbability, although that way you can probably disprove your own existence if you try hard enough. Outside of NASA the opinion is already hardening on an explosion, either a fuel accident or some kind of weapon that went wrong. That's a somewhat wild idea."

"Crap is what it is." Chas was beginning to get exasperated. The logical insanity of superpower politics got you just everywhere you went. "What makes you say it might not be so bad? We're still getting nothing at all over their Selenos-10 satellite."

Two and a half seconds, then a nod. "There's been no restoration of telemetry over the satellite, but around forty minutes ago they got one of the S-band antennas right at the base working again. They're both sending and receiving from Earth. We can't decode the telemetry stream – or so CSOC says – but at least we know they have a voice channel back home."

"Do we know if it's actually on the base or if it's maybe someone in one of their landers there?"

A long pause while Maclaughlin listened to someone out of shot, nodded, and then turned back to the camera. "The signal strength is higher than anything previously observed from a lander vehicle, so it has to be on the base. At least a part of the base is still intact and functional and at least some of the people in it are alive. That's all we know right now."

"Well at least that's something."

A delayed nod. "I guess we have to hang fire until CSOC decides to move an orbiter around to take a look at the place or until we decide to put our Transiter in an appropriate orbit when it arrives. Unless Moscow tells us all something. Right now I have a press release to discuss, so that's all for the moment. Could Beverly wait right there? Someone wants to check back on the seismic data."

Maclaughlin moved out of her seat and disappeared from the field of view. Paul Coseriu, one of the regular duty communicators, came into shot and slipped into the chair.

"Beverly? The people down here have checked on your estimate for the event energy and they come out with the same – between one hundred and two hundred fifty million joules."

Beverly nodded while the others started distributing themselves around the control center. "Nice to know I'm right. Have they got anything for the second event? I didn't bother yet."

Time-lagged surprise. "Second event? What second event?"

"Around a half hour after the first, at sixty-nine-point-seven south, one-thirty east. An obvious meteorite impact, just a little bit larger energy value, maybe." Coseriu was still looking skeptical. "It's there on your tapes of the seismic responses. Tell them to take a look."

Coseriu was looking around at people out of shot. He returned to the camera. "Guess I shouldn't still be on visual. I'll tell the seismologists, Beverly. But right now they're busy squeezing data out of the important one for the Defense Department. Okay, going over to sound only now. Bring Cherryl back, huh?" The screen went blank.

Beverly glanced at Chas, and Chas was looking sour.

Extract by permission of *Aviation Week and Space Technology*:

Mare Orientale, whose name paradoxically means "eastern sea", is located on the extreme western limb of the Moon as seen from Earth. The major formation lies exactly south of the equator and all but a small portion is located on the Far Side and thus permanently hidden from observers on Earth. Mare Orientale is a dramatic target-like feature 560 miles across, composed of a central plain of basaltic lava surrounded by three concentric mountain rings, of which the innermost is only partially distinct.

The Soviet base is situated on the extreme eastern periphery of Mare Orientale, i.e. on the Near Side of the Moon, on the ridge of the outer Cordillera Mountains at 14°S 79°W. The main complex is sited on a small level plateau to the east of the highest ridge and enjoying an unobscured view towards the Earth above the base's eastern horizon. The base complex comprises two parallel and fully interconnected rows of five units each. These square-plan units are 26 feet across and have two floors. The northeast corner unit contains the control center on an additional upper floor, and is thus the tallest building on the Moon.

The base has some solar panel arrays but its main power source is three nuclear-powered thermal generators with an output of 250kW each. Latest information released in the USSR is that a 1,000 kW generator will be installed at the base within approximately one year. Other elements at the main complex include two surveillance dishes, and a 39 inch optical telescope, with a 118 inch multimirror telescope in construction. A road, i.e. a flag-marked track, runs west from the main complex, over the ridge and down the concealed western slope of the Cordillera Mountains. It connects with an outstation located 30 miles away in the deep ring between the concentric Cordillera and Rook

Mountains, the main ramparts of Mare Orientale. This out-station consists of two units together with a single 250kW generator. According to *Pravda*, basalt processing for mineral and water recovery is planned there.

It is to be noted that the outstation is permanently unsighted from the Earth by the Cordillera Mountains. A new structure is being built out from the main complex and is extending down the mountainside towards the outstation. It consists of approximately six miles of raised track or pipe with a further six miles of support posts still awaiting track. This installation, which *Pravda* on two occasions referred to as a "monorail", is the cause of some concern in Government circles. Many experts are convinced that it is not a transport system but instead a weapon intended for so-called Earth-interdiction applications, consisting of either a laser guide tube or an electrically powered projectile-launching track functioning on the principle of the railgun. The serious threat posed by such an installation to United States space defense interests would be difficult to exaggerate.

Leonid Steffanovich Shalyapin, stocky and a little over-weight, married with two children, was forty-seven years old and was the oldest man on the Moon. This was his fifth visit, including the first time when he stayed on board the orbiting *Vladimir Komarov*, this was his fourth tour at Luna Base and his third as commandant. He had been in residence again all of seven weeks, and the privilege of being here provided a very deep and quiet joy. The Moon, to sum it up succinctly, was magnificent.

He sat behind his desk, wedged between it and the wall in his tiny cabin on the midfloor of B1, the northeast corner block, and hurriedly scrolled performance data on his desk-top screen. Number one power unit was giving some concern to Yelena Blochina and Mikhail Charotonov, and they wanted to talk to him over lunch about the merits of a servicing shutdown. Lunch was a more or less communal affair, and was just about due.

It was like blinking, but bright instead of dark. It was a momentary brightness across his bunk at the other end of the cabin. It was a flash from outside the little window.

A flash from outside? On the Moon?

He went from his desk to his window, no distance at all in the box of a cabin. As he completed the first step the base shuddered.

The second step brought him to the window. Outside should be the pale night, with the half-Earth shining fat and belly down above the eastern horizon. But he didn't see a thing. There was an instant *crack* in front of his face. When he opened his eyes again the window was opaque, its outer safety pane starred like a spider's web of damask lace.

Then there was a *crash* overhead. And the hissing sound of escaping air.

Up above the midfloor cabins in B1 was the control center, the brain of the base. He forgot the window with its inner pane still intact, and turned instead to the door. He had to *tug* open the door, like wrestling a summer wind in the open-windowed study of his dacha. His ears popped. He stepped out onto the diamond of floor around the central ladder.

A wind was blowing upwards, into the control center.

The pressure on his ears hardened. The hissing was louder. Down on the lower floor the emergency doors to the neighboring blocks slammed closed, sealing off B1 and anyone inside it. He stepped over the updraught hole and started to pull himself towards the control center hatch in the ceiling.

The hatch came down over his head.

It bounced out of its seals and the wind resumed.

Maria Alova would be alone in the control center on midday watch. Leonid reached over his head to push the hatch open. The wind helped. Nothing came back into his lungs.

Upwards through the gap, he saw her in mid air – *jumping* onto the hatch.

The hatch slammed against his hair. The latches locked home.

Leonid hung easy-handed on the ladder, dizzy. Air pressure must be halfway down. Indirectly, angrily, he heard the hissing from the sealed-off control center. The pressure in there was still falling. He wrapped his free hand around the latch handle.

Maria Alova had sealed herself inside. Her decision. For a reason. He should wait. Or help her?

Her decision. For a reason.

Swallowing stopped his ears from hurting. Above the hatch above his head, the hissing was fainter. It would die away as the air pressure in the control center dropped to zero. Waiting the seconds. Cold seconds now the expanded air had swallowed its own heat. Down the ladder beyond his feet, the lower floor was condensation misty. Seconds of foggy breathlessness.

A rapping on the hatch cover.

Leonid wrenched the latch handle. The hatch ripped from his fingers and slammed right over. Air whooshed upwards to equalize internal pressure. His ears almost burst.

Maria lay on the floor beside the hatch. Blood spread out from under her face. She lifted her head and blinked as he climbed up beside her. Blood poured out of her nose. She lifted her hand and pointed through a white haze. She collapsed, but the hissing went on.

Leonid waved his way through an icy fog, and found the leak. Up above the instrument consoles, right at the top of the wall, a torn off strip of computer paper was plastered flat into the angle with the ceiling. Right in the angle, at the fold in the strip, the paper was puckered into a crack as long as his forearm.

The paper fluttered, air pressure alone holding it in place. The hissing went on viciously. The paper was going to tear.

He rushed through the bright lights fog to the computer desk, snapped open the printer cover and ripped out a length of paper. He crossed back to the crack, folding the strip double and double again. He reached up and fitted the double fold against the crack, and opened the paper so that it could smooth itself like a flexible magnet against wall and ceiling surfaces.

And the crack still hissed viciously.

His ears had compressed springs inside them, and swallowing didn't help. His legs quivered, his head was as fogged as the control center. Through the haze, all around, warning lights and red alarm eyes flashed at him. The crack hissed and the air was still going, slowly. When the pressure had dropped even further, the sheets of paper would come un-plastered and free the crack. And that would be that.

Beside the ladder top, on the back of the central console, was the oxygen cylinder with integral mask. Maria hadn't even had time to use it. Leonid pulled the cylinder out of its clamp, laid it down in front of Maria's bloody face, and put her hand around the mask and trigger. Her eyes flickered.

Then he dropped down the ladder again. Behind him, the crack hissed vehemently.

When he returned less than a minute later, with a plastic sheet to make a better seal, and medical tape to secure its edges in place, Maria Alova was back on her feet. Blood was still running down her chin and soaking the front of her overall, and she was dosing herself from the blood-smeared oxygen mask – but she was checking through with the other blocks to list up the extent of the damage to the base.

Leonid Steffanovich Shalyapin was forty-seven and felt it. Moscow Time ruled at the base – 02:00, thirteen hours and twenty minutes after the explosion. Those intervening hours had been long and hideous, and it would be at least another complete day before he could even think of finding time to sleep. He had Maria Alova to thank for that option. Alone in the control center, she had sealed the hatch from the inside instead of trying to escape to the floors below, and had halted the depressurization of the entire block. Then she'd made an emergency repair in time to prevent a complete depressurization of the control center, thus keeping it operational at the one time when they needed it most. She had even retained enough presence of mind to rap on the hatch cover to tell Leonid he could open it again.

Leonid would never have got to the leak in time. If Maria had chosen to flee downwards from the control center, it would have caused just enough delay for too much air to escape from B1, and neither of them would have survived. Maria was the reason he was still the oldest man on the Moon.

He pulled his teeshirt over his head, such an effort after such a day, and tucked it into his pants. Going out in a suit made such a mess of you, obliging you to shower and change when you came back. He had walked the whole area around the base buildings, he had been up to the ridge to inspect the monorail pylons, he had checked up on all the major and minor emergency repairs that had been made to the external structures. Good people. They were all good people. He couldn't have wished for a better team. If it had to happen.

On his desk in a plastic frame, because nothing heavy-weight goes as a luxury to the Moon, was the picture of Tatyana with her arms around Andrei's and Marianna's shoulders, all of them smiling. People always asked if Andrei was named after Andrei Tsherbakov, which was ridiculous. The Moon landing and the *Vladimir Komarov*'s first mission had been a little over five years ago, while Andrei Leonovich was seventeen years old and had been born long before Leonid even met Tsherbakov – and he didn't like the man anyway. Marianna was named after Tatyana's mother. They would know he was alive and unharmed, of course. That information had got through shortly after the rooftop S-band antenna was repaired and a first link to Kaliningrad was restored. But they hadn't heard his voice and wouldn't do so for days. Personal messages had zero priority as long as the total available bandwidth was still so limited.

He pulled on his overall jacket, then stepped out of his cabin onto the midfloor diamond around the central ladder. Taking hold of the ladder, he stepped out over the midfloor hole and then started to haul himself upwards hand over hand and easily into the lights of the control center above. B1 was the only building on the Moon to boast three internal floors.

Eight metres square, the control center filled the whole of the top floor and enjoyed an all-round view from the pair of little windows set in each side. The windows showed only reflections against night, with a ghostly half-Earth suspended forlornly amid the phantom scenes in the two eastern windows. Nelli Ulyanova was there, Vitali Zorin and Maria Alova.

Major Maria Alova of the State Committee on Space Defense was thirty-three, blonde and slightly built, and the senior of the pair of resident communications specialists. She had washed her face and neck, and had showered after a spell in a suit repairing antennas on the roof, but the front of her overall was still covered in a brown mess of dried blood. At some time during the last five or six hours, someone had finally found a moment to wipe the trodden smears of her blood from the control center floor. Maria had been far too busy the whole time with the priority task of restoring telemetry with Earth.

The ground shock from the explosion had snapped the foot of the thirty-metre antenna mast which stood free at the north end of the double row of blocks. Even in lunar gravity the mast added up to a couple of tonnes of lattice girder, dish antennas and omni arrays, and it had come crashing down across the roof of B1, wrecking both itself and all the rooftop antennas mounted above the control center. It had also cracked the wall and ceiling joint up between the two windows on the north side. Air started rushing out of that crack.

Maria hadn't had a pause for breath since it happened. First she'd spent four hours in a suit, working with Vitali Zorin up on the roof to repair the S-band antenna, while Elena Naumova ran the control center side of the task. Then there were the rest of the immediate repairs that were needed in order to restore more than just a single channel voice link with Earth. Slumped in a seat in front of the communications board, she looked utterly exhausted.

She pushed herself upright in the chair when Leonid appeared, the correctness of military training asserting its modest tyranny. "We've got double the telemetry now," she said. "The K-band up and down link to Selenos-10 is restored, and there's no more trouble with the K-band to Earth."

Leonid nodded. He put his hand on her shoulder as he passed behind her chair. It wasn't a military gesture, but then he wasn't a military commandant. He felt a fraction of exhausted tautness evaporate from the woman's back. He walked around the central console that protected the access ladder, and stopped at the eastern side. On top of the console was a clipboard with the scribbled sheets that comprised the temporary list of the damage done and the repairs achieved. When the emergency was finally under control he would transfer the scribble into the computer file in a more proper form. He picked up the clipboard. Across the control center, Vitali Zorin was watching him. Vitali shrugged.

Only the top sheet mattered at the moment. The rest listed minor damage to the base structure, such as dents in the outer walls or cracks in the commandant's cabin windows caused by flying rocks, or detailed precisely the base functions which had been affected by the explosion and had been wholly, partially or not yet restored.

The top sheet listed the big damage.

The antenna mast was down and the rooftop antennas were all out except for the repaired S- and K-band dishes. B9, the block at the southeast corner, had been holed by a piece of rock the size of a man's head and was depressurized and useless, along with the stores and cabins inside. Repairable at an indefinite future date. B10 had been depressurized when the connecting sleeve to B9 was split by a combination of the ground shock and the structural distortion caused to B9. The stores and gymnasium inside were useless. Repairable at indefinite future date. The roof of B1 had its crack, now sealed by two plastic sheets one over the other, both fixed around the edges with adhesive tape. Welding or plate bonding repair required. The number three nuclear power unit to the south of the base had been tipped over by the shock and written off. Replacement needed. The six-metre astronomy and surveillance dish had been buckled on its mounting by the whip of the ground shock. The mesh of the three-metre dish had been punctured by flying debris. Verdict pending on both. The hundred-centimetre telescope was skew in its mounting. Verdict pending. The half-built three hundred-centimetre had collapsed. Verdict pending. One lander had been wrecked by a boulder that had punctured its roof. Not repairable – replacement priority one. One rover vehicle had been crushed by debris. Not repairable. One liquid hydrogen tank had tipped over, cracked, and emptied itself. Repairable – content replacement priority one.

The visual inspection seemed to show that the monorail

from the base right up to the ridge a kilometre away was intact. So was the radio relay mast on the ridge that connected the base to the outstation down in the wide valley plain between the Cordillera and the Rook Mountains. Here at the base they still didn't have a working antenna lined up on the relay mast, but that could wait, after all. They could talk to Earth, and Earth could talk to the outstation, just fifty kilometres from the base, over Selenos-10. Everything down at the outstation was in perfect order, of course. Kaliningrad had told the two people there to get into suits and drive up to see what had happened at the main base. But just after they started out they were told to return again because the voice link from Luna Base back to Earth had been restored.

The deaths had been at the main base.

Vladimir Krushinski was inside B9 when it was holed, and hadn't had a chance. Yelena Blochina was killed when B10 lost pressure along with B9. Like Leonid, she was a veteran of the first lunar expedition. She had a husband and children to mourn for her. The rest were all survivors – two at the outstation, and Leonid and thirteen others at Luna Base. And what caused it all?

That wasn't a mystery. You could see it from any window on the east side of the base if you dimmed the interior lights. One hundred metres away southeast, in cosmic terms not even a hair's-breadth distant, was a new crater. Just twelve metres wide and two metres deep, but big enough all the same.

Something small and hard and fast had landed there and vaporized itself with the force of the impact. It had sent a shock wave through the ground, and thrown up a shower of dust and debris that had more or less blanketed everything for three hundred metres around, including the base.

Leonid put the clipboard down, wondering what job to start with next.

Vitali Zorin crossed the control center, walking round the central console. "I've been talking to Vitali Raisman." Raisman had been commander on the Moon landing five years ago. Now a general and based in Star City, he was in charge of personnel scheduling for Luna Base. "He says everyone agrees that the best thing to do with the bodies at the moment is to leave them where they are inside the damaged blocks. In vacuum they'd stay fresh forever, obviously. They can wait until someone thinks up some way of preparing them for transport back to Earth. They might even end up buried here." Vitali paused. "Did you take a look while you were out there?"

Leonid nodded.

"And?"

"They both look a mess." Leonid shrugged. "Explosive decompression makes a mess."

They looked past each other at images of alternative deaths – their possible own.

Over in the opposite corner, Nelli Ulyanova turned her chair away from the geology science board. "I've been looking at the traces recorded at the seismograph stations. Kaliningrad wants to know whether there were any other impacts – whether it was a single meteorite or part of a shower."

Leonid nodded. "And?"

"There's just one other impact apart from our own, but it's about thirty minutes later and in the south polar region on Far Side. Difficult to see how that could possibly be related."

"Unless we got some data on the path of our meteorite," Vitali suggested. "The exact shape of the crater and the debris blanket. Might that tell us where it came from?"

Nelli shook her head. "Unlikely. Meteorites make symmetrical craters when they explode, regardless of the impact direction."

"Mikhail was talking to me a while ago," Maria Alova said. "He had a look at the crater while he was inspecting what's left of number three generator. He said he thought the crater was slightly elongated, northeast to southwest."

"Well," Nelli shrugged. "It wouldn't be the *only* one on the Moon that wasn't perfectly symmetrical."

Vitali was taking a long look at Leonid again. "Leo, you look even more exhausted than the rest of us. Like a little laugh to cheer you up?"

"One of your jokes?" Leonid said, balefully.

"No, something we just heard from home. They say the American news programs have aready carried the story that something nasty has happened up here. *Our* television still hasn't broken the news back home, I think. Anyway, it seems that someone at the Pentagon has said that one of the nuclear warheads we apparently have up here has gone and exploded. So now we know. It wasn't a meteorite after all. We blew ourselves up. Comes as a bit of a surprise, doesn't it?"

Leonid just shook his head, so Vitali shrugged and wandered back to his work watching over the power system monitors. Leonid turned to the blank little window in the east wall between the shut down astronomy consoles.

He stared through his own reflection, through his ghostly and troubled forehead, at the Earth. Belly down and flat topped, it hung in the blank black frame like a lightshade of swirling patterned glass. A lightshade planet on a string, eleven degrees above the invisible horizon of craters and mountains and plains. If he ordered the lights turned down, an eerily beautiful landscape in shallow earthlight would appear, the view that he had never ceased to love, that had been stolen from his cabin window. Stolen by a little shadowed hole which had suddenly appeared out there fourteen hours ago. By sheer random chance? As an experienced cosmonaut and pilot, as a trained scientist and engineer, he had a full appreciation of randomness and the statistics of probability. But as a human being born with the curse of rationality his mind rebelled against reasonless results, against an objective lack of true causality, against a simple supervention of event upon event instead of chains of directed intervention. People want things to have happened for reasons. What was the old answer against reasonless events – act of God. Well if there really was a god and it really was his or hers or its act, what was the sense in meddling with the material universe just to score a direct miss next to the base? Why not do the job properly? Why bother at all?

The Moon is silent, and from moment to moment is a

perfection of peacefulness. The catastrophic event was no more than a tiny craterlet frozen in time. Static. He gazed at the faraway Earth, half brilliantly lit and half invisibly dark. Out there beyond the window reflections was a motionless moonscape, by earthlight.

With bodies.

5 DOWN TO EARTH

19 *Return Transit*

It came as a shock. When the ELTS-19 mission arrived three days after the impact or explosion or whatever – after the *event* – at the Soviet base, Beverly Ryle had been at Armstrong for exactly three months and was exactly halfway through her tour of duty. Her scheduled journey back was booked for ELTS-22. But she was ordered back immediately on Mission 19. Reason? Explanations? *Any* coherent explanations at all?

No explanation. NASA's Space Force partner in the financing and running of Armstrong and of the entire Earth-Lunar Transportation System and its supporting infrastructure wanted it that way. Space Force pulled the military clause in all its relevant contracts with the space agency, and said nothing about its motives. So Beverly was recalled, and the only accompanying information was that Space Force would meet the costs of replacing all the ADV propellant expended in lifting her up to meet the Transiter.

The Transiter arrived and entered an orbit that took it over Mare Orientale so that it could photograph the Soviet base by fading earthlight. Moscow protested and reaffirmed that it didn't need any American help, thank you. The Transiter regularized its orbit, landed Slams loaded with supplies at Armstrong and at Aldrin, and rendezvoused with Aldrin's ADV to rotate out two of the personnel there, resuming the dislocated schedule at the Far Side base. It also rendezvoused with one of the ADVs from Armstrong and took on board its extra passenger. Andy Bakum flew her up, pulling rank on Morris and on Cherryl Donahue to get the chance of flying an extra orbital mission. Morris preferred it that way – it meant he was free to watch her go without having his hands full keeping an eye on a spread of instrumentation. Morris looked as shocked and upset as Beverly felt. He was very tender.

So she left Sinus Aestuum at the sudden untimely end of what she had hoped would be the first of a series of half-year visits, the beginning of a career of careers as one of a tiny clique of top experts on lunar science. She didn't know what to think of the punishment. Had she done something wrong, *said* something wrong? Made some blunder that compromised her security clearance at NASA's DOD office and that might take her off astronaut duties for good? When she left Armstrong she left a Bay of Fears and Troubles and Misery.

The Transiter was the same vehicle that had brought her out from Earth three missions previously, and it had another military crew, plus two military passengers rotating down to Earth – Colonel Alan Browning and Major Greg Bleazard. Just like on the journey out, the pair were polite but terse, close, almost unfriendly. Bèverly spent three free-fall joyless days in social isolation, keeping up with the relayed television and radio newscasts from the remorselessly approaching Earth. The Earth and all its personal and political troubles were returning far too soon, a welter of unwanted things. Taxes, pollution, the Third World problem, nuclear weapons, racism, communism, Islamic radicalism, South Africa, lasers, Soviet militarist aggression. And advertising. Being American can be a burden.

One of Space Force's smaller TAV shuttles took them down to Vandenberg. During the hours she was there Beverly saw no single other civilian on the base. Wobbly and strained in one hundred per cent Earth surface gravity again, she was pulled straight in for the routine returnee's medical. The medical officer measured physiological parameters – ECG, respiration, blood sugar, cholesterol, adrenalin, insulin, haemoglobin – while she lay down for ten blessed minutes and then had to treadmill stoically and stubbornly for a further exhausting fifteen. She had just enough time to dress before she was sent across the corridor into another room. Space's soldiers were really in a hurry with her.

The room was bare, with a water cooler, a table and four chairs, and a window that looked out across the staff car park. A woman in Space Force uniform, a lieutenant colonel by the name of Gruber, was waiting for her. Immediately after her arrival the door opened again and in walked two male officers. The lieutenant wore the name Alderson on his uniform. The one-star brigadier general with the crewcut in steel gray bore the name Reeber. They didn't introduce themselves – she took their identities from their name strips. They sat around the table, Reeber opposite her with his back to the bright window, Gruber to her right and Alderson to her left. On Reeber's uniform were pilot's wings in Air Force style, which told her which service he'd belonged to before Space Force was formed, as well as astronaut flashes with Shuttle, TAV, Columbus and Pilgrim ribbons, each with several mission bars. The brigadier general was a highly experienced pilot astronaut. Lieutenant Colonel Gruber had astronaut flashes with Columbus and Pilgrim ribbons with two bars each. Lieutenant Alderson didn't have anything. Beverly sat in her chair, weighted down by Earth and waiting for her fate.

"You know about the seismic event at the Soviet base," Reeber said by way of an opening remark. "In the last couple of days, have you picked up any news of the way things are proceeding on that?"

Beverly shrugged. "Some. A little."

A curt nod. "Well, the important issue is as follows. The Soviets are denying there was any *explosion* at the base and are claiming it was a meteorite instead. That's ridiculous. The chances on a meteorite hitting right in one place are less than negligible, whereas they have all kinds of explosive and potentially explosive stuff up there. Also, our radars and visual scans picked up no rocks flying around, and absolutely no meteorite shower is known that was due to have crossed space in the vicinity of the Earth or Moon at the time. The Soviet claim is not credible, and we're saying so. In fact Washington has demanded confirmation of the claim in view of the seriousness of the incident. It's a gross violation of treaty agreements to go putting any kind of weapon, offensive or defensive, on the Moon. Washington would be very reluctant to have to respond in kind by stationing anything up there. The idea is to embarrass the Soviets by exposing what they're doing, and so to get them to cancel their plans and remove their shit from up there."

"What are they doing there?" She felt so naive, fresh from the scene of the crime instead of having kept down to Earth where the true action was. "Before I was rotated up for my tour I heard all the fuss about them allegedly having a laser at Mare Orientale."

"Allegedly," Gruber said, shaking her head slightly. "That's good."

"But I thought – the assumption was just an overreaction to the South Africa business. Wasn't it?"

"It wasn't." Reeber was flatly emphatic. "We have clear evidence they used one or several lasers on South Africa. But that isn't what exploded up there, and that's the problem. It was a weapon of some kind – we're guessing either a stockpiled warhead or propellant in its delivery system. It would be a weapon for use *on* the Moon – in other words against people like you at Armstrong or Aldrin – or in lunar orbit or approach. Or it's for use against targets in near-Earth space in what we call an Earth interdiction mode. They launch from the Moon, the direction our space defenses are *not* looking in, and they wipe them clean out – which would leave the United States wide open to a major missile attack by Soviet Earth-based nuclear forces. That's the biggest and the most total threat to the continued existence of this country. The Soviets are mounting one of the most massive efforts in their history to establish themselves on the Moon, and they're not doing it for fun, that I can assure you. They intend to pursue an Earth interdiction strategy. That's the reason for the strong Defense Department interest in lunar activities – so that we're in the position to respond with our own version if necessary. That's unfortunate but unavoidable. When Moscow's around things just get nasty."

Alderson, the lieutenant, nodded quietly. Reeber cleared his throat to continue.

"We know approximately what they're doing, and the task is – the task of the group I lead – is to find out *exactly* what they're doing, and to prevent it. Or to provide the Defense Department and the politicians with sufficient information so they can expose to the world what's going on up there, and so they can force Moscow into changing its plans. Now this explosion is a real mess for Moscow, and we're making the most of the opportunity it offers. We're not buying any crap about meteorites. Did you hear any news from today? Guess you were too busy with the transfer to the TAV and the descent and the medical and all here. Well, the White House has issued a flat challenge. If it was a meteorite, Moscow should fly a couple of neutral astronauts up there to inspect the hole it left and the nature of the damage – check for radiation and chemical traces and that kind of thing. We've suggested a couple of ESA personnel, maybe a French and a German. A Brit wouldn't do because they're too much in our pocket and Moscow wouldn't play. We'd accept a Jap or an Indian or even a Chinese. The odds are Moscow will go along because they're so in a hole over stockpiling nuclear weapons on the Moon –"

"It can't have been a nuclear warhead." And there she was, daring to interrupt a brigadier general. "There wasn't enough energy in the seismic wave. I know – I worked it out."

"Oh it could have been. We have little things down under the one kiloton size – not very efficient, but very real. But that's not the point. They're so in a hole, with so much to lose diplomatically, that they'll probably accept. Of course, by the time the inspectors finally get there, they'll have cleaned it up so much it really does look like a meteorite. That'll be interesting – the longer it takes before they allow an inspection, the worse the mess they must have made of themselves. But now we're getting to the real issue. Whatever went wrong at their base, it's critical and it's part of something real underhand that's going on. We have a damn good idea – we've been onto this for some time – but we haven't fixed it yet, we're not ready to put the finger on them with hard evidence. We've been working for several years, and we expect it's going to take another one to two years to sew this up. At least we just got a breathing space from the way they went and disrupted their own program with something going off right in their own back yard. Must have made a real mess – been eight days now, and they still haven't gone public on casualties."

"But – what I don't understand – why tell me all this?"

"There are Soviet nuclear and other weapons on the Moon. I'm not authorized to disclose what other weapons, since that would help them figure out how much we know, and maybe how we found it out. But for example, that installation running out from the base that they call a monorail – no one would be more surprised than me if it ever got used as a *transport* system. The whole thing is a matter of the gravest national security risk for the United States. We have to land that vital evidence, which is the task of my team. But that's delicate and risky, too. Appallingly risky. If Moscow ever finds out how close we are, and how it is we're getting there, that will be the end of our operation. We'd never get that evidence, and we might even be compromised doing something they could claim to the whole world was dirty. They'd be able to go right ahead with what they're doing, and they'd score a major propaganda victory on top. There's also considerable risk to the American personnel involved. So you'll appreciate how it's absolutely vital that even the *existence* of my team, never mind the area we're working in or the state of our knowledge, cannot possibly be revealed. *Nothing* can be leaked."

"But –" Now she was completely confused. "How could I leak anything – except what you've just told me?"

"Unfortunately, without realizing the significance of it, you happen to have stumbled on something." Reeber placed his hands on the empty table, palms down and fingers spread. "You did so because your attention was caught by the seismic record of the explosion." He leaned a little forward, a little eagerly, a little like a steel-haired eagle that had spotted its prey. "Begin to see what?"

"The – second impact? Event?"

"Exactly." The eagle had found its prey, and was satisfied with that. Reeber leaned back again, his hands still on the table, but resting relaxed upon the edge. "Let's just say it was an instrument of some description, which unfortunately was affected. Flash radiation or debris impact – we don't know yet. This coincident damage caused it to malfunction and crash instead of returning to Aldrin."

"A satellite or something?"

"Something like that," Gruber said, and almost allowed a smile on her face.

"That's not the whole of it," Reeber continued, "but it's close enough not to be fooling you more than I absolutely have to. Now, the Soviets won't know about it because with an explosion right at their base they won't have been doing any seismic science right at the time. It's important that they *never* know, because otherwise they might go looking. If they looked like doing that we'd have to get there first and clear the site, because nothing lying around up there on the Moon is going to decay or wash away or anything. The evidence stays. But you read an estimated position through to Houston on this second event. You and several other people know where it was. Where what was? What second event? What location? Get my meaning? The information could wreck our whole operation and any further chance of unmasking what they're really up to. So that's why I'm talking to you now."

Beverly nodded, transfixed by his seriousness and by the sideline eyes of Gruber and the silent lieutenant.

Reeber echoed the nod. "Next to no one knows about it, and that's the way it has to stay. I cannot impress that on you enough. It's vital to national security that you don't even think of talking to your colleagues, to anyone at all – not even your husband. About the seismic event at the Soviet base, the meteorite claim and counter theories, sure – otherwise your lack of interest is going to be suspicious. But the truth must be absolutely secret. Everything I've said – we didn't even meet – and *no* second seismic event. The very few people at Houston who got what you said have each been given exactly the same interview by myself or another member of my team. NASA has seen the necessity of closing up on the data, and has handed all seismic records from the relevant period over to us – for analysis, they'll tell you. The other people at Armstrong who might have picked up something from you will also be debriefed when they're rotated down – and none of you will ever talk to each other about it. But you're so important because of your knowledge of the approximate location, that we had to get you back here right away. As for cutting your tour of duty clean in half, all we can do is apologize – but the issue is absolutely crucial. Once rumors start they spread exponentially, until finally someone hears who you just don't want to have heard – in other words, Moscow. Obviously someone sometime will open their mouth, but if we can stop that happening for at least a year – two would be more comfortable, but a year might do it – we'll have a good chance of cleaning up that piece of compromising evidence, and at the same time fixing the Soviets for what they're doing." Reeber leaned forward again, fingers tensed on the table edge. The eagle had decided to swoop. "So – can we count on you?"

There was a seat all lined up for her on a machine waiting to fly to Los Angeles – they didn't want her waiting around and seeing or overhearing things at Vandenberg. Then the next surprise – her pre-paid flight from L.A. wasn't going to Houston. Returnees from the Moon always spent six days at Johnson Space Center on post-tour debriefings coupled with routine medical monitoring of their readjustment to life at one gee. Instead she had a flight straight back home to New Orleans. She'd come back so suddenly, so early, that NASA simply had no work for her to do, and her six weeks of post-tour vacation could start right away. It had to be a device to keep her away from the temptation to talk with people about the hot news from the Moon until it had gone good and cold again. Helping her to do her bit for America.

She had time at the airport to call James at the city laboratories in New Orleans. James knew, of course, that she was due in today and he was expecting an evening call at home, but he wasn't expecting Beverly herself for another six days. Nice surprise, huh? James was surprised all right. He seemed confused and hurried, and almost displeased in a kind of way. There wasn't enough time to clear it up on the phone – there wasn't so much change in the NASA travel wallet she'd been given, and she wasn't able to call the city laboratories collect at long distance rates. He was probably in a hurry because of something going on right then at the lab. They had their emergencies in the pollution monitoring business.

Beverly got home from the airport in New Orleans in the

afternoon, taking a cab for the long drive across Pontchartrain Bridge to their home on the nice side of Covington. It was a neat house, fruit of James's modest and her own excellent salaries. James wouldn't be back from work for another couple of hours. And then came another surprise. There was a woman's rouge and foundation powder and cleanser in the bathroom on the shelf under the mirror. In the bedroom there was white underwear with frills, all of it clean, a sweater for the cool of evening and the early morning, and a stranger's bathrobe over the chair on her side of the bed.

Beverly fixed herself a martini as big as the glass would hold, her very first alcoholic drink for four months. Astronauts lead a hard and taxing life. Exhausted by it all, squashed by her leaden earthly weight, she stretched out on the couch downstairs, her feet up on the cushions, and tried to suppress wandering wonderings about who had maybe been smooching with James right there on her couch and how recently. It was a new development this, that he brought his sanctioned extramaritals home so that they were almost live-in visitors, leaving a couple of days supply of fresh underwear lying around. She had to keep reminding herself that she was fresh from the sideline advantages of an open marriage, too. Adult respect for each other's freedom was a very important virtue. But it didn't help.

She went through her collection of symphonies and put on the First, a young Beethoven in a cheeky mood and demonstrating just how much fun a true genius can have with a nice little tune. If that didn't cheer her up, nothing would. The martini on an empty and unaccustomed stomach helped, too.

When James arrived home he explained straight out – nothing hidden from your partner in an open marriage. The clothes and makeup belonged to Karen. Yes, one and the same Karen like the last two times Beverly was away. Karen's exchange semester to France had been canceled at the last minute, it seemed. James seemed somehow caught out, but he was brave about it. He had, therefore, spent most of the last four months with his French literature girlfriend and hadn't said a single word about it. But then she hadn't teased him with Morris, either. Another martini and a marvelous meal helped a lot – James could *cook*, too, producing flavors as exotic and dark as his complexion – and it turned out to be good to be home.

The next morning, James took Karen's things away in his car when he left for work. Well, home was home and wonderful, but it wasn't exactly a perfect homecoming.

Frank Simons, Cape Town

The whites are fleeing South Africa and the Republic is disintegrating. They have no farms any more, no gold mines and no industry. Their savings are worthless and their property useless. When they leave the country, thousands every day, they take nothing more than their hand baggage and the clothes they are wearing. They are as destitute as their former laborers and servants and street sweepers. They will arrive to destitution, too. They are too many and their exodus too sudden. The United States and Britain are less welcoming than they were two and three months ago. Coloured US politicians, or the ethnic community in the UK, are making their voices heard. Supporting the fight against communists in southern Africa was one thing, but taking in a flood of white racists is quite another. The stunned and bitter refugees standing in line amid the burned-out ruins of the docks in Table Bay, or amid the wreckage that used to be the airport terminal, do not understand the troubles awaiting them.

The Boer Republic has next to no army, it has no air force, its navy is useless, its stocks of ammunition are all but gone. Only the major city enclaves are left in white hands, acres of burned-down houses and shops, factories and office blocks. The mood has hardened in the four months since final disaster overtook the white regime with such crushing and complete suddenness. It has become one of grim fatalism among those destined to remain: the soldiers, and the poorest civilians who cannot afford a ticket out. Those doomed to stay who have a gun in their hands – there are an astonishing number of guns among the white civilians of South Africa – are adopting an almost theatrical determination to make a glorious last stand. They are going to take a lot of ANC communists with them, they say. The bravura seems a thin veneer. If not, the end will be bloody indeed.

The ANC's commanders seem to have elected to leave Cape Town until the very last. When they have finished in the rest of the country, it will take some time to move their forces here for the final attack. The government of the Republic has already abandoned Pretoria for the temporary safety of Johannesburg, and is making plans for new accommodation here on the Cape of Good Hope. Where the leading politicians will go after that is still not clear. Washington's commitment to them is too high simply to strand them here, but which nations might be prepared to take them is far from clear. The most likely candidates are in South America, where another brand of fascism is at home.

The fall of East London two weeks ago came as a shock for the people here. The cities and towns of the interior might have gone down in rapid succession, but East London was different. Like Cape Town, it lies on the coast. The ANC could not attack it from all sides, nor cut off supplies coming in on ships under American escort. East London should have held out like Port Elizabeth, Durban and Cape Town, untakeable fortresses of white dominion from which the reconquest of the black interior could one day begin. It was only a matter of time, after all. For the Boer mentality it is nothing less than a fact that black Africans will never be capable of running anything as complex as a national economy, never mind organizing the recovery of a war-savaged land. The ANC will fail in a matter of years, they are prophesying here, no matter how much aid they receive from Moscow and from the Organization of African Unity. To the last, white South Africa expected still to be around to reclaim what it believes to be its own. But now East London has fallen, and standing with your back to the sea is suddenly no protection any more.

Pietermaritzburg fell last week and the way to Durban is open. The rocket and mortar attacks on Port Elizabeth have increased. The ring is closing around Johannesburg. In Cape Town, General Klerk still promises to hold the guerrillas at the line of trenches and bunkers, but fewer believe him now. And everyone saw how pitifully few escaped here from East London, a few hundred civilians and a handful of police and soldiers. No one knows the fate of those left behind. Even if a more orderly

withdrawal can be arranged from Cape Town, the fear remains
that the very last to stay may be massacred. With or without
eventual reinforcements escaping from Johannesburg with the
hoped-for American airlift, with or without their additional
strength to delay the end, General Klerk will one day be forced
to choose between a fight to the death or the risk of surrender.
Today, in the devastation of what once was prosperous Cape
Town, that day does not seem far.

Frank Simons stood on the charred and cracked asphalt of
the junction and held a fire in his hand. An old, cold fire.
Around him was a dry and windy silence, a sunstruck desolation. Beside him, at the corner of the junction, was the
house that didn't burn, very possibly the last house still
standing in Sea Point.

This whole arm of the city had been burned to the ground.
The conflagration had raged from Bantry Bay in the south
to Green Point in the north and had destroyed everything
between the Atlantic seashore and the sharp slopes under
Lion's Head and Signal Hill. Everything but this single house
at the intersection of Biederkop Drive and Pieter-W.-Botha
Avenue, alone but for the dirty signs still bearing the street
names. Everything else between Main Road and High Level
Road, the main traffic arteries of this long seaboard suburb,
was ruins – nothing but the blackened brick rubble of
burned-out houses ringed by the blackened skeletal corpses
of garden trees, laced together by telegraph pole stumps and
street lights buckled, bent and deformed by the merciless
heat of the firestorm of four months ago. And here in the
middle of it, this one last house still standing, blackened by
smoke, windows smashed and doors broken down, wrecked
and abandoned but whole, a landmark among the rows upon
rows of shamble plots marking the long lines of cracked and
blistered streets. The hot clear sun shone on it all so pitilessly.
There was no smoke in the air to hide the city's shame, there
was nothing left to burn except one lonely shell of a house
in a suburban crematorium.

He held its fire, its failed fire, in his hand.

The intersection with its verges and sidewalks had protected it on two sides, its own treeless garden, the clay tennis

court at the rear and the double width drive at the side – a gravel drive, that hadn't caught fire like tarmac – had protected it with a fire break from the immolation of the neighboring properties. It was stripped bare, of course, a rich prize for the looters. Only the scattered garbage was still there at the rear, picked over so many times by people and dogs and cats and rats that there was nothing edible or decayable left. It was almost sterile, it didn't even stink especially despite the heat.

He knew all the stories of the way the fires started – enough people had escaped to tell the tale. Not every house had caught light, just random rows and isolated buildings, but the fires had been so densely spread that the flames had jumped from house to house until they consumed everything. Extinguishing so many simultaneous fires had been an absolute impossibility – many residents had been able to put out their own blaze before it took proper hold, only to see their house overwhelmed by flames springing over from a neighbor's garden or roof. The fires had always started in the kitchens or at the backs of the buildings, as though the black servants had all one day cast tribal voodoo spells while at work, woven little metaphysical packages of pyrotechnic hatred made from sulphurous resentment and saltpeter of subjugation, little imaginary time bombs left behind in the master's and mistress's kitchen cupboard, one in almost every house in every city in South Africa and timed to go off in a flash of incendiary magic at midnight.

It was impossible, of course, to set fire to the entire country from one end to the other, city centers, suburbs and wide open bush and grassland and wheat fields. If it wasn't metaphysics, it certainly couldn't have been fire-raisers – not unaided fire-raisers, anyway. The urban guerrillas could have penetrated the white areas by day, sneaking in among the hordes of laborers brought in to do the dirty work and to keep spick-and-span the domestic opulence that their sweat and poverty paid for, but they could never have survived in sufficient numbers at night as the police and the vigilante patrols combed the streets. And as for the open countryside where the miles upon miles of fire lines had wiped out the army – well not even the ANC had that many members. It just couldn't be done. So if it hadn't been metaphysics it must have been Moscow. The trapdoor devil on the Western world's political stage had to make his entrance again, not from below this time, but still in a flash that reeked of brimstone, a flash as bright as anything imaginable. Moscow must have turned its lasers on South Africa. The American government said so, after all, and they had their CIA and their National Security Agency and their spy satellites and so they really ought to know.

Frank Simons held a little piece of metaphysics in his hand. He had found it with the garbage, where all metaphysics belongs.

The dustbin behind the house was plastic with a plastic lid, the modern world's petroleum-consuming answer to the depletion of metal ores. Plundered and emptied, it lay on its side against the wall at the back of the little roofed-over alcove beside the kitchen door. Its base was designed to stand clear of the ground, raised on a thick rim strengthened with a hoop of aluminum – just an inch-high hiding place under all the household's solid kitchen waste, all the plastic and paper and lovely inflammable things. And stuck to the base, adhering to the PVC with a strip of sticky tape, he had found the tiny time bomb.

It was a plain little box, for all the world like those old once-upon-a-time packets of ten cigarettes. The wrapping was dried out and tore easily. He started taking the contents apart before he realized what he was handling. His finger and thumb pulled out a little metal tube with a detonator cap wired to it. The cap dangled on a spring of wire as his hand shook.

He disarmed the thing by placing it on the ground, laying a brick on top of it so that the detonator cap was trapped under its edge, and then ripping the metal tube free.

Inside the torn open packet was a plasticine-like substance in a clear plastic wrapping that had been punctured where the detonator had been pushed home. He hadn't seen anything like it since Northern Ireland. When he unscrewed the top of the little metal tube he found a sealed plug of plastic no bigger than a pen cartridge, and a miniature battery. Timer circuit and power source, something to fire the detonator and ignite the few ounces of incendiary material, to set fire to the garbage and with luck to burn down the house. Could that really burn down a house? Yes, if unnoticed for the first few minutes in the middle of the night until the flames had spread to the walls and the roof next to the bin, to the garage with its car and its tank full of petrol. If the same thing was happening at a thousand neighboring houses at once.

Like that you could burn down cities.

The sealed up, obviously customized timing circuit was something he'd never seen before. A little piece of microelectronics, it had to be, sophisticated but probably mass produced and immensely cheap, and reliable enough to time its ignition to minutes over a period of days or weeks – or even longer, if the devices had been started up and synchronized before they were even delivered to the guerrillas who were to plant them. And if the things were mass produced – and they had been mass produced, because of the numbers that had been used – then it wasn't just one of them that had gone wrong. Hundreds, thousands of them must have failed. Most would have been consumed in the spreading fires, but some, like this one in his hand, would have survived.

He couldn't possibly be the first man to have found one.

South African secret service people had combed the devastated cities searching for evidence on the way it had been done. Even in defeat, you cannot face the apparently impossible without trying to explain it. And two weeks after it all happened, little teams of Americans had turned up everywhere. Some of them had worn military uniforms, but the majority had gone about their quiet business in ordinary clothes. It was an open secret that they had come from the Pentagon, the CIA and the State Department's Bureau of Intelligence. In twos and threes and in the company of South African escorts, they had picked their way through half the civic areas in the country. How many failed little incendiary time bombs had they found? For how long had they known what form Moscow's help had really taken? And why hadn't they said so to the world, why still talk of ground lasers and orbital mirrors and a laser up there on the Moon? Perhaps the Soviets had used their lasers to help the ANC, but not in the cities.

The mechanism was so obvious, so simple. With good enough timing devices you could plant your invisible little bombs over a series of weeks, hundreds of saboteurs each planting dozens every day, until you could set fire at once to all the domestic garbage, all the industrial garbage, all the office block waste, all the diesel tanks of the civic buses, all the pumps at all the filling stations. Who was it who collected the garbage, a heavy and filthy and stinking job? Blacks. Blacks from the townships, bussed and train-loaded into the white areas every morning and then thrown out again every night. Day after day, a commando troop of your enemy returning to your own back door, your vulnerable point where you shit out the materialist effluent collected from your magnificently wealthy way of life. Your most intimate sphere. All the rich whites in their domestic paradise, burned by their own garbage, set alight by the people on whose backs they'd climbed in the process of producing it. It was certainly a kind of justice, if you could bring yourself to think in terms of collective social guilt and to forget all the images of individual suffering. Children had died here, too, just as they had during all the years of vigilante raids on the black townships, and a war is a horror beyond any qualification.

But a war produces stories. And journalists are paid to catch them. All he needed was time to trace the evidence. One single failed fire in his hand wasn't enough, it didn't carry the background, it implied but didn't confirm the broader truth. To put his story together he had to find more of the things or he had to find someone who would talk. But the Americans must have picked most places clean, and no one had talked for four months and perhaps they never would.

He stood with a fire in his hand at the intersection of Biederkop Drive and Pieter-W.-Botha Avenue, looking down across rubble heaps and ruined shells, tree skeletons and street light sculptures to the surf of the South Atlantic Ocean, around him a desolation of hot sun and windy silence.

21 *Briefing*

Excerpt of press briefing with Barbara-Ann Schwaetzer, White House spokeswoman, July 29th.

SCHWAETZER: Ladies and gentlemen, the statement concerns the Soviet insistence that the explosive event at their lunar base on June 27th was a blameless accident. The statement is as follows.

A close and careful study of photographic evidence, obtained by United States Space Force and NASA facilities, has been found to corroborate the evidence presented at an international press briefing in Moscow on July 23rd. Our own independent assessment of the extent of damage to the Soviet lunar facility, as well as the size and form of the new crater immediately adjacent to the facility, leads our experts to the conclusion that the event could without doubt have been caused by the impact of a very small bolide on the surface of the Moon at the Soviet site. The Government of the United States of America is therefore willing to concede the truth of the Soviet claim that the cause was indeed the impact of a very small bolide, and considers the issue as to the cause of the event closed. Accordingly, the Government of the United States of America withdraws its demand of July 3rd, reiterated at the United Nations on July 5th, that the Government of the Soviet Union permit an on-site inspection by neutral parties in order to establish the cause. The Government of the United States wishes to reaffirm its statement of July 11th expressing sympathy and commiseration at the tragic deaths of the cosmonauts Yelena Blochina and Vladimir Krushinski.

That's the end of the statement. Before we proceed, are there any questions on that?

Unidentified: What's a very small bolide?

(*Laughter*)

SCHWAETZER: That's another one of those darned technical terms again. Well, I had to ask, too. As I understand it, bolide is a term for all the things flying around loose in the Solar System. Bolides are things like comets, stray lumps of rock and so on. I guess the asteroids are a kind of bolide, too. A very small bolide is a little lump of rock a few feet or less across. I guess anything bigger would have wiped out the entire base. I'm told this one probably would have done, if it had hit any closer.

LENNERT, *NBC*: Is it possible that this business is going to have some effect on the course of the election campaign of the president or of the Democrat rival?

SCHWAETZER: I can't actually see how, except maybe the positive aspect that we clarified the issue by our firm insistence that Moscow should come up with some hard evidence. The White House certainly won't be taking it over into the campaign. We'll be fighting through into the fall on our established platform.

CAGE, *Transworld-Telenews-2*: Does the new development in any way change the White House position on the moon-laser theory?

SCHWAETZER: Not directly, no. We can now be certain that it wasn't any part of any laser installation they have up there that exploded, but beyond that it has no material effect that a meteorite caused all the damage to their base.

WILLIAMS, *Time*: Is the president firmly of the opinion that there is a laser weapon at the Soviet base? Two days ago we had the statement from the Bureau of Space Affairs, at the State Department, that on the basis of the available evidence there is definitely no laser installation at the base.

SCHWAETZER: Personally I'm not impressed by the assessment from the undersecretary for Space Affairs. The State Department doesn't have the necessary expertise. Their area is the diplomacy of space. Now I wouldn't for one moment deny undersecretary Hyland's personal competence in aerospace and related questions, which I highly respect. But assessments on an issue like this really belong within the competence of the Pentagon. I would stay with the Pentagon's view of the probable nature of that so-called monorail track the Russians have up there. It could be the start of a surface mounted railgun they're building, or it could be the light guide from a major laser installation buried underground somewhere down the far side of the mountains, where we can't observe it very readily. That's where it leads from to come over the ridge up to the base. And where it stops it's pointing right here at the Earth.

James left the bed and padded over towards the bedroom
door, bare brown feet on white deep-pile carpet. "Don't go
getting yourself uptight about it." And he stopped halfway
through the door, one hand holding the door handle, the
other the tissue bundle. Naked, his deep brown body was
solidly athletic and should have been reassuring. "Sex is
supposed to relax you, not just put a punctuation between
your worries. Just calm yourself down, and try telling me
about it. It's late, and tomorrow's Monday, and I have to
drive in early morning, but I'd rather you talked about what's
getting at you than you stayed awake for hours worrying
about it. Okay?"

He went out to the bathroom.

Beverly squeezed her legs together to keep the little towel
in place, then twisted onto her side, reached out and turned
on the bedhead hifi with the volume low. One of the
Beethoven discs was loaded and played part through. The
Pastoral, the Sixth, seeped into the room, the soft second
movement beginning, the scene beside a brook. Lyricism
surrounded her, soothing as sliding water. She stuck her feet
under the rumpled covers and drew the sheet and coverlet
up over her hips, she folded her arms behind her head on
the pillow and closed her eyes. Over the last five weeks her
hair had grown long enough for her to have it cut and restyled
sufficiently to undo most of the well-meant amateur damage
from the Moon, so in spite of everything she should feel
good. Outside was a hot and sticky Louisiana delta midnight
at the start of August. Inside the bedroom was air-
conditioned coolness, with softly shaded lights bathing her
eyelids from the wall over the bed. Life allows you sweet
and lazy moments.

James came back, naked, and got onto the bed beside her.

He plumped the pillow and stuffed it against the headboard, and then settled down half sitting there beside her. The plain sheets and pillow covers were coffee cream color, a shade exactly halfway between her pale and his dark body. His hand resting across his hip, James stroked her shoulder. "You know, maybe you should take the pill after all. It's much more aesthetic."

That was the end of another romantic moment.

"Do we have to discuss that again? Once a year you get your attack of aesthetics. I am not going to put myself permanently on that hormone trip. Long-term use produces too many side effects. Okay?"

"But it's okay for months at a time up there on the Moon."

"Yes. It is. I should get pregnant? That isn't long-term exposure. Using it every month every year would be."

Silence but for Beethoven bathed in the peacefulness beside his brook. But she didn't want a fight, dammit. Not another one, not at midnight.

She fished out the little towel from under the sheet, folded it crudely together, rolled over and put it down on the rug beside the bed. She lay flat again and looked up at his uneasy eyes. "Besides." She pouted just a little.

"Besides?"

"Well, then we couldn't do it so nicely two times, one right after the other, could we?"

"Couldn't we?"

"Well – the stuff as goes in first time gets pumped right out again the second time, doesn't it? Makes an awful mess on the sheet." She lifted her head to peer over his hip. "Your little friend with his big ideas makes quite a splash, doesn't he?"

James grinned. "You're getting obscene."

"If doing this sort of thing with you is obscene –"

"I just don't want to be heard!"

She laughed. "I was going to say, be decent."

Peace restored. He stroked her shoulder again. "So, then." His fingers moved with the music. "What's troubling you?"

What's really troubling me? You. You are. And his fingers moved automatically with the music, oblivious of her thoughts. Since I came back, I'm not really here. I'm here all day on this sit-around and do-nothing vacation, but I'm not really quite back in our home. You're distant, somehow. Maybe it comes from me, but I have the feeling it comes from you. In bed you're wonderful, you're marvelous to me. But all the rest of the time you're kind of irritated or guarded, or dissatisfied, or I don't quite know what. But the last thing we need is a fight or a standoff or a silence until morning.

So she decided to talk about the other thing, the safer thing, the thing that was outside of them. Well, outside of him, anyhow.

"I have only one more week of vacation, don't I? And there's still been nothing from Houston about where I'm supposed to turn up Monday week or what I'm supposed to do next. Almost as if I've ceased to exist as far as NASA's concerned. The whole thing worries me – especially with that statement from the White House last week. I'm beginning to wonder if my memory's right. Did I go loony on the Moon, or something?"

"I don't think you're loopy. Well – no more than when I first met you."

A masking smile for him. She'd told him about the crazy talk at Vandenberg, of course, and had explained as much of the background to it as he'd listen to. James had lost all patience and interest in geology and seismology over the last year, as if her doctorate and her job and her knowledge had suddenly become a trio of rivals competing either for her or maybe just against him. It made no sense, but it seemed like that.

"Well," he said. "Guess I don't see the problem."

"Well now, that guy Reeber said they were challenging Moscow to make them go as far as taking European astronauts up there to prove to the public it wasn't a weapon exploded on the Moon. The whole point being, he meant it most certainly was, and the trick was to trip up Moscow. And now Washington suddenly backs down and says it's a meteorite after all. No checks, no inspections, no pushing the Russians into a corner. So exactly what was all that about a weapon of some kind, a small nuke or something? What was all that about national security, about not disclosing the presence of a team trying to figure out what the Russians are up to, about not wanting them to find out about any second impact and so on?"

"What second impact?" James yawned. "Oh yeah."

"Yes. And – well – what's it all about? And if it's all for nothing, why bring me back three months early? That'll have messed up the crew rotation and science schedules for the rest of the year. The Defense Department must have had some good reason if they were going to lean hard enough on NASA for the Agency to okay that. And then the whole thing just kind of dissolves."

James settled down to lie in the bed, covering himself with the sheet and coverlet. He lay sideways on the pillow, facing her. "Maybe it's just some kind of blind. Let's suppose the Russians are really building a system up there to launch things from the Moon. A what do you call it?"

"A railgun. Or a Clarke launcher, if it's for transporting stuff. Clarke's the man who invented the idea."

"A railgun. Or a laser. Everyone who knows anything is saying that's what it is. They'd use it to hit our lasers up in space, zap the Transavs and the space stations and that kind of thing. What do I know? Be real dangerous for America. So we make them think we've given up on the issue of the explosion. It was a bomb they have stockpiled up there, but we make out we can't prove it and we're satisfied with their story about a meteorite. That way we don't alarm them into accelerating their program by letting them know we've found out, and at the same time we go ahead as fast as we can with catching up on them, because we have to get our own counter-system up there to balance things as fast as we can. Maybe the only quick answer, something to fill the gap until we can put something better together, is something that threatens the Soviet base directly and is banned by treaty or something. So we don't want to get Moscow suspicious and get them snooping on us. We put something up there we could use in a crisis to zap their base before they could get around to zapping our bases or defense satellites. We have to be able to do *something* about a threat like that. Otherwise we just wait until they put their gun to our head. Or maybe we could try throwing rocks at them. There are an awful lot of rocks on the Moon. If we don't build ourselves a *technological* weapon, rocks is what we'll have to throw at them."

James turned over to reach the console in the wing on his side of the headboard. The theme of the Sixth was just emerging, rediscovered, at the end of the second movement. James canceled the music without waiting. Goodnight, Ludwig van Beethoven. He checked the alarm was set and then switched off the light over his side of the bed. He lay with his back to her in a bedroom consigned to half darkness.

"I'm still worried by it, James. It doesn't hang together right. I've been getting more and more confused over it. And what Reeber said. I'm sure it couldn't have been a nuclear bomb, neither the first nor the second event. They just didn't have enough energy."

"Let's get some sleep, huh?" he said over his shoulder. "Maybe it was the Russians throwing rocks. Testing something and it went wrong. The first bang at the base was the launcher exploding and the second one was the rock landing thousands of miles away. Or what the hell? Who knows? Maybe it went so wrong they bombed themselves. Who cares?"

"Reeber said the second impact was something like a surveillance instrument – a satellite or something like that – coming down. He hinted at that, anyway."

"Who cares right now? You going to go on all night?" He turned around to her in a flurry of bedding. "Look, fuck all that about mustn't talk to anyone. Can't do any harm to talk to someone who already knows, can it? Well according to the schedule, four of the others up at Armstrong at the time were rotated down last week. Right? They'll have had their post-tour debriefing by now, so they'll be home all day. So call one of them tomorrow."

"Chas Watkins, maybe."

"Yeah. Now put the light out. Let's sleep, for God's sake."

"Merryn Watkins, Clear Lake. Who's calling, please?"

"Beverly Ryle. Morning, Mrs Watkins. Is Chas – is Charles at home? I'd like to speak with him if he has the time."

"Well – he's kind of tied up right now with the kids. Only

got his first day at home instead of the debriefings Saturday. But I'll see. Hold on a moment."

A moment could be a long time in Clear Lake.

"Hello, Beverly? Chas. Sorry that took so long. We're messing around in the pool. I'm trying to get them to swim properly. Pete's getting the hang of it – he's four. But Kim, she still just doggy paddles. Hey, but they've *grown* in half a year."

"I can believe it, at that age. How are you? How's Merryn?"

"Oh fine. Just dandy. How about you and Jim?"

"Oh – things are kind of strained, some way or other. One of those phases, I guess. Do you have a couple of minutes right now? I just want to check something with you."

"Beverly, for a colleague and co-worker I always have time. You got kind of pushed around with that early recall, didn't you? I could see you were thrown right over by it. So would I have been. And the whole of the last month Morris was looking quite lost without you. Beyond comfort, he was."

"Really? He was? That's nice."

And a short moment in Covington, Louisiana, near New Orleans.

"What did you want to check, Beverly?"

"Um – yes. It's connected with the meteorite impact at the Soviet base."

"Ah."

"I was brought down in a TAV to Vandenberg and given a special debriefing or whatever you'd call it. Were you?"

"I was, yes. But we're not supposed to talk about it."

"Chas, I *have* to talk about it. With having my post-tour debriefing canceled and going right into vacation without even *seeing* Houston, I feel like I'm isolated from everyone. So I wanted to check I wasn't the only one got the treatment from this guy Reeber and the other two."

"Other two? I only got a talk from Reeber. Maybe Madge and Tania saw the others. I haven't spoken with Andy Bakum since we disembarked at Vandenberg, but then he's Space Force and they have a totally separate ground organization. Tania got a talk from some lieutenant colonel name of

Gruber, she said. Don't know who Madge saw. Tania didn't say much about it. She was just told not to say anything to anyone about the event at the Soviet base – national security attached to it. And please not to start any stories – least of all with the media. Let the people in Washington play it their own way without the media on their backs. About the same as Reeber said to me."

"Sounds a lot less hair-raising than what he said to me. He went on about the Soviets having maybe nuclear weapons up there, and about some secret intelligence operation. Didn't he say that to you?"

"Well, sort of indirect, maybe. Should we be talking about this? I only spoke with Merryn about it. She says it sounds kind of cloak-and-dagger, but what the hell."

"Did Reeber say anything to you about the second impact?"

"Second impact? Oh yeah – you spotted that, didn't you?"

"What did he say? He hinted to me it was some kind of DOD satellite that crashed."

"Nope. He just told me there was some interesting debris to collect if we ever wanted, and that we don't want Moscow to know we know it's there. I asked him if it was some kind of Soviet satellite or launcher vehicle, and he nodded. Don't recall he said anything."

"Well that doesn't tie up."

"Yeah – well. Who says it has to? The thing that matters to them is just that we don't go and tell someone something that's important, but we don't know it's important. That's how I read it."

"Guess so. Guess that makes sense. Nice to be sure I don't have to feel singled out on this any more. Thanks for discussing it with me."

"Nothing to thank, Beverly. Any time. Any time at all. Guess I'd better be getting back to the kids before they start pulling Merryn into the pool. She's planning to do some shopping."

"Better go rescue her, Chas."

"Sure. Okay – so keep in touch, Beverly. Be sure to keep in touch until next time we meet on a tour together. Okay now?"

"Okay, Chas."

"That's the way. Have a nice day now."

"You too, Chas. Bye."

"Guaraldi, City Environmental Laboratories. Can I help you?"

"That Sam Guaraldi? We met once about a year back. This is Beverly."

"Beverly?"

"Yes. Is James Heaton there? I'd like to speak with him."

"'Fraid Jim's out right now. Can I help?"

"Do you know when he's due back?"

"I don't rightly know if he's due back at all today. Might be gone the whole afternoon. Wait a moment. I got a note here somewhere. Jeez, his desk is even more of a mess than mine. He's over at the university somewheres. Loyola."

"The university?"

"Yep. We like to keep on good terms with the other institutes in town, case we ever need their facilities if anything big turns up. Train load of industrial solvents derailed right next to Tulane Avenue or something. We always leave the number where we're at, case there's an emergency. Here it is. Got it. Nope, I was wrong. He's not rightly at the university. You can reach him with Karen Flitchen. At her home office, I guess. The number –"

"*Who?*"

"Karen Flitchen. That's F-L-I-T-C-H-E-N. Guess she's one of their chemistry people. For theoretical chem you don't have to sit in a lab or department all day. The number is –"

"Never mind the number. It isn't – it isn't urgent."

"Okay. When next I see him, who should I say called? Beverly?"

"Yes. Beverly Ryle. His wife."

"Okay. Have a nice day now."

South Africa was on the television screen, pictures from the slow piecemeal battle for Johannesburg. Pictures of the dust and crackle and sudden dirt clouds of fire fights and mortars on the perimeter where it meandered through the shambles that used to be suburbs and satellite towns and bits of industrialized open country immediately around the capital. Pictures of dead ANC twisted on the street where an attacking unit got too far and didn't get back. Pictures of South African army units pulling out under fire, just a scatter of soldiers while an armored car burned, some of the soldiers hardly kids, some of them scared-eyed at the camera. Picture of a lone spotter helicopter spiraling down, its single remaining rotor blade looping lazily, spiraling down and vanishing behind some apartment house shells. Not even an explosion. Pictures of the immediate aftermath of rocket hits in the outskirts of the city itself – freshly thrown-up rubble, some smoke, fresh bits of people stuck to the ground with a paste of dust and blood, whole people and bloody people standing around in shock. Pictures of US Air Force Hercules transports coming down steeply, landing and taxiing around shell-craters in what was left of Jan Smuts Airport. Pictures of the blackened wreckage of one that caught an ANC anti-aircraft missile. Pictures of long lines of people queueing with bags in their hands and on their backs, or shuffling into the gaping tail doors of the aircraft. Picture of a Hercules climbing crabwise into the sky, hardly shrinking at all, transfixed like an ugly butterfly in a telephoto frame.

Pictures. Pictures of the execution of white South Africa.

Beverly reached over from her chair onto the couch and touched the button of the remote control to mute the sound. They had to talk. A wordless standoff can't go on for ever. Pick the less critical subject first, to show you don't want a fight.

"I called Chas Watkins this morning, and now I'm really confused. The others who were rotated back down also got talks from Reeber and his people, but not so detailed talks. And they weren't told the same story – at least, Chas wasn't. And when I think about it, and about how apparently I'm the only one who's been pushed around to *isolate* me, I get really worried."

James sat in the center of the couch, toying with the remote control with his left hand. "How do you mean, isolated?"

"No contact with anyone else. I should talk with no one, my post-tour debriefing is canceled and my vacation starts right away instead. And now it's the last day of my vacation Friday – in four days, for God's sake – and I still haven't heard a word about what to do and where to go next Monday."

"Well instead of eating yourself up about it, *ask* them, for Christ's sake. Try talking to someone who can tell you something. Someone on personnel for Lunar Operations. Or go to the top in Lunar Surface Operations."

"Maclaughlin?"

"Why not? When your employer fucks you around, you don't just let them. You ask them if it's you who's done something wrong or them who're making a mistake. Go see Maclaughlin. Go right to the top where you can get some answers."

Then silence with a mute television panoply of news shorts and intercut ads for chewing gum and instant hair color, while the sun sets outside, abdicating from a hot and sticky Louisiana August evening.

"I tried to call you at the lab this afternoon."

"You did? I was out."

"You were at this woman Karen's home. You're still seeing her."

James stared at the silent television. Soundless crunchy cookies were capering through a gateway of massive white wicked-eyed molars, until a slimy colored caries blob suddenly stopped the fun.

"Are – you – still – seeing – her?"

James nodded. He spread his hands out left and right on the couch.

"Me Sunday night and her Monday afternoon. You can't keep it still, can you? What does she do – pass out when you screw her? Or *she* screws *you* unconscious? When am I planned in next?"

Arms splayed, James pushed the fingers of each hand down between the cushions of the couch each side of him. He buried his fingers up to the knuckles, slowly shoving them carefully and viciously deeper, both hands, a thrust at a time.

"She was never really supposed to be going on any exchange semester, was she? James. Why have you started lying to me?"

Fingers safely buried, James turned his head towards her.

"Is this an open marriage we have here? Do you own me? Are you going to pretend you never used it when it suited you?"

"I never —" Ripped by his ice-hard eyes, "I never did anything at —" Rising from the chair on an updraught of incomprehension. "Anything at — *at the same time!*"

Beverly rushed out to the hall and slammed the door behind her so hard the entire house shook.

"The director is extremely busy, as I'm sure you'll appreciate, Mrs Ryle. Are you quite certain it's a matter for her, and not for our personnel office or maybe the crew scheduling manager?"

"I'm entirely sure. It's something important concerning my tour at Armstrong — which was cut short, like I say, immediately after that accident at the Soviet base. I could probably have passed this on at my post-tour debriefing, but that was canceled. Among other things, I want to know why it was canceled. I feel I know something the director should know urgently."

"Very well, Mrs Ryle. I'll see if the director is too busy right at this moment, or if she has time to take a call. One moment please."

It took so long. She had to be getting the brush-off by Maclaughlin. The unit counter on the phone steadily clocked up the cost of silence. It took so long.

"Mrs Ryle, I'm putting you through." A click.

"Good morning, Beverly. I hear you have some kind of a problem? By the way, has anyone told you NET were very pleased with that short talk you did for us from Armstrong? And our public relations people were delighted. You came over great, just the image we like to push these days."

"Good morning. No, no one's told me. No one's told me anything, like why I was pulled back early or why my post-tour debriefing was canceled. That's one of the things I'm calling about. Also —"

"Isn't that rather a matter for the crew scheduling manager? I have too many things to take care of to go into details on all of them. I'd have thought you were clear about the reasons, anyway, having been involved in the arrangement."

"Arrangement? I was just told, put on a Transiter, landed at Vandenberg, briefed by this General Reeber and sent right home."

"Come again? *Who* debriefed you at Vandenberg?"

"It wasn't a *debriefing*, it was more of a briefing. Reeber told me a whole lot of things about national security and pep-talked me about the need –"

"Who? *Reeber*? A one-star general? He's something in Space Force's Special Operations Divison, I believe. Are you sure you have the name right?"

"Brigadier General Reeber. And a lieutenant colonel by the name of Gruber, and a lieutenant – Alderton or Alderson, I think. They said they'd also talked to your people at Lunar Operations Control, so I assumed they had the okay of Lunar Surface Operations. Um – didn't they?"

"They certainly wouldn't have gotten my okay to wreck our personnel scheduling for Armstrong just so as to pep-talk you on national security. Space Force asked us to pull you back for an urgent debriefing on what you observed of the seismic event at the Soviet base – you being the only person who observed it more or less in real time. Six weeks ago they were still really worried the Soviets were placing nuclear weapons up there. I guess the information they got from you helped confirm our own photographic data and the claim by Moscow that it was a meteorite impact."

"But they didn't *get* any information from me. Reeber just gave me this pep-talk on not saying a word to anyone about anything connected with the impact events. He didn't want anything *from* me."

"That doesn't tie up. Maybe someone here at LSO fouled up on the information passed through to me. Do you happen to know if there's been any more of these briefings?"

"Yes. Reeber told me he'd talked with people at Operations Control, like I said. And I called Charles Watkins yesterday –"

"Hold on. Watkins, Zavaroni, Sheldon and Bakum were landed by TAV at Vandenberg, but that was just the regular payload sharing we do with the DOD. Nothing was said to us about the DOD wanting to debrief them."

"Well, I called him at home, and he told me he had a little

talk with Reeber at Vandenberg, and so did the others. Zavaroni and Sheldon, that is. They all got more or less the same pep-talk as I did. But that wasn't what I really wanted to talk with you about. There's this business about the accident or explosion or whatever it was at the Soviet base, and I've kind of got this feeling that –"

"Look – ah, sorry to interrupt you. But I think I'd like to check up on a thing or two, soon as I can. And I'd like a better chance to talk with you. I have a manager's meeting to run in a few minutes, so I'll have to cut you off here. Could I ask you maybe to come over to the office sometime? It's kind of a long way for you, I know. I'm right, aren't I – you live in New Orleans?"

"Out of town, yes. I guess it's maybe a five-hour drive. But it's worth it to me if you have the time."

"I'm checking right now. Tomorrow's out. I'm in Washington in the morning and Kennedy in the afternoon. Thursday looks tight as well. Could you make Friday? You could get here by early afternoon, I guess?"

"Friday would be fine. What time in the afternoon?"

"Let's see. Science schedule talk-through at two. Should take around an hour. Then the expansion program discussion on Armstrong at three-thirty. That'll be open ended, probably go on late. How about three?"

"Friday?" he said, and shrugged. "Yes, why not Friday? You want to drive the whole way? Take a flight. On your salary you can afford that just for a half-hour talk."

"I'll drive. What's the point in me having a Mercedes if I never use it?"

"But there and back in a day. It's not like driving there so as to have the car available all week. You'll be starting early and returning late. That's a lot of driving. At least five hours each way."

"Five hours, maybe six. I can use the time to think. I got a lot to think about. Don't I?"

"Whatever you say."

"So Friday. I'll be leaving some time after eight, right after you start for work."

"And you'll be back late."

"Guess so. Nine. Or ten, maybe."

"So would it be okay with you if I stay in town Friday evening?"

"Huh? Why not. Who with, James?"

"The guys from work. Well – Maggie, and Sam Guaraldi from our lab, and a couple more from the lab next door. Maggie's husband, Sam's girl, and I think one of the others is bringing his wife along, too. I was going to ask you case you wanted us to go along, or we'd not bother. But rather than stay here alone, if you're going to be late?"

"Sure. Why not. What do I care?"

23 *A Nice Day*

Beverly left right after eight, just after James had driven in the direction of the Pontchartrain Bridge to get into New Orleans.

She got into her air-conditioned everyman Mercedes and drove away from home on a day already starting out sticky in the relative cool of the morning, with a low and hazed sun blaring out of a white sky. She picked up Twelve right south of Covington and turned west on it, with heavy morning traffic the whole of the way through to Baton Rouge. Then she picked up Ten and crossed the Mississippi and took off on the long, easy, smooth freeway drive. She pushed a little over the speed restriction and passed Lafayette in two hours, Lake Charles in only three, not quite making the kind of time she would have expected if she was traveling on a Sunday evening and due to check in for work at Johnson the next morning. The Mercedes was small and compact. It had a stick shift to give her something to do, it had all the traditional advantages of a passenger cage with modern shock absorbing all-synthetic fenders front and rear, and James called it her German pocket battleship. It was cool inside, quiet, a dream of a car to drive, and the highway was flat and straight and generous for the amount of traffic on it. She played music disks the whole time, mostly Bach, the whole of the St Matthew Passion plus some of the cantatas – "Ach, lieben Christen seid getrost" . . . "Jesu, der du meine Seele." You don't have to be a churchgoing or any other kind of a Christian to love such music, any more than you have to be a paid-up pagan to go to the Moon.

She got hungry right after crossing the Texas border at Orange, and by the time she was approaching Beaumont and signs appeared for both Bobby Robbino's and the Magic Pan, all she had to do after coming off the highway was make her choice. The Magic Pan won because it turned up first on the route she took through Beaumont.

It was midday hot, with the white-sky sun planishing tarmac and flat-tile roofs and the metal tops of parked and cruising cars. She ate, freshened up, returned through the outdoor instant sticky heat to the cooled car interior, and drove off looking for a filling station. It was twelve-thirty and the place was clogging up with traffic. The entire area for miles around Houston was getting more and more of a sprawling strip and satellite development region, a bloom of light and service and information industries around the big city in line with the continuous economic rise of Texas. And these days lots of people were getting the habit of using flexitime working to extend the weekends, or were taking advantage of working at the home terminal connected to the office computer and were staying away from the office outside of core time. So right inside Beaumont she was caught in a rush-hour squeeze and crawl at midday Friday.

She got stuck in the right side lane on a packed stretch of stop-and-crawl road heading towards some distant lights far away through a sun and exhaust haze. Right behind her she had a real asshole, a scruffy guy with sunglasses in an old Eldorado Biarritz, its front all chrome fender and ancient chrome fireplace grill like a make-believe Rolls, plastered all over with gleaming chrome-framed spot and fog and what the hell else lights. He bounced around impatient in his seat, a stupid puppet in her mirror. He revved the whole time behind her. A real macho vehicle for a pseudo macho type. What he couldn't do his machine made up for. With some-one like that behind you in a jam, you hate them very quickly. Either he couldn't get his dick to do anything at all, or it fired so fast it was no use to any girl, so instead he asserted himself with his big gleaming automobile with all its phallic fucking stupid lamps on the front, ramming them at her ass all the time, hanging back and then lunging close, almost trying to push her when the car ahead of her braked.

The queue was passing a filling station. She left a space in front so she could pull off cleanly into the entrance. From behind a hoarding at the entrance, another car shot out right across her nose and into the second lane. She stamped on the brake. Jolt –

Her head hurt from the headrest and she was winded, and there went the bastard who cut in, forcing his way along *between* the second and third lanes, cutting into the third and then the faster flowing fourth, and disappearing.

And the motherfucker behind had gone and hit her.

In the mirror he'd backed off and was pulling out to pass her, heedless of the confusion he was causing in the adjacent lane. She slammed in the gear, hauled the wheel and reversed in a curve outwards to block him off, her nearside front mounting the kerb. She pulled on the brake and jumped out into the din and the awful heat.

The motherfucker had his head out of the window. "What in hell you doing!"

"Traffic laws! You don't run into me from behind and leave me carrying the bill. Pull back into the side and let's exchange insurance details!"

He did so, cursing inside his car. And his fucking lamps up front were all smashed and she'd driven backwards onto a carpet of glass. And traffic horns were hooting at her to get out of the way. She got into her car, straightened up forward, then reversed to park right into the side short of the filling station entry and tight in front of the motherfucker's pride and joy. She got out.

The pride and joy had its front all damaged. The fender was bent and the grill dented and the chrome all chipped and scratched, all the lights were cockeyed and glassless and shards were spread around everywhere. Her pocket battleship Mercedes had slight scratches and a few dirty marks on the shock absorbing plastic of the deep fender that stuck out below and inches beyond the tail lights. So she was unharmed and the guilty party had made a real mess of himself. She started scuffing some of the glass into the gutter.

The motherfucker was out of his machine and slapping his fists against his thighs in fury at the appalling damage done to his compensatory dream. "What kind of a mess you made of my car!" He pointed straight-armed, rigid from the shoulder with a furiously fluttering index finger, at her NASA sticker inside the rear windshield. "You flying fuckers with your asses on fire! You can't even drive!"

"Hey! What kind of a motherfucker are you? You smash into the back of my car because you're too dumb to brake. You're totally absolutely hundred per cent legally in the wrong. *You* pay!"

He bent over suddenly like a mad priest. He slapped and punched the injuries of his pride and joy. Even the bodywork was buckled where the supports of the fender passed through it. In a frenzy of foot and finger work he danced around again to get to the driver's door. "You smart-assed fuckers with your fucking rockets!" He took two tries to tug open the door. "Can't even drive!"

"Hey! Who's paying? You paying cash or is your insurance paying?" Crazy question, because another glance at her own vehicle confirmed that it hadn't cost her a cent.

"You play castrator with someone else, lady!" He got in, pulled out right in front of another car, and stammered away with the creeping traffic in a series of wild revvings and brake squeals.

Now don't go getting furious, Beverly. He's all smashed up, he has hundreds, maybe even a thousand dollars worth of repairs, and all you have is a couple of scratches and some dirty marks to clean up on a non-corroding paint-free fender.

Then she noticed that the nearside rear tire was half down and deflating steadily. His fucking glass she'd reversed over!

With the tire squelching fearfully, she drove off the road into the filling station and parked beside the big hoarding where the original rally driver shot out from. She got out into the heat again, took a look, then opened the trunk and got ready to change the wheel.

The station attendant came across, obligatory rag in hand. "Hey lady, this is a business here. You can't park and go do your shopping or get your hair fixed."

"Here! Come here! See! I've got a flat tire. Should I change it in the middle of the highway? And don't worry. When I'm through I'll even fill up here. Okay? That okay?"

"Sure, lady. Sure." He went back to his pumps.

She opened aside the floor of the trunk to get at the car jack. No chance of assistance with the power jack from that jerk, and it was so hot and humid and she was sweating before she even started. Hope to God the place had a decent washroom with soap and a towel or a dryer. She got down to insert the jack properly.

She noticed a little straight black wire dangling from under the rear of the car. Oh no, don't say the motherfucker damaged her after all, broke a cable to the lights or something. She got right down on her hands and knees on the heat-sticky asphalt and ducked her head to the ground to take a look underneath.

The short and stiff little wire dangled from an oblong package wrapped in black and stuck on clear of the inner underedge of the fender, neatly fixed against the ribbed underfloor panel.

A bomb or something? It couldn't be, not so small as that. Maybe an incendiary designed just to set off the gas in the tank, radio-controlled with a little wire aerial to pick up the firing instruction? Then it clicked what it was.

She tugged at the plastic-wrapped thing. From the way it insisted on sliding free and tried to jump back, she could tell it was held in place by strong magnets. In her hand it was heavy, a solid package longer than she could span with her fingers. She knelt there with her weight on her heels and brushed pieces of grit out of the side of her hair. She looked at the anonymous package with its dirty plastic wrapping and its short and black and near invisible aerial. It had to be so heavy because of the batteries inside and maybe also little accelerometers to sense which way the car turned and how it accelerated and slowed all the time. That way they didn't have to stay right behind. They could sit in a surveillance car miles away and follow her on a map, never losing her but never being seen.

It was a radio tracker.

She couldn't take it apart here. She wouldn't throw it away. She wanted to know who owned it. She should take it along and see what Maclaughlin had to say about that. NASA had to work closely with the Defense Department, space also being a strategic area, but Jesus God Almighty. What kind of a filthy trick?

She put it in the trunk.

A big and square thing, a Toyota Land Cruiser, rolled into the filling station and parked at the pumps, CB aerials swinging gently as it stopped. The driver got out and started filling the tank. It had shaded windows, but she was sure there was another person inside who had turned around and was staring at her. Didn't they ever see a woman who could change a wheel before? And now she was getting too dirty to drive without filthying up the steering wheel and the whole of the inside of the car, and she was still two hours away from Johnson Space Center.

Furious with a boiling feeling of outrage, Beverly drove on to Houston. She came in on Beaumont Road to Denver Harbor, headed south through Jacinto City and Park Place, then took the Gulf Freeway out past the airport and Ellington Air Force Base. Everywhere the fucking military. Who else would put a tracker on her car but the same people who wanted her to keep her mouth shut in the interest of glorious goddam national security? At least she lost the Toyota Land Cruiser with the CB aerials on the way through Houston before she turned onto the Gulf Freeway. She didn't have to begin to believe the vehicle really was tailing her.

She got to Johnson shaving the time for the appointment. The guy on the gate didn't just glance at but *studied* her NASA pass before letting her in – they must have had a security blitz here as well. She drove through the Center to the new Moon Program building and parked, grabbed her shoulder bag, took her little passenger from the trunk and wrapped it in a tissue and stuffed it into the bag, and went inside. On the door her pass was checked again. She took the elevator up to the floors occupied by Lunar Surface Operations. She freshened up as well as she could, and it was five after three when she knocked on the door of the office of Maclaughlin's secretary.

Maclaughlin wasn't there.

It was ten minutes before Rosemary Maclaughlin marched in direct from the overrun of the science talk-through, and took Beverly straight into her office. She parked Beverly in one of the easy interview chairs around the coffee-high conference table, and started unloading papers and folders onto her desk. Maclaughlin was wearing dark gray cotton pants and a white blouse with gray and black lace panels over the bodice and around the cuffs – she looked cool and severe today, an executive woman you'd better not tangle with. Her hair was blonde, and even enough in color to suggest it had been dyed to cover over any grays. It was cut very short, tapered to a point at the back of the neck and with points in front of the ears, it was a little longer on top and fluffed up and blowdried back except for a feathery fringe of strands coming down over her forehead. The style was simple, conservative and careful, but friendly and fresh. Maclaughlin was forty-five, very successful, and single.

She came back and sat in one of the chairs across the little discussion table. "Did you have a smooth journey over?"

"No. I was rammed by some idiot in Beaumont – his car damaged, not mine – and got a flat from his broken glass. I fixed the wheel, which is when I found this." She opened her shoulder bag. "Under the back of my car." She leaned forward and put the tissue wrapped thing in the middle of the spotless table. She unfolded the tissue. "What do you make of that?"

Maclaughlin looked at it for a long moment, not moving at all except for a single twitch at the corner of her mouth. "I'd say it looks like someone's put you under surveillance."

"Just like that? Put a bug under my car? Isn't it *illegal*?"

"Not for a suitably empowered authority, if it also obtains the necessary court or police order. Whether the FBI and CIA are subject to the same restrictions, I don't know."

"But – you mean it's *all right* that someone does that to me?"

"No, I do *not* mean it's all right. NASA is a security sensitive organization because of the work we do ourselves and because we're continually sharing transport and facilities with the military. Sometimes that partnership gets too close for comfort. People like me get security vetted at regular intervals. There have also been instances of our employees being put under routine or even close surveillance. Some of them even turned out actually to *be* spies, though they've always been dealt with by dismissal and extradition to keep it out of the public eye. But now putting you under surveillance, one of *my* people, without informing *me* is not acceptable. And if they had informed me and the reason had not been good, I'd have kicked up a real fuss and passed it higher up. Some people in the Pentagon have security paranoia – okay. But they don't have to expect us to get ourselves infected."

"So." Beverly spread her hands to let out some of the helplessness she'd been feeling. "What are we going to do about it? Can I do something – call my lawyer or what? Can you do something?"

Maclaughlin looked at her watch. "I still have ten minutes until the meeting. But they can't exactly start without me, so I can spare an extra five. Okay, then – let's see what reasons we can dig out. You were given this security pep-talk, right? And you're unhappy about the general treatment you've been getting. Well let's take easy points first. Have we been mistreating you?"

"Well – well – it's the feeling of being kept out of the way. For example, today's the last day of my vacation, and I still haven't heard anything on where I'm to report for what work."

Maclaughlin nodded. "I've been looking at your details this morning. Your vacation still has a week to run, after which you'll be wanted here to co-work on a backlog of lunar geophysics results. The six-week vacation was planned as normal. We'd been given to understand they wanted you in Vandenberg for several days of debriefing, so we wrote those off as equivalent to our six-day session and added your vacation start on after that. If Reeber gave you the impression your vacation was starting right away, he misinformed you. Nothing to worry about there."

"He misinformed me on a whole lot of things, I think. He told me the second seismic event was caused by one of our satellites crashing as a direct result of the explosion at the Soviet base, which it was observing at the time. When he told me that, he already *knew* it was a weapon that had exploded, but since then Washington have said it was a meteorite without waiting to hear what any neutral inspectors might have had to say. And –"

"I've seen our own photographic evidence, plus all the

material released by Moscow. It undoubtedly was a meteorite. We have to know about that because of the risk to our own installations. We want to see if we should introduce any safety features or procedures – maybe even a radar watch so we could at least get the people into suits ahead of any sudden depressurization to the base from impact damage. It was a meteorite."

"Well – anyway, Reeber apparently told Charles Watkins last week it was a Soviet satellite or carrier rocket that crashed to create the second event."

Maclaughlin nodded. "I already called Watkins Tuesday afternoon, also Sheldon and Zavaroni. Sheldon got a similar pep-talk from your Lieutenant Colonel Gruber to what Watkins got from Reeber. Zavaroni got a version from a Major Macklin that was so vague it would fit either version on the second event the other two got, or probably also the one you appear to have been told. Reeber was also still talking about the explosion of a Soviet weapon installation – that was a couple of days before the Washington statement. The Defense Department already had the evidence by then, so I don't quite understand that. We can't assume that Reeber's an idiot – quite the opposite, in fact. I guess the best thing is for you to brief me now on this second seismic event, on what you know or have been told, and on what you think."

"There's not really so much I know or have been told – or that I've thought. Beyond that it doesn't tie up, and it makes no sense bringing me back early for absolutely nothing, and it also doesn't make *any* sense putting me under secret observation like I was some kind of criminal or spy." She looked at the bug on the table. "With this – this – this disgusting thing."

Maclaughlin shrugged. "I'm terribly short on time, so just tell me the facts. Especially the seismic data. I've asked our people here and at Ames, and at all our university contract departments for the data, and no one has it any more and no one can remember it. It doesn't surprise me at all that no one looked at it closely at the time once we knew there'd been an impact at the Soviet base, but I'm still trying to figure how the Defense Department pulled the trick of intercepting it before it even got into our records. I'm looking for someone who I'm going to fire – unless they have a damn good excuse for handing it over, like a secret order from the president or something equivalent. So now, as quick as you can, tell me."

"Well." And there really wasn't anything much to say, once it was boiled down to the few bare facts. All the rest was just impressions clouded around it. "There was a second seismic event recorded around thirty minutes after the one at the base. It was also located at or near the surface. It was also a very low energy event, although I didn't have the chance to analyze the trace or even just subtract the resonance component of the first event. I think it was slightly more energetic than the first, but at that scale of event there's a huge proportional error involved anyway. It was located on Far Side, somewhere towards the south pole and almost due south of Aldrin, but I didn't see the need to commit the coordinates to memory at the time, and I'm vague on it now. As for what Reeber told me, in retrospect it seems like just a lot of persuasive nonsense. He gave a good impression of it all somehow meaning something or other that he couldn't disclose, and beyond that he just set me up to draw my own conclusions. But he did clearly say that the first event was an explosion and not a meteorite, and that the second was the crash of an American surveillance instrument that was caused to malfunction by the explosion. And he certainly said there was a team he headed which is involved in some sort of secret and diplomatically risky operation on and to do with the Moon, with the aim of discovering what's going on at the Soviet base."

"He told you Space Force are running a secret operation on the Moon? Are you sure?"

"Sure I'm sure. He said it right out."

"Well it isn't at Armstrong." Maclaughlin stood up abruptly. "So if it exists at all, it must be what they're doing since they effectively took over Aldrin."

"He said they'd been working for a couple of years on it, I think. He said I shouldn't be saying a word about it to anyone."

"That doesn't surprise me." Maclaughlin walked past her

desk and over to the long window, and stared out through the lace curtain into the blank afternoon.

"As for me!" Beverly turned her gaze to the ugly plastic wrapping of the radio transmitter on its tissue setting on the table. "I've been feeling like a dupe or some kind of a dope, but that's all pushed into the background by this – this *thing*. This tracker or tracer or whatever the name is. To think that people have been doing *this* to me ever since I came back from Armstrong. It makes me feel dirty. Really dirty." Did they put it in place under her car by breaking into her garage some time, or did they do it deftly while the car was parked somewhere on a street. Had they broken in secretly, untroubled by the locks, into her home sometime before she even got back from the Moon, fucking up her life silently in the dark downstairs by placing bugs everywhere, while James was fucking up her life energetically in her bed upstairs by fucking Karen and falling infatuated in love with her or something stupid or even stupider?

Rosemary Maclaughlin stood silent at the window, staring out and thinking. She stood there for well over five minutes without even moving her weight. Then she turned around, decisions made.

"One. I'm suspending you on full pay as of now until further notice. Don't panic. Just don't panic. I'm going to make as much of a fuss about this as I can get together, and if I can claim one of my science astronauts is so harassed that she's unable to carry out her duties, that's a valuable reinforcement of my complaint. You people are *expensive* to train and employ. Two, I'd like you to leave the radio tracker here with me. It won't have a name or an organization's logo on it, but its components might carry serial numbers we can trace far enough to figure out who we can embarrass. I'll embarrass them if I can. Space Force have well and truly messed up our programing. They've insisted on an all-DOD crew at Aldrin for the last four months and they're still insisting for the next rotation. The whole time we haven't had a single science specialist up there, the science program is completely out of schedule and two ongoing experiments have been shut down. By insisting on having you brought back early they've thrown the entire science and work schedules at Armstrong, complicated the personnel and equipment scheduling for at least the next half year, and left the place short of one astronaut for three months. Sure they have the power to do it. It's all in the agreements NASA's been having to make with the Pentagon all along the line, with us as the junior partner ever since the space defense thing got off the ground and Space Force was established. If they didn't need our engineering skills to help them run things, and our science and exploration angle to help legitim- ize space and the Moon and provide non-secure areas usable as publicity for the electorate, I guess the Pentagon and the White House together would have squeezed us out of the business a decade ago. Did you know there was a move preparing to put NASA under Pentagon control? That wasn't torpedoed until the Russians went to the Moon and Washing- ton realized how much they still needed us. It's called the joint civil and military exploitation and development of space, but an equal partnership it most certainly is not. It hasn't worked out anything like the way I once expected it would." Maclaughlin paused suddenly and looked at Beverly more acutely. "That's a purely private opinion, with no correspondence in public or professional life, you under- stand?"

Beverly nodded.

"Good. Next point, don't be tempted to go to the police, a lawyer or the press over the radio tracker. The police will be blocked internally – no one who does this sort of thing is so dumb they don't cover themselves against discovery. A lawyer will be stonewalled because you can't issue a writ against persons unknown, and any press story will be dis- credited with a severity you can't imagine. You can't take on elements of the Government any more without hard evidence. This is the end of the twentieth century, not the middle, and things have changed. All that I can do right at the moment is send you home again. You'll get notification of the suspension early next week. *Don't* disappear in a get-away-from-it-all fit. I need to know I can get in touch with you directly as and when required. Feel free to call me here any time. If I'm not in my office, my secretary will take a message. If you have any more trouble, call me or get me to call you back. Incidentally, if there's a tracker on your car, you'd better not go assuming anything you say on your phone goes unheard. The cases I ever met of close surveillance always involved the interception of mail and phone calls. Sometimes they also wire a person's home."

"Oh God."

Maclaughlin looked at her watch again. "They've been waiting more than ten minutes for me downstairs. When I wasn't in charge I always really hated it when the boss wasn't punctual. I intend to start things moving in the agency's central hierarchy just as soon as I can, and that thing you found there is one of the things I need to do it. But as you know, we've developed quite a bureaucracy over the years and things can get stuck, so I'm also going to try outside contacts – strictly unofficially. Something's going on, and I've already asked a couple of people here at Johnson to see if they can dig anything out, and I'm still waiting. For the moment, though, this has to be it. I have to get to the meeting, and we can't do anything right this minute anyway. Thanks for tipping me off that something quite inexcusable is being done, both to NASA – at least to this division – and to NASA employees. Don't worry too much about the suspension. You're not going to get fired by me, and I'm not going to go losing my job and leaving you stuck. So, now. I hope you have a nice – and a trouble-free journey back home. Take care, and have a nice day now."

Beverly drove out of Johnson Space Center feeling pushed around, mistreated, cheated by her husband and her country, then rolled over and bounced out again by Maclaughlin. A *suspension*. A suspension was a suspension, and it stayed on your record for ever. Out on the highway and looking in the mirror, she saw it a couple of hundred yards and a handful of cars behind her, a Toyota Land Cruiser with shaded windows and CB aerials. It was the same color as the one that tailed her from Beaumont to Houston. At least, she *thought* it was the same color. Why didn't she write it down, make a note of the number? This lookalike was too far away to see its plates through the intervening traffic. It followed her for around a mile into Houston, then turned off at an intersection. With a radio available, the people inside only had to report that she'd left the Space Center and everyone could guess she was heading for home. A home with maybe a telephone tap and bugs all over it? What can you do? How can you know? How can you get rid of them? Phone the FBI?

It was a very long drive home, broken by stops to fill up with gas and a break at a diner in Lake Charles. It was a very long drive with plenty of time to get very bitter. Very bitter indeed. A miracle she didn't drive off the road.

The meeting on the expansion program for Armstrong lasted long enough, all right. Rosemary Maclaughlin got back to her office shortly before seven. Her secretary had left but there was a note on her desk saying that Cliff Daley, the ELTS Mission Scheduling Manager, had called and could she call back. She got no answer from his office so she packed her briefcase with the weekend's work and headed for home. She lived in Galveston now that there had been some new changes and Galveston was chic and in again, but was expensive enough to ensure you didn't share your street exclusively with colleagues from work. She drove to a home which was an elegant, comfortable and completely empty house, just herself and no one else. At forty-five she was the head of Lunar Surface Operations, the bigger half of the Moon Program and by itself as expensive as the Transav and NASA's share in the space stations put together. Lunar Surface Operations was the most important of the prestige manned spaceflight programs, the forward mover whose further development would feed all future expansion in space. That was success indeed. But the price is high in a world still preferentially geared up towards men making careers. Rosemary Maclaughlin was single, and she was celibate sexually, emotionally and domestically. She lived alone.

She called Daley at his home. "Cliff? Rosemary here. Sorry to spoil your evening, but do you have something for me?"

"That's okay, Rosemary. We just finished eating. Yes, I have something. Not much, but it might help."

"Okay, Cliff. I'm listening."

"Well, it starts with the ELTS-16 mission. That's the one where they first pulled their security precedence, and put two new DOD astronauts on for Aldrin instead of the scheduled NASA guys. The two replacements were Bleazard and Browning, right?"

"That much I know."

"Well, Browning and Bleazard are both with the Space Force Special Operations Division. Also on Sixteen, Space Force switched some of its payload due for Aldrin. They put on two of their black box containers. Those went up from Vandenberg by TAV just a day ahead of Sixteen's departure from Pilgrim. They also put a couple more black boxes on ELTS-17 a month later, supplementary payload of seven hundred kilogrammes each."

"Nothing like a launch vehicle for a test firing, maybe?"

"You mean the proposal to put rocket vehicles with war-heads on Far Side, for if the Russians ever put weapons up there aimed at our facilities? Well the black boxes on Sixteen were long and thin and had flammables. Those on Seventeen were pallet blocks. I was thinking maybe that's just what it was, a couple of test vehicles, and then a package of launch and monitoring equipment. Aldrin's been locked to CSOC ever since the Sixteen mission, and it's still an all-military crew up there. Browning and Bleazard came back on Nine-teen, but they were replaced by DOD non-scientists, weren't they? Could be they were planning a test firing – although I thought the system was on ice right now – and then decided to pull back their firing crew instead. After all, they wouldn't tell *us* what they were planning to do up there."

"That's for sure."

"But it would tie up. They plan a test firing and have to cancel. They bring back the operators but leave the stuff up there, and only let their own people go anywhere near it at Aldrin. With rocks landing on the Russians, you don't want to go firing off missiles they could point at and scream about."

"No, I wouldn't think you do."

"Apart from that, they're still tying up the personnel allocation for Aldrin for the next two rotations. Two DOD guys each time. I figure they're still up to something. They insist we put only military pilots on the Transiters for missions Twenty-One, Twenty-Two and Twenty-Three. Rosemary, those guys are going paranoid."

"Cliff, they already are paranoid."

"The only other thing is a payload rescheduling they've pulled on ELTS-21. They've put one of their Torus-12 orbiters on board for launch into lunar orbit. The reason is, the one they already have there is locked in a polar orbit and is clean out of maneuvering propellant. They've been shunting it around so much since the impact at the Soviet base, they've used up its entire reserve. They must have looked at the whole Moon with it. They had to keep us informed every time it could affect the Transiter orbits. It was all over the place, I can tell you. But they're paying for the rescheduling – okay so let them. That's about all I have for facts. The rest would be just rumor."

"Cliff, that's already a lot more than I had up until now. If I need the rumor I'll get back to you. I really might."

It was late, getting past eight. Rosemary fixed herself a drink, took a pizza out of the freezer and put it ready to go in the microwave. Hungry and in a hurry, and she would need some part of the evening soon to relax in. She got out her address book and started calling Washington. If it was late in Texas, it was even later in the Federal capital, and it took her ten calls and a small fortune to track down the party she wanted.

Beverly got home at almost ten. By then she had driven all of twelve hours in one day. Out on the driveway, head buzzing and dizzier than she'd realized, she took the air for a couple of minutes. Solid, squeezable, breathless air. A gibbous moon, going towards its third quarter, was hanging bloated and bulbous above the eastern horizon in a sticky subtropical sky. The creeping, searing sun would be halfway down from the zenith at Armstrong. Up there were people she knew, one of them very intimately. Up there were splendid places she'd seen, the highest ground she'd ever walked upon. And all of it so trouble free.

She found a note from James in the kitchen: "The guys booked a nightclub table. Guess I won't be in a state to drive home after. Sam offered me a bed at his place. Expect me Saturday afternoon after tennis workout. Hope you had a nice day."

She threw the note in the trash can. Why did he bother? Why not just write he was spending the evening, night and half of Saturday with Karen? It had been one long, hot, bitter, nasty, bastard, shocking, wearing, exhausting hell of a sickening awful nice day.

6 HIGHEST GROUND

24 *Ventersberg*

Frank Simons met up with them at the prefabricated press center which had been erected on the side of the street between the shell of Government House and the ruins of the Houses of Parliament. The briefing had been a vacuous exercise. The interior minister, having jealously kept political and economic freedom for himself all his professional life, while denying anything more than a semblance of it to the non-white races, a man now without any interior left to administer, had merely repeated the rhetoric about erecting a fortress around Cape Town to stem the communist tide for the sake of the Free World. It was all bullshit. The evil of these people had turned into a sad and sorry farce. Laughable, except for those thousands of human beings they would still arrange to kill.

Shari Laurin and Jim Walters had been one of the last news teams to leave Johannesburg during the helicopter evacuation, two days before the final collapse of resistance in the city. They had to leave their latest satellite aerial behind in Jo'burg because the American aircrew refused to waste lifting capacity on the weight. In Durban, they were told by their bosses that a complete sender was available and waiting in Cape Town, the inevitable scene of the last act of the drama. So they hitched a ride on a US transport plane from Durban's cratered airstrip to Cape Town's bouncily repaired main airport runway. They disembarked after taxiing – just in time to see a rocket come screeching over the lines from somewhere out east and plant a new crater in the tarmac. No more aircraft coming in to unload supplies and collect evacuees that day.

They picked up the sender and went searching for something to transport it in, their pockets bulging with dollars. They found themselves an old but roadworthy Range Rover, and yes, the former owner was even willing to take handfuls of dollar bills that had just been counted through – been *touched* – by Shari. By a black. She'd loved every minute of it. So now they had wheels, and even had masses of the only currency with which you could still get gas. All they didn't really have, locked up inside the Cape Town enclave, was somewhere to go.

"Which is why," Shari said, leaning on the hood of the dirty and once white Range Rover parked in front of the burned-out shell of City Hall. "Which is why we're going to take a little excursion out of this place." She stared glumly across the cracked and buckled tarmac of Darling Street and down a rubble-strewn side road towards the ruins of the main railway station, and screwed up her nose. "Looks like it's been nuked or something."

"Out?" Frank said.

Jim nodded. "Use our wheels to get some country air."

"What's the one thing no correspondent has ever done in this war?" Shari straightened up and brushed dirt off her elbow. "Go out there and talk to the enemy. See what they have to say."

"It isn't worth the risk." Frank shook his head. "This is a war purely about racism, and we're all on the wrong side."

"But me – I'm the right color, aren't I? So we're going to get the scoop before the war runs out on us. First across-the-lines interview with an ANC general. A full colonel would do, I guess. That's worth the risk, so off we go. First light tomorrow."

"Just like that? Drive across our lines and head their way?"

"If the Boers will let us out. Don't have transport, do you?"

"Me?" Frank shrugged. "My car was wrecked when we escaped from Valsfontein."

"Okay then, Frank. So you can drive."

"*What?*"

"You can drive. You were born in another of these countries where they have vehicles with the steering wheel on the right. Crazy habit. I just can't get the hang of it with a stick shift like this thing has. And Jim's way of winding the window down every time he wants to change gear doesn't exactly inspire me with confidence. So you can drive."

Jim just grinned.

"What makes you think," Frank asked, "that *I* want to come?"

"You got us out of Valsfontein. So we owe you a favor. We get the world scoop for TV, you get it for the gentlemen of the good old written press. Deal?"

The camp lay in a hollow in the flank of Ventersberg, up amid the bare peaks of the Hexrivierberge. Below, about a mile distant, the main road from Cape Town wound up into the mountains at the start of its long cross-country journey towards Johannesburg. The only traffic on the road was in the other direction – old trucks overloaded with supplies, and long lines of marching guerrillas. The ANC was slowly moving up its forces for what would be the last battle, the assault on Cape Town.

The camp was small, just a scatter of widely spaced tents. Around it were sandbagged positions with heavy machine guns and hand-held anti-aircraft missiles, enough to defend the camp should an air attack ever come, but not enough to draw particular attention to it. In the best tradition of guerrilla forces long subjected to an enemy's total command of the air, the camp was arranged to present a dispersed target and seemed of no importance, set as it was on the high ground away from the road, several miles into the mountains from the junction town of Worcester. The camp was at present the headquarters of all ANC forces operating in the Western Cape.

They had driven out through the South African lines at dawn the previous day, passing through the perimeter in the outskirts of Belville. No one tried to stop them – suicidal correspondents are no one's concern. The road east of Cape Town ran through countryside devastated by the major fires and the scattered fighting that had followed. They made very slow progress along the cratered tarmac, not daring to leave it for fear that the ground alongside might have been mined, and having no wish at all to charge down upon the positions of the ANC. It was not until they crawled into Kraaifontein, a razed township looking like a disordered cemetery, that they met the first guerrillas. They were searched, and then made to wait under guard. Eventually a captured troop carrier appeared, loaded with guerrillas, and they were told to follow it. The imbalanced convoy trundled slowly for another fifteen miles. In Paarl they were interviewed by a group of ANC officers, and then escorted to a shed and locked in for the night. The journey resumed under escort at dawn. They reached Worcester at midday, and the head-quarters camp an hour later.

The overall commander of ANC forces in the southwestern Cape was Aggre Maubane. A commissar of the newly formed Democratic People's Government of Southern Africa, Maubane spoke with an excellently refined British accent that few Oxbridge graduates could have equaled. He had been educated at the Funda Centre in Soweto, back in the days before the South African authorities had decided that Johannesburg would be safer if Soweto ceased to exist. The ANC had spirited him out of the country to study at Nairobi University, and from there he was sent to Oxford to take a further degree in political science. Aggre Maubane was as cultured a man as you could wish to meet. He was also one of the ANC's most experienced commanders, and had been closely involved in the preparation of the military coup which had turned the war into virtually an overnight victory earlier in the year. He was going to figure prominently in the political makeup of the future black state that had seized for itself the colonial inheritance at the southern pole of Africa.

The flaps were open at each end of the ridge tent, and the side walls were rolled up so that the breeze blew through unimpeded. South Africa it might be, but it was rainy season mountain air, and almost cold. Outside, in the out-of-focus background, were aides with communications equipment and guards with Kalashnikovs. Under the stilted, flapping roof of the tent, Frank Simons and Shari Laurin faced each other across a rickety map table. Between them, seated on a canvas chair, was Aggre Maubane. Jim Walters crouched in the entrance to the tent, his camera zoomed out to capture the complete group, and then zoomed in to concentrate on Maubane. Perched on the map table were the microphones of the sound camera and of Frank's cassette recorder.

Maubane was affably answering questions without even insisting on a preparatory vetting. After all, no one would be able to leave until any offending passages had been wiped from all the tapes. So the commissar and general was sitting at ease in his combat jacket, legs comfortably crossed, and exuding public relations skill.

"I think such predictions by the whites that our government will fail are quite ridiculous." He smiled tolerantly. "First of all, we've been running most of the country for years, so we already have the experience. Secondly, all twenty million of the native peoples of this country are on our side. You might say it has been a very popular war. Furthermore, we share our land borders with Black African neighbors who support our cause wholeheartedly, so this time the United States will be unable to try its trick of conjuring up an insurgency movement and invading us by proxy. The Nicaraguan model simply won't work here. We'll be left sufficiently in peace to repair the economy, and our people will be free to return to the daily business of normal life."

Shari, according to the deal, still had a couple more questions to go. "Will you be interested in trading contacts with the West?"

Maubane nodded. "Certainly, if the West is interested in trading contacts with us. South Africa has for decades been an advanced industrial country. We should know, after all. We were the ones who did most of the work."

Shari checked off another of her notes. "Up until six months ago the ANC was being rolled back by Pretoria, but then Moscow pitched in and helped in a big way. Presumably your major source of economic aid will now be Moscow. Your dependence on Moscow seems to be extreme."

"Oh now look," Maubane protested gently, waving a patient hand. "The governments of the major Western nations have always in reality supported the Pretoria regime, either by refusing all pressures to apply sanctions or other means against the white government, or by permitting your industries to do unrestricted business with the white-run economy. Western Europe invented representative democracy. Britain was the first nation completely to abolish slavery. The

United States proclaims individual freedom and equality as the cornerstone of its constitution. But whose side were you all on? Pretoria's. *You* people, through the governments *you* elect and tolerate, have helped to deny us the very principles you claim to live by, because you found it economically profitable. Who were we to turn to? Instead of offering finely worded assurances of sympathy, the Soviet Bloc has provided the support we needed to be able to free ourselves from racial injustice. In the end it is practical results which count – a friend in need is a friend indeed. The politics of this war were programed in advance at least half a century ago."

Shari checked off another note, and glanced at Frank.

Frank met Maubane's disconcertingly self-confident eyes. "Can we concentrate for a moment on the assistance you had from Moscow? At the end of February you started fires from one end of the country to the other. How much of that could you achieve yourselves, and how much of it was done for you by the Soviet Union?"

Maubane reapplied his tolerant smile. "I still haven't got over my own amazement that people were so *surprised* by it. South Africa is an extremely dry country, and therefore it burns easily – especially when the rains have virtually failed. All you have to do is light so many fires that no one is going to be able to put them out. It's a simple matter of coordination. Even a black man who grew up in Soweto or Crossroads and was destined to fulfil his human potential by cleaning out the white man's drains in the big city – even that black man had to be able to read a watch, so that he could catch the train to paradise in the morning and back to his ghetto in the evening."

"So you laid the fires yourselves?" Frank asked. "How?"

Maubane shrugged. "By pouring gasoline on the ground every hundred yards for several miles, and setting light to it with matches. In places we even had soldiers running along with burning torches in their hands. The only trick lay in collating accurate information on local wind directions so that we could line up the fires and pick the right night to do it on. A major help was weather satellite data sent to us from ground terminals in Nairobi. Nothing mysterious about that."

"And military airfields, and other defended targets?"

"Incendiary rockets. Saboteurs. That sort of thing."

"And the city areas?" Frank put his hand in the pocket of his bush jacket. "The patrols were far too intense. You couldn't have sent large numbers of fireraisers undetected into the cities at night, could you?"

"I must admit that was a trickier problem." Aggre Maubane tipped his head back slightly, waiting for whatever the British reporter was going to produce and the American colleagues clearly knew about. His manner, for a moment, was guarded.

"Your people weren't in the cities that night, were they? Instead you planted thousands of little incendiary bombs that were all timed to go off together. You planted them all over the cities, days in advance of the actual burns, didn't you?" Frank took the little exhibit from his pocket and placed it on the map table. A battery, a control circuit chip, detonator wires, and a compact little block of plastic explosive. "What you used were little bombs like this."

Jim Walters zoomed in on the disassembled device for a long moment, and then opened up the shot again to include Maubane once more.

Maubane could see what Jim was doing with the zoom lens drive, and waited patiently until he was in shot again. Then he nodded. "I see you managed to find one that the CIA missed. Most observant of you, Mr Simons. Yes, that was the little trick we used. You know, the mistake the whites made was that they couldn't bear to get their hands dirty, and so they couldn't live without us. They were far too pure and dainty to collect their own garbage, and right through the war it never occurred to them to take over from the smelly kaffirs who came to their doors every week to remove the awful stuff. So – we just put our little incendiary bombs under their dustbins, in their garages, under their porches. We planted thousands of them, and if only one in ten worked well enough to start a real fire, well it was still far too many simultaneous fires for anyone to have a chance of stopping it before everything had been burned to the ground." He pointed to the dismembered bomb on the table. "That thing you have there appears to be one of the ones that didn't work."

"And you used tens of thousands." Shari jumped in now that Frank had landed his little coup. "Did Moscow supply them?"

"Well now." Maubane dressed himself in whole new layers of self-assurance. "Let's just say that obviously the timing circuits were specially made, and we don't have any electronics factories, do we? But I really don't think it's my business to discuss who we might have purchased them from."

"So Moscow supplied them." And Shari didn't waste time waiting to see if that assertion would be challenged. Maubane was far too astute to indulge in pointless denials. "And what about the use of lasers to start some of the open country fires. To what extent were lasers used?"

"Oh, we certainly didn't use any lasers." Aggre Maubane shook his head, a smooth declaration that the subject was going to change with the next question. "After all, the ANC hasn't actually got any lasers. I'm afraid you're asking the wrong person about that."

25 *Joint Space*

Mid-September was not a popular time to be stuck in Washington on the drudge of committee routine, and with the presidential election revving up for its final phase, there was no lack of excuses for empaneled members to absent themselves on constituency business. Entire committees had gone into recess for the duration. In the new extension building across from the Capitol there was a surplus of suites available for hearings of newly formed special subcommittees. This spacious chamber, though, was somewhat wasted. The five-member subcommittee occupied the middle of the bench amid flanking arrays of empty places. Facing them across the entire length of the witness table were just three invited experts, unaccompanied by any retinues of legal advisers. The public benches at the rear were deserted – no media, no citizens observing the mechanisms of democratic government. The ushers overseeing the recording operation were the only audience.

This hearing was in closed session, strictly private and confidential. These proceedings were secret.

The parent of the subcommittee was the Joint Space Activities Advisory Committee, whose business was to monitor closely all United States and foreign activities in space, and to report its findings regularly to both the Senate and the House. Space had become far too important for Congress to get along any more without a coherent overview supplied by one single authoritative body, but until the advent of the Joint Space Activities Advisory Committee, the monitoring of space had remained splintered among dozens of other committees, ranging from the prestigious Senate Foreign Relations down to the most mundane housekeeping instances that never got into the news. The committee was still new, and had yet really to try out its muscle, but one day Joint

Space was going to be powerful. Its field of responsibility was growing almost exponentially, after all, and it encompassed the highest ground.

Today's subcommittee had been voted into existence by Joint Space barely a week ago. Empaneled in order to conduct a secret and specific investigation, it was burdened with the title of Joint Space Activities Advisory Special Subcommittee, shortened to Joint Space Sub. The protocols of reporting exactly what to exactly whom still had to be worked out, but that could wait. The passing years had seen some changes for congressional committees, with a dilution of the powers of subpoena for open sessions, together with an imposition of security restrictions which led to more and more closed sessions and an ever decreasing publication of evidence heard and findings made. The impetus had come primarily from the Department of Defense, and the measures had been pushed through by successive Administrations. But when Congress gave, it also knew how to take. The renegotiated procedures allowed committees operating in closed session to move quickly with wide powers to identify where the real paydirt was to be dug. The ceaseless battle about who really ran the country, the people's elected representatives or the people's anointed administrator, was never lost and never won. The dispositions just shifted around some.

A programed timer pinged on the wristwatch worn by Senator Bryant J. Pallas, Republican, and chairman both of Joint Space and of this subcommittee which it had spawned at his instigation. He was getting old, he was getting more ill, he was losing the weight battle, and he was getting frightened of what the hypertension was one day going to do to him. But he wasn't going to retire for love nor money, least of all when he had a committee which could keep on throwing sticks between the legs of the Administration. That it was a Republican Administration didn't matter a damn. It was a mixture of newfangled and Nixonesque, both of which he detested, and as good a target as any for those checks and balances which had to be played if Congress was going to stay Congress and not turn into a rubber-stamp national assembly like they had all over Europe these days.

Bryant J. Pallas took his pillbox out of his jacket pocket, swallowed a capsule and washed it down with water, then pocketed the pills. He set the glass precisely down on its little ring of water against the front balk of the committee bench. These days, when he lifted the heavy carafe to top up the glass, his hand trembled. It didn't used to. To hell with that. He cleared his throat. "This special subcommittee has been empaneled to pursue a matter which surfaced during a session of the Joint Space Activities Advisory Committee some days ago." He eyed the three witnesses across the other side of their long table – Disney, Maclaughlin and Ryle. Astronaut Ryle looked nervous, never been up in front of a committee before. "I remind all present that these proceedings are in closed session. There are no restrictions of any kind operating on what we choose to discuss here, no legal or national security restraints and no right of silence. Conversely, everything that is said before this committee is uttered in confidence and will be kept secret outside the doors of this room. The penalties for breaching that confidentiality are mandatory, and can be severe. I trust that is clearly understood."

It seemed to be. It was only Ryle he had to impress – the Maclaughlin woman already knew the form, and secrecy would be second nature to Lyal Disney.

Pallas looked around at his fellows on the bench. On his left sat Robert Mecklen, a veteran of the House Appropriations Committee and a space finance expert. Beyond him sat Sam Caldicott, a Democrat from the House. On Pallas's right sat Senator Jacqueline Monzione, a Democrat and the subcommittee's vice-chairwoman. On her right was Daniel Shane, a fellow Republican in a technocrat's light blue suit, and one of Joint Space's factual heavyweights. "Mr Shane, would you like to summarize how we come to be here?"

Daniel Shane nodded and bent his microphone towards himself so it could pick up his voice clearly. "In the course of taking routine evidence on the current level of NASA and Defense Department mission activities, Joint Space heard from Mr Cliff Daley, ELTS Mission Scheduling manager in Houston. I put some supplementary questions to Mr Daley concerning details of secret DOD payloading since March of this year, and we also discussed personnel scheduling for both lunar bases. It emerged that there have been secret briefings by Space Force officers given to NASA command and science astronauts rotated down on ELTS missions Nineteen and Twenty. Also, all lunar seismic data collected at and around the time of the meteorite impact on June 27th have been placed under a security order. The order is so strict that as yet we've been unable to obtain those data by subpoena. This subcommittee has been set up to pursue as a matter of urgency the possibility that Space Force may be conducting some operation of which neither Congress nor Joint Space have been informed. It is the business of Joint Space to be aware of everything the United States does in space, irrespective of sensitivity or national security."

What Daniel Shane chose not to say, though everyone present must know it, was where the tip-off to Joint Space had originated. At the State Department's Bureau of Space Affairs they had no more than rumors, some hunches and a whole lot of curiosity. But as soon as Undersecretary Joseph Hyland had acquired his first reliable facts plus the private assurance that certain NASA managers, including Daley and Maclaughlin, would cooperate, he'd passed the whole lot on to Pallas and Shane.

First to give evidence was Lyal Disney. He wore a dark blue suit and tie, as perfectly and wholesomely American as his name. It was reassuring that such upright and right-thinking people were to be found filling the ranks of the Central Intelligence Agency. Disney was being concisely and precisely helpful, just as the committee had been promised. The information Joseph Hyland was shunting through to them from the Bureau of Space Affairs was limited in scope but golden in quality.

"That's correct," Disney affirmed. "Certain people were put under full passive surveillance after their return from duty tours at Armstrong Base on the Moon. In order of task starts, those people are Beverly Diane Ryle, Charles Watkins, Tania June Sheldon, Madge Zavaroni. Also scheduled for such a task is Richard Sullivan O'Carr when he returns from Armstrong at the end of this month. Sheldon is currently transferred to one of our overseas desks, on account of she's presently vacationing abroad."

Senator Jacqueline Monzione nodded a little wearily. "And are any other people the subjects of associated surveillance?"

"Not that I'm aware."

"And what's the nature of the surveillance?"

"Telephone and mail interceptions, plus observation."

"Does observation mean tailing?"

"Not close tailing, just checking on movements and whereabouts and contacts. We put a radio direction tracker on each subject's private vehicle so that our people don't have to drive right behind them everywhere they go. These devices were however removed from the vehicles of the other subjects after Ryle discovered the device on her vehicle. That device has not since been replaced." And he talked about Ryle as if she wasn't sitting six seats away from him on the other side of Maclaughlin.

"Were listening devices installed in the houses of the subjects?"

"Only in the case of Ryle, who was the main subject of the operation. After Ryle discovered the radio direction tracker it was decided to remove the voice pickup devices from her home as a precaution against possible embarrassments. Sometimes people get a little hysterical and haul in the police or lawyers or the media."

"Isn't that hardly surprising when people are suddenly confronted with the idea that their private life is being eavesdropped?"

"Yes, it's probably an understandable reaction when people are unaware of our discretion. Our computers screen tapes for key words and pre-identified voices and so on, we do routine auditory checks on the taped material, and we transcribe and further process those time frames considered relevant or of possible further importance. But we're not interested in most of what we get – all the purely domestic stuff."

"Don't you consider this an invasion of privacy?"

Disney raised an eyebrow. He was going to be straight with the committee on the condition that the committee was going to stick to the facts of real life and not get into bleeding heart liberalism.

"Not at all, Senator. After a routine surveillance task is ended we wipe all the tapes and shred all the transcripts not of potential value in other contexts."

Monzione nodded again, resigning herself for the sake of expediency to those facts of real life. "What was the purpose of the operation?"

"We were given to understand by the Defense Department, who became our client in requesting the operation, that there were certain specific sensitive matters about which it would be preferred that the subjects didn't talk with anyone. Our task was to ascertain if they did so, identify with whom, and further the information to our client, specifically to intelligence officers of the US Space Force. I'm not aware what action they would then propose taking."

"And what were these specific sensitive matters?"

"The DOD was concerned that none of the subjects should at any time discuss the destructive event at the Soviet base or any other event relating directly to it. In the case of Ryle we were particularly requested to monitor any exchanges concerning seismic data collected at or about the time of the destructive event. Space Force were anxious to maintain the security blanket placed on this data, I believe."

"Are you able to tell the committee what it is about the seismic data that makes it particularly sensitive?"

"That we weren't told. From my own familiarity with the Ryle material, I'd say it centers on the identification of two seismic events in close temporal proximity, the one coincident with the destructive event at the Soviet base, and also one other. Further than that I can't say."

"The subjects obviously did talk about this."

"Certainly. Ryle, Watkins and Zavaroni each discussed their Vandenberg briefing with their respective spouses, Sheldon discussed it with her cohabitant partner. Ryle also discussed the seismic data to a limited extent with her spouse. We didn't consider it relevant to inform our client of this. Ryle also had further discussions by telephone with Watkins and also with Maclaughlin. Watkins subsequently discussed the Vandenberg briefing with Maclaughlin by telephone at the latter's instigation, as did Sheldon and Zavaroni."

"And at this stage did you inform the Defense Department?"

"No."

"Why not, Mr Disney?"

"Well – let's say we were reluctant to get involved in cleaning up a mess for them when they had neither consulted with us about the advisability of doing it in the first place, nor were they prepared to tell us what had happened. From the general circumstances, the unspecific nature of the surveillance task passed to us, and from the nature of the subjects – security vetted science astronauts with a clean record on political, criminal or other irregularities – it was quite obvious to us that the DOD, specifically Space Force, had gotten themselves into a mess and let's say they didn't want to get caught with their pants down. Anything they are or have been doing which they don't like others to find out about has to be a hot issue, and at the Agency we're very concerned to preserve our credibility by keeping our hands as far as possible clean. You might say we're very image conscious these days."

"Was the Defense Department in fact at any stage informed of the activities of the subjects?"

"Yes. When Ryle discovered the tracker on her vehicle while on the way to meet with Maclaughlin, we informed the DOD that their subjects were discussing the relevant matters and that our surveillance operation had been jeopardized. We've since been regularly recommending that we terminate all tasks but our client has not as yet concurred. We've reduced the surveillance in the meantime to only telephone and mail intercepts – I'm not as yet in possession of a confirmation that we have a phone intercept operating at Ryle's new address."

"You don't seem to be too enthusiastic over the issue at the CIA, Mr Disney."

"We're not too enthusiastic, Senator. Maybe someone higher up could tell you exactly why we're soft pedaling it, but as far as I'm aware it's just caution on our part and a reluctance to waste resources on a pointless task. There's no sense in plugging a leak after the water's already poured out."

"I suppose there really isn't. One final question, Mr Disney. Why did you refer to the meteorite impact at the Soviet base as a destructive event and not as a meteorite impact?"

"That's the term we're using on it at the Agency. We've been involved in the whole issue of determining its possible cause, and I believe we selected a cause-neutral term, is all."

Disney might or might not have been a busy man, but he stayed in the room to hear the evidence of the other two witnesses. The CIA was obviously concerned to learn as much as possible about whatever the mess might be that the Defense Department was suspected of having perpetrated.

Rosemary Maclaughlin had the next turn. She wore a cotton suit, a jacket and pleated skirt, in salmon and covered with leaf-and-flower patterns in greens and soft yellows, and under it a salmon silk blouse. She looked cool and authoritative and at ease. As if she wasn't at all upset to learn that conversations she'd had with other people over their own tapped phones had been recorded and analyzed by third parties, maybe. She took the committee through everything she had found out about the handing over of all copies of seismic data related to a time window of twelve hours centered around the impact at the Soviet base on June 27th, and the subsequent impounding of it by USSF departments under CSOC at Peterson Air Force Base, Colorado. She explained how infuriating it was for NASA's lunar science program that Aldrin was completely blocked under a DOD/USSF defense priority order, and how insulting it was that the Defense Department had declined to give any explanation whatsoever. Not even head office or the directors of the relevant programs had been told why.

"And when," Robert Mecklen wanted to know, "did you become aware that underhand – or we'd better say untoward – activities were going on with respect to Space Force interference with NASA programs and astronauts?"

"Specifically when Dr Ryle contacted me at the beginning of August, although by then I was good and alarmed about the program consequences of the continued blocking of Aldrin."

"What seemed untoward?"

"CSOC had told us that they wanted us to rotate Dr Ryle down three months early so that they could debrief her on observations made at the time of the impact at the Soviet base. That made sense since Dr Ryle is a seismology specialist, and since at the time there appeared to be good grounds to suspect that the Soviets were holding weapons of some kind on the Moon. That would have been directly relevant to the security of our own lunar facilities, so I and my superiors felt we should comply with the request. It was only when Dr Ryle talked to me that I then learned no such debriefing had in fact taken place, and that she had been given nothing more than a ten or fifteen minute pep-talk on keeping her mouth shut on the seismic record. It seemed to me they could have told her that over a normal secure voice or telemetry channel to Armstrong without having to pull her back from her duties there. I also learned from Dr Ryle that Space Force had given comparable talks to Watkins, Sheldon and Zavaroni without having the courtesy to inform us at Houston. I was further surprised to hear that the most senior officer involved in these so-called debriefings was Brigadier General Reeber, who I happen to know is with the US Space Force's Special Operations Division. What finally convinced me that something downright underhand was going on concerning the treatment of my own astronauts, and by extension Lunar Surface Operations and the whole of NASA, was Dr Ryle's discovery of a CIA radio tracker under her car. I didn't at the time know precisely who it belonged to, of course. We still have it safe at Houston, and I'd be glad to return it to the CIA if Mr Disney could maybe give me the correct address to mail it to."

Unruffled, Lyal Disney smiled.

"What action did you take?"

"Initially I was concerned to alert our own people discreetly that other astronauts, ground, science or administrative personnel might also be subjects of surveillance operations of which NASA's management had not been informed, so I therefore contacted the other Moon Program division directors and my immediate superiors. Also, out of purely personal interest I contacted my old friend of long standing, Undersecretary Hyland of the State Department, who of course is especially well informed about all matters concerning United States and foreign space activities. He wasn't able to help me at the time, being just as much in the dark. But of course the committee will know that from him directly, I presume."

Mecklen smiled. Senator Pallas, apparently preoccupied with preparing to swallow some kind of a pill, nodded to himself. Daniel Shane stepped into the continuing pause. "Miss Maclaughlin, you'll be aware that we've had no success in serving a powerful enough subpoena on the seismic data that seem to be at the center of this. Might you perhaps know what they contain that is of such concern to the United States Space Force that they have to keep the data locked away somewhere?"

"As far as I'm aware the entire time interval contains only the two impact events, the one at the Soviet base and the one approximately thirty minutes later. Otherwise the traces are empty."

"And it is now confirmed that the event at the Soviet base was not any kind of explosion but instead a meteorite impact?"

"I've seen all our own photographic evidence, everything released to us by CSOC and everything that the Soviet authorities have released to date. It was certainly a small lump of rock that hit that base. The crater and the ejecta spread show all the features you'd expect of a small meteorite. The only unusual feature is the slight elongation of the crater, which is sometimes associated with a low angle of incidence and a relatively low impact velocity, which allows the meteorite body to more or less plough through the ground for a fraction of a second before thermal and mechanical stresses cause it to disintegrate explosively."

"Have you seen any photographs or other data on the second impact?"

"I wasn't even aware there'd been any second impact until Dr Ryle informed me about it."

"Would you like to continue the questioning?" Pallas said to Shane.

Shane nodded. "You are Dr Beverly Diane Ryle, presently science astronaut with NASA's Moon Program?"

"I am." And don't sound so nervous, dammit.

"Of one hundred-and-four Hickory Fields, Covington, Louisiana?"

"No, that's my former address. I just moved as of last week. Right at the moment I have an apartment in Houston – two-twenty-eight Bayou Meadow, in Willow Bend."

"I see. Is the reason for the change of address the harassment – that is the close personal surveillance – to which you've been subjected?"

"Partly, yes." She looked across at Disney, who was listening intently but looking elsewhere. With his *familiarity with the Ryle material* he would know exactly and word perfect what the rest of the reasons, the messy marital reasons, were. The neat looking man made her at least as sick inside as James Heaton had started to do. Had Disney himself put the bugs inside her house and then taken them out again, secretly and some time in the night?

"Very well, Dr Ryle. First of all we'd like to hear what you can tell us about the briefing you received at Vandenberg from Brigadier General Reeber, and then everything you know about the seismic data which has been placed under a security order. You do understand fully that this is a closed hearing of a congressional advisory committee and that all testimony given here is strictly confidential and thus exempt from any restrictions imposed in the interest of national security?"

"Yes, I understand." Beverly glanced across at Maclaughlin, who had put on her reading glasses and was apparently studying a sheaf of notes on the table in front of her. It was all right for Maclaughlin – in the first place she was used to committees, and in the second place it wasn't her who'd started the whole thing rolling by upping and talking to someone about it. Beverly had half expected all kinds of trouble. What she had never anticipated was that she would land up in front of a secret committee hearing in Washington.

They pumped her out on Reeber's briefing, taking about

three to four times as long as the original had lasted. It was the vagueness of her answers, or rather the vagueness of Reeber's statements that she reported that so irritated them. Shane led the questioning but the other three kept joining in. What interested them most of all was the brigadier general's confusing hints about the nature and cause of the second seismic event she had observed, and especially his assertions about some sort of undercover intelligence work being carried out by Space Force and directed at the Soviet base at Mare Orientale. Didn't he say anything firm about what the Soviets were doing there or exactly what kind of weapon installation Space Force had uncovered? And as for some operation that had been underway for several years and was expected to run for a further one or two years and whose existence threatened the diplomatic integrity of the United States – what was that supposed to be about?

Bryant J. Pallas turned to his fellow committee members. "Any one of us ever heard of a covert operation being undertaken on the Moon, for God's sake?" He just got headshakes. "Mr Disney, do you people know anything about this?"

"Not that I'm aware. There's certainly no direct CIA involvement. We're strictly earthbound by decree of Space Force." He said it as though he resented the fact intensely.

"Miss Maclaughlin?"

Rosemary Maclaughlin shrugged her shoulders. "They have their established programs of observation directed at Earth and also at the Mare Orientale facility, but I never heard of their Special Operations Division being independently active at Armstrong or Aldrin. A high proportion of the Space Force astronauts who make lunar tours are from Special Operations, but they've always previously been booked on work associated with the normal DOD monitoring programs. Of course, I have no information on any new programs they might be carrying out currently at Aldrin, but the blocking of the base only goes back six months, not the year and a half since it was established."

Pallas frowned. "Dr Ryle, are you sure Reeber said he had a *team* engaged in some covert activity up there?"

"Yes. He said it was the activities of his team which were

in danger of being exposed if the seismic data were leaked."

"Well." Pallas shook his head. "Well. I guess we're just going to have to get right on with exposing that as soon as we can. Let's get on. Mr Shane, let's move on to the seismic stuff so we can wind up for today."

The decor had changed repeatedly over the years but the ambience was still excellent. Something else that was new was the number of fellow diners Joseph Hyland was obliged to exchange a word or two with both in the bar and in the restaurant proper on the way to their table. Fortunately the table itself was tucked away privately in a deeply recessed alcove, otherwise they would probably have had no peace at all during the meal. Dining out in Washington with one of the better known and most influential undersecretaries at the State Department was an even more complicated business than it had been with the man in his previous incarnation as a representative and active aerospace lobbyist. And of course, right back when she had first met him here all those years ago, they had been just another two people in a crowd.

They had skipped starters and had just finished the salads. Rosemary had ordered a gourmet salad *à la nouvelle cuisine*, more because of the smaller quantity than the delicate flavors, and Joseph had dealt with a full-sized king prawn salad with just about everything. The waiter cleared the plates away and set the table ready for the next course. They'd decided against wine and stuck to cocktails. Rosemary had a tumbler with the remaining third of a Blue Lagoon – she was *thirsty*, because since they met in the bar he'd been making her do nothing else but report in detail on the day's proceedings at Joint Space, that route being much quicker than waiting for Shane to pass illicit copies of the testimony transcripts over to him. Joseph had a Black Russian in a conical champagne glass. He was fifty-two and graying patriarchally, and gaining weight. He took hold of the stem of the glass with his brown fingers that ended in perfectly manicured nails, and he smiled. "Black Russian is what someone at the Pentagon decided to christen me the other day."

"Really? I guess they don't like you across the river."

"Let's say my Bureau of Space Affairs is practically at war with the United States Space Force over this business. Hostilities started earlier this year when we took diametrically opposed views on the issue of any completed or completing combat laser at the Soviet base at Mare Orientale. Now we've got an interdepartmental shooting war starting up, fortunately just restricted to my bureau and Space Force. The other services at the Pentagon are even more jealous of the newcomer than ever, it getting all its spending proposals through no matter how big, and they getting theirs either capped or cut the whole time to pay for Space Force – and they're also all of them as displeased as you could imagine with the way the defense secretary handles it. He's nothing more than a totally pro-Space Force man and the president's functional extension on space defense policy." Joseph Hyland sighed. "The only extension of the war, I believe, is going to be between the secretary of state and the defense secretary. Unless the White House is insane enough to get involved on the side of the Defense Department when this comes out. But I guess the president is going to play it surprised and sober, and pull the diplomatic responsibility line to dampen things down."

"When *what* comes out?" It was a warm late summer evening, it had been a positively successful day in front of the committee, and the long cool drink was so relaxing. But the informational vacuum was getting on Rosemary's nerves. "I still don't see exactly what it's all pointing at."

"Neither do I. Not yet. But the secretary of state is getting ready to get livid, and when she does she's going to lynch somebody, and if the White House is smart they'll make good and sure it's the defense secretary. Of course, it'll be a private and discreet lynching. No one is going to breathe a word of this until long after the election, I'd expect. But when the Administration is returned, it's going to be with a new secretary of defense."

"Joseph – breathe a word of *what*?"

"I don't know yet, but I have a nasty feeling all my hunches are going to turn out correct. When I know more facts or just pointers to facts, I'll tell you right away. You tipped me off on the way to get a handle on this business. We couldn't get anyone to take our hunches seriously until you let us know Space Force had got the CIA involved, and that Reeber had gone and told one of your astronauts enough to get the Joint Space committee up off its collective ass and hunting. The situation was all poised to roll, but it needed something to give that first push. Well that was it, okay, along with seismic data being put under wraps and mysterious payloads to Aldrin and secrets about second impacts. I still don't see how it adds together, Rosemary, but it adds to something."

"That seems to be sure." She sipped her cocktail, running down her reserves. "The CIA were incredibly forthcoming. Thought I was dreaming when I realized the implications of what Disney said – that they didn't bother to tell Space Force the cat was coming out of the bag until it had already gone so far that Ryle being under surveillance was also out in the open. And then he said he figured Space Force had been up to something and had made a mess of it. The CIA were happy for this to leak, weren't they?"

"Only too happy. Our own Bureau of Intelligence was involved from the start on two issues. Whether or not Moscow used lasers in South Africa – which looks to be the case in spite of this story that broke last week."

"The Maubane interview and the follow-up stories."

"Exactly. And also whether or not Moscow has a laser installation on the Moon which could have exploded and damaged their base. All that junk about nuclear bombs up there is just public smoke screen, of course. So anyway, we had close contacts with the NSA because of their signal intercepts and with the CIA because of their competence on the ground, so we know how they're feeling. Both issues had been mixed up by the Defense Department and the White House in line with this idiotic belief that Moscow used a Moon-based laser on South Africa. That's just projecting their own stage-three Earth interdiction strategy proposal onto the other side, as far as I can see. And then it seems that Space Force pulled the CIA into it again on the other side of the already mixed-up issue by asking them to snoop on your people. Well neither the CIA nor the NSA like that one bit – having to help clear up a mess after someone else produced it by doing something without consulting them in the first place. Both of them got their noses out of joint and a hate up against Space Force years ago. The NSA was restricted to Earth-based antennas and satellites up to and including geosynchronous Clarke orbits while Space Force keeps the monitoring dishes up at Armstrong entirely to itself, and the CIA failed to get its remit extended to include space and lunar activities, again to the benefit of Space Force. Add to that the fact that the Army, the Navy, the Marine Corps and above all the Air Force are sick as hell at what they see as virtually a usurper in their camp at the Pentagon, and you have a regular viper's nest of interservice and inter-agency rivalries."

"Sounds like just about everyone but the White House is going to be on the side of the State Department."

"Oh they are. They're just dying for a chance to jump on Space Force and its patrons, and this looks like it's going to be it. Whatever they've gone and done up there, it's either very stupid or even worse, and everyone wants to know. Provided the investigation and the results are held strictly under wraps and kept right away from the media, they're going to be falling all over each other to help pull this thing out into the open. It's going to go fast when it goes, that I promise you."

"Well – it's about time Space Force got a brake pulled on them. You know, with the way they can meddle, rearrange and substitute when and how they like in our programs, plus the fact that they've been doing so more and more often and more and more heavy-handedly over the last five years, at NASA we've started referring to the DOD liaison office as the DOD's command bunker. This latest business with the science wipe-out at Aldrin has been the last straw for us at Lunar Surface Operations. For me, anyway. Congress should just never have weighted the joint NASA/DOD sharings the way they did in the wake of the strategic defense initiative. It most certainly isn't the way you and me wanted things to go when we started promoting the highest ground idea."

Joseph Hyland just shook his head.

The main course arrived, lamb casserole Provençale for Rosemary and lobster thermidor for Joseph. Joseph ordered more cocktails.

"Joseph." Rosemary eyed the pile on his plate. "You really are putting on weight these days." Then she looked at her own plate. "So will I be if I eat many more meals this size. A girl gets to be forty-five and she finds her waistline is waging a regular war with her. How's your family? Gloria over the operation yet?"

"Sure, sure. She's picking up again." He was hovering with the fork and wondering where to start the attack. "She keeps trying to eat things she shouldn't and gets sick as a dog, but she's getting a diet worked out that keeps her feeling well. And it's healthy – you wouldn't believe. Low fat, high fiber, moderate protein intake. When I get back to Seattle for a few days or she's over here she gets me down to a reasonable weight in no time flat."

"And Denise and John?"

"Denise is getting on just fine at MIT. John's career is perfect and his private life is a disaster."

"Come again?" She stabbed the errant slivers of beans again and then set to at the meat that parted like butter under the knife.

"He just got promoted to a research leader – at *his* age. And he just got divorced – also at *his* age."

"Oh there's plenty of divorce about. Beverly Ryle, my star witness – she seems to have gotten landed in this mess of being more or less persecuted in the name of national security at the same time as her marriage is starting to dissolve before her eyes. Seems like one of those classic problems. She has a prestige career and a fat salary, he has a modest career and a lower salary – and a lower qualification – and a male compensatory requirement, in other words another woman. Tarzan fears himself confronted with second-ratedness and all that."

"That's a problem you've always hit up against, isn't it? How's life now you have that chic house on the coast?"

"Single." And now don't go letting that come pouring out.

Switch to the positive, and fast. "My career, though, is fine – so long as no one develops a hate against me as a result of all this, which I'll give them no reason for because no way am I going to be so crazy as to breathe a word to any outsider. I'm sitting pretty at Lunar Surface Operations, and after the next three years of expansion we're going to take over not just as the lead but the controlling element of the Moon Program."

"That's just been decided at last?"

"That's just been decided. With me in the saddle, I might add."

"Congratulations." He said it quietly, and meant it.

"That means we'll be NASA's biggest program division. Unless there would be some kind of budget *catastrophe* in Congress, when I retire I'll be saying goodbye to my very own self-supporting and fuel-exporting lunar base. That'll be a dream come true."

He nodded. "It will. It really will."

"*If* we all of us survive the troubles of the moment, that is. So where does it go from here? What's the next move?"

"That's with Joint Space Sub. They have some subpoenas to issue."

"And who do they subpoena, for God's sake? About *what*?"

Joseph Hyland shrugged. "The answer to that involves a short digression." He put down his knife and fork and leaned forward, elbows on the table. It was a conspiratorial pose, and almost funny from a man who masterminded a real live information network. "Remember Ruth Buchannan of the House Appropriations Committee?"

"I'll say. First time I tangled with her was over our stage three program allocations – right before the Russians went and landed on the Moon. Violently opposed to space spending."

"Right. Well, she's had to keep a low profile these last five years, but now she has the chance to let rip at something big. She's still on House Appropriations, and she's chairing their subcommittee on Earth interdiction strategy funding."

"*She's* running EIS Sub? That must have taken some maneuvering. You have anything to do with that?"

"I helped out with her lobbying some, which means she owes me a favor. Which I've called in. And so somewhere in this little city tonight, Buchannan is dining with Daniel Shane."

"Aha." The information network was woven closely. "And is telling him – and Joint Space – what?"

"Well now, EIS Sub is looking at Space Force's funding proposals for the Earth interdiction strategy. They have the three generally known systems to choose between – EIS-1, EIS-2 and EIS-3."

"EIS-1 is a little rocket vehicle. It's already developed, but put on ice, right? Space Force would deploy it at Aldrin so launches would be out of sight from Earth. It would carry a nuclear warhead, and would be for use against Soviet space defenses in Earth orbit. It would take days for the warheads to arrive from the Moon, but the launches would be secret so there'd be no warning. It's supposed to be an interdiction weapon. You use it first and take out the other side's space defenses so they can't shelter behind them."

He nodded. "The EIS-2 system is a king-sized railgun built on the lunar surface. It would also be deployed at Aldrin so the thing couldn't be detected when it fired – there's no flash or flame with a railgun, but there's an awful loud pulse of electromagnetic radiation. The EIS-2 would fire off a swarm of kinetic munitions, too small to see with telescopes or radar, and all of them launched on trajectories so they'd each collide with one of the elements in the Soviet space defense system orbiting the Earth. A complete wipe-out with no warning, but again a two or three day delay between launch and strike. The EIS-3 is an absolutely gigantic laser installation to be sited at Armstrong. Doesn't matter that it's on Near Side, so it's visible from Earth and you could see it fire, because a laser kills instantaneously. That instant response time is the big plus. It also happens to be hideously destabilizing, and about the ultimate perversion of the highest ground idea. The big minus for EIS-3 is the cost – ten times even the EIS-2 railgun, which itself is ten times more expensive than EIS-1."

"And Buchannan is opposed to funding an EIS system."

"Most everyone outside of Space Force is. But what's going to decide it is whether the Russians have one of their own, or are maybe engaged in building one."

"Ah – I see." Rosemary nodded for her own benefit. "So EIS Sub has been taking a look at all the evidence for the claims and counter claims about the Russians setting fire to South Africa with a laser up at Mare Orientale."

"Exactly. EIS Sub has been taking an extremely close look."

"And which way has the evidence been pointing?"

"Just the same as we've always maintained. The city fires and most of the open country burns were started by ground action. Defense Intelligence, the CIA – everyone who went to look confirms that. There's just around ten per cent of the open country burns that aren't accounted for by ground mechanisms. And for those, the NSA has signal intercepts which show exactly which of the Soviet defense lasers were bouncing shots off exactly which of their orbiting relay mirrors at exactly the right time. As far as the South African burns are concerned, the case is closed."

"And just how does this digression into EIS help decide what Joint Space does next?"

"EIS Sub had a witness up the other day, an Air Force colonel with Defense Intelligence. And the Air Force just do not like Space Force, do they? The colonel's evidence was about burn patterns in open country. She was asked if she knew of any evidence that a Soviet Moon-based laser might exist and might have, been involved. She said she wasn't aware of any evidence, but relevant material might have been in the package the defense secretary took with him when he went to talk with the president about the Skyrock Option."

"And what's that?"

"They asked. The colonel said she didn't know, but she believed the code name for the operation was Blue Bolt. After that she clammed up, like she'd let out something she shouldn't. Of course, it was the Air Force deliberately doing it to Space Force."

Rosemary nodded slowly. "And what is Blue Bolt, exactly?"

"As soon as Joint Space tells me, Rosemary, I'll tell you."

"Brigadier General Reeber," Pallas intoned, putting the authority of a political lifetime into his voice. The chairman of Joint Space Sub feared he probably looked as old and sick as he felt, but he wasn't going to let this space hero from the Pentagon get the idea he could take the subcommittee lightly. No sir, he wasn't. "We understand you are on the staff of Space Force's Special Operations Division, and that you are head of Lunar Section. You personally also have extensive space experience. Is that correct?"

"That is correct, Senator." Reeber had his hat on the table in front of him. His hair was a crew-cut of steel stubble, he sat in an easy but straight-backed posture, correct, sharp, and with knife creases in his perfect uniform. The documents were looked after by his aide, Lieutenant Alderson, on his right, and on his left sat Major Greg Bleazard, the alternative witness summoned because Colonel Browning was apparently not available at short notice.

"And you were principal overseer of operation Blue Bolt?"

"My section was responsible for mounting Blue Bolt. The field commander was Colonel Browning, who was supported by Major Bleazard here."

"Thank you. Well, Mr Shane, let's get on with taking testimony." Bryant J. Pallas reached for his first fix of water.

Daniel Shane leaned forward, his elbows on the committee bench. "As we understand it, Blue Bolt is a case of the actual realization of the Skyrock Option. What is the genesis of Skyrock?"

"The term Skyrock dates back to a study completed in January of last year. It was a proposed adaptation of the EIS-1 system."

"To check, General. EIS-1 is an Earth interdiction strategy

system. It involves a small rocket-propelled launch vehicle to be deployed on the Moon for the purpose of delivering nuclear warheads against targets on the Moon, in lunar orbit, or in near-Earth space. The current status of EIS-1 is that twenty launch vehicles have been stockpiled at Vandenberg, pending a decision at some future date to go ahead with deployment at expanded bases on the Moon. Correct?"

Reeber nodded. "That's correct. The deployment is proposed for PLSF-2 Aldrin. Initially it would involve six vehicles."

"And there has as yet been no EIS-1 deployment. Except, of course, for Blue Bolt."

"As yet, no."

Shane nodded and folded his arms on the bench. This was going to go smoothly step by step, just the way Hyland had said it would. "What is the Skyrock Option, exactly?"

"To be direct," Reeber said, without a flicker in his expression, "It's a way of circumventing the moratorium on stationing weapon systems on the Moon. From a military standpoint you have to be able to defend the facilities up there, or there's no sense in spending a bare cent on them. The idea behind Skyrock was to achieve some degree of workable defense at Aldrin, but without recourse to deployment on the Moon of nuclear or conventional warheads."

"And how would that be achieved?"

"By using kinetic rounds. The launch vehicle would be used to accelerate a purely kinetic munition for use in collision mode against targets orbiting above the Moon. Alternatively, the vehicle would deliver its payload mass as a purely kinetic warhead against ground targets there. If you like, in concept Skyrock is a rocket-propelled cannonball."

"Did the study of twenty months ago also consider Skyrock as a mechanism for covert applications – so-called invisible use? I refer to appendix two of the study."

If hinting at the degree of detail the subcommittee had on supposedly secret Space Force documents was supposed to unsettle Reeber, it failed. The general had a steel-alloy composure. "That was the conclusion of appendix two. If one were to deploy the kinetic munition, and include into the operational mode a separation of the munition from the carrier vehicle – plus a subsequent burn, so that the vehicle did *not* proceed with the munition to its target, but flew off someplace else – then the munition alone would impact on the target. Of course, there would be the disadvantage that less total mass arrived at the target, transferring less kinetic energy and therefore having less destructive potential."

"And the advantage?" Shane asked.

"That you could engage and destroy a target, and have it look like a pure accident, just a collision with a lump of passing debris. No explosion, no residues, no technology visible in the form of a carrier vehicle. In fact if the kinetic munition were to be made of a naturally occurring substance, it would look like a natural accident if anyone would retrieve the debris and examine it for traces of a suspicious origin. You would have a collision or impact event, and any investigation would only reveal that the object responsible was of mineralogical composition."

"In other words, a lump of rock."

"That's correct."

"And this so-called invisible weapon, as detailed, would have its application for covert use in peacetime."

"Certainly." Reeber almost allowed himself a shrug. "Otherwise its non-detectable status would be of little purpose."

"And returning for a moment to the unmodified EIS-1 system." Shane turned over his sheet of notes. "The basic advantage of the EIS-1 is that it could be used for a pre-emptive strike against any Soviet EIS system on the Moon, such as a railgun or laser, before this could be used to attack our own space defense systems in Earth orbits?"

"Precisely. If we don't have our own railgun or laser on the Moon capable of taking out the Soviet space defense screen, but they do have an EIS up there, we have to be able to take it clean out with a pre-emptive strike. Otherwise they could strip our space shield clean away while retaining their own."

"And for such an eventuality, the Skyrock invisible weapon would be ideal as a system to execute such a pre-emptive strike, hopefully without precipitating an immediate fullscale war."

"That was the idea, yes. Of course, in an acute political crisis you couldn't expect the Soviets to check before they'd start shooting. But in a lower level crisis, you could use the invisible weapon mode in a climate where they could be expected to check closely before initiating a war. Their close check would then reveal only the characteristics of a natural accident – a debris collision or a meteorite strike."

"And this response was in fact decided upon in the context of the assumed intervention by Moscow in the South African war – that is to say, their subsequently verified use of missile defense lasers against ground targets."

Reeber nodded. "Yes."

Shane sat back in his chair while Reeber waited unperturbed, a military man secure in the armor of his uniform, his rank and his duty. Alderson and Bleazard, his aide and his field officer, sat safe on his flanks within the shield of his immunity. They, like their general, were guilty only of carrying out orders.

Pallas glanced at Shane to check he was finished, then nodded at Monzione. Senator Jacqueline Monzione took her pen in her hand and held it vertical like a little joystick on the bench. "Why was that so, General? Why was the response decided on?"

"The motivation was two-fold, I believe. I should point out that's a question for my superiors, Senator. Not Major General Waterson at Special Operations – I mean the chief of staff of Space Force and right on up to the president." And that was a careful uploading of any blame that was coming, clarifying from the start that the orders had originated right at the top.

"And those reasons would be?"

"First of all the requirement to teach Moscow a lesson by giving them a major setback, just as they'd given us a major defeat by turning the South African war right around and winning it for their surrogates. I believe it's called maintaining the geopolitical balance. The second and dominant consideration is purely strategic. It was considered vital we prevent the Soviet EIS system at Mare Orientale completing before we are in a position to commission our own EIS system with comparable capabilities. In other words, we should delay the construction work at the Soviet base. Otherwise, we are about to enter a phase where the Soviets have the one-sided capability to eradicate our space defenses and subject us to total nuclear blackmail. Against that kind of threat you really have to do something. That's basic military logic."

Monzione tested her joystick, forward and back. "I take it you're convinced that the Soviet Union is indeed constructing a railgun or laser at their Mare Orientale site?"

"Is my personal opinion of any relevance?"

"General, we'd be very interested to hear your personal view. As head of the Lunar Section of the Special Operations Division, we would assume you have a particularly shrewd opinion."

"Very well – but this is strictly personal. I don't believe the Soviets are building any free electron laser up there. What they *are* building is a railgun, an equivalent of our EIS-2 proposal. They have ten kilometres of track already erected, and posts ready for a further ten kilometres. It employs the natural upward inclination of the inner slope of the Cordillera Mountains, and rises to their base, which will be the power, control and aiming station. Once they have the full length of track laid they should be in business. With a twenty-kilometre track, they'd need to apply something of the order of thirteen gee to accelerate a munition to a velocity sufficient for it to escape the pull of the Moon and cross over onto a course to engage a target in near-Earth space. They could power that with around five or ten megawatts, depending on the munition mass. According to their own press releases, they were intending to install the first one-megawatt power reactor in a few months. I'd say that if left to do what they like up there – in blatant defiance of the lunar weapons moratorium – they would have had an operational EIS railgun in around one year."

"You rule out the possibility that the Soviets are actually building a monorail, just as they claim?"

"They didn't go all the way to the Moon at the kind of cost you have to pay for getting there, just for the fun and the science. That you can be sure of. No more than we did.

It's the highest ground, it's a matter of purely strategic necessity."

"Ah – some of us out here in the real world are still laboring under the illusion that we went to the Moon for the fun and the science, as you put it, and the long-term materials return advantage. Purely peaceful purposes."

"The strategic capability to cancel out your enemy's attacking potential is purely peaceful, Senator Monzione, but it's also somewhat realistic."

Jacqueline Monzione disengaged her pen joystick, turned it end over end, and planted it vertical again on the bench. "Can you tell us how the Skyrock Option was turned into Blue Bolt?"

"I wasn't involved directly until the go-ahead had been given and operational planning was handed over to my section. As far as I'm personally aware, the decision process dates back to a memorandum our division's own South African Enmod Response Group sent to the chief of staff on March 13. A consideration of the Skyrock Option was one of the recommendations listed. My section was pulled in shortly thereafter on the orders of the chief of staff, and we were detailed to get the system modified and deployable."

"And when was it deployed?"

"We were able to place two modified EIS-1 launch vehicles on the ELTS-16 mission, one for eventual operational use and the other as a backup. Major Bleazard, with Colonel Browning as field commander, went with the launch vehicles on Sixteen to Aldrin. The launch and guidance equipment went up on the ELTS-17 mission."

"Wasn't that extremely rapid?"

"Well, we only had to put it together and send up two of our guys who knew how to use it. At that stage we'd been waiting for fourteen months for a go-ahead with EIS-1, so we were good and ready. The modifications for a covert Skyrock mode are very simple and were already detailed. It only requires a payload separation facility on the vehicle, and a reprograming of the propulsion burn to give a second kick after separation."

"And when was operational deployment completed?"

"May 21."

Monzione was circling her joystick pen, winding it up. "When was the operation officially designated Blue Bolt?"

"I believe before March 31. The designation would be chosen because it was planned as a surprise coming out of an empty sky so the Russians wouldn't know what hit them."

"That consideration, I would imagine, must have been paramount." The joystick stopped, wound up and quivering. "You are aware, General, that Blue Bolt is nothing other than an act of war committed against the Soviet Union?"

"For details such as the legal status you'll have to ask the appropriate authorities. My concern was – and is – exclusively with the execution of the operation, and not with any political implications it may or may not carry."

"It carries them. My God, but it carries them!" Monzione snapped her pen flat on the bench.

Pallas cleared his throat, punctuating the pause. He drank a little water, with the glass shaking slightly in his hand. He set it down again very carefully behind the front balk. "When," he said, "was the final go-ahead for Blue Bolt given?"

"June 25."

"It must by then have become clear that at least no laser on the Moon had been used to start the catastrophic fires in South Africa. Was that taken into consideration?"

"I wouldn't know," Reeber said flatly. "I wouldn't in fact know whether at that stage the relevant intelligence data had already been collated and analyzed."

"Who gave the order to execute Blue Bolt?"

"That went over the normal chain of command. Colonel Browning launched it, I ordered him to, and I received the order from Major General Waterson at Special Operations Command."

"How high," Pallas asked almost absentmindedly, "did the order originate?"

"The committee's guess is as good as mine. The operation had by then been discussed at a joint chiefs of staff meeting, had been considered by the office of the secretary of defense at some length, and an informational package had been presented some time earlier at the White House."

The senator's wristwatch timer peeped. Pallas fished in the

pocket of his jacket. "The president was involved personally?" He brought out the pill box, fumbled a capsule out of it, and then stuffed the box back in his pocket.

"I would imagine the president was involved. You can't go throwing rocks at the Russians without obtaining permission first. And since the whole sense of Blue Bolt depended on its invisibility, and therefore total secrecy, I don't see how anyone could have gone to Congress for a vote on it."

Pallas lifted the glass again, put the capsule in his mouth, and washed it down. Again, he set the glass down very carefully exactly where it had been, forcing precision into his fingers. "Can you tell us what measures were taken to hide the true nature of Blue Bolt from the Soviet authorities?" His eyes jumped from the taming of the glass and settled sidelong on Reeber. "You realize the possible consequences if they ever figured out what actually happened on June 27th?"

"I realize fully, Senator. The principal measure is inherent in the concept. The launcher vehicle injects itself and the attached payload into a trajectory to take it direct to the target. It then has to separate from the payload, reorientate, fire a further burn and boost itself out of the target trajectory into an escape path. The escape path should take it clear of the Moon and ultimately of the Earth-Moon system so that it disappears irretrievably into deep space. All burns have to take place over Far Side so that they cannot be observed from Earth, and they also have to be timed so they don't coincide with the overflight of a Soviet observation satellite in orbit around the Moon. Beyond that, you just have to be as shocked and horrified when you hit the target as you would be if it was a real accident."

"Do we gather that the White House claim that a Soviet weapon installation had exploded at Mare Orientale on June 27th was not ignorance but a deliberate bluff?"

"That's correct, as far as I'm informed. The Soviets would believe from the start they had been hit by a natural meteorite, and the trick was to make them back their story with the strongest possible evidence, at which point you back down and accede. That way Moscow convinces the entire world it was an accident."

"And the payload, General." Pallas shifted uneasily in his seat, as if preoccupied with getting comfortable. "The kinetic weapon you threw at their Mare Orientale base. What was it exactly? A rock?"

Reeber nodded. "Exactly. A rock. We would have liked to use a meteorite core, but all the real meteorite cores are in the geology departments of museums and universities, and you'll appreciate we couldn't get hold of one of those without stirring up questions. What we used was a lump of rock collected for the purpose right on the Moon at Tsiolkovsky and machined down to a form to fit the EIS-1 vehicle's payload cradle and with a mass of exactly one hundred fifty kilogrammes."

"If my science is up to it, wouldn't that be suspect? Small traces of the rock would certainly be recoverable from the hole it made where it hit. They would demonstrate that a rock of lunar and not meteoritic origin had done the damage."

"Our science advisers recommended we should ensure that no leftover traces would be identifiable as part of the impacting rock, and not just pieces of rocks that had already been lying there at the site in the first place. They suggested we select a piece of anorthositic gabbro. That's a rock that occurs in the lunar highlands and is of a lower density than the basalts. I can give you the exact composition if you wish." And on cue his aide produced a piece of paper covered with figures.

"No need, General." Pallas gave up fidgeting and looked left and right at his committee associates. "I suggest we take a short break so we can catch our breath after the extraordinary nature of what we've been hearing."

"Enormity," Monzione muttered. "That's what it is."

"Any objections? No. Very well – we'll adjourn for fifteen minutes, then resume with Major Bleazard. We'd prefer it if you remain for the rest of this hearing, General."

Reeber nodded, and actually smiled.

Alderson, the aide, studied papers as he listened. Reeber sat with his back straight, his legs crossed, one arm stretched along the backs of the empty seats beside him – clean uniform, clean jaw and clean conscience. In contrast, Major Greg Bleazard wasn't comfortable giving testimony in front of the committee, closed hearing or no closed hearing, and he was visibly pale under his negro complexion. But he had his general to look after him, so he soldiered on valiantly.

"No, sir. On the Moon that's no problem for four men to erect – Colonel Browning and myself and the other two at Aldrin. The EIS-1 missile is designed to be able to escape from lunar gravity and be able to engage targets in near-Earth space, but it only has to overcome one sixth of Earth surface gravity. The missile itself has a maximum diameter of seventy-two centimetres and a total assembled length of four hundred twenty centimetres. Empty of fuel it weighs only two hundred twelve kilogrammes – that's the Earth surface weight. On the surface of the Moon it weighs only around thirty-five kilogrammes. Two men can handle the whole thing without any trouble. Same goes for the launcher assembly. That's just an open guide track with four rails plus a support frame. Colonel Browning and I had the whole assembly mounted and the missile ready to fuel up and program with the predetermined course instructions by May 21st. Then it was just a case of keeping the systems in trim until the launch order came through."

Robert Mecklen made a note, and then nodded. "And the order came through on June 25th?"

"Yes, sir."

"Why was the launch delayed until early on June 27th?"

"We were ordered to launch on June 27th at the precise time we did in fact launch. It's a matter of orbital configurations, sir. It was necessary to be able to launch the missile such that neither the launch itself, nor the trajectory of either the warhead or the vehicle would be at any point directly observable by any Soviet orbiter using visual or radar sensing for surface mapping or intelligence or other purposes. I understand it was also required that we hit the Soviet base during their midday and not during their night routine. I should add they're linked to Moscow time, so they're nine hours ahead."

"And why was that necessary, Major?"

Bleazard turned to Reeber. "Sir?"

"Expediency," Reeber said to the committee. "We felt that in the event of an exact bull's-eye on the crew accommodation of the base, which would disrupt all the base units, we'd have a good chance at around midday in their routine that one or more of their personnel would be outside in suits and at some distance from the damage center. Conversely, if we hit them in the middle of the night and destroyed the crew accommodation, that way we'd kill them all. The decision had come down to attempt maximum damage to the base but to avoid wiping out the entire personnel if at all feasible. If the base had in fact gone and they'd been stuck with a couple of people outside in suits, we'd have let NASA mount an ADV rescue operation from Armstrong to haul in the survivors before they ran out of air."

"Very commendably cynical, General," Monzione said.

Reeber shrugged.

Mecklen addressed Bleazard again. "What was the launch time, Major?"

"Exactly o-two-thirty-one and twenty seconds, sir, by Aldrin and Houston time."

"And the impact of the warhead – the rock – was at o-three-forty and twenty seconds, striking the ground three hundred and twenty-five feet from the accommodation structures of the Soviet base. Is that correct?"

"Yes, sir."

Mecklen nodded. "Thank you. That was all my questions."

Pallas looked at Monzione. "You want to take up here?"

Jacqueline Monzione nodded. "I guess we could conclude that Blue Bolt just about missed, since it only killed two Soviet citizens, thank God."

Reeber shook his steel cropped head. "We had a grade two success according to the operational goal assessments. We created a major impairment of their ability to continue weapon construction up there. We holed two of their base modules and did minor damage to several more, we wrote off one lander and one of their surface vehicles, we destroyed a whole bunch of communications antennas, damaged both their big radio surveillance dishes, destroyed the big optical telescope they were building, and above all we took a two hundred fifty kilowatt nuclear power unit clean out. Before they've repaired or replaced all that, considering the payload penalty they'll incur transporting everything they need out from Earth, they'll have lost nine to fifteen months on their construction program."

"General, as I understand the details I've seen of the damage achieved, apart from the two deaths it was largely their astronomy instrumentation which was destroyed."

"Senator, an astronomy capability is also at one and the same time a military surveillance capability. That's the way we also work it on the Moon."

Monzione turned her attention to Bleazard. "Major Bleazard, if the first seismic event of which we've heard in previous testimony was the rock hitting the ground at the Soviet base, what was the second seismic event approximately thirty minutes after that? I mean the one Brigadier General Reeber has been at pains on several occasions to keep secret."

"The operation – wasn't quite a pure success. Not in all respects." Bleazard glanced at Reeber, and received a nod.

"Would you care to elaborate on that, Major?"

"The launch burn proceeded according to program and put the missile into a low inclination orbit. At T plus three hundred seconds a second burn was programed to place the missile into a high inclination elliptical trajectory with the perigee located within the radius of the Moon. That means that the missile, in following the orbital path, would in fact crash into the ground at the point where the path intersected the surface of the Moon."

"I can assure you, Major, that everyone on this committee is well experienced with elementary celestial mechanics. You mean the missile put itself and its payload into a trajectory which would crash it into the ground at its target, the Soviet base."

"Yes, ma'am. The initial trajectory change was so that in the event of the Soviets obtaining some sort of track on the approaching rock by chance, they at least wouldn't discover a flight path that would project back to a launch point at or anywhere near Aldrin."

"Commendable thinking. Presumably they'd conclude that since they hadn't fired it themselves, and it apparently didn't start exactly at Aldrin, it must have been sent up by some Martian vandals on a day trip to the Far Side of the Moon?"

"Senator," Reeber said politely but flatly, "my section was responsible for the execution, not the conception, of Blue Bolt."

"Point well taken," Monzione said, letting enough cynical satisfaction show at the exercise in buck passing. "We're just fact finding here. So, Major?"

Bleazard cleared his throat. "The T plus three hundred burn obviously went as programed because of the strike accuracy of the warhead at its target. The program was for the missile to separate from the warhead payload at T plus three-forty, and then reorientate and fire a third burn at T plus three-sixty to put it into the planned escape trajectory. It would have crossed out over Near Side near the lunar north pole and then proceeded on to a trajectory ultimately putting it into independent solar orbit at an inclination of three-point-seven degrees to the plane of the ecliptic. It would not have come within radar or visual detection range of the Earth or Moon again for something in the order of four hundred years."

"But that didn't quite happen?"

"No, ma'am. Separation obviously proceeded according to program, as did the third burn initiation."

"But, Major?"

"But – the burn must have had the wrong orientation or the wrong duration, or both, we assume."

"You assume. Weren't you monitoring the progress of the missile?"

"No, ma'am. It was way over our horizon at Aldrin, but not yet around the limb of the Moon and visible from any Earth or any Earth-orbital station. The missile was dependent entirely on its own on-board guidance."

"And this went wrong?"

"It seems so." Bleazard cleared his throat again. "Seems so."

"And the consequences?" She had the man squirming.

"The missile launch vehicle failed to inject as planned into an escape trajectory."

"And instead?"

Bleazard looked pleadingly at his general.

"That's all right, Major." Reeber squared up to give the answers. "Instead it apparently entered a very high inclination trajectory passing over the north polar region in an approximately to-Earth direction. We don't have exact data because we didn't know where to look for it when it failed to appear at the pickup point of the visual track we intended to run from Pilgrim. In contrast we had a clear track of the warhead rock obtained using the hundred centimetre telescope at Armstrong as it traversed part of Armstrong's sky. The trajectory of the missile vehicle after the final burn took it approximately north to south across Near Side, over the south polar region, and on in an approximately south to north direction over Far Side."

"And the second seismic event at something like one thousand miles south of Aldrin on Far Side?"

"That was the impact of the carrier vehicle." Reeber said it very calmly.

"It crashed on Far Side?"

"It did."

"Where exactly?"

Alderson held a sheet of paper so that Reeber could read it. "At sixty-nine point seven degrees south, one hundred thirty degrees east, at exactly o-four-o-nine and forty-nine seconds." Reeber looked up from the sheet. "That's on the inside of the north wall of a major crater formation known as Schrödinger."

Monzione nodded. That was what they'd been working towards for over two weeks now.

Pallas tapped the bench a couple of times with one over-weight finger, then cleared his throat. "I assume there's no point in asking anyone but the Russians whether *they* know about this second impact or have any reason to suspect what it was. Presumably the impact crater is visible?"

"With good enough optics and camera systems, yes. We believe they orbit good enough systems up there."

"And, ah, have they actually orbited one over the site?"

"I believe they have, yes."

"They've had time enough, I guess. Is it possible for them to get to that site and examine it? Or is that unnecessary – is there going to be enough wreckage to see from orbit?"

"It wouldn't be possible under any circumstances to observe the wreckage of such a small vehicle from orbit. From a high orbit the pieces will be too small to resolve with any camera. In a low orbit you traverse over the site with too much angular track to resolve any details at all without lateral smearing. It would only be possible to identify any wreckage by going there."

"Will there in fact be any wreckage at the site?"

"I doubt that. The vehicle impacted at orbital velocity. It obviously isn't a compact and coherent structure, since it comprises empty tanks, structural members, pumps, exhaust venturi and so on, so it would collapse and fragment on impact without sufficient heat transfer efficiency to vaporize the entire material. There could be small melt-damaged fragments buried there. But that's essentially irrelevant because you would only need to find microscopic metal alloy globules in the ground to be sure the impacting object was artificial in nature. However, the risk that the Soviets might recover any evidence is essentially zero. The site is halfway round the Moon from their base, and it's virtually inaccessible by direct landing. Besides, there's no way they could prove anything they dug out of there wasn't evidence they'd planted themselves to frame us."

"That, General, really is not the point. The real question is not what they're going to say, but what they're going to *do* if they ever figure out what we've been doing to them up there." Pallas shook his head. "Do you at least know what went wrong?"

"Presumably a fault in the guidance computer. We've checked over the programing every way there is and find no error there. The technology failed us. The manufacturer has no explanation."

"General, do you mean to try telling me you don't realize that military technology is not exempt by any kind of divine decree from Murphy's Law, for God's sake? Even tested systems still go wrong, but this one wasn't even *tested* first."

Reeber shrugged. "I don't personally see how we could have gone throwing one rock at them just to see if we'd be able to throw a second rock. By its very nature, Blue Bolt had to be a one-shot option."

Flanked by Banners and Seals on the wall behind him, encompassed by the brown leather wings of his own personal executive chair, barricaded by the gleaming expanse of his workdesk, Defense Secretary Willard Arthur Mackover sat in a glum funk, gazing disconsolately out of the wide windows of his private office. A smallish man, both very devout and very dedicated, he tended to depressions. High public office conflicted perpetually with his fundamentalist instinct for intellectual and material modesty and a sense of acute personal responsibility for his fate in this world and the next. And now other people were trampling on his fate in this one, and his righteously indignant anger at their temerity made him fear for the inadvisable consequences in the one to come. So he buried the prideful fury under a smothering blanket of misery. Now self-pity was a sin, too, but sometimes things just got the better of you and you had to give a little and sink under the gloomy clouds of comfortless introspection, turning your back on the perfidy and betrayal of this corrupt human existence.

Backing up the Pentagon on the landward side was the Arlington National Cemetery, its lawns laid with the heroic dead the Pentagon generals had expended over the years in the service of national pride and of the freedom of the established economic order. Half a mile on the other side, across the highways, was the Potomac River with the Lincoln Memorial on the opposite bank and The Mall running towards the Capitol. Across The Mall lay the White House, flat-browed behind its iron park railings. In the Pentagon, if you had a more metaphysical than megatechnological imagination, you were caught between the White House you served, the Capitol you contested with, and the dead the three of you had accumulated in the process. And through the middle of that metaphorically contoured landscape ran the river that washed the frontage of the Watergate Building. Sometimes things really just got the better of you and you really had to give a little and sink under the gloomy clouds.

"Beg pardon, sir?" Edward Hirayama, youngly middle-aged, comfortably compact and cleanly executive efficient, sat in one of the easy chairs arranged in the discussion horseshoe. "What's that about Watergate?"

Mackover straightened up some in his chair, hating himself for sagging into a weak and awful body posture. "Watergate?" He shook his head. "I say this isn't going to be a Watergate."

"No, sir. No one's going to go public on this business. Too delicate by a long way."

"That's right, Ed. That's good to know you think that way, too. No one's going to go public on this. With the election due everyone's going to keep the lid on. No one wants a little thing like this to get into the media. They'd blow it right out of proportion as if we'd been running a war up there. The whole thing's going to stay under, even in Congress."

"That goddam committee leaks like a sieve." Major General Matthew Newell, on permanent secondment from the office of the chief of staff of the United States Space Force, picked a thread from his uniform pants where he sat in the discussion horseshoe opposite Hirayama. "Just five active members, and five active leaks. I hope – I just *hope* – everyone they're leaking it to keeps the lid on tight."

Hirayama shrugged. "If they didn't leak, we wouldn't know what's been said and what's still unsaid."

"The CIA." Mackover counted the perfidious. "The NSA, some of those science fetishists at NASA, even some of our own kind of people right here in the Pentagon. Falling all over each other to testify in front of Joint Space or EIS Sub. Whose side are all those people on?"

Newell grunted. "The CIA are pissed because they never got a look in at Space or the Moon. The NSA are pissed for the same reason – the highest they get to go is to their elint channels on some of the geosynch satellites. They're all jealous. Specially the other services right here in the Penta-gon – at least, *some* of the officers involved are. They've all been jealous as hell for over a decade because of the money and prestige pumped into Space Force. As if we could have gone along putting together a coherent space defense frontier with the Air Force and the Navy fighting over who got every cent, and the Army and the Marine Corps bitching the whole time about their nuclear missiles and their flyers and their communication needs. They're all pissed and jealous, and now it looks like we've fucked something, they're all piling up out of their holes to dish the dirt."

Mackover didn't like words like pissed and fucked at all, and he'd fry in mortal damnation rather than use them personally. But Newell was a general and would go on using a general's kind of language. At least, as a go-ahead and modern thinking and strategically up to the minute Space Force ranker, that was the only thing traditionalist about him. The others now, all those jealousy crazed traditionalist generals and their trained up subordinate officers, they were all out of date with their belief in men and guns and ships and tanks and aircraft – even nuclear armed missiles – as being the *key* to effective deterrence. Those were all just so many backups, and *armies* and *navies* didn't count any, anyway. When nuclear weapons can hurt you mortally there's no Godly sense in a whole lot of soldiers and sailors swarming all over the Earth – not even in rows and ranks of nuclear missiles you could have hit back with if you hadn't been hit and wiped out first. With that setup you could only achieve anything by hitting first, which was immoral and un-American, and only to be done if you couldn't get out of the corner some other way. The only *deterrent* which made sense was a total invulnerability to nuclear attack, which was what this and previous Administrations and Space Force had been trying to put together now for over a decade. And then when you've just about put it together right, the Russians go and start building what might turn out to be an Earth interdiction weapon up there on the Moon, a weapon with which they could conceivably wipe the whole of your shield out of existence – at least shoot it as full of holes as a turkey after Thanksgiving – and they just had to be stopped before they put their EIS launcher together at a time when you still didn't have your own already working and ready to use. So you *had* to hit them out of the blue and secretly, because you could hardly go asking them to stop and wait until you caught up. You *had* to hit them first just a little bit, which was underhand and immoral and un-American and absolutely unavoidable.

Well now all the blind fool traditionalists right here at the Pentagon, all the jealous agency rivals outside, all the meddling self-interested and liberalized and diplomatically fixated numbskulls at the State Department and in Congress were having their party. Here was their chance to get up and really do what they'd been wanting to do for years – to wreck the funding of a major Space Force project and maybe even precipitate a general block on further expansion of space defense systems. And what project did they pick to ruin? The Earth interdiction system. And if the United States didn't have one of those, well it was just *vital* to make good and sure that Moscow never got its own EIS working up on the Moon. Creeps. Lousy creeps, every last one of them. Thank the Lord at least it was all going to stay firmly under wraps.

"Beg pardon, sir?" Edward Hirayama said. "I'd say it was going to stay under wraps, too, sir. No one could afford it politically."

"That's right, Ed. Good to know you think that way, too. No one can afford it politically."

"It's Hyland," Newell said. "That Black Russian bastard. The tip-offs went through to him on his private network, and he's steered the whole thing since. Contacts everywhere, fingers in everything. One of the cleverest pro-space lobbyists there is, but he's turned into one of these dove types and seems to be taking the whole State Department with him. He used to be on our side when we were all trying to get space going big again. Good God, the man's a Republican. And now he brings the State Department, the CIA, the NSA, and half the bastards right here at the Pentagon down on our necks."

"Terrible." Mackover winced slightly at the sharpness of the general's language. "Terrible disloyalty. It's even got into Space Force. There are weaklings and back-stabbers everywhere the minute the going gets tough. This man

Reeber. I've always had the greatest respect for his abilities and experience, I congratulated him myself when he made it to head of Lunar Section at Special Operations. He was right in here – right where you're sitting now, Ed – advising us on Blue Bolt with Waterson and the chief of staff. How many times? Half a dozen times, Ed?"

Hirayama nodded. "A good six or seven times, sir."

"And then he goes in front of that committee last week, and does he cover? No. He blurts it right out. The secretary of defense and the White House. *Me* and the president. That hurts so. That kind of disloyalty really hurts a man."

Newell shook his head. "I don't like to trash a colleague, but if I had Reeber I would wreck him. But I'm afraid we have to cope with the cold facts, sir. Reeber isn't high enough to risk sticking his neck out like that. He was doing just what someone told him. I wouldn't want to say who, but I guess you just have to accept that for some people – right up to the very top – departmental and service loyalty is the only issue when you take it right down to the wire. They'd see a political head roll any day to protect their own."

Mackover nodded despondently, his head feeling precariously loose. He leaned back against the cool leather of his personal executive chair. All the rest of the opulence of this office belonged to the Defense Department, but the chair was his very own.

"I guess the critical issue," Hirayama said carefully, "is that this whole thing holds long enough for us to get finished and tidied away up there. Then even if some fool goes public on it there'll be nothing solid for the media to get their hands on, and above all nothing that Moscow could dig out and use at us. Then the big embarrassments are saved and the heads don't have to roll. The ELTS-22 mission boosted out of Earth orbit yesterday, so we'll be clear in another month."

"You think someone's going to go public on this, Ed?" Mackover asked dismally. "You think it's going to get so far that it turns nasty for us?"

Hirayama pulled off a doubletake so smooth you couldn't see it no matter how close you looked. "I don't think anyone's going to go public, sir. The risk is just too high. No one directly concerned with diplomacy is going to open it up because it would be a diplomatic catastrophe."

"I'm not so sure, Ed. The secretary of state wasn't just livid at the White House yesterday, she was screaming blue murder over us going behind her back the whole time."

"But she won't blow it open under any circumstances. Neither will any of her people. They're the ones who have to deal with Moscow, sir, and they have their work cut out without feeding the enemy things to hit them with."

"That's true, Ed. That's true right enough."

Newell grunted to express his distrust. "But those politicians there at the Capitol. They're so pissed, and half of them aren't even on the Administration's side in party terms. The politicians have to be a danger."

Hirayama shook his head. "I doubt I'd agree. The election's the key there. Absolutely no Republican is going to blow it open before the election because of the risk of lousing it up at the last minute. Simple and straight. But no Republican is going to blow it *after* the election either because of the consequences if it would blow up domestically and diplomatically and cripple the Administration for its whole second term. That's why I don't think even Hyland would talk on it. If the election went to the Democrats he'd be out of a job, and if the second term was crippled, well as undersecretary for Space Affairs over there he'd have sunk his own ship. Besides which, my analysis of Hyland over the years since he got prominent on the back of the space lobby shows him as a patriot, even if he doesn't understand a flexible contingency response like Blue Bolt so well. He wouldn't blow it open because he just isn't un-American. He's just a traditional patriot who wants things done the right way, in the old-style way he understands."

Mackover nodded. "You know, I think you're right there, Ed. He's arranged for it to come out and get spread around, but he's arranged for that to go ahead strictly under wraps. That's true."

"That's it, sir. If he'd wanted he could have leaked it round a couple of corners to the media." Hirayama didn't actually give a flying fuck about Hyland's motives and possible alternative actions. His only concern was to coax the defense secretary at least a little way out of the gloom so that they could get back to some of the daily business of running the executive of the Department.

"But the Democrats, now," Newell said. "They're a threat that could sink us right when we're getting ready to take the election."

Hirayama shook his head mildly, hiding his thought that the major general was not very subtle in his awareness of the defense secretary's needs and at times was fuck all help. "I disagree there. The election's the key to the whole thing. What's the big issue, the big concern, the story of the decade right at the moment?"

Newell shrugged. "South Africa. Has been all year. Now that Durban's gone, it's going right down the toilet."

The defense secretary winced at the image-rich language.

"And the mood in the country?" Hirayama asked. "Well over half of Congress, well over half the entire electorate is sick at a communist victory, is furious at seeing Soviet imperialism swallow the last big chunk of genuinely pro-Western democratic Africa, and is hopping mad at the way Moscow mixed in there and set fire to the place. It's materially the same as if they'd invaded. Now the attitude in the country is very hard on that. Sure, there's the racist side issue, which is why the Administration could not at any stage put in ground troops and roll those ANC Marxists right back where they came from, and which is why the South Africa issue is a balanced thing and doesn't itself work for or against the president for the election. But the Soviet intervention is different. People don't like that. Now – any Democrat who leaks Blue Bolt has to realize that people are most likely going to *like* it, are going to approve and say that was giving the Soviets just what they deserve. A Democrat who leaks it risks a landslide for the Republicans, I'd say. So in my view, sir, I can't see anyone risking breathing a word until it's politically safe in self-interest terms one way or the other. For everyone involved out there, the backlash effect is just too strong to take the risk."

Mackover was nodding vigorously. "You know, that makes a lot of sense, Ed. That really does make a lot of sense. There really is a motivation for everyone to be sure and see this whole business stays safely behind closed doors. It could stay that way for years with self-interest playing such a big role." He shook his head at the moral perfidy and selfishness he'd observed.

"I'm confident myself we'll weather the storm, sir. Joint Space have asked the White House to send someone down for a clarification on what authority was given for Blue Bolt, and once they have that to their satisfaction, the issue's just going to fold. The president will make sure it's capped."

"Who's the president sending down, Ed? Do we know yet?"

"We know as of this lunchtime, sir. It's Challis. He's told the committee he has time for them tomorrow."

Mackover was surprised. "Challis?"

"That's right, sir."

Newell pulled a face. "Oh that's shit. The president has to arrange that the White House doesn't carry the can for any bad decisions. Challis is a cold-blooded bastard. He'll make sure someone else gets nailed for any fuck-up on Blue Bolt."

Defense Secretary Mackover recoiled visibly, and not at the language. His fragile optimism burst, and now Edward Hirayama had to start all over.

Vernon C. Challis was black, forty-six, and son of a software consultancy sole-owner from Chicago. Son, in other words, of a new-rich middle-class black family that had taken the economic success option and shortcut the interminable wait for the true realization of civil rights. Such a family was inevitably Republican and had given him the ideal start for a career as an incisive, no-nonsense managerial fixer and troubleshooter. He had degrees in law and in economics, and a perfect familiarity with math, logic and computers that had its roots in his childhood. His career as the background man who made things work had been brilliant and ruthless, until four years ago the new president elect had taken him off the policy development team and made him chief of staff at the White House. Vernon Challis was the president's organizer, the president's closest adviser, and the second most powerful human being in the United States of America. What was sent to the president went through Challis, what was decided or desired by the president was ordered by Challis. At the president's wish to be free to work on policy and politics, Challis had restored the office of chief of staff to the unfettered shadow authority it had been in the Nixon era, modified only by two critical considerations – pick your people carefully, and keep your hands scrupulously clean.

Challis was the biggest gun the president could send to sort out the Joint Space Activities Advisory Special Subcommittee after they had requested someone to deliver a clarification on a whole list of issues associated with Blue Bolt. He was elegant and cool, a brown-skinned man in a perfect charcoal gray suit, with a white shirt and a pale patterned gray silk tie. A monochrome cloak of shadows surrounding a glimpse of shielded light. He came alone, without assistants or legal advisers, without even a briefcase full of documents to support his memory. He was going to take no nonsense from the committee, and was going to exercise the practically absolute authority he certainly didn't have constitutionally but might as well have. He was going to tell them exactly what he and the president wanted them to know, and fence or flatly refuse any questions probing beyond that limit. And since he was a busy man in a tumultuous world with the added complication of an immediate and still accelerating electoral run-up, he wasn't going to take any more time than necessary over it.

Senator Bryant J. Pallas put on his calm and weary tone, an experienced heavyweight squaring up quietly to a serious opponent. "I guess we can take the reasons for outward secrecy on Blue Bolt as given, Mr Challis. Also we can follow with adequate precision the route taken by the Executive and responsible military authorities in circumventing the Legislature in such a weighty matter as the perpetration of a planned application of force – that is to say, the deliberate taking of lives of citizens of a foreign power and the destruction of the property of that foreign power. We're also aware that covert operations of an ethically questionable and sometimes downright illegal nature are unfortunately nothing new. We'll also for the moment ignore the question as to the sanity of perpetrating such an act against a foreign power as mighty and as potentially dangerous as the Soviet Union. It seems grossly ill-advised, to say the least, but it has happened. What concerns us is the need to clarify *who* ordered it and *why* it was ordered, and to inquire as to how in God's name the mess that the military have gone and made of it can be kept under control, so that either Moscow doesn't find out, or one way or another – but God alone knows how – can be kept from throwing a fit over this. The nightmare I have in front of me the whole time is what we would possibly do if we found out they had been bombing one of our bases and killing our astronauts up there."

Challis sat alone and perfectly still at the table facing the committee. "The questions, Senator?"

Pallas sighed, the involuntary sigh of a sick old man. "The first one is simple, Mr Challis. Please explain to us the involvement of the White House and the president in Blue Bolt."

Challis nodded. "The CIA, the Pentagon and the NSA were able to supply the White House with digests of collated data on the South Africa burns within forty-eight hours of the war turn-around. By March 11th we were getting a detailed picture of the full extent of the burns and their consequences, together with firm indications of laser use by the Soviet Union. By that time the United States Space Force had established a special assessment group to cover the enmod burns in South Africa, in view of the potential direct relevance both for the capabilities of and necessary defense against space defense weaponry in ground conflict situations. The office of the chief of staff of Space Force was able to report to the White House on March 14th that in its assessment, Soviet lasers had probably been employed against South African combat forces in the field. This was in accord with the improving CIA and NSA analyses. At that stage on-the-ground investigations were not yet possible, due primarily to the chaotic state of affairs in South Africa, and so there was as yet no indication of possible ground-based local mechanisms that might have been employed by ANC forces." Challis paused. He showed no trace of even the slightest amusement, but he was deliberately ripping into it almost faster than they could take notes.

Pallas didn't wait for the others to catch up. "What was the opinion on the possibility that a Soviet laser installation at Mare Orientale on the Moon might have been involved?"

"The Defense Department's opinion at the time was strongly that a Moon-based laser use was probable. Preliminary analysis of monitoring data on Soviet relay and battle mirrors collated with NSA signal intercepts and general data on the extent of the burn starts, most critically the time resolution, indicated clearly that Soviet ground-based lasers were not involved to a sufficient extent to account for more than one tenth to one fifth of the burns in fact observed. This tipped the balance in the Pentagon against the orthodox view that the Soviets were building a surface-mounted railgun at Mare Orientale for the purpose of Earth interdiction, and gave strong support to the previously minority view that it was a laser EIS system and that it was already operational."

"Hard information on the actual mechanisms used by the ANC – incendiary devices, simple torches, poured gasoline and so on – were not at that time available?"

Challis shook his head. "To get that data required evidence gathered on the ground, which was not exactly an overnight job in a state of rapidly proceeding collapse such as obtained in South Africa. No really satisfactory data came through at any stage from the South African intelligence agencies, which were basically just disintegrating at the time. Our teams from the CIA, the State Department and Space Force had difficulties establishing themselves on the ground, and the first firm analyses were available towards the end of April. The actuality of any use of a Moon-based laser was not finally ruled out until late May, when on-the-ground mechanisms had been fully elicited and collated against the burn patterns. The observed ground-based laser activity enacted by the Soviet Union transpired to be of the correct order to cover the unexplained proportion of fire starts."

"As we understand it from previous testimony, the equipment for Blue Bolt was fully deployed and operational at Aldrin by May 21st. Was this as a result of orders originating from the White House?"

"No. Space Force had transported its equipment and its team for Blue Bolt on Transiter missions at the end of March and the end of April. At that stage Space Force was acting entirely within its own competence."

"Without orders, in other words. When did the president learn of the existence of Blue Bolt?"

"We requested information on appropriate responses to the South African turn-around from all relevant sources at the beginning of March. At no time was the State Department able to suggest any credible means of using diplomatic pressure to prevent the Soviet Union from doing the same thing over again somewhere else at some future date. The major fear – apart from the extreme case of an attack on the United States – was that they could hit us right in our back yard in Central America. They would also be able to take out, for example, every oil terminal in the Persian Gulf or elsewhere in support of pro-Moscow guerrilla or terror organizations. The DOD and Space Force came through with a discussion memorandum to the president on April 17th, which outlined a modification to turn the so-called Skyrock Option into an invisible use weapon. As this concept of a modified EIS-1 system utilization was the only available countermeasure short of putting nuclear warheads down on laser installations on Soviet territory, this minimal force option appeared worthy of further discussion. The president requested further information, and the DOD came back two days later with Space Force's details on the non-nuclear non-weapon mode for EIS-1 they'd put together, and an outline of a possible operational use code named Blue Bolt. When we requested their reaction time on a possible deployment, they advised us on April 22nd that a precautionary deployment of the modified system was already under way."

"Did that not seem somewhat precipitate?"

"Not at all. The dimensions of the system are so small that it could be hidden adequately under an aluminum foil sunshield at Aldrin, therefore not alarming Moscow. Further, we live in a world where a global nuclear war can be started in minutes. In those terms the Blue Bolt deployment was almost exaggeratedly slow, I'd say."

Pallas felt as though he wasn't getting a foot on the ground. If he let that go he was tacitly conceding that Blue Bolt was a careful, reluctant and well-considered operation, if he said the comparison was ridiculous the whole alarm about it being an act of war against the Soviet Union was out the window. Challis was one tough young bastard, and no mistake. But what the hell. Go to the core issue. "About the final go-ahead, Mr Challis. Lunar Section of the Special Operations Division received the order to execute Blue Bolt on June 25th. Did this order originate from the president?"

"The president authorized the DOD to execute Blue Bolt if circumstances were favorable. That decision went out on the morning of June 25th. The order to execute would then have originated with the defense secretary or the chief of staff of Space Force."

That caught out everyone on the committee. Challis had just said the president ordered the go-ahead on Blue Bolt. They had expected a claim – probably a claim that could never be challenged successfully – that either the Defense Department or Space Force had acted without authority at the crucial time. The obvious tactic should have been for the White House to throw the blame back down the ladder and let it settle at the level of either the defense secretary or the top echelons of Space Force, leaving the two candidates to fight it out for themselves.

Pallas couldn't think of a follow-up question at all right then, so he turned to his deputy on the committee. "Like to take up the questioning, Senator?"

Jacqueline Monzione looked quickly over the list she'd prepared. "Ah – why was the order given to attempt to destroy or damage the Soviet Mare Orientale base as late as June 25th, when it had been clear at the White House since – according to your own statement – late in May that no laser was there at the base. We'll leave out the issue of the White House and the Defense Department still claiming in public right up to last week that it was possible that Moscow had an operational laser up there."

"I don't recall," Challis said flatly, "stating that the White House was at any time categorically advised there was no laser at Mare Orientale. At that time only its involvement in South Africa had been ruled out."

"Then at what point did the Defense Department or Space Force directly inform the president that there is no laser at the target selected for Blue Bolt?"

"At no point. Our advisements from the DOD had stabilized on that issue by mid-June." Challis finally shifted in his seat, turning just a little sideways and placing one forearm on the table in front of him, but still sitting upright rather than signaling any tension by leaning forward. "Perhaps I should remind the committee that only the Defense Department, and in particular Space Force, are in any way competent to advise on matters concerning Soviet military activity in space in general and on the Moon in particular. They are the only authorities in possession of the necessary data. The president is as fully dependent on their assessment as is everyone else here in this room. About the only check we have against faulty assessments is the power to fire people if they foul up."

"That might prove to be a power in need of being exercised, Mr Challis." Monzione shook her head. "And so what was the Defense Department's assessment on the laser?"

"That with a ninety-eight per cent probability, the Soviets would complete and make operational a high capability EIS system at Mare Orientale not later than April next year. The installation would either be a free electron or undetermined technology laser, or a kinetic munition railgun, with the respective probabilities roughly equal at forty-five to fifty-five per cent. In either event they would have such a system years ahead of us, since neither our EIS-2 nor EIS-3 proposal has yet been voted funding."

"Didn't anyone consider the possibility that there is *no* major weapon system up there?"

"That view is strongly represented in *Pravda*, which is not a reliable source, and at the Bureau of Space Affairs at the State Department, which has no military competence. But it has absolutely no representation at the Defense Department."

"But." And here she had to have hit a chink in the man's charcoal gray armor. "Are we to understand that the president authorized Blue Bolt, knowing full well there would be no operational weapon up there – if at all – earlier than next spring?"

Challis nodded. "That's correct."

"And why?"

"The DOD urged that some action to prevent the installation completing and becoming operational was imperative. A high capability EIS system at Mare Orientale, if operational in the absence of a comparable US system, would be highly destabilizing in its effect upon the belligerence of its operators. In other words, Moscow might choose to use it while it had a clear field. At present we have no possible defense against an EIS. An EIS could cut our space defenses to ribbons before we could respond with any pre-emptive nuclear attack against the Soviet Union or against its own space defense systems. We would then be totally naked to nuclear attack while the enemy remained essentially invulnerable."

"We've already heard this argument a time or two in the

past couple of weeks, let me assure you. If the consequences are so alarming, why hasn't anyone thought of them before?"

"They have. They're becoming obvious now because of the shock caused by the demonstrated effectiveness of space weapons in a ground conflict – South Africa – and as a natural consequence of the detailed EIS proposals only now becoming sufficiently mature to go before Congress for budgetry inclusion. When dollars are at issue people finally take notice. The awareness itself is not new, although the awareness of the Soviet lead is very recent. Beyond that I do not propose to waste time discussing the genesis of strategic concepts."

He told her to shut up and get back to the point. He damn well did. Who was running this testimony anyway – Challis or the committee? "How does any such potential threat – however real – warrant an outright attack on a Soviet facility?"

"Perhaps you don't quite realize the implications." He let her have a trace of a smile, but then erased it. "The fact of the Soviet Union having such a weapon up there would instantly turn the vast financial *and political* investment in space defense over the past almost decade and a half into just so much gold-and-diamonds trash. It would precipitate the political collapse and ruination of both the Administration *and* the Congress that permitted such a state of affairs to come about." And they were going to jump up at that, so he raised his voice to shut them up. "We are talking about a total investment to date of approximately one hundred forty billion, of funding presently running at twelve billion per year, and long-term contract runs into the next decade totaling around another one hundred to one hundred twenty billion. The consequences of a cessation of the major development and procurement programs tied to space defense – a necessary result of it suddenly acquiring a worthless status – are limitless. Such a major cash withdrawal would cause the total collapse of the entire aerospace industry and related technologies, and around half the remaining defense-related industries. They have become tied and committed exclusively to space defense activities. That would mean the total excision of an industrial complex vital to the

United States and its defense capabilities in all areas, and would be of such financial proportions that it might very well precipitate a major collapse of the entire US economy through debt default chain reactions. At the very least, the appalling loss of confidence would be worse in its effects and its persistence than the Wall Street collapse earlier this century. The affair is that serious, let me assure you."

"If that is the case – *if* it is – shouldn't the current Administration have maybe taken steps over the past four years to alter the total dependence of aerospace and related industries on one single primary income source?"

"We couldn't very easily undo the irreversible space defense commitment introduced by the eighty-four Administration and extended exponentially ever since. The best we could do was concur with the DOD on the need to put together as fast as possible an EIS proposal that would match anything that Moscow floated. It was the previous Democrat Administration that let the Soviets get to the Moon four years ahead of us, Senator Monzione. We've been catching up as fast as we could."

"However, Mr Challis. Is the appropriate response really to commit what any sane victim on the other end would just have to judge to be an act of naked aggression? An act of war, my God."

"Whether or not it's an act of war is immaterial. Perhaps Moscow didn't intend its use of lasers on South Africa to be discovered for what it was, nor their supplying the ANC with literally millions of tailor-made incendiary devices. That, though, was most certainly an act of war against South Africa and also against the United States. Two hundred and seven of our advisers and logistics support personnel were killed in the fires and a further three hundred nineteen were injured. However, if you're afraid of a Soviet response to Blue Bolt, consider that *we* are not, in response to South Africa, launching strategic nuclear missiles against the Soviet Union. We're essentially playing low key but firm here. They decided to risk playing tough so we demonstrate the will to play tough as well, but we keep it to a measured response. Two Soviet cosmonauts against two hundred and seven of our service personnel, plus a small setback at Mare Orientale against the total loss of South Africa, is little more than a token response. A sense of proportion might seem in order here. The issue is less dramatic than it is being painted in some quarters."

"Mr Challis, the issue is not merely the execution of Blue Bolt as a covert operation in response to South Africa and so on." Monzione was getting angry enough to let it show, and also exasperated. "The issue is also that of the God-awful mess that Space Force made of it. And of course the possible diplomatic and even more serious consequences. Wasn't consideration given to this at all?"

"I can assure you, Senator, the defense secretary and the people from Space Force didn't tell us in advance that they wouldn't be able to do it right. The president is hardly likely to have authorized an operation whose architects advised it was likely to fall down."

"Then you consider that Blue Bolt was ill-advised?"

"I consider that the White House was badly advised on the feasibility and undetectability of Blue Bolt. The experts for the system and the operation at the Pentagon appear to have fouled up dismally."

"Blue Bolt was a complete failure?"

"Blue Bolt was a success insofar as work at Mare Orientale has been delayed by approximately one year. It was a failure insofar as the invisibility aspect has been jeopardized by some kind of allegedly mysterious and inexplicable guidance system failure, for which no one from manufacturer to end operator appears to accept responsibility. So far as I'm informed, Space Force blames the manufacturer's hardware and the manufacturer blames Space Force's operation programing, together with stretching the carrier vehicle beyond its attested design capabilities by requiring three separate propulsion burns from a basically single-use system. It seems to me that the Space Force people have tried to stretch EIS-1 through Skyrock and finally into the Blue Bolt application without realizing they had to redesign their basic system. An aviation parallel would be with the Starfighter, if any of you remember it. However, the question of blame in that respect will have to be cleared internally at the Defense Department."

"But at the very least an abort option should have been built into the vehicle." Monzione spread her hands, gesticulating from the committee bench. "A destructive explosive charge, maybe."

"The DOD assured us it was totally unnecessary." Challis shrugged his shoulders, and such a gesture from that virtually motionless man was totally dismissive. "Besides which, no one could put a constant radar track on the vehicle without spotlighting it for the Soviets with radar scattering, if they just happened to be looking that way. Without tracking, you have no way of knowing when you should use your abort."

That had brought Senator Jacqueline Monzione to a dead end.

Pallas was ready to try again, this time on the open-ended issue of the practical consequences of the mess. He cleared his throat. "So – the only cover for Blue Bolt was the White House's diplomatic action to chain Moscow to a firm claim that the object which struck their base was a natural meteorite?"

"Exactly. Our part in the concept went flawlessly."

"And what about the part that didn't? How much of a risk does that represent?"

"Risk of detection or risk of conviction? No evidence presented by Moscow could be proved to demonstrate a genuine US origin. The pro-Moscow regimes would vote with Moscow, the allied governments would vote with us."

"The risk of detection, Mr Challis. I mean the risk that Moscow will find out we did it. Irrespective of the follow-on in world opinion, can they go and get actual proof?"

"The EIS carrier vehicle apparently traversed Near Side and then the south polar region and proceeded on over Far Side. It crossed over the Schrödinger formation on an approximately west of north track. It was destroyed when it impacted against the inner slope of the mountains which form the north wall of Schrödinger, striking just below the crest. As a matter of interest, I'm advised that the impact site represents the highest ground for miles around, and that if the vehicle had cleared the mountains it would have continued on in a low orbit. It would have been visible and recoverable by anyone interested enough – parked up there in orbit for the Soviets to collect, you might say. The situation could have been a whole lot worse."

"We're concerned here with the situation as it is, Mr Challis." And that felt good, getting a little one in against the man. "Is it conceivable that the Soviets might be planning to visit the site at Schrödinger and inspect it for debris? They've recently been maintaining a doubled schedule of transport missions from Earth, and in spite of the repair and reconstruction they have to do, they might well be mounting the effort for such a mission."

"They certainly know of the Far Side impact site, and have overflown it several times with some of their lunar orbiters. It is still entirely possible they think of it as a natural meteorite, which would also explain their interest. Our scientific advisers inform us that the odds against two unrelated meteorites striking the Moon within twenty-nine minutes are so enormous that if the Soviets still believe both events were caused by meteorites, they will conclude that both meteorites must have come from the same parent swarm. They might then consider it possible to obtain enough data from two such impacts to be able to project an approximate direction of arrival, and then to look for the parent swarm further along its path and so fix its orbit around the sun. That way they would be able to predict any eventual return of the swarm, and so gain some warning and possibly at least an idea of the future risk from meteorite impacts. I can't discuss that in detail since I'm no astrophysicist. The scenario is of course fictional."

"Is there, or is there not, reason to believe that the Soviets are going to go look? We already understand that if the site is at all accessible, there's a very real risk of them finding confirmation that the United States did it. There doesn't have to be any rocket fuselage panel with the Stars and Stripes painted on it lying out on the ground. Droplets of advanced metal alloys would be enough to indicate that technology was involved. And we're the only credible culprit."

"Obviously," Challis said, unperturbed. "Space Force's Special Operations Division has studied the mission that would be required. They consider a landing by ADV – or of course a Soviet lander vehicle – at the site would be extremely dangerous and highly risk-loaded, but it would also be possible for a sufficiently experienced pilot. The Soviets could conceivably do it, either from orbit or from their base at Mare Orientale."

"And what's being done to pull this mess out of the fire?" Pallas was right on the verge of losing his temper at this ice cold and blatantly unimpressible backroom policy-maker who played brinkmanship games with, in the final analysis, the fate of the entire nation. "This incredible and insane and irresponsibly conceived and executed mess! What kind of contingency does the president have, or has the Defense Department cooked up, if the Russians actually go there?"

"We're going there first."

Bryant J. Pallas just opened his mouth, and then clamped it shut again. The rest of the committee were equally speechless.

Too cool to show even a hint of satisfaction at pulling off such a big surprise, Challis proceeded to put the Joint Space Activities Advisory Committee in handcuffs. "The operation is appropriately code-named Clean Sweep. Two DOD astronauts will make a suborbital hop from Aldrin by ADV and will attempt to land at the site. They will then attempt to eliminate any accessible evidence. For the event that the Soviets should spot Clean Sweep from orbit, or fly to the site later and find footprints in the area, our cover story will be the science mission I just outlined as a fictional scenario. We will have been seeking to gain data on the parent swarm of the two meteorites so that we can judge whether there's any danger of a future encounter with the swarm and thus further impacts. After all, our people up there are as at risk from real meteorites as are the Russians. The science mission cover story is compatible with the use of Space Force personnel because of the risk involved at such a difficult site and the imperative need to send the best ADV pilots we have. Consideration is being given at the moment to the formulation of a press release giving appropriate fake data on the approximate path of the meteorite involved, and asking Moscow to release any data they have on the path of the one which impacted at Mare Orientale so that a collation of the data could be attempted. Our fake data will be tailored so that any genuine or credible data they could provide would combine to indicate a source for the meteorites that is nowhere inside the Earth-Moon system. At that stage the complete cover-up of Blue Bolt will have been restored, exactly as originally intended."

"And when –" Monzione stopped herself. "My God, *if* this operation succeeds, this Clean Sweep notion. How much would it cost, and who pays? It wouldn't have been necessary without the mess made on Blue Bolt."

"Space Force haven't as yet given us a figure on that. However, it will be covered entirely within their approved budget allocation, seeing as it has been necessitated by their mistake on Blue Bolt. Other than that, the cost is immaterial when the security and the international credibility of the United States is at stake."

Pallas shook his head emphatically. "The credibility of this Administration, Mr Challis. Of the president and the defense secretary, but I hope to God not of the nation. You people and Space Force have been running an entirely private war."

"Construe it however you like, Senator. The issue now is that of avoiding at all costs – both operationally on the Moon, and diplomatically *and informationally* on Earth – any association of the United States with the impact at the Soviet Mare Orientale base." Challis fixed his eyes on them one at a time. *Informationally* was the key statement aimed at the committee – keep quiet, or be condemned for doing it to your country.

Pallas shook his head once more, not emphatically, not even furiously – just a little helplessly. The taut sick feeling was following the rise in his blood pressure, and he needed one of those capsules again. He didn't want it to kill him or cripple him just yet. He started to fish in the pocket of his jacket. "And when will Clean Sweep be attempted?"

"The Transiter operating the ELTS-22 mission arrives in lunar orbit just about now, I believe." Challis lifted his arm, pulling back his jacket sleeve and white shirt cuff from his wristwatch. "Clean Sweep is already underway."

When Challis left the hearing a few minutes later, he left a committee whose hands had been firmly tied. All essential answers had been given so that there was nothing left to investigate, and they had been informed in advance of the catastrophic consequences of any leak now or at any future date. Anyone who went ahead and perpetrated such a leak while being in the know on the Clean Sweep operation would be pilloried as a culpable villain by Congress, the media and the nation. As far as American internal politics was concerned, he had closed the stable door for his president and had managed to arrange that for months or even years no one would dare to suggest that any bolted horse was not safely back inside. Any possible leak into the public domain had been plugged before it had a chance to happen. Vernon Challis left the committee room upright and unassailable, a man in perfect possession of himself and of the situation he constructed around himself. The next step was going to be the briefing of the secretary of state on Clean Sweep that afternoon in the Oval Office, tying the hands of everyone at the State Department. Then there was the business of persuading the president why the secretary of defense would have to be replaced immediately after the election, and why Hyland had to be kept employed and sweet at all costs in spite of the trouble the man had caused. Vernon C. Challis was a brilliant and ice cold man with every prospect of getting exactly wherever he wanted to go, because he understood that in any struggle of whatever nature, the secret of survival and eventual victory is to take and to hold the highest ground.

30 *Tsiolkovsky Night*

Excerpted from *The Conquest of the Moon*, NASA/DOD Joint Informational Publications:

PLSF-2 Aldrin is located at 19.5°S 128°E in the 190km (118 miles) wide crater Tsiolkovsky, and is sited on a strip of mare-like basaltic lava midway between the central mountain and the lower slopes of the north wall.

At the time of publication Aldrin comprises three modules of the same type as at Armstrong interconnected in a north-south line, with module M1 at the north end facing the landing area and M3 at the south end. M1 and M3 have end airlocks and M2 has a single side airlock. The base control center is in the upper level of M1. There are stores and two private cabins in the upper levels of both M2 and M3.

The main power supply is from two 100 kW Nuclear Energy System units. Supplementary power is supplied from steerable photovoltaic arrays ("solar panels") on the roofs of M2 and M3, backed up by battery stacks. For the purposes of radiation safety, both NES units are placed individually in small craters some distance to the southwest of the base and connected to it by buried cables exactly as at Armstrong. Maintenance work is done remotely with robotized machinery known as a "handyman". Due east of the base is a 2 metre radio telescope dish and a 60 centimetre optical telescope (at half the distance). An expansion of Aldrin is planned for the future to establish a major radio astronomy facility taking advantage of the interference-free location shielded from the Earth by the bulk of the Moon. The DOD plan to establish surveillance antennas on the peak of the central mountain, and Aldrin is also the proposed site for an EIS-2 concept railgun installation.

The base is regularly staffed at present by four personnel, normally resident for three months and rotated in groups of two at intervals of one and then two months. These personnel include the base commander, a doctor or medical technician, and usually a geology and geochemistry specialist and a supplementary scientist or engineer. All personnel also double as base systems specialists. The personnel at Aldrin are all male: this policy will be suspended after the next planned expansion. There are at all times at least two ADV pilots at the base. The personnel always include two, and sometimes up to four, DOD Space Force astronauts. The base commander at Aldrin is always a DOD astronaut.

It is quiet here. Aldrin is permanently shielded by the Moon from the gabbling radio flux emanating from the Earth, and during its two-week night it is screened from the ceaseless radio noise of the sun. It is bathed in a special silence.

There was the five-second time lagged communication over Troy-1 back to Earth, of course. But since the end of March everything that went over the satellite had been channeled exclusively to CSOC in Colorado, with no more chatter to Armstrong or to NASA in Houston, and the CSOC staff were by disposition not very talkative. And being just four people locked up together, periods of quiet inside the three modules of the base were frequent and sometimes long. You only had to stay three months on a regular rotation at Aldrin, and that was enough.

Morris Gates only had to stay for one month before he got his delayed Transiter ride back to Earth on ELTS-23. He should have been rotated back down on ELTS-22 at the end of his six-month tour at Armstrong. His plan was to use his post-tour vacation to see if he could track down Beverly Ryle through NASA, find out her address and what assignment she was currently working on, and see if they couldn't get together for a meal and a talk and a how are you doing, husband or no husband. But that had all been postponed by the order that had arrived a day ahead of ELTS-22. He went up in the ADV to dock with the Transiter all right, but after the four personnel rotating in for Armstrong had gone down to the surface, he stayed in his suit with his effects bag in his hand, transferred to the new ADV bound for Aldrin, and flew it down to the surface at Tsiolkovsky on Far Side. Back on the Moon for an extra month. It was still an exclusively Space Force crew at Aldrin – Morris himself and Major Vic Gillworth, a science officer who had flown down with him in the ADV on rotation up from Earth, together with two guys from Special Operations Division's Lunar Section, Lieutenant Colonel Ron Beazly and Colonel Alan Browning. The colonel was forty-two and wore a crew-cut that made his hair color almost irrelevant, and he veiled a kind of personal intensity that contrasted with his quiet and strictly matter of fact way of talking. It was Browning who had the explanations for Major Morris Gates.

Static and lightless Tsiolkovsky night outside, close and thoughtful attention inside. Browning called a map section up on the console screen.

"Okay, this is the location. Sixty-nine point seven degrees south latitude, one hundred thirty degrees east longitude – just about due south of here, right up on the crest of the north wall of Schrödinger. Now Schrödinger's a big formation, around three hundred ten kilometres across, half as wide again as Tsiolkovsky. On Near Side with the stronger lava flows there it would have turned into a little mare, I guess. Here it's just a big empty crater. It stretches from seventy to eighty degrees south, biggest single feature in the south polar region. The EIS-1 went into a near-as-dammit circular orbit inclined at eighty-three degrees, crossed the north polar region, all of Near Side and the south polar region, and then it came in over the southeast wall of Schrödinger. It tracked over the floor and then slammed right into the top of the north wall mountains without clearing the ridge crest."

"How close to the crest?" Morris asked.

"Around seventy metres down."

Ron Beazly whistled softly. "Goddam."

"Why couldn't it clear the top?" Vic Gillworth said. "Just a lousy seventy metres."

"We're lucky it didn't." Alan Browning tapped the screen. "This here is the only piece of ground in the way that was high enough to catch it. Without it the thing would have gone into a parking orbit, just ready for the Soviets to go and collect any time. This way they can't get at it any better than we can, and since there's no reason at all they should know what it is, they'll most likely not want to try."

Then a picture on the screen, a monochrome photograph of jumbled ground hammered full of crater holes.

"These pics are all from our Torus-12 sat. This is the north wall on the outer side. It's a mess of broken ground with craters and craterlets and all kinds of rocks and big boulders. The point is, the ground slopes steadily up to the crest in this area, in spite of all the breaks in the ground. The slope averages eighteen degrees, so we can't set down on that with an ADV and be able to take off again. Sure, some bits will be fifteen degrees or less – even flat – but we haven't had a Transiter over this area to radar map it and figure out which bits. We didn't want to alert the Soviets by putting a Transiter into such an untypical orbit, so we haven't had a chance to find a piece of ground that's level enough and looks clean enough for a landing. The nearest place on the outer slope where it looks worthwhile going for a landing is over here, around eight kilometres away east and three or so down from the ridge northwards. But that's no use. If we want to do any useful work at the impact site, we can't go walking eight or nine klicks there and the same distance back the whole time. There's only a six-hour oxygen and water load with a thirty-minute reserve in those PLSSs, so we'd get not much more than one hour of work time each trip. Ideally we'd take a buggy strapped on the ADV and drive up, but for this mission we need a maximum propellant reserve to cover inspection time over untried ground before we go in and land. If we had one of those big Soviet landers I guess it might be a different story."

Another picture, this time filled with zebra bands of shadow.

"This is of the southward slope, the inner side of the north wall at the site. You can see how sharp the ridge is along this section, although it's clefted. The wall goes down in a series of scarps and terraces, mostly irregular, right the way down into the crater floor. Over five thousand metres right here, so that's one big drop – over half the height of Everest in a single fall. Then the crater floor runs away south for around sixty kilometres to the Cat – that's the unofficial name we're using for the concentric little inner wall around the central plain. This region's never been mapped in detail or visited by anyone, of course."

"Why call it the Cat?" Beazly asked.

"I guess because the inner ring's broken, so it forms a C on the map."

"Uh-huh," Gillworth said. "That'll be after Schrödinger's Cat."

"Schrödinger's Cat?"

"That's right. Schrödinger was one of the founders of quantum theory – well, of the wave mechanics approach. Schrödinger's Cat is one of the ideas he played with to try explaining things."

"I guess so."

Another picture, filled with the bars of stark shadow cast under the serried escarpments by the north sky sunlight.

"Well this is a close-up of the south slope under the ridge crest. This first terrace is around two hundred metres down from the ridge and four hundred metres broad. The front edge is around six hundred out horizontally from the ridge. It runs for three klicks west, getting narrower all the way, and another kilometre and a half east until it's cut by this deep gully here. But right at this point it's nice and wide, it's good and level at its outer edge with around a six degree slope only, and it's apparently free of boulders and junk. We have some more close-ups of the ground there on the terrace that we can study for the actual landing. That's where we're going for, the outer edge of this first terrace, five thousand metres up on the side of one hell of a mountain wall. That's tough enough. Add to that the fact that we don't know exactly in fine detail if the ground really is smooth enough, and that we're coming in from the north so we only see it at the last minute, and that's why they picked you, Morris, and seconded you to Special Operations for the job. I can fly an ADV, Ron here is one of the Division's best ADV pilots, but you're the most experienced ADV guy Space Force has on offer. You and me go on the mission, with Ron making our backup in the second ADV while Vic stays here to mind the base."

"Always knew it," Morris said. "Making that landing up on the peak here was about as dumb as volunteering. Just had to catch up on me one day."

"That's the way it always goes, Morris. Okay now – the impact is up here, seventy metres under the crest. It's right on the face of this slight bluff, with a talus slope under it down to the terrace. You can just make it out in the shadow."

Another picture change on the screen.

"Here's a closer shot. This has been processed to get rid of the contrast. Light is going to be a real problem on the mission. At that high latitude the sun's only twenty and one half degrees up in the sky at noon. We have to go there over the noon period so we have good light on the part of the terrace where we want to land, otherwise the shadow of the crest is too long and we won't be able to see where we're going. Only thing is, once we're sitting down there in the sunlight, when we look towards the impact site we'll be looking straight up into the shadow and into the sun itself. But there's nothing we can do about that. Okay now, this shallow looking craterlet right flat on the steep slope around two thirds of the way up, right here between the talus slope and the crest, that's where it hit. The whole impact feature is around twenty metres across and gouged maybe two or three metres into the slope. See how the edge has collapsed here at bottom left? That's an indication that the slope is relatively unstable. It's soft broken material, fairly deep piece of regolith for a mountainside. Any pieces of wreckage – if there are any real chunks instead of just droplets of metal – will be bedded into the regolith there. But this isn't a recovery mission, it's a clean-up. What we're going to do, Morris, is load up with seismic charges and rope, climb up there, and bring the whole of that mountainside down over the site. We're going to erase that crater and bury the debris too deep for anyone to find."

"And, ah – how do we get up there, exactly?"

"Here on each side of this shallow bluff where the crater is, are these two gullies. The one on the east looks more promising. Probably only a forty-five degree slope at the worst in there – it's damn near fifty degrees average straight up to the site, and worse still just above it. The idea is we place seismic charges with radio detonators inside the crater and on the slope above it, either by climbing right up, or by going down on a rope anchored by a partner up above on the bluff. Be my job to go down, so that Morris, who's the better pilot, is still alive to take off again if the rope breaks or something nice like that happens. We place the charges, return to the ADV and set up ready to lift off on a minimum countdown for the hop back here to Aldrin. Then we fire the charges and hope it brings down the slope. It should work the first time, but we'll just keep on trying the trick until we get it right."

"When does the backup come into effect?" Beazly asked.

"That's you in the number two ADV. We have thirty-six hours around the noon slot to do the mission and return. The problem is, we're going to be too far eastward at the site to see the Troy-1 comsat – it wouldn't be over our horizon even if we were right up on the ridge instead of parked down underneath it. There's no way we'll be able to contact either Earth or Aldrin. So Ron and Vic wait thirty-six hours from when we lift off from here, and if by then we haven't hopped right back again, Ron, you consult with CSOC on a go-ahead for the backup. That will involve lifting off into a polar orbit over the site so you can take a look and get some radio communication with us while you fly over. You'll be able to report back with CSOC every half orbit while you're crossing over Near Side. If we're stuck down there but could talk you down for the final descent, and if CSOC agrees, the backup mission might involve landing at the site to pick us up, so study it good, Ron. If you get no response from us, whether or not our ADV looks intact, there will be no landing. We'll count as dead and the site will count as too dangerous. CSOC and Special Operations and Reeber will just have to dream up a new mission to clean up the EIS-1 vehicle and what's left of us. Clean Sweep is no picnic. It's no suicide mission, but it's high risk. Virgin ground, a tricky site to land, no direct communication and not much of a backup prospect. But that's just the way it has to be."

"When do we go?" Morris asked.

"In nineteen days – six days after sunrise. That way we

get optimal lighting, and we also get finished and back safely ready for the arrival of the next Transiter. That's our rotation back down to Earth, Morris."

The control center was just like the one at Armstrong, located on the upper level of M1, but with some gaps around the circular wall where consoles and control computation for new systems would be installed as the base expanded. The place was silent but for the sigh of the air.

Morris had no music of any kind along with him, and the others were not very musical, although Vic sometimes ran jazz tapes in his cabin next to Morris's. Ron seemed totally unmusical and Alan Browning almost appeared to dislike the art form. It wasn't one bit like his previous visit to isolated and lonely and confined Aldrin, when almost non-stop music had been preferred by the personnel, old rock classics, jazz, pop inanities, classical – anything other than the silence. A silence was so ominous. And coupled with the dark it was oppressive.

It was midnight in the two-week night at Tsiolkovsky. Outside was pitch darkness – no sun, no glorious Earth, nothing but the marginal illumination of starlight on the blank and barren ground. Here on Far Side you were on the outside face of the highest ground in the Earth-Moon system, and around you was the vacuum that extended unchecked out past the stars and to the utter and incomprehensible edge of spacetime, to the end of the universe. During the long night the only real light outside the base came from the paired red and green points of the orientation lamps mounted at the sites of the outlying functions on the sunken plain of Tsiolkovsky. The surrounding ring of mountain grandeur was just a blackness under a field of stars. Morris Gates peered out the window, his hands shielding the sides of his eyes from the interior lights and pressed up tight against the plexiglass pane. All he could see were little split color points floating in pitch blackness. There was no array of lights out on the landing area to the north – all their competence and experience on the Moon still wasn't up to contemplating even a landing in a darkness so total it was bereft even of earthlight. There were no EVAs either during the dark half of each month at Aldrin, and they had to stay locked together inside for fourteen days.

"Taking a break, Morris?"

Far away in his thoughts, he hadn't even heard the man come up the ladder in the silence.

Alan Browning nodded towards the illuminated console screen where flight program parameters glowed to themselves. "You got that good and fixed by now?"

"I know every step both ways as well as the computer. I could set it up again blind. That's going to be okay." Uneasy, Morris leaned against the end of the console mounted to the wall right next to the window. "When the sun's back we should get over to the ADV and start checking it through. I want to check *everything*, as many times over as we have the time."

"We'll have the time, Morris. I'll help you right through. That's the only thing we have to worry about come sunup – getting this mission so smooth it's polished. Cleaning up that mess there is about *the* number one issue for the security of the United States right now."

"I was thinking more about making goddam sure we get back okay. Have to admit I'm not all that personally concerned with the security aspect."

"It's *the* aspect, Morris. Believe me." Browning let go a little smile. "Reeber and Waterson wouldn't send anyone on something like this if it wasn't so critical. This one has come straight down from the chief of staff, the defense secretary and the president. It's a security-dedicated mission. Could be about as big a thing as avoiding a war with the Soviet Union, which is what might result if they find out about Blue Bolt and go and flip right out over it. The issue is that big. In the final analysis it doesn't matter if we get back, so long as we wipe out that impact site. Our lives don't matter, just the mission. That's important, Morris."

Morris shrugged. "Guess I just feel this question *why*?"

"Why you and me?" Browning shook his head. "Well – we're Space Force and we're military, so we're the people to do it. Have to confess, though – when I take a personal view, I'd prefer if those dumb imbeciles from the manufacturer were landed with pulling it out of the fire and cleaning up the mess. You'd think they might have told us where their system reached its limit instead of waiting for us just to find out. But they couldn't do a mission like this, so it has to be us."

"I don't mean that. I don't mean why I have to be assigned. I'm proud of being rated as the best ADV pilot, and I can see why they couldn't ask anyone else to fly the mission." Escaping the intensity hidden behind Browning's gaze, he looked down at his hand resting on the console, a brown hand on white plastic cladding. A perfectly steady pilot's hand. "I also don't mean why this particular mission to clean away the mess. I've studied it enough to see there's no other way we can do it. And I don't mean why do Clean Sweep at all – once Blue Bolt came apart, well obviously you have to pick up the pieces and keep the whole thing hidden. And I don't even mean why did Blue Bolt go wrong. Things go wrong, it just happened and that's all. What I mean is –" He risked Browning's glance again. "Why Blue Bolt? Why go throwing rocks and trying to kill the Russians? *Why*, Alan? You were operation chief on Blue Bolt, so they must have told you. Why was Blue Bolt necessary?"

Browning smiled gently, because that one was easy. "The strategic imperative, Morris. The consequences for the United States if the Soviets get their EIS railgun completed ahead of us. Either we get a major collapse of our domestic economy, or we get a wipe-out strike against our space defenses followed by a nuclear assault coming right down on our heads. Either the economic collapse or the nuclear annihilation of the United States. That's quite a serious issue, Morris."

"You really believe that would happen?" And the thing about Browning's gaze was the pure conviction in it. What he was keeping hidden behind a quiet exterior of professional perfection was a certainty that the military system, from commander in chief right down to the nuts and bolts at the bottom, was infallible. For Alan Browning it was a system of belief.

"I believe my superiors right up to the president, Morris. I guess they know what they're doing and why they're doing it. If they saw the need, it had to be done."

"But why Blue Bolt? Couldn't they have figured out some other way? Diplomacy, pulling a hard line on the lunar weapons moratorium? Or speeding up our own EIS programs? *Why* take the aggressive option right out? It just doesn't make any sense to me."

"I guess after what they did in South Africa, you just have to get tough with Moscow for your own protection, Morris. That's never happened before, a whole country just destroyed overnight." Browning shifted his weight slightly, glanced at the glowing mission parameters and then back at Morris. "In the military we have to understand military solutions to problems that require them. That's why we exist."

And outside was a star dark blackness that didn't care whether they existed or not, an absolutely cold vacuum over bare rock ground on the airless and lifeless Moon in an empty vastness called the universe. Human lives are visitors here, insignificant in space, in time, in their actions and in the consequences of those actions. Let them kill each other or kiss each other. That material, physical, self-sufficient reality out there, supreme and sovereign, didn't care.

After three and a half months of priority work the base had been largely repaired. They had a new antenna mast, blocks B9 and B10 had been made safe again and the stores inside which had been ruined by vacuum were being cleared out. The replacement for number three nuclear power unit was due in on the next ship. The three-metre dish had been repaired and the six-metre mounting replaced. The hundred-centimetre telescope was operational again, while the three hundred-centimetre multimirror had been written off with a new construction start planned in six months. A new lander vehicle and a new surface rover were parked outside, and the debris of the wrecked machines had been cannibalized for spares. All minor damage to the other accommodation blocks had been repaired, and now he even had a new and transparent outer pane in his cabin window on the east side of B1, on the mid-floor below the control center.

Leonid Steffanovich Shalyapin, aged forty-seven, was now five months and one week into his fourth tour at Luna Base, his third as base commandant. He looked out at an eastward scene lit blindingly by the overhead sun. Broken ground, with all its features blanked out, fell away towards Rocca crater and towards the Earth. The planet hung at half full a few degrees clear of the horizon, a bow on its back with north at the left and south at the right, painted in as a half-disk in brilliant white and color streaks in the middle of a backdrop of perfect blackness. It would grow gradually as the sun sank behind the base. They would have a full Earth after sunset, failing gradually through the long lunar night to a ribbon crescent just before the blinding solar dawn. Three days after that dawn he would be riding up to the transit ship for his trip back to splendid Earth, to see Tatyana and to see Marianna and Andrei again, to live family life once more. Somewhere far enough away from Americans and the kind of thing they did on the Moon.

Vitali Zorin was there in his office cabin, sitting on the single additional chair between the desk and the door, listening to *Rhapsody in Blue* which was sweeping and rolling along quietly on the cassette deck. Leonid left the window and edged around his desk in the cramped cabin. He sat down in his chair behind the desk with his back to the wall charts of work details and system dispositions. Computer graphics were all very well, but he needed his wall charts to keep an overview of everything at once. Leonid, pilot cosmonaut, shuttle veteran and now most experienced and senior of the Luna Base commandants, was something of an old-fashioned super-technocrat. He liked a bit of hands-on control in his decision making, the very same motivation that had put him at the flight controls of those supreme achievements of technology known as spacecraft.

And he was old-fashioned enough to be glad he could hardly see the shallow little crater out there in the flood of flat sunlight, that little crater one hundred metres away southeast that had received so much attention in terms of measurements and the careful excavation of debris in and around it. He was old-fashioned enough still to be so upset by what it represented. Until now he had believed that despite the overwhelming encroachment of military interests in space – spying on each other and getting ready to shoot down each other's swarms of insane missiles – a bond of special comradeship still held between all spacefarers irrespective of nationality or political creed. He had hoped at least that military concerns would never triumph here so far away on the Moon, so high above the Earth that the mad confrontational pettiness didn't matter any more. He had always believed the Moon was safe. But five days ago Andrei Tsherbakov arrived on the latest ship along with documents and computer disks full of data to back up the conclusions already sent up from Kaliningrad. Now that fond illusion was shattered, another victim of the impact and as dead as Yelena Blochina or Vladimir Krushinsky.

"There should be some vodka up here," he said into the middle of the music.

"What?" Vitali shook his head. "Not a chance. Cosmonauts have to be heroes of the nation. No indulgence in alcoholic beverages. Corrupts the brave proletariat and all that. You're too morose, Leo. You knew perfectly well what the results would be in the end, as soon as the geologists and the meteorite experts started getting their first measurements and things together a couple of months ago. Good grief, the day it happened Mikhail Charotonov spotted that the crater wasn't quite circular but a bit elongated. It's just been a matter of waiting for the picture to clear, that's all."

"Vitali, do you know how many times I've met American astronauts? I've been to their Johnson Space Center and the Kennedy Space Center. I was there when Vitali Raisman put a commemorative wreath on the Challenger crew memorial. I've helped play host to astronauts in Moscow and Star City – knowledge of English is always in demand at shows like that. Who was copilot on our ship for the joint shuttle-shuttle rescue rehearsal in ninety-four? Me. I must have met hundreds of civilian and military astronauts. And there still just aren't *thousands* of astronauts any more than there are thousands of cosmonauts. That's years away. So there's a good chance I've spoken to whoever it was fired that thing at us."

"Oh don't blame the little people who only do what they're told. Blame the politicians, Leo. They cause all the trouble and they never get into it themselves."

"They should. A general couldn't do that all by himself. Their defense secretary or their president must have thought it up."

"Oh, politicians are always far too clever." Vitali looked at him intently across the desk for a moment, then lifted his head. "Look, one day the general secretary and all the important ministers are flying in a plane from Vladivostok to Moscow. They're flying over the middle of absolutely bloody nowhere in Siberia when disaster strikes – the bottom falls out of the aircraft and the Central Committee are all sitting there terrified in their seats, with nothing but air under their feet. The pilot comes on the intercom and says they're in trouble and losing height, so they have to shed some weight. The Central Committee throw out all their baggage,

their patent leather shoes, fur coats and hats – even papers
and documents, state secrets and all. Then the pilot says
sorry, we're still losing height. So they grab hold of the
baggage racks, unbolt the seats from the side, and let them
fall out. The entire Central Committee is hanging there for
dear life, and the Siberian forest is sliding by thousands of
metres below their dangling feet – and it's coming closer.
The pilot says sorry, we're still losing height. The steward-
esses have just sacrificed themselves for the good of the
nation and jumped out, but we're still too heavy. So – the
time of inevitable decision has come. They all look round at
the general secretary, hanging there by his hands from the
baggage rack like the rest of them. He looks very serious and
says, 'Comrades, the situation is serious beyond measure.
Someone must sacrifice himself for the good of the government and the nation. Such a supreme sacrifice is no trivial
matter. I cannot demand it of anyone else, therefore I myself
will lighten the load by letting go.' He looks round at all
his ministers hanging there, and of course *they* all start to
clap . . ."

Leonid let Gershwin punctuate the punch line for a few
hectic bars. "Vitali," he said across the music, "that joke's
so old. It must go back to Breshnev."

"Oh further, I'm sure. But it's true right enough."

There was a knock, the door opened slightly, and Maria
Alova looked in. "Excuse me. It's time for the decision
from Moscow. The colonel's already upstairs on the line to
Kaliningrad. Do you want to hear it yourself?"

Leonid nodded. He stood up and edged round the end of
his desk, Vitali moving his knees aside to make room. "Turn
the music off for me, Vitali. Then come up and listen,
too."

In the middle of the afternoon they had the canteen, an open
space eight metres by eight, to themselves. They sat around
one of the tables, three military and three civilian
cosmonauts, fully one third of the entire present population
of Moon Base. Colonel Andrei Tsherbakov and Lieutenant
Colonel Alex Stechlin were fresh up from Earth, Major
Maria Alova, Vitali Zorin, Nelli Ulyanova and Leonid were

all longer residents whose tours were due to end in one or two months' time.

"I'll summarize once again," Tsherbakov said. "If you don't mind, Leonid?"

Leonid just shook his head.

Tsherbakov nodded, an acknowledgement more than a thank you. "In short, the results of all the work done on the impact crater are as follows. The object must have been traveling at a velocity of between one thousand and two thousand three hundred metres per second, with a highest probability centering around one thousand five hundred. That's more or less orbital velocity for a low altitude orbit, so it most probably came from the Moon, and not from just over the horizon but from much further away. The elongation of the impact crater, plus the axial distortion of the fan of ejecta thrown out by the impact, point to an approximately northeast to southwest trajectory with a very shallow angle of impact with the ground. Incidentally, the way it threw out material, if it had struck at one hundred metres northeast instead of one hundred metres southeast, it might have smashed holes in all the blocks and killed everyone here at the time."

"Nice thought," Vitali said.

"The probable velocity and the apparent direction rule out a launch from the American base at Sinus Aestuum but accommodate fairly well the possibility of a launch from their base at Tsiolkovsky. That fits with common sense, since they wouldn't launch any kind of rocket from Sinus Aestuum for fear that we were looking at them at the time. Finally, the rock. To throw stuff around the way it did, involving an energy of one hundred and fifty to two hundred million joules, the rock must have been anything from seventy to three hundred kilogrammes, depending on the velocity. Now with the energy fixed, the bigger the rock the slower it was traveling, and the more of it that should have survived as recognizable fragments instead of being atomized or whatever. The identifiable non-local glassified pieces sieved out of the crater are of a size apparently most easily compatible with a rock of something like one hundred and fifty kilogrammes traveling at one thousand five hundred metres per second. Again, that supports a launch at or near Tsiolkovsky. Also, those pieces were unequivocally anorthositic gabbro before they were glassified, which means that it's hardly credible that it was any kind of meteorite. Whatever possessed the Americans to use a piece of rock just lying around at their feet, I don't know."

"Huh," Nelli Ulyanova said. "Proves their military did it by themselves without consulting any real scientists. Any competent scientist would have told them to use a real meteorite core from the Earth, or else a lump of water ice so that it would look like cometary debris. Only the military could get it that wrong." She smiled quickly at Tsherbakov, Stechlin and Maria Alova. "No offense meant, of course."

"What I can't understand," Maria said, moving on quickly before Tsherbakov could decide to jump, "is *why* did they do it at all?"

"Why else?" Alex Stechlin shrugged. "To get their own back for South Africa, because it went our way. As usual, just like South America, they backed the oppressors instead of the mass of the proletariat. Like that, history will always be against them. With such a large population of negroes at home, you'd have thought they'd have backed the blacks right from the start."

"That would have put us in a real corner." Vitali actually could smile cynically. "If we'd found ourselves having to back the whites we'd have had to do some pretty amazing ideological conjuring."

"Let's come back to the decision from Moscow," Tsherbakov said. Idiotic political speculations were a waste of time and effort, apart from also being distasteful. "The point is that the time association between the rock that struck here and whatever it was that smashed into the mountainside at Schrödinger is just too suspicious. It might have been the rocket they sent the rock up on, though why they went and let it crash back onto the Moon is anybody's guess. We suspect they used one of the EIS-1 vehicles they've developed and are always claiming are *not* stationed on the Moon. Not that it matters much."

"No rocket that hit the ground is going to be in big enough pieces to have any intelligence value," Stechlin said. "You'll probably find pieces a centimetre or two in size, but that's all."

"The point is that if we go there and *do* find any pieces, that will confirm it once and for all. I don't personally see what good that would do in diplomatic terms. Washington would claim that any evidence we produced was faked."

"We'd be able to inform them we knew precisely what they'd done," Nelli suggested. "We could demand a public apology and compensation for the families of the victims, and for all the extra transport and equipment costs we've incurred."

"Or what?" Maria said. "Either that, or what?"

Nelli shrugged.

"It's important to know whether they really did it," Tsherbakov said, "so that we know what kind of people we're dealing with and what the new rules of the game are. Their president is going to be re-elected now, that's for sure. So we'll have the same game players on their side for the next four years. We need to know exactly what we're up against. That's why Moscow has decided to go ahead with the Schrödinger mission. And if we're going to do it, we'll do it as quickly as possible."

Maria brushed nonexistent fluff off the sleeve of her overall. "And when is that?"

"When it's midday there," Leonid said, looking straight at Andrei Tsherbakov. "You need the best light you can get for climbing around on that slope. So near the south pole, you only have a high enough sun angle at noon."

Tsherbakov nodded. "We fly a lander there at local noon, work at trying to recover debris for one or two days, and then fly back before the Americans have time to notice us."

"We don't want any trouble with them." Alex Stechlin shook his head. "Not now we know they're being aggressive."

"It's like science fiction." Vitali had decided to move from cynicism to ironic disgust. "Aggressive savages discovered on the Moon. Stand by your blasters."

"It is not science fiction." Andrei Tsherbakov's voice was very quiet, and it left a small silence.

"If we fly there and back at local midday," Nelli said after a moment, "it's going to be night here. That's tricky for the landing."

Tsherbakov shook his head. "We'll have full earthlight here for liftoff, and still almost full for the landing. We have the base radar, the lander's own radar, and we can arrange a landing target of lights in the set-down area. That won't be a problem."

"But the landing site at Schrödinger will be," Leonid said.

"It will. It's out of all possible contact with Earth or with the base here. The ground is terrible everywhere within reasonable range of the impact site. The outer slope of the north wall is fairly shallow, but it's badly broken and cratered. On the inner side there's an impossible pattern of escarpments and terraces and gullies. However, there is one small area about eight kilometres east of the site and three kilometres down the outer slope from the ridge. It's level enough and fairly clear, although there's enough craterlets and enough boulders sticking up out of the regolith to make it dangerous just the same. But that's the only landing site there is, so that's where we'll try. Once we've selected our crews for the mission we'll get down to studying the photographs."

"The lander will carry a rover to drive up to the ridge," Stechlin said. "That way it's possible to cart enough equipment up to the ridge to be able to climb down to the impact site."

"We'll go with three people. That gives us a broad propellant margin for the landing there and for the landing back here at the base. Also, having only three people along means a real chance of being rescued – a backup mission by a lander carrying just a pilot and a copilot could bring all three back, again with a good propellant margin. Alex is going to command the backup mission. The State Committee insists that we have military command responsibility on the backup, too, in case whatever has happened to the first team turns out to be American. We'll select a copilot for Alex later."

"And the primary mission?" Nelli asked.

"I go as one of the pilots. Then I need two more people, another pilot and a third pair of hands for the climbing and digging. On no account will the second pilot climb down that slope. He or she has to be alive to fly the lander back if there's an accident. The slope is possibly unstable." Tsherbakov paused and looked at Maria Alova. "I've been intending to ask you to make number three. I've known you since you were attached to me as a trainee five years ago, and you've proved that you react well in an emergency. You don't have to decide now, though, so please –"

"I've decided," she said. "Who's the second pilot?"

Tsherbakov watched her for a moment, then turned to the question. "That's a problem. I'm a very good pilot – almost as good as Alex. But that doesn't mean we want to take along a pilot who's merely competent if we can find a better one. The landing site is a *risk*, I'll stress again. The difficulty is that all the pilot cosmonauts up here at the moment are rated on paper at around the same level of competence. Leonid, you know most of them better than I do. Who would you suggest?"

Leonid shrugged. "No one. I'm not going to put anyone in the position of having to volunteer because I suggested them. I'll go."

"You're the base commandant," Vitali protested. "You can't go."

Leonid was looking at Tsherbakov. "I'm a better pilot than you, probably even better than Alex. So I'll go." And just a little barb for the cold-mannered military man he'd never learned to like. "Unless being forty-seven or being a civilian prejudices my reliability?"

"Nothing prejudices your reliability, Leonid."

"Thank you, Andrei."

"Um – forgive me for the thought." Maria made a little apology with her hands. "But doesn't that create a command problem? On the mission, I mean."

"No." Leonid shook his head. "He's the military and the mission expert. I'm the flying expert and the expert on lunar ground work. I have twice as many hours here, don't I? We're both grown men with enough sense to respect each other's skills. We can cooperate and share the responsibility."

Tsherbakov nodded. Then he lifted up a plastic box, one of the items of special payload he and Alex had brought with them from Earth, and placed it on the table. "Before you commit yourself, Maria, remember that there's a small but real risk we might bump straight into the Americans. If it really is their rocket, they'll certainly know all about it. So we're taking precautions for our own safety." He opened the lid of the box. "They've already killed two of us and tried to kill everyone else who was here at the base at the time."

Inside the box was a gun. For a moment it looked like an antique pistol, but its ugly functionality was too modern.

"This is the newest weapon in the armory of the Soviet Republics. The first prototype was tested four weeks ago. There are now about twenty in existence. It's a rushed design, but they've kept it simple, so it works."

He took it out of the case. The barrel tube was about eighteen centimetres long and ended at the rear in an empty rectangular metal frame. At the upper rear corner of the frame was a hammer, at the lower rear corner was a pistol grip, and in front of the grip under the frame was a trigger inside an exaggeratedly wide guard. He took hold of another piece made of four short tubes welded together in a bundle, and snapped it into the empty frame. Assembled, the thing was a long and fat-barreled revolver with four oversized chambers. Two more sets of reload chambers lay in recesses inside the plastic case.

"It has a very basic revolver mechanism." Tsherbakov pulled the hammer back with his thumb, and the chamber rotated one turn and the trigger moved slightly forward. The gun was cocked. He squeezed the trigger and the hammer snapped home with a little click. "It's a hand-held shotgun. You need to use both hands. It has an eighteen millimetre bore, with a choke so the shot doesn't scatter too wide. It fires simple buckshot, but steel instead of lead so that it penetrates better. It's supposed to be very easy to use – I'm going to test it tomorrow – although at one sixth of Earth weight you have to remember to brace yourself firmly. Otherwise, inertia or no inertia, it'll knock you over backwards when you fire. A shotgun like this doesn't have a very high muzzle velocity, but for use in a vacuum the shot will arrive at its target as fast as it originally left the barrel. And at one sixth gee, the trajectory will be flat enough to fire aimed shots over four hundred metres. You also have a very good chance of hitting the target, since you're firing a diverging cloud of buckshot. And only one single piece of shot has to hit a man. If it puts a hole through his suit, he's dead." He looked at Maria, oversized pistol at a slope in his hand. "Still want to come?"

"I'm an officer. I'm not afraid of a gun." She took it from his hand, cocked the long weapon, and pulled the trigger. Click. "What would it do against a vehicle? A lander?"

Alex Stechlin shrugged. "Probably pepper it with holes. A lander's built as flimsily as possible to save weight, isn't it?"

Leonid was looking distastefully at the weapon.

Tsherbakov took the thing back from Maria and snapped the chamber out of the frame. "We'll carry them strapped in a pouch on the stomach of our suits. The chambers are too awkward to load with cartridges while wearing spacesuit gloves, so we'll each have two spare sets of pre-loaded chambers. Twelve shots each should protect us from anything. We're not exactly expecting a war."

Leonid was still glowering at the gun as it disappeared in two pieces beneath the lid of the box. "So – this is what it's come to. I've never used a weapon, and I don't want to start."

"Blame the Americans." Tsherbakov snapped the lid closed. "They're the ones who started playing cowboys and Indians here on the Moon."

Sunrise came as a cold caress of incandescence.

Conjured out of nothing night, the highest peaks of
Tsiolkovsky's north wall caught silent fire – an irregular jewel
string along the fringe of heaven, diamond hard points that
grew to a necklace of searing jagged pearls. Then the light
came down across the void above Tsiolkovsky and struck
flame to the central peak, a tiny broken pyramid of brilliance
suspended in black nothingness. In long slow hours, the
liquid light trickled down the raw slopes of the mountain and
spread onto the jumbled floor. By then the north wall was a
shadow-clefted mountain range that ran sunlit westward,
then curved south to sink below the horizon behind the flanks
of Tsiolkovsky peak. The giant crater had emerged from
night once again, a walled plain girdled with ramparts of
frozen fire.

Morris Gates and Alan Browning were inside one of the two
ADVs parked on the landing area north of the base. They'd
walked across in suits, but since this was going to be a
servicing and check-through visit lasting several hours, they'd
pressured up the ADV interior. They had removed their
helmets and the Snoopy caps with the built-in earphones
and microphone, and had removed their gloves from the
snap-rings at the wrists in order to make manipulation of
controls, locker latches and inspection panels easier. Outside
of the two forward windows they had a clear view of the base
two hundred metres away, its three circular modules almost
end on with their solar panel rooftop sails tipped up to face
the sun. The shadows cast by the base fell long metres
westward, over the parked and patient buggies, over the
supply dumps, over liquid hydrogen and liquid oxygen
storage tanks draped with crinkled aluminum foil that was

never rustled or disturbed by any breeze. Beyond, sharp and unsoftened by the perfect transparency of vacuum, the broken flanks of the boulder-strewn and sun-combed mountainside rose incredibly sharply to the saw-ridged central peak. Tsiolkovsky was dramatic and daunting, the most imposing human habitation on the Moon. The vulnerable little buildings of Aldrin were dwarfed by it all like little children's toys, or models on a film set.

Below the twin forward windows was the forward landing leg with its pad resting on the dusty ground. A short ladder was mounted on the slope of the leg. Apart from the ladder and the egress platform right above it, the entire exterior structure of the ADV was wrapped in gold-sputtered mylar film to protect it from the heat and the photochemical degradation of the sun.

The ADV was a single-stage development of the original Apollo Lunar Excursion Module. It had four angled legs mounted at the corners of a square box lower section that contained the main cryogenic motor, the feed pumps, and four spherical liquid hydrogen tanks. Outside on the flanks of the box was provision for external loads secured to strap-racks. The upper level contained the pair of liquid oxygen tanks housed outboard left and right, the life-support systems, equipment storage space in the rear recess, and crew space center and forward. The crew space was just a cramped standing area for up to five people. In the front wall at floor level was the egress door, and above it flight instruments and computer panels. Left and right were two stand-up pilot positions with flight controls and instrument displays, and a forward looking window for each pilot for landing maneuvers. Above were two small ceiling windows with calibration marks for orbital docking. In the center of the ceiling was a docking hatch, and at the rear over the stores recess was a small back window. Two tiny side ports looked out over the housings of the liquid oxygen tanks. Mounted outside on the upper section were dish and omni antennas, reaction control jet clusters, and little navigation lights. It was a cramped machine to live in, with just enough space for one man almost to stretch out on the floor and another to sling a mesh hammock at halfway height.

Browning switched on the interior light. The reflected sunlight wasn't bright enough yet to do detailed work inside. He turned his head, rubbing his chin into the empty helmet snap-ring as he looked around the tiny compartment. "No ice. Good thermal surfaces in these things."

Onboard air was stored dry. Morris could feel a hard dryness in his nose as he breathed. "Take a couple of hours of habitation to humidify the air."

Browning nodded absently. Then he stooped in his bulky suit and picked up one of the tool and equipment boxes they'd dumped around their feet. "Morris, there's a safety precaution you should know about right away so you don't have to worry about things." He opened the box. Inside it was a pair of automatic pistols. He turned, placing the box up on top of the storage recess in front of the rear viewing port, and lifted out one of the guns.

"What are those for?" Morris asked. "Duelling?"

"They started life as nine millimetre Berettas, the things the Army's using these days. Our development people at Special Operations modified them for suit gloves and for vacuum." Browning held the gun to show it to Morris. "The trigger guard's extended, the safety catch has bigger tabs so you can slide it easier, and so on. They've put in a new lubricant that won't degrade when the thing fires but is resistant to vacuum. They wanted to modify the barrel – make it smooth bore and up the muzzle velocity – but then there would've been trouble with the ammunition."

"And that's the latest in space weaponry?"

"Don't knock it, Morris. It could save your life if the Russians turn up there looking for what hit. If they have enough suspicions to come looking they'll be hopping mad, so you can bet they'd shoot us down as soon as see us. Russians are unscrupulous." He hefted the weapon in his hand, a featherweight thing on the Moon. "Kill anything it hits, even if it just wings a guy in a suit. Depressurize him. Up here it has such a flat trajectory it'll reach as far as an M16 on Earth. And with no air to mess the trajectory it'll fire as accurately as you can point it, so remember to use it two-handed. Have to lean right into it or the kick will knock you clean over backwards."

"We're really going to take those things with us?"

"Yes. Carry them in one of the equipment pockets on the thighs of our suits. Easy to reach."

"Huh. Seismic charges and modified pistols. Real starship troopers."

"The things work, Morris. You can't shoulder a rifle in a spacesuit. And forget the crappy science fiction. Tried and simple technology is best."

Simple handguns and simple lumps of rock, the ideal ways to kill human beings on the Moon. Morris had joined the Air Force to fly, and had transferred to Space Force to fly spacecraft and to see the Earth from orbit and to get a chance to walk on the highest ground, the Moon. He didn't join the military in order to *kill*. He looked out through the forward window, across the rock-littered and pock-marked ground laced with long hard shadows, past the base to the steep flank of Tsiolkovsky mountain rising up tall and sharp against infinite black. Liftoff in three days.

There weren't going to be any Russians at Schrödinger.

33 Schrödinger

They flew the mission in shirtsleeves with their suits stowed in the equipment recess behind them. They stood in the ADV in gray-green Space Force overalls, the nearest approximation to an in-space uniform for Defense Department astronauts. Standing at liftoff was no problem – the ADV pulled enough power to push them up at all of one gee acceleration, exactly like standing easy on the surface of the Earth. Two minutes and thirty-three seconds of normal weight, then the thrust shut down and they had free fall – floating in a dream in a metal machine above the rolling cratered face of the Far Side of the Moon. The halfway point was when they passed over the east rim of Carver, with Roche and Pauli on the eastern horizon and Van der Waals out on the western edge of space. The halfway point was at nine minutes and thirty-six seconds from liftoff.

Morris floated at the left-hand position, watching the flight parameters as the computer counted through its mathematical map to tell them exactly where they were. At the right side position, Alan Browning, mission commander but ADV copilot, prepared to send their sign-off message over Troy-1 to CSOC in the United States, telling them they were commencing the descent just before the ADV sank below Troy-1's horizon into radio silence.

They crossed over the cratered northwest wall of Planck. They picked up the long straight chasm of Rima Planck, converging on their due-south course as it grazed the western rim of Planck's walled plain. The southwest wall of Planck passed below with Rima Planck right under them, a steep-sided chasm angled slightly to their direction of flight. Its sides already falling away, the chasm ended ahead in Grotrian, a mere forty-kilometre crater. The raised rim of Grotrian came sliding down off the horizon. Morris watched the flight data progressing on the screen. "Deorbit in twenty-five seconds. Due to orient – now."

The computer fired the pitch thrusters to tip them over with their backs to the Moon. It fired again to halt the rotation and hold them there.

Browning opened the channel through the narrow beam dish antenna the computer was keeping trained on Troy-1. "Clean Sweep ADV to ground. Deorbit in five."

Five seconds, then the main engine fired automatically as they crossed south of Grotrian, back there on the Moon behind them. They landed standing on the floor at one gee. The deorbit and descent burn would run for one hundred fifty-three seconds.

The time-delayed answer returned from CSOC. "Copy Clean Sweep. Good luck and take care, now." That was the voice of Reeber himself, wishing them well from the safety and comfort of faraway Colorado.

Browning glanced at Morris, and received a nod. "Deorbit and descent nominal. We're go for landing. Closing down." He switched off the channel before they could lose Troy-1 and get only static. Loss of signal has an ominous finality.

Forty seconds into the deorbit and descent burn, velocity down to one thousand one hundred metres per second. Morris was nothing more than a computer caretaker and Browning only a passenger until they got an eye view of the landing site. The sun was sending little burning rectangular patches in through the ceiling docking windows and onto the floor, patches that were slowly swinging forward as the ADV pitched to keep the burn aimed down the curving trajectory. The sun patches reached the forward wall each side of the egress door and started to elongate, climbing upwards to the instrument boards.

Ninety seconds into the burn. The sun was shining in through the docking windows and straight out again through the forward windows. The lower structure of the ADV was obscured by its own shadow. The forward landing leg was just a faint gleam against black space.

One hundred seconds into the burn, velocity five hundred and twenty metres per second. A curved lunar horizon swung up in front of them from under their feet. Bright ground as

they looked down the path of the shallow sunlight, with the
shadowed leg and landing pad silhouetted against it. That
was the floor of Schrödinger, a smooth plain running to the
low and jumbled inner ring of the Cat.

One hundred and ten seconds and tipped up far enough
to see the north wall over the lower rim of the windows –
just a lip of ground ending in a jagged edge, with zebra-
blended bars of bright terrace and black shadow beyond it
and falling to the plain. An impossible landing.

Morris put his hands on the vertical trigger-grip control
stick and the main engine throttle, watching the instruments.
Browning had his forehead pressed against his window,
peering down at the tipped up mountain world below. "Going down the line, Morris?" That was the coolest of questions.

"Down the line. Radar altimeter."

Browning threw a switch. "Altimeter on. Oscillating reading." With the ridge, terraces and deep floor in the beam, it
wasn't going to give a useful reading until they were closer.

One hundred and twenty-three seconds in, thirty seconds
of burn to go, descending at two hundred and ninety-four
per second, altitude four thousand four hundred on inertial
track. Tipping over nearer to the vertical, normal to the
Moon. Couldn't see the north wall terraces below any more,
just the expansive and expanding floor of Schrödinger.

"Rotating." Morris fired the thrusters to spin the ADV on
its vertical axis. A slope horizon rolled around outside the
window, climbing. Sunlight struck in on his chest and
stomach. Rotated through one hundred and eighty degrees.
He fired a correction thrust to stop the spin. The horizon
was high ahead, all sun shadows on long mountain slopes,
on chaotic climbing rising ground coming up towards him
and disappearing under the forward landing pad. The pad
glittered golden in the sun. Ignore the view, watch the count.
One hundred and forty seconds, descending at one hundred
and twenty-seven per second, inertially computed altitude
over target nine hundred and fifty-five metres.

"Good reading." Browning watched the altimeter.
"Stable. Nine forty metres. Eight fifty. Seven eighty. Seven
forty. Seven hundred."

The sun was shining on his face and chest. A landscape of

craters and hollows and rocks and craterlets was coming up towards them. Seventy per second down, inertial altitude two hundred and forty-five metres.

"Two ninety metres on the altimeter. We're going to come out high."

"About fifty high." And there's the ridge, the break, the cutoff edge of the upsweeping mountainside, a jagged tear of black shadow across the ground. It rose like a blind tide in front of them. Crags and slopes were vague guesses inside the shadow.

The ridge rose, the distance tipped away and disappeared. The crest reared above them. Forty per second down, inertial altitude seventy-nine metres.

"One twenty metres." And twenty per second down. "Sixty metres."

There was the shadow edge on the rubble-strewn terrace in front of them, a bright sunstruck messy flatness and a web of rock shadows. The blank black shadow wall rose up to the sun.

The automatic throttle went back to sixteen point five per cent and the hover light came on. He flipped to manual.

"Forty-two metres," Browning said.

The propellant reserve was counting down to the red line where they had only enough left for the return journey. Two hundred seconds. The abort readiness light came on. Push the abort button now, and the pre-programed flight computer would throttle out to full and fire them automatically into a return path back the way they'd come. "Give me a steady altitude count."

"Forty. Constant at forty."

He fired the thrusters forward to give them drift velocity backwards. Balancing on the hydrogen flame of the main engine, the ADV glided away from the shadowed scarp and out over the edge of the sunlit terrace, out over the next abyss in the downward steps of Schrödinger's wall.

"Sixty metres. Seventy. Ninety. One ten. One twenty."

He fired a correcting thrust.

"One forty. Constant at one forty."

Hovering over the next scarp drop, with the front edge of the terrace out there ending abruptly in a shadow fall. One

hundred and fifty seconds to the red line and the abort. Now
look at the ground and all the rocks and pick a flat and clear
piece to land on. You can judge the scale of the rocks because
you know the distance – the shadow of the rearing ridge
where it falls across the terrace ground is around one hundred
metres away, the front edge of the terrace forty metres. It
looks kind of level, as level as expected. But craterlets and
rocks and boulders are scattered everywhere. The ADV
needs a space eight and one half metres across to land, and
one single rock under one landing pad can tip it too steeply
and it won't be able to take off again. Ah *there*. There's a
possible place, just left of ahead. "Patch of ground fifteen
degrees left of ahead, around halfway in to the shadow line.
Check?" One hundred and twenty seconds to the red line.

"I don't see anything better."

He fired thrust aft to start them moving forward, balanced
in a vacuum above the abyss. A touch of right thrust to give
them a slight left component.

"Altitude one twenty. One ten. Ninety. Seventy. Sixty."

The sunlit terrace edge slid under them again.

"Fifty. Forty. Thirty-eight. Thirty-six."

The piece of approaching ground was looking good. Ninety
seconds of propellant before the abort line.

"Thirty-six. Thirty-five. Thirty-five."

A crack, a whole fissure in the ground on the far side of
the clear patch. What's clear? It was littered with little rocks.

"Thirty. Twenty-seven. Ground sloping up more."

The target swung directly in front of them. Fire left thrust
to halt the leftward drift. Forward drift continues. Sixty
seconds.

"Twenty-three. Twenty. Seventeen. Fifteen."

It was a rubble carpet but no real rocks. No rock-choked
crevasses either. Should be stable enough to take the weight
of the ADV. The forward leg and its footpad end almost
bisected the target patch. Looking steeply down, you see the
ground through the almost invisible outer envelope of the
hydrogen flame from the main engine. Forty seconds to
the red line abort.

"Eleven. Ten metres. Ten."

Sharp rocks right ahead, and a big slab at the edge of the

shadow thrown by the ridge. The ADV is right over the clear patch. Fire forward thrust to stop the drift. The rocky dusty ground is almost stationary. Just a fractional residual drift backwards. Twenty seconds. Ease back the main throttle from sixteen point five to ten per cent. The ADV begins to fall.

"Nine metres. Eight. Seven. Six. Five."

Dust blowing out under them. Throttle out to twenty per cent, then straight back to sixteen point five.

"Four point five. Four dead."

Ten seconds to the red line. Throttle to eighteen per cent.

"Three point five. Three point five. Three dead."

Throttle to fifteen per cent. Four seconds to the line. Dust blowing in a radial fan out from beneath the ADV.

"Two point five. Two point five. Two dead. Contact light forward."

The forward footpad scraped up a little wash of dust. Red line. Over the red line. The ADV still settling, tipping backwards – three degrees of tilt. A rock squeezed out from under the forward footpad and wobbled. Five seconds over the red line, five degree tilt.

"Contact light right."

Eight seconds over – eating into the hover reserve for landing back at Aldrin. If the tilt goes on you have to abort. Teetering back left – eight degrees, nine, ten. Twelve seconds over the line.

"Contact light left. Contact light rear."

Main throttle to ten per cent. Tilt angle twelve degrees. Steady at twelve degrees. Main throttle to five per cent, and a vague spray of dust still fanning out from under the ADV. Still steady at twelve degrees. Firm touchdown. Throttle to zero and the dust fan dies. Pump out. Valves closed. Still twelve degrees. Hydrogen tank pressures all steady. Oxygen pressures steady. Valves all confirmed closed. Not losing any propellant. Can afford to sit here long enough to run a preliminary post-flight. "Okay. We're down."

Browning nodded.

Outside was the blinding sunstrip in front of them, and the shadowed terrace and the scarp wall beyond. No more dust fan or little rolling chunks or chips of rock. Everything was

as motionless as time again, the eternal static world of the
Moon.

"You went –" Browning looked at the frozen figures for
the propellant reserve mass and at the time counter.
"– twenty-two seconds over the red line."

"I was sure the site was good. It is. Twelve degrees is
okay."

Browning nodded. "Leaves us with seventy-eight seconds
hover time back at Aldrin."

"I can land at Aldrin on less than that." A man who can
set down on Tsiolkovsky peak, or on a ledge on the vast
inside slope of the north wall of Schrödinger – maybe he can
do anything. Aldrin, with a ground radar track to help all
the way, was easy if you stayed careful. That was all you
had to do – stay very, *very* careful. "Okay. Let's do the
post-flights."

One hour after touchdown they had run the preliminary and
then the full series of post-flight checks. The ADV was in
perfect condition and its computer was happy and knew
exactly where it was sitting on the Moon. Its return flight
program was read in and holding, and once they initiated the
twenty-second final countdown the computer would be able
to run the liftoff and ascent burn automatically, throwing
them on course back to Tsiolkovsky. They just had to do the
pre-flight checks, and then initiate the countdown.

The view out of the tiny left side port showed the terrace
narrowing away and vanishing totally into shadow. The sunlit
lips of other terraces were arrayed further west and far below.
Out of the right side port they could see how the terrace
broke up a thousand metres away where a huge gully cut
down through the shadowed mountainside. The view behind
was of the floor of Schrödinger far below, running downsun
southward to the jagged little lumps of the low inner ring of
the Cat. The Cat should have caught the EIS-1 vehicle – it
might have been an easier job there.

In front of the pair of forward windows was sunlit rocky
rubble, and then the shadow edge thirty metres away. Right
at the edge, bisected by the shadow line, was a huge flat slab
of rock. It must have come tumbling down from above,

shaken loose by the tremor of a moonquake or of some large meteorite impact far away, and slammed down to rest here on the gentle slope of the terrace. It had been lying here ever since, the forward edge of its flat top tasting the heat of the sun for forty or fifty hours every month, every noon, and otherwise in perpetual darkness. It had never made it out into the light, it had ground to a halt still gripped by the shadow. How long ago? A year – a thousand years? A thousand million years? Such changeless times were possible on the Moon. Schrödinger could be two or three or four times older still. A mere human lifetime is meaningless here.

Looking straight from the sunlit ground into the shadow, they could see nothing, they were contrast blinded. But if they let their eyes adapt long enough they could see dim details in the backwash light from the surrounding bluffs and crests and terraces and from the vast white-lit plain below. With eyes shaded from the foreground and from the point fire of the sun, or better still through the narrow field of binoculars, they could see their target two thirds of the way up to the sun-rimmed ridge above them.

"You put us down perfect, Morris. It's right up there in front of us."

A steep slope of scree and boulders, apparently a slope of talus cascaded down from the crest and compacted together over time, rose from just inside the shadow line. The huge flat slab was its vanguard in an abortive attempt to slide out into the sun. The talus started up gently but got steeper and steeper, rising to halfway up to the ridge before it met the even steeper breast of the shallow bluff above them. A little way up that upper slope was the fresh impact crater. *Any* crater is fresh for ever on the Moon, unless it is hit by another meteorite and rubbed out or buried, but no normal impact could make a circular dent in a hillside as steep as that. The object that produced it had been traveling almost horizontally – two hundred and twelve kilogrammes burn-out weight of modified EIS-1 rocket, Browning's and Bleazard's, Reeber's and Waterson's errant bird finding somewhere blind to roost.

"The regolith on that slope has got to be poised to come down, Morris. Must already have been unstable enough to be ready to make a landslip, and the impact will have shaken it some. The crater's undercut some of it. The upper rim looks ready to collapse."

Morris peered through his own pair of binoculars. If two hundred and twelve kilogrammes striking at one thousand five hundred and seventeen metres per second, a mile a second or thereabouts, didn't bring it down, then maybe Colonel Alan Browning was being over-optimistic until they'd tested the precariousness of the slope. The impact crater was a rough feature, all churned up regolith, all dirt and rocks. There seemed to be no melt features – the total impact energy had been low, and the ground already broken and unconsolidated and absorbent. A softer part of the Moon. Was that a tiny gleam of something in there?

"We'll take the long way around. The talus slope looks too risky to get up under it if we don't have to try. We'll take the route up in the gully to the right."

Morris swung his binoculars to look into the shallowly recessed and slope-sided little gully.

"Must be talus in there, but not so steep and loose, maybe. We go up to the ridge, onto the bluff, then I go down on a rope and place a bunch of charges. Then we come back and fire them."

Morris swung the field of view back to look at the crater. "How do we communicate when I'm on top and you're down under the slope? Set the EVA antenna here to relay?" There was a tiny point gleaming inside the crater. He was sure.

"That's what we'll have to do, Morris."

"I can see something glinting in the crater. Real small."

"Uh-huh. Your eyes must be better than mine. Don't see a thing."

"Maybe it's a piece of the vehicle. Is there debris up there?"

"No. Should be smashed into pieces smaller than your fingernail."

Then Browning was moving around. Morris took the binoculars from his eyes and blinked to get used to focusing at the cramped arm's length distances inside the ADV.

Browning put on the interior light, turned away and stooped to open the storage lockers in the side wall. He lifted things out, twisting and putting them up on top of the rear stores recess in front of the tiny viewing port. Two pistols, an ammunition box, and a thing the size of a hospital doctor's pocket pager.

"What's that?"

Browning looked round, looked up at Morris over his shoulder. "A radio detonator. I'll carry it with me."

They were supposed to be detonating the charges from inside the ADV, so that they could lift off immediately if it turned out they'd created a major landslide. "Why?"

"Just in case, Morris. If something happens and we can't get back to the ADV. If the Russians turn up and cut us off, maybe. Or an accident. I want to be able to fire those charges." He turned back to the lockers. "That's what it's all about, Morris. Firing those charges and burying that hole."

They could see well enough under the shadow of the ridge. The backwash light of noontime Schrödinger was far brighter than tropical moonlight on Earth. It was the contrast that blinded you. If you looked out at the brilliant plain below, then back into the shadow, you had to wait minutes until your eyes had fully adjusted again.

The first part of the ascent was an easy walk over rocks among the bigger boulders that littered the tipped-up terrace. But it grew steeper as the ridge reared above them under the stars – you could see a few hard pinpoint stars when you were so effectively screened from the blinding imperial light of the sun. Halfway up, and it was a struggle. Morris was weighted down – even in one sixth gee – by a coil of one hundred metres of four millimetre-diameter rope, a much more slender rope than you'd need to go mountaineering on the Earth. Browning was carrying a bundle of six seismic charges, things the size of a tall and fat aerosol can, each packed with a radio receiver circuit, an arming lock, a detonator, and five thousand Earth weight grammes of explosive. They still had another twelve stored on the external strap-racks of the ADV, but six should be enough.

From halfway up it was worse than a struggle. They were clambering over rubble and scree and outcroppings of rock.

Loose scree slid under their boots, and at each bad patch
they scrabbled with hands and feet to get inches higher to
the next firm handhold so they could haul themselves up and
clear. Their suits started out white, with Space Force shoulder
patches, double red arm and thigh rings for Browning and
single rings for Morris. Now the suits were dusted all over
and were filthy up to elbows and knees. No scree channel
could stay poised at such an angle in the gravitational field
of the Earth – it would spill down like a river of stones. No
boulders could have come to rest wedged so precariously in
a cleft on a terrestrial mountain – they would have gone
crashing on, bounced right across the terrace, and hurtled
away to the plain five thousand metres, almost seventeen
thousand feet, below. Here everything hung defiantly, daring
the prohibition of the vertical. It was an impossible world.
On Earth it would have been an impossible climb.

It was two hundred metres straight up, a mere six hundred
and fifty feet, and it took them two and one quarter hours.
They tottered up over the lip of the gully into the visual blast
of the sun and snapped down their gilded visors. They picked
rocks and sat on them, feet splayed, two filthied white
spacesuits facing each other, reflecting each other tiny in
the convex miniaturized worlds of the sunvisors. Your own
breathing rasps in your throat and bounces back at you from
the inside of your faceplate. A second symphony of gasping
breaths sounds in your ears direct from inside that other suit.

They climbed up the easier and sun-slanted slope westward, onto the narrow and boulder-strewn top of the shallow
bluff that jutted from the ridge. A view! A perfect circle of
exquisite scenery, razor sharp in the harsh light that knew
only two tones – brilliant, and shadow-black. The crest of the
north wall marched away, broken and almost imperceptibly
curved, to east and west and vanished on the sudden horizon.
Right around the north lay an empty and cratered terrain
that fell rapidly away and then blended into a jumbled chaos
of shadows and sunlit rims and ridges and pyramid peaks,
all of them stopping abruptly at the broken edge of the world.
And south was the inner plain of Schrödinger, made smooth
by the low-angled sun at their backs – an arcing plain that
extended out to the crumbled, jumbled ring of the Cat over

sixty kilometres distant. As far again beyond the Cat was the center of Schrödinger. The rock that blasted this giant crater in the face of the Moon two or three billion years ago would have been the size of a large asteroid, bigger than any ordinary flying mountain. Nothing like the puny, idiotic one hundred and fifty kilogrammes of Blue Bolt. It was a splendid, motionless, lifeless, eternal scene in slow-frozen noon. Just himself and another spacesuit to look at it all, and the gold-glittering ADV perched on the sunlit edge of the first terrace down below like a patient sentinel from the stars. And above it all a black cowl of absolute nothingness.

Browning was casting about down the slope that tumbled over to the escarpment drop. He was lining himself up with the glittering marker of the ADV. He stopped. Morris jogged down the slope towards that mechanical man who had thoughts only for Clean Sweep, a mission more vital and precarious than the Blue Bolt operation that had preceded it. Morris slid and skidded to a halt with dug in heels at the point where the shadows of the little rocks started to mesh over the ground. The slope was convex, about to tip over into the steep drop to the talus pile one hundred metres further down. That would kill you outright even in the gentle gravity of the Moon, even without a rupturable spacesuit around you. It was a dizzy drop into a contrast pool of impenetrable shadow.

Browning's suit turned to look at him, then turned away and crossed to a flattish chunk of rock a couple of metres across and bedded into the thin debris of the regolith, of the thin mountaintop soil. Browning climbed around to the upper side and pushed at it hard a couple of times, his breath coming loud and sharp in Morris's ears. Then he straightened up. "Guess this is solid enough. We'll tie on here. Then you take the rope for me and over I go. Switch to the ADV's EVA channel, Morris."

A click in his ears, and Browning's breathing vanished. Looking down at the instruments mounted on the chest of his suit, he turned the frequency control until the preset channel showed in the readout window. Click, and Browning's lifebreath was back.

Browning went over the edge and on down carefully while

Morris paid out the anchored rope. Sometimes Browning had enough purchase on the slope to support himself, sometimes Morris was taking part or all of his weight as he abseiled down a section. That wasn't difficult – Morris could have held him one-handed. A man plus suit, plus PLSS on his back, weighed no more on the Moon than a third of what the man alone would weigh on the Earth. That wasn't the danger. The danger was from dislodged rocks coming down on top of Browning. He had to pick a straight route down that didn't stretch the rope over or around anything that looked unsafe. He had to keep coming back up a section and start over again. It took forty minutes before he got down beside the impact crater. They had a maximum of six hours, plus a thirty-minute reserve, in the PLSSs on their backs, and soon it would be time to start around for the haven of the ADV down there.

Still on the rope, Browning crossed the slope sideways into the crater. He found that the upturned floor was of loose material with unconsolidated rock fragments, some of them freshly sheared and splintered. Out of sight but talking over the ADV's relay antenna, he instructed Morris to take in the rope and hold him while he got up inside the upper rim excavated by the impact of the EIS-1 vehicle. He bedded the six seismic charges in a line under the rim, placed so as to bring down the stuff poised above the crater. The ground collapsed in bucketfuls as he worked. He said it was kind of tricky – it must have been awful, an impediment and a constant danger. The man was no second-rater, and that was for sure. Morris had never heard Colonel Alan Browning swear – the man said nothing acute or in any way uncouth, and though he talked smoothly and easily he said little more than the necessary and relevant at any time. But down there on the end of the rope, he cursed over and over again.

It took a mere fifteen careful minutes to haul him up, and another five to coil the rope neatly. Browning held something out to Morris, a piece of twisted and shiny metal with sheared edges, no bigger than the palm of his glove. The glinting thing had been a part of the EIS-1 rocket after all, lying there on the upturned floor of the crater, some anonymous fragment of plating skin stripped clean to pure bare metal by the flash heat of the impact. Morris put the souvenir into the thigh pocket of his suit, the one holding the modified gun, and zipped it closed.

They walked down to the point where the gully dropped away into inky shadow, went over the edge and then paused until their eyes had adjusted to the absence of the sun again. Carefully, not wanting to plunge headlong or else get caught in a rockslide, not wanting to tear their suits or crack their helmets, smash their PLSSs or just break a wrist or ankle, they took an hour getting down.

They climbed the egress ladder mounted on the front leg of the ADV, squirmed through the egress door, stood up inside and started brushing themselves down and sweeping the debris and dust of the Moon out through the door. Then they closed the door, pressured up the ADV, and got out of their suits five hours after they had begun the EVA. They were tired, with the muscles of their arms and legs, backs and shoulders aching as if they'd spent an entire day working out in some maniac's fitness center. They exchanged the spent oxygen, CO_2 scrubbers, batteries and filters in the two PLSS packs for fresh units, and then they ate cold rations and drank a litre or two of sweetened fruit juice. It would all come out again at the other end, but that was what the ADV's supply of urine bags was for. Life together in an ADV is very intimate.

Nine hours after they touched down. The preflights were through, and the countdown on the pre-programed computer had been run to a hold at T minus two seconds. At T minus one point eight the oxidant and fuel pumps would start to run, at minus one point four the tank valves would open, at minus zero point eight propellant mix would start to flush into the combustion chamber, and at minus zero point two the ignition arc would fire. Morris just had to press the hold key again to release the countdown, and exactly two seconds later the ADV would start up vertically out of the way of any landslide rushing down towards them. There was nothing left to wait for.

Browning was peering up at the impact crater through binoculars. "Doesn't look as if any of the charges have fallen out." He lowered the binoculars, then put them back in a sidewall locker and latched the door closed. "Okay to go, Morris?"

Morris nodded.

Browning tapped computer board keys on his rightside panel, calling up the preset detonation signal and opening a channel through one of the ADV's antennas. "Okay. Close your eyes for the flash, and then open them right away to see what's coming at us. Stand by. Firing - now."

The faint click of the computer key. A little flash seen through closed eyelids. No other sound. He opened his eyes.

Up there in the shadow, a plume of dust and debris was bursting out of the slope a third of the way down from the summit. A symmetrical bloom of striated feathers spreading up, out, forward and down. It expanded into a spray of arcing things inside a cloud of dust – no turbulence because there was no air to tumble through. Some of the pieces arched up into the sunlight and caught glinting fire as they turned their facets over and over. A silver haze of parabola dust reached into the sun's realm and made its lightstream visible. Ejecta from the explosion expanded out and down towards them. Rocks struck back onto the slope below the crater. With no buoyant air to keep it afloat, the haze of dust fell back into darkness. Pieces of rock hit the sloping ground at the back of the terrace. A bright lit little piece came spinning down and dropped soundlessly onto the ground a few metres in front of the ADV, kicking aside a wave of dust that flopped back in a tiny parabolic loop.

Morris put his finger over the hold key. Browning shook his head at Morris and looked back out.

. A boulder came bouncing down the talus slope in a stream of dust and rubble. It started to roll on down towards them amid plumes of sidethrown dust. It rolled. It slowed. It stopped, still a good twenty metres above the foot of the talus slope.

. And that was it. Morris looked at the little rock that had landed in front of them. It was only the size of a grapefruit, but after flying that far it could have crippled the ADV or even ruptured the crew compartment and killed them. A cold little reminder of personal mortality.

Browning looked up at the crater. He took out the binoculars and inspected it for long minutes. The dust had settled as suddenly and silently as it had sprung out from the face of the scarp. Dust settles very quickly on the Moon.

"Hell," Browning said quietly.

"Not good?"

"It's slipped some, but that's all. And I'd have thought a good cough would bring that whole hillside down."

Morris shrugged. "It's stood for a couple of billion years or more. Compared to that, Mount Everest hasn't even been born. Maybe it's a tough slope." And that was a stupid notion. It could just as easily poise undisturbed on a feather balance for a billion years or two, waiting for a little push.

"We'll have to try again. Be tricky this time. That ground's really got to be ready to go now." Browning took his eyes from the binocular cups and looked round at Morris. "We'd better get some sleep. Shifts – one of us has to watch that slope the whole time to be ready if it suddenly goes spontaneously. We don't want to be caught asleep and swept back over that edge behind us. Four hours each. Like to take the first turn, Morris, or the first watch?"

The edge of the shadow had crept closer to the ADV, swallowing the flat slab boulder, returning it to its absolute-cold hibernation for another twenty-six days. The sun had moved past noon.

They took all twelve remaining seismic charges. Browning took his radio detonator, they each took a gun zipped into the thigh pocket of their suits. Browning had decided they should split up for this attempt. Morris was to go up the gully again and onto the summit of the bluff, then work his way as far as he could down its face and lower four charges bundled together on a length of rope. They would dangle against the slope immediately above the impact crater, giving the material poised to slide there an extra kick when the charges were fired. Browning took eight charges and started straight up the talus slope at the back of the terrace towards the crater. He intended to put the charges in a line in order that the new blast would so undercut the loose regolith on the slope that it just had to come down. He didn't like the prospect of climbing up that loose and probably unstable and rubble-littered slope with a mountainside hanging over him, but the mission had to go through and they *had* to get it right. A second mission in another month, waiting until the light was right, might run right into Russians. Their luck couldn't hold every time, and the United States was depending on them.

Part way up the gully, struggling and sliding, Morris paused and looked west through the shadow. There on the talus slope around one hundred and fifty metres away was another white spacesuit, already filthy again, scrambling and clawing its way slowly upwards, half the time slipping back almost as far as it had advanced. They should have come with two or three ADVs, a fully equipped mountaineering team, and above all the time to string lifting and safety ropes. Whoever it was in the Pentagon, whether Reeber of Lunar Section or Waterson of Special Operations – whoever it was who'd dreamed up Clean Sweep and then done it to their loyal and dutiful Colonel Alan Browning and had seconded Morris and mixed him up in it, they were insane. A secret low-profile, two-man mission in a hurry. And all just to clear up the idiotic mess they'd made of Blue Bolt, which didn't make any sense anyway. It took your automatic confidence in Space Force and squeezed the life right out of it. There was Browning flinging himself dedicatedly up an all but lethal hillside, not to rescue any comrade from danger, not to save any American man, woman or child from the threat of invasion and death. Just to do his best to save a bunch of generals and politicians from embarrassment. It was cynical and utterly senseless.

Morris turned his gaze back into the towering cleft of the shadowed gully. He dug his gloved fingers into the loose soil, stamped a grip of sorts with the side of his boot, got his knee onto the slope and hauled himself up towards the next protruding rock. No sense at all.

It took him only two hours to climb the gully this time. Once he was out high enough to see down to the ADV again he checked over the relay with Browning. The man had just got past the top of the talus and was on the steeper upper slope above. At least there the material was better consolidated and the going was safer, mostly. He was climbing with hands and feet over jammed-together rocks. Some of them kept coming loose, though. Kind of nasty.

Morris got up onto the narrow summit of the bluff. He ignored the magnificent view. They were in a hurry – it was already nineteen and a half hours after liftoff from Aldrin when they had depressed the ADV to begin this second EVA. He moved down the front face of the bluff a little way until his shadow was so long it reached right over the edge into empty space. Following the messed-up multiple tracks of their footprints from the first visit, he got down to the rock where they'd tied on the last time. Going down there, Browning had come out beside the crater, so Morris cut to the right across the rock-strewn slope, moving some way

west to bring himself level right above the impact crater. He
picked a big pointed rock that seemed firmly bedded, tied
on the rope, and then with the rope in one hand he set off
down the steepening slope. Dust flopped aside from his boots
as he dug his feet in at every descending step. Little pieces
of rock rolled and bounced away over the convex edge ahead
of him. The shadows of the rocks and rubble merged on the
slope as it curved away from the sun. His feet went into
shadow, cut off at the ankles. He took it further carefully,
until he judged the slope had reached forty-five degrees, and
he was half supporting his weight on the rope, and he was
up to his knees in darkness. If the sun had been a point, not
a little disc, he would have been able to wave to his own
shadow way down there almost at the lip of the next precipice
in front of the golden glittering ADV. But his shadow blurred
out across all those slanted metres of vacuum. He daren't go
any further. He made a bend in the rope, snapped the loop
into the carabiner on the front of his suit harness, and sat
down with his legs splayed and his heels dug into the loose
and treacherous soil of dust and rock chips. When it moved
under your feet it moved silently, no chinking and clinking
and klirring of little rocks rattling down a scree slope in the
lee of a mountain top on Earth. There was no air to carry
any sound. He was up above a vast amphitheatre of perfect
silence, a quieter and a more eternal place than Olympus,
and much, much higher. Higher than any earthly gods had
ever been.

He unhitched the bundle of four charges, twisted and
locked their arming rings, and tied them to the end of the
rope. He swung the charges right out in front of himself and
let them drop onto the slope and slither a little further down.
The bundle stopped about ten metres below him. By shaking
and whipping the rope he got the bundle to slip, slither and
roll further until it was out of sight. From then on he could
only work by feel. When the rope went slack as he paid it
out he knew the charges had snagged on something, and he
had to jiggle and shake the rope to free them. They snagged
every few metres. Sometimes he had to stand up and whip
the rope from side to side with wide arm movements to free
them again.

It took a long time to pay out fifty metres of rope.

He opened the relay channel and called Browning. "Alan, how you doing?"

A click as Browning switched on his transmitter in response. "Fine, Morris. You?"

"Got the charges placed, I hope. Can you see them, maybe?"

"Hold on while I get back from here." An interlude of exerted breath as Browning moved around down there. "Yeah. That's good, Morris. Real good. They're at around ten to twelve metres up above the crater, nice and central. Just tie off the rope there. That'll do fine."

"Okay. How are you making out?"

"Fine." There was a pause, with breath. Morris looked down at the ADV, sunlit and golden right on the margin of the advancing shadow as the sun slowly moved down the sky. Behind and below the ADV were the sunstrips of other terraces, and five thousand metres down was the floor of Schrödinger. "Just have the last two charges to put in. I'm right inside the crater. Our first blast near excavated it, Morris. You should see this. There's real wreckage here. Mostly little pieces, but some regular chunks. Right beside me there's the casing from a fuel pump. There's a piece of piston shaft from one of the motor gimbal actuators. There's around half the combustion chamber flange, and pieces of sheeting or ribbing buried in the ground. Half of the EIS-1 must be here in recognizable pieces. Must be the combination of collapsible structure plus soft ground here did it. I'd have thought it would end up like matchwood."

"That's another point where the guys who dreamed up Blue Bolt were wrong." Morris opened his thigh pocket and took out the little piece of shiny buckled metal – his private souvenir.

"Guess you could always look at it that way, Morris. I'm just about finished here. I put four charges in a line across the slope under the crater. Each one's under a biggish rock so it can blast it out and encourage more to collapse, maybe. The other four I'm putting inside the crater under the upper rim again. Two are in and just two more to go. The rim's mostly been undercut by the first blast and overhangs some now, maybe a metre and a half at the widest. With four charges right along under that, this time we'll bring something down okay."

"Sounds good." It meant they could fire the charges, then lift off in the ADV and arc on back to Aldrin.

"It does, Morris. We're at just on a hundred seventy minutes into the EVA. Maybe you should start on down."

"Okay. I'll check with you next time I'm far enough down the gully to see the ADV."

He tied off the rope and left the spare coiled up right where it was. There was no danger about a Soviet expedition turning up one day and finding the rope, footprints and the ADV landing pad marks. They already knew of the impact crater – what mattered was that they never found any evidence to link it with an unnatural cause. Traces of an American scientific expedition trying to gather data on a meteorite impact were no threat to the international credibility of the US Government.

Morris climbed up along the rope to where it was tied around the boulder, then he struck ahead straight up towards the brow of the slope. He came up west of the crest of the bluff and headed up and around the north side of it to go more or less over the top. He came up just short of the very top, and figured he had five minutes to spare on the view. Such a magnificent view a man never saw before – well, just he and Browning around twelve or so hours ago, and Browning apparently hadn't been too interested. But apart from at Tsiolkovsky, and maybe any exploratory hops the Russians had made into the interior of Mare Orientale, no one had been anywhere much on Far Side before – certainly not *here*. And no one had ever been so near to one of the poles.

He should have had a camera to photograph the panorama, the details, anything and everything, the breathtaking sight of the golden ADV sitting down there with a sheer drop almost at its back and a vast crater floor five thousand metres further down behind it. NASA would have sent them here with cameras. The Pentagon sent them with explosives and guns. Wasted, a wasted opportunity. He gazed around the magnificent sweep south into Schrödinger, printing it onto his mind to keep for the rest of his life. He looked along the ridge of the north wall running barely curved out to the west, a deep rampart of trapped shadows dropping onto the enclosed plain. Around the north, a crystal clear chaotic landscape of craters and valleys and peaks shadow-stroked by the slowly sinking sun. The ridge of the north wall again as it ran off in sweeps and breaks into the east, closing the huge circle around Schrödinger.

Something glinted. Some little glass-bright speck. Something kilometres away, down north of the ridge in among the foreshortened jumble of craters and chasms. Some bright little point of mirrored sunlight. It hadn't been there the last time he looked, not the previous time he was up here – it was too bright for both of them to have missed it. Must be six or eight or more kilometres away – that would put it a good two and a half or three kilometres north of the ridge. Three kilometres north of the ridge on the outer slope of the north wall, eight kilometres to the east of the target site. That was where there was a piece of ground level and clean enough to land on. Except from there they would have needed a buggy to get up to the site in reasonable time, and the ADV couldn't carry a buggy on this long-hopping mission.

But a Soviet lander could.

That tiny brilliant speck had to be the reflective flank or the flat window of a big Soviet lander. Then he noticed the line.

A tiny little line was laid across the lifeless land in sections going up and down, disappearing into and reappearing out of folds in the ground. He lifted his sunvisor to let the blinding dazzle flood his face, and screwed up his eyes to look at that line. It had to be the wheel tracks of a vehicle driven towards the site, climbing slowly over the broken terrain on a diagonal course up to the ridge. The track disappeared one last time into a sharp dip in the northward sloping ground, no more than a thousand metres away.

Jesus Christ. They were going to come up out of that dip any second and see him, a figure in a white suit in the sun standing up on the skyline in front of them. And get off the skyline! He started to move, and then stopped.

If he headed down the east slope towards the head of the
gully, he would be caught out in the open if they appeared
before he was safely down. Any second now. What do you
do? Kneel behind a boulder, draw your gun and wait until
they're the ones caught in the open a hundred or two hundred
meters away, then pick them off all bunched together on
their buggy? Kill them just for driving towards him? That
was no option, even if he could shoot straight enough. There
was nothing else for it but to back off on the blind slope to
the west, go down to the dip between the bluff and the next
rise in the ridge, and try to find a way down to the terrace
and the ADV.

He turned around and fled from the skyline, his feet
skidding inside slopping dust sprays on the steepening slope.
He paused to look down to his left. He couldn't see the ADV
yet so he couldn't call Browning on the relay. No time to
mess around – get on down and call him just as soon as the
ADV was in line of sight again. Both of them had to get
back to the ADV and lift off out of there.

Morris ran down the slope into the dip on the ridge and
cast about over the scarp. He was still unsighted from the
ADV by the breast of the bluff. He looked back at the
skyline above as if Soviet tanks or something were going to
appear there. They weren't going to come shooting – why
should they? Because of what we did to their base, that's
why. Right below was what looked like a possible way down
the scarp, so he set off running.

Within twenty metres he was completely out of control on
a sliding cascade of dirt and rocks and grinding grains that
carried him down like a carpet of dark gray water. He fell
on his side, scrabbled with his arms, went bouncing and
tobogganing down in a one-man avalanche. Then he jolted
to a halt on the top side of a boulder that twisted around
under him. Dirt, rocks and rolling slabs were going past him,
pebbles rattling on his helmet and shoulders. He pulled down
the visor over his faceplate to protect it. Something sharp
slammed into the visor and cracked it. Through the cracked
and crazed visor a sloping river of stones ran darkly and
dustily down right in front of his face. Something huge rolled
past and disappeared. He hung onto the pitched-up face of

the Moon like he was going to fall off into the empty cosmos.

After a few minutes the last trickles had dried up and everything around him was motionless. He lifted the broken visor, feeling dust grate in the hinges. Jesus Christ, but this was a dumb way to try to get down. He lifted his body away from the slope. The boulder his feet were planted on moved some – then caught again. He breathed once more, a heavy breath that bounced off the inside of his faceplate. He seemed to be around halfway down to the shadowed terrace. The slope looked a little less steep further below. Still no sight of the ADV yet. He was shaking. He was *shaking* as he half sat, half lay and altogether more or less stood there. He'd found the part of the scarp that did come down in a landslide if you as much as coughed. Get over the shakes for a couple of minutes – the hurry isn't so much that you should kill yourself in a fall of moondust. Wait, then go on down. And *slowly*. Slow and careful, go on down.

The lander flight was all right – the liftoff with backs to bright earthlight, the midcourse orbital transfer burn, the descent burn, the long hover over the allegedly easier piece of ground, the maneuver towards a minimal gap between boulders and craterlets, the final cautious touchdown. All that had been under Leonid's own control. But this was different. Tsherbakov drove the rover as if he was obsessed with some race against time.

They sat on the open vehicle, Tsherbakov driving and Leonid in the webbed seat beside him, with Major Maria Alova on one of the pair of seats behind. At the back of the vehicle, behind the power packs and the dish aerial mast, the loading racks were filled with ropes and climbing equipment. Their suits were connected by umbilicals to the rover's own life-support systems and they were plugged into its direct communication circuit. And Leonid clung to the grab bars as Tsherbakov sent them bouncing around craterlets and between boulders, steadily tracking upwards and nearer to the rearing ridge line. Time after time the rover went diving down into a fold in the mountainside and then shot up out of it again, mesh wheels spinning and dust shooting around in plumes in all directions. Twice on the way down into a gully he thought the colonel from the State Committee was going to let the vehicle tip right over and somersault to the bottom. Once on the way up the other side the front wheels came off the ground and he was sure they would tumble over backwards. The mad rush was because Tsherbakov had seen something – *something* – while on the way down for the landing. Leonid had been too busy with the landing site and Maria too concerned with watching how he brought them down safe. But in a momentary glance along the north wall towards the impact site, Tsherbakov had thought he saw *something*.

They came up out of the bottom of the last big gully, Tsherbakov snapping the steering joystick around and turning the wheels against the crabwise slide of the rover, correcting to go up the slope, catching the crabwise falloff again. Dust shot everywhere. The rover leaped up out of the gully onto the upper canted mountainside. Tsherbakov throttled back the power and drove them to a halt just under the brow of the ridge. They stopped tilted sideways below the final ridge on ground that fell away to the right, to the north, towards the sun. In front of them another dip in the ground cut across the ridge, and on the other side rose the low-browed bluff, the very highest piece of ground, below which was the impact crater stamped into the face of the escarpment that dropped down into the walled plain of Schrödinger. Tsherbakov lifted a gloved hand and pointed across towards the sunlit flank of the bluff.

"Footprints," said Maria Alova's voice direct in Leonid's ears. "Lines of footprints."

"Someone's here," Tsherbakov said. "Or been here. We'll continue on foot. Switch to radio communication."

"Is that a good idea?" said Maria's voice. "If the Americans are still here they might pick up our transmissions and –"

"They don't use the same frequencies." A click as he disconnected the communication lead from the socket of his suit.

Leonid disconnected his own lead and switched to the radio channel, using the wheel and button controls on the upturned little panel on the chest of his suit. He opened the locking ring where the umbilical joined the left side of his backpack, and disconnected it. He checked the chest instruments to be sure that his backpack had automatically taken over all the life-support functions, then let the umbilical wind itself back under the seat. He clambered out of the vehicle and stepped onto the sloping gritty dirt of the Moon – literally the dust of ages under his feet.

Tsherbakov in his ears. "You two go around the ridge here, and see if you can get a view across to the impact site down on the face. I'll go onto the bluff and see where those footprints lead. We can relay to each other over the rover's transceiver, but it's better if we keep in direct sight of each other. If you get right over the horizon and out of radio contact, get back again. Constant communication has the first priority until we know what's been going on." Tsherbakov's suit turned to them, a dulled sun reflecting down off its dark visor. "And be careful. All right?"

"Yes," said Maria's voice.

"Don't go beyond the top of the bluff," Leonid said. "See what you can see, then either you come back or we'll drive up to you."

"Right," Tsherbakov said. Then his tall white suit turned and set off at a fast jog, down the slope into the dip below the bluff. You can cover ground very quickly by jogging on the Moon, bouncing along like a long jumper with all the ease of a fitness fan making a morning circuit of Gorky Park.

Behind his own sunvisor, Leonid turned his head to look across at Maria Alova's visored suit where it stood waiting beside the rover, with the ridge crest and the black sky beyond it. "Come on," he said, and started walking towards the falloff at the end of the ridge.

Tsherbakov's voice spoke in their ears two minutes later. His white-suited figure was hurrying up out of the dip onto the sun-slanted side of the bluff over there, its hugely elongated shadow stilting upwards beside it. "The footprints are all trampled together. Looks like at least two sets going each way. The tracks break off in the dip towards the edge of the scarp. Might have tried getting down that way."

Maria, answering. "They couldn't have gone down over

the front of the bluff. It's too steep. Not without ropes,
anyway."

The bluff fell in deep dark shadow from its brow into a
face that dropped down at something like seventy degrees
or more. It plunged out of sight, cut off by the convex fall
of the end slope they were starting to descend. Between
them and the bluff, down out of sight, was the gully that cut
up steeply into the scarp from the terrace below. They could
see past the raised bluff and right along the slightly curving
sunlit ridge to the west – no tiny American figures wandering
about far away up there. The scarps and walls below the
ridge on the inner slope were all lost in deep black shadow
cut by an occasional terrace or tumbling promontory that
reached out into the shallow sun. Left of them was the open
expanse of Schrödinger and the jagged little hills of the inner
ring, sixty kilometres away and isolating the center of the
vast circular plain. It was a breathtaking, brilliant sight.

They came so far down and forward that they could see
the sunlit strip of terrace edge that protruded out of the
shadow below the bluff. And they could see the little technological glittering thing parked between the shadow margin
and the next sheer drop. Leonid stopped, his heels skidding
slightly. In his ears Maria's breath caught, and her suit
stopped suddenly beside him in the edge of his visored field
of view.

"Oh," she said.

Colonel Alan Miles Browning had just placed the last charge
into the hollow he'd scooped with his hand into the compacted regolith right under the overhang that stretched across
the top of the tipped-up crater on the steep and sheer
mountainside. Its radio receiver and detonator circuit cap
protruded neatly, marked dimly red-and-white for danger in
shadows lit only by weakly backwashed sunlight. He slithered
carefully down clear of the overhang, straightened up, and
turned to survey the crater scar with its churned-up roof-
pitched floor of rocks and grit and pieces of metal, fragments
of that darned malfunctioning carrier rocket that had brought
him to this ridiculous and ridiculously dangerous place. The
Moon was someplace where duty to your country coupled

with your own personal perfectly matched skills might bring you, but it wasn't any place you liked to be. Least of all halfway up a mountainside that was poised to collapse around you. Well, he had four charges in a line below the crater, four along the upper edge, and four more placed by Morris against the slope right above. That would move the mountainside okay and bury this wreckage and the mess it had made once and for all. Time to get back to the ADV down there.

Morris's voice in his ears over the relay circuit. "Alan, you hear me?"

"Hear you, Morris. How far down are you?"

"Right down. I'm on the terrace around six or seven hundred metres west of you. Can't see your position yet."

"*West* of me? How –?"

"There's a Soviet lander parked along the north wall, east of our position. Maybe eight or nine klicks, over on the north side. Must have come down while I was busy with the charges up there."

"They're here?"

"They're sure coming. I spotted a ground vehicle trail coming up towards the bluff. Most of the way there. They'll be here any time. Finish off up there and start on down to the ADV right away. We have to lift off out of here."

"We have to fire the charges and check the result."

"We can fire them right at liftoff, Alan. Just get on down to the ADV."

Russians. The damn Russians got here after all. Well not fast enough, just not quite fast enough. "You get along there, Morris. Run, man. You'll get there ahead of me. Set up for an immediate liftoff. We'll go without pressuring up or getting out of the suits. Just stay in the shadow so they don't see you on the way across the terrace. You reckon they'll be up on the ridge right now?"

"They have to be heading for the bluff over the site. They'll see our tracks up there."

He started moving carefully across the sloped mess of rock and metal debris that littered the interior of the crater, both feet and his left hand to steady himself as he moved towards the shallow rim of the impact scar. "Morris, if they pin me down up here, if I can't get to the ADV – you lift off. You have to lift off back to Aldrin, and as you go you have to fire these charges. Is that clear?"

A pause. "I don't think I can do that to you, Alan."

"Morris, that's an order. You fire the charges if I don't get down from here."

"I don't think I could do that. Just get on down."

He reached the canted lip of the crater and looked up towards the blindingly illuminated ridge high above him to the east. "Get to the ADV and clear for liftoff. I'm checking the ground above me right now." And what was wrong with Morris Gates? Was he too soft for the job? An officer should have enough sense to obey an order in a crisis, with or without tears in his eyes, and not debate it. He looked up at the blindingly bright, fire-spilled crest above the looming shadow around him, destroying his dark adapted vision for a moment.

And he saw two even brighter specks, little figures on the end slope across the top of the gully there, around seventy or eighty metres above him and a hundred and twenty or so along the north wall. Those were the Russians up there, and they had to be able to see the ADV in the sun on the terrace below, and when they shaded their eyes to search the shadows they would see him, too. He was so high, so very high up above the plain of Schrödinger, so nearly at the crest of the wall. But they had the highest ground of all.

There was no other option. He had to try to get down to the ADV alive and unhindered. There was a real risk that Morris wouldn't have the guts to fire the charges if he had to lift off alone, and firing the charges was the only sense in the entire business. So he couldn't just set off down the steep and exposed talus slope below the crater and hope to dear God they didn't start anything from up there. He had to move first while he still had the brief advantage of invisibility and surprise.

He unzipped his right thigh pocket and pulled out the automatic pistol, a solid thing but shrunken slightly in the bulky spacesuit glove. He cocked it and slipped off the safety catch. He steadied himself on the rim of the crater, his weight on his left knee and shin, with his right leg stemmed straight and the boot dug into the loose sloping dirt. He lifted the gun and took aim with both hands. They wouldn't hear the concussion of the shot, the whine of the bullet or even the thud of the impact if he missed and hit the ground – there was no air to carry a single sound. They wouldn't have any idea where he was firing from. Just aim steady and it's a perfect ambush. Ducks in a barrel. At that range on the Moon you should be able to point the gun straight, no need to compensate. Just aim steady and easy.

One of the white figures was now a little further down the slope, the other a little higher to the right with its arms raised to its helmet to shade its eyes and start searching the shadows below.

That one was the target.

Maria Alova had moved further down the slope towards the convex fallaway. Leonid stood higher up with a flat-topped boulder to his left, a chunk of rock flung here improbably onto the last slope under the very crest, perched up here for millions upon millions of years. There were rocks and boulders everywhere, debris ejected by a sparse billion-year rain of meteorites large and small, and not one of them ever hurled in anger before. He had his visor up and his hands raised to his faceplate, his right glove cutting out the sun and the bright flank of the bluff, his left hand held flat to screen off the immediate foreground, with forearm and elbow extended to cut out the plain of Schrödinger. He was trying to penetrate the shadow, searching for people. He could see the impact crater, more or less, side on and almost at the top of the steep breast of the bluff, up above the start of the talus slope.

Maria's voice in his ears. "See anything?" She was shading her eyes, too.

"Not yet." Although there was a little shadow of something on the crater rim there.

Tsherbakov's voice. "Only one line of footprints goes on down the far side of the bluff. Doesn't seem to come back. Apart from that one, they must have come up using the gully on your side."

Is that really a figure down there on the slope, a brighter spacesuit in the deep shadow?

Then a pinpoint flash. And a silent spurt of dust right in front of his feet.

A *bullet*? Burying itself into the ground, into the regolith, on the slope in front of him?

He sidestepped left. The boulder was to his left. "Maria!" She hadn't moved. She couldn't hear anything, of course, couldn't see the spurt of dust on the slope behind her, and wouldn't have seen the muzzle flash unless she was looking right at where the gun was fired. "He's shooting at us!"

"Who? Who's shooting?"

Another spurt of dust short of his feet on the slope. The man down there was aiming slightly too low. Aiming at *him*. "Maria! Get back here into cover!" He ran behind the boulder and skidded on his knees on the slope, turning.

Maria was facing him now and running up the slope, ploughing dust with her boots. Her visor was up and her face inside the helmet frightened. A spurt of dust burst right in front of her – the bullet had gone past her into the hillside. She veered towards the boulder. And then pitched onto her face on the slope.

A *plume* of sunlit gas fountained up from her back, a shimmering spray of air condensing into droplets and freezing in the vacuum. Her suit lay with its arms outstretched and its faceplate in the dirt. Her voice wailed in his ears.

The signal stuttered and the wail stopped.

The plume of escaping gas died back and disappeared.

"What happened?" Tsherbakov's voice. "What happened?"

Maria's suit lay motionless on the sunlit slope, no air left inside it to escape into the infinite vacuum.

"*What happened*?"

"Maria." Impossible. Completely impossible. "She's dead."

"*Dead*?"

Completely impossible. "Some bloody fool down there shot her. He punctured her suit. That killed her, even if the bullet wound didn't. Some bloody, bloody fool!"

"Fuck. I'm coming back." Andrei Tsherbakov's breath

was already uneven as he started to run. Across on the crest
of the bluff his blinding bright figure was running down the
flanking slope.

Leonid pulled down his visor to stop himself being blinded.
The world right around him came back into bearable visibility
again – the falling away and rock-littered hillside, the motionless spacesuit lying on its face. There was a pounding in
his throat like a flux of molten metal. It could have been
me.

"Can you get into cover? I can see you by the boulder.
Can you get into better cover?"

On the wide open hillside in the sun? "Not if the fool
down there keeps shooting."

"Can you shoot back?"

"Into that shadow?" And he'd forgotten he even had a
gun. "I can't even see him." Through the visor the shadow
was opaque.

And then a miracle.

Maria's suit moved. Its arms pulled in and then pushed
against the ground. The dead woman got onto her knees and
started crawling up the slope towards him.

"Maria? You're all right?" And no answer at all. Was
her radio dead? Just her radio? But the long plume of
air?

A spurt of dust blossomed on the ground immediately
beside her, another bullet burying itself in the regolith that
had accumulated over a thousand million years.

"Maria! Don't move!"

But she couldn't hear him and she crawled on desperately.
Another spurt right beside her. The bastard down there was
trying to murder her.

Leonid snapped open the buttons of the stomach pouch
attached to his suit. With one hand he pulled out the long
and clumsy and ridiculously fat-barreled shotgun-revolver,
lightweight on the Moon. With the other he pushed up the
sunvisor. With screwed up eyes he could see into the shadow.
He could see the little crouching figure at the edge of the
crater rim on the slope. He cocked the hammer and pointed
the revolver out over the top of the boulder two-handed.

He fired before he'd realized it and the silent gun knocked

him back into a sitting position on the ground above the boulder. He looked again, and the figure down there had gone.

Maria crawled the last metres up towards him and stopped on her hands and knees. He couldn't see her averted face because of the top of her helmet. He stuffed the gun back into its pouch and scrambled across to her.

Half sitting against the slope, he pulled at her shoulders. As she straightened up, her face appeared behind the face-plate. It was contorted. He took hold of her helmet with both hands, leaned forward and pressed his faceplate hard against hers.

"Maria? Are you hurt? How badly are you hurt?"

"Something –" Her muffled voice, transmitted from air to faceplate, to faceplate to air, cut off. Her eyes opened and blinked at him, centimetres away. "Something's pushing into my back."

"Can you feel blood?"

"No. But it hurts. It *hurts*."

Tsherbakov's panting voice. "What's going on? Did you get the bastard?"

"I don't know. He stopped shooting. Maria's hurt but she's alive. Her radio's out."

Maria blinked at him with unclear eyes. "My whole suit," said her muffled voice. "It's out. What happened?"

"You got a bullet in your back. Must have smashed right through your backpack. Let's have a look." He moved his helmet away and looked down at the dials mounted on the chest of her suit. Oxygen zero, coolant water zero, no power reading, coolant pump, air pump and radio dials all dark. She had no radio to talk with, and no oxygen to feed into her suit as she consumed what was left in the air inside it. She had no air pump to circulate the air through the CO_2 scrubber to clean out the accumulating gas that would knock her out and kill her even before the oxygen level had dropped too low. She had no pump working to circulate the coolant fluid in the inner garment that prevented her cooking slowly in her own body heat inside the insulated shell. In that state she would only last a few minutes. He leaned forward and touched helmets again. "How do you feel?"

"Hot. And dull. All sort of fuzzy. I've got too much CO_2, Leonid. I'm starting to suffocate."

"I know." He kept the faceplate contact so that the frightened woman a hand's width away in front of him could hear what he said even if she was deaf to Tsherbakov's replies. "Andrei? How far away are you?"

"Three – four minutes."

"Well keep running. Maria's suit is completely out. We have to get her back to the rover where she can use the umbilical. We'll have to carry her. If she tries to walk, the heat and CO_2 production will kill her in minutes."

"Understand." Tsherbakov was panting. "Can you start off? Carry her? Until I can help."

"I can start."

Maria's eyes blinked at him. He pulled her to her feet on the high sun-dazzled slope, and then pulled his visor down into place. With his backpack in the way, he had to carry her like a bride across a threshold. On the Moon, a woman plus spacesuit plus life-support backpack is still a manageable weight. But she was so bulky and balanced on his outstretched arms, and he was perched on a mountainside of loose grit and rubble, and he kept stumbling at every step.

There had been a simultaneous spray of dusty feather-fountains across the slanted slope in front of him. And a sharp sting above his right knee as if someone had tried to stab him with the point of an umbrella. And that was all except for the faint hissing noise.

Alan Miles Browning sat on the steep rubble of the impact crater, his right leg drawn up and bent double at the knee. Rocks and grit and the little metal shards of an errant rocket were scattered around him, above him was an overhang of regolith and rock and then half a mountainside above that, there was a dark drop to the barren terrace below and to the sun-dazzled ADV parked right out there on its edge – and beyond it all was the splendid open stony desolation of Schrödinger. The two suited figures had left the slope of liquid light which hovered up there to his left against the perfect black sky. It was a lonely, a very lonely place to die.

The itching, wriggling, bursting sensation in his nose finally

broke and blood ran over his lips, salted. It dribbled from
his lips in pulling drips, then the warm wetness soaked into
the Snoopy cap and ran over his chin and down his throat.
That was the depressurization. Swallow as often as he liked,
the pain in his ears persisted – and he couldn't catch the
falling pressure in his suit. The hiss transmitted through the
remaining air was barely audible, but under his glove, under
his right hand clamped tight over his right thigh just above
the knee, a knee he'd bent as far as he could so as to stretch
the suit fabric taut over his leg – under that glove, the air
was still escaping. Escaping far too fast, from such a tiny
hole punched through the suit, a little puncture clean through
the Kevlar-Teflon-Dacron anti-abrasion layer, the bonded
Kevlar layers, and the polyurethane-on-nylon pressure
bladder. Pressing so hard on the hole made the wound inside
in his thigh hurt like hell. But that didn't matter.

Blood went on streaming from his nose. When he licked
his irritated lips it flooded his mouth with sharp saltedness.
Blood is something that sticks around your teeth. He
swallowed it away. He looked at the chest instruments. Suit
pressure down to twenty-five per cent, oxygen valve fully
open and the gas flow rate maximum, twenty minutes oxygen
left at normal consumption. Two or three minutes only at
the present rate. When the thirty minute normal-use oxygen
reserve came on automatically, it would extend his life to a
full five or six minutes. The air inside his suit had to be almost
pure oxygen by now, the bulk of the normal nitrogen having
been flushed out. At a quarter – now less than a quarter –
atmospheric pressure, he'd be passing out if he wasn't on
almost pure oxygen. Pressure down to twenty-two per cent
and the hungry vacuum outside still winning, and it isn't
going to stop in time. Oh shit, this is really it. Better get it
said before the blood running down his chin ruined the
microphone in the Snoopy cap or something.

"Morris? You hear me?" Blood flowed stickily into his
mouth.

"Yes." And the panting breath of a runner in his ears.

"They got me, Morris. I've had it. My suit's holed." With
his left hand he unzipped his left thigh pocket.

"Your suit's holed?" The breath was still panting but the

words were no longer jogged. Morris Gates had stopped running somewhere down there on the terrace.

"They got the drop on me. They fired something at me. Some sort of shotgun, I guess. One little pellet went clean through my suit."

"They were *shooting* at you?"

"Just that one shot, but it went and did it. I saw them first and opened up. Got one of them, no sweat. Flattened him. But the other went and got me. Now he's picked up the dead one and run for it. So the way to the ADV's safe for you. I'm not going to make it."

"Alan, get on *down* here."

"Morris, I can't. I have just – just nineteen per cent pressure in my suit, and oxygen for maybe four minutes. The reserve just came on with its feed wide open." He swallowed the slimy blood swimming around his teeth. He lifted out the little pager-sized radio detonator and placed it carefully on the slope of his right thigh. "I'm not going to get out of this. And I don't want to –" Little black specks swimming and then shrinking away. "Uh, guess I'm getting into oxygen deficit by now. Getting kind of dizzy. I don't want to go this way and leave the mission half finished. Don't want to waste myself, you could say." With the thick gloved index finger of his left hand he tapped the *on* switch and then the *ready* button. The only two other keys on the device were *cancel* and *fire*. "Has to have some kind of sense."

"Alan, I can't get up to you in less than thirty or forty minutes. Maybe longer. Come on *down*, man. Down's easy – like a mud slide. You'll be down in ten minutes."

Black specks rotating in front of his eyes again, and shooting in and out through his thoughts like voids entering from the vacuum that waited outside his suit. "Pressure fourteen per cent and falling. Won't be more than a – minute or two before I pass out. So I – going to fire the charges, Morris. Has to work. You look out for yourself. Don't get caught in the slide."

"Alan, that's crazy!"

"Rather go the quick way." The flecks had grown to patches, holes in his sight. "Charges have to be fired, Morris." Even the taste and texture of blood had faded away. His legs were dissolving in a tingling mush. "Don't have any family of my own. Didn't work out so good. That's years ago. But my sister's – married with a couple of – couple of growed-up kids, and my father lives with them all now in Riverdale." Stupid, but he'd started to shiver. Was going to drop the dumb detonator any second. "Morris, I want you to explain to them. What this was all about and why it was so important. I want you to tell – to tell them what – what you can. Allow for security. That comes first. But tell them – everything you can, Morris." He placed a reluctant finger, seen through a web of night-nothings, over the firing key. "You do that for me, Morris? You do that, now?"

"Sure, Alan. I'll tell them."

"Good man, Morris." The first attempt to push the key didn't work. Concentrate on your hand, your finger. "Good man."

Tsherbakov came up to him at a run across the slope and ploughed up dust as he stopped abruptly. Leonid set Maria down on her feet, steadied himself as his foot slipped – and then grabbed Maria by her arm as she started to sag. Tsherbakov grabbed her other arm. His reflective visor showed Leonid's own helmet and visor, which showed Tsherbakov's tiny in a double convex image – an infinite series of two cosmonauts anonymous in sunlight on a mountain ridge on the Moon. Maria half hung and half stood between them, her visor up and her face flooded with harsh sunlight, her eyes closed.

Tsherbakov in Leonid's ears. "What *happened* to her?"

"Some fool was firing bullets at us. One hit her in the back. It must have wrecked the whole life-support systems. All the power is off and the whole oxygen reserve came out. That's why I thought she was dead. But it didn't puncture the suit."

"Obviously. Is she injured?"

"She might be. The bullet must have been stopped by something. Perhaps it's buckled something and driven it into her back."

"Bloody mess. Let's get her to the rover."

Then the ground trembled under their feet.

Leonid turned his head inside his helmet. He saw a white mist out in space in front of the bluff – like smoke blown into a sunbeam, its bottom edge a sharp diagonal line. It wasn't smoke. It was dust and debris. He snapped up his sunvisor and stared into the shadow, ignoring the dazzle from the ridge and the foreground and the far distance. He turned on his feet so as to shade the sun out of his eyes with the side of his own helmet.

In the shadow of the scarp below the bluff and silently, the mountainside had exploded. Plumes and streamers of it were shooting out into the void like a bursting cascade of water let out of the pipes at the base of a high dam. A springing surge of dust and rocks leaped in perfect arcs, out and over the terrace below. And under all the flying dust and debris the face of the mountainside was slipping, sliding, slithering down, a gathering cascade of rocks and rolling regolith tumbling and spilling off the inside of the north wall.

"Bloody hell!" Tsherbakov's voice was so loud it crashed through the headphones. "What have they done?"

"Rubbed it out." Through the plunging dust he watched the rolling avalanche sweep down across the terrace, a huge spill of vomited mountainside racing for the endless drop beyond the next edge. "They've rubbed out the evidence. They've killed themselves to do it." The avalanche reached the sun and the parked lander vehicle. The lander turned a little, slid backwards, tipped, and disappeared over the second scarp. "They've killed themselves. They're crazy."

The dust arcs were coming down out of the sunlight into shadow, rocks and rubble were rolling over the new talus carpet across the halfway filled-in terrace. Some of them followed the little spacecraft over the edge. Above the stalling landslide, bare rock jutted out of the stripped face of the bluff. No more impact site, no possibility of any wreckage to find. But who needed that kind of proof now anyway?

"Hey!" Tsherbakov said. "Maria!"

Maria Alova had collapsed between them and they didn't even notice as they held her. A human body is not so heavy on the Moon.

Morris Gates, Major Morris Elwood Gates, pushed with his arms and lifted his body up from the ground. Dry, perfectly dry dust streamed past the sides of his faceplate as he got himself clear of the dirt. He sat on his heels and pulled his hands out of the grit and rubble. Handfuls of the soil of the Moon. He let the dirt run through the fingers of his gloves, like alien time in an alien place, draining away. The gloved palms emptied. He brushed off the last dust grains that stuck halfheartedly by electrostatic attraction, patted and swept down his arms and shoulders, rubbed dust from the instrument windows on the little board mounted on his chest. Still alive, pressure in the suit one hundred per cent, and everything still working. How much luck do you need to survive without even a rip in your suit when so much rock and gravel falls on top of you and rolls right over you?

Not enough luck.

This time Browning had brought down the face of the mountain. Well – the powder on its face. All that was left up there was bare rock right up to the blinding crest of the bluff. So much suicidal success. Far too much success. He had seen the tide of streaming stone flow around and under the ADV, lift it, and carry it smoothly over the edge of the next precipice. So Browning had killed him, too. Two Russians at their base with Blue Bolt, another Russian up on the ridge with his gun, then himself, and now Major Morris Gates, aged thirty-three and never going to get a single day older. His instruments told him he was two hundred and twenty minutes into the EVA time. The PLSS on his back carried oxygen and power for three hundred and sixty minutes plus an independent thirty minute reserve. He had one hundred and seventy minutes left to live. Less than three hours.

He stood up, brushing dirt from the legs of his suit. In the right thigh pocket he had a gun, in the left thigh pocket that little piece of the EIS-1 rocket, the last bit of it still accessible to anyone at all. A self-defense weapon and a souvenir, and neither of them any use. He was as far away from anywhere as you could get, on the Far Side of the highest ground that could possibly matter to Earth. He was far too far away from everywhere. At least he was going to die in front of a marvelous, a magnificent, an indescribably monumental view. A little less splendid but also a little less alien – that might have been nice.

Maria Alova was unconscious by the time they got her strapped into one of the rover's seats and coupled to an umbilical. Plugged into the rover's communication circuit they could talk to her and try to get through to her. It was more than ten minutes before they got any response. It was another quarter of an hour before her head became halfway clear as the life-support unit scrubbed CO_2 from the air in her suit and renormalized the oxygen, and before its coolant circuit pumps gradually got her body temperature back to a safe level.

Tsherbakov thought he was crazy.

What was the point? The mad Americans had killed themselves, and what had they bloody well tried to do to Maria? What had Leonid shot one of them for – for fun, or to save Maria's life and quite probably his own? But Maria was safe on the rover's umbilical, and they would have to wait at least another half hour before she had recovered sufficiently to be more or less in control of herself again. So they couldn't drive away yet, anyway.

But he couldn't see anything. Standing almost on the lip of the precipice, next to the scuff and scrape marks in the dust where Maria had gone crawling for her life, his visor up and his hands shielding his eyes from the glare, he couldn't see anything in the shadow of the escarpment. Just the new loose ground down there, as motionless as if it had lain like that for a thousand, for a million, for a thousand million years. Would it stay undisturbed for so long a time, or would someone one day come here again, searching for bodies preserved perfectly in vacuum? Victims or heroes or however you looked at them, more corpses from the first little war ever fought on the Moon. The buried bodies and the wreckage would literally last for ever. In an eternal place like this the human race was really making its mark on the universe. Stamping its imprint into time. An imprint all too truthful.

It was a long time before he realized that by looking into the shadows he was searching in the wrong place. *There* was the shape, a piece of scalding white in the sun at the very edge of the terrace. He snapped down his visor against the glare. Two hundred metres below and at least three times as far away, a space-suited figure was sitting right at the edge of the next scarp in the gradually shrinking strip of sun. Perhaps he or she was looking down over the edge to where the wreckage of their lander lay, but it was almost as if the American was peacefully enjoying the magnificent view south into Schrödinger.

Leonid turned the selector on the instrument dial of his suit radio and rolled it back to the first bunch of frequencies the Americans were assumed to use. They weren't NASA frequencies, but the people who had come here were military astronauts, that was certain. Of course, the exercise was a complete waste of time if the American's radio was damaged, or even just switched off. He summoned up his English from its all too easy sleep and spoke into the ether. "Hello. Can you hear me? Answer on one-one-seven if you can hear me." The figure didn't move. The sun didn't move. Seconds slipped by. He rolled the frequency selector a fraction. "Hello. Can you hear me? Answer on one-one-nine if you can hear me."

The figure didn't move. The sun and the mountain and the Moon didn't move. Seconds slipped by.

Stravinsky's *Rite of Spring* came drifting down from the control center. Among the people working up there was someone with a semblance of culture, but how well did you have to know a piece of such disturbing and penetrating music before you could use it just as background sound? Perhaps the human being has a limitless capacity to trivialize.

Outside the little window, a dark moonscape swept somberly, secretly, to a black horizon. You peer from the strict confines of your own life at the dark material reality out of reach beyond. It was a tapestry of shadow and thin milk-white highlights, almost too alien to be beautiful, but too beautiful to be strange. Balanced a hand's-breadth above it was the brilliant sickle arc of the Earth, a silver rainbow on its back, a bent bow of cold fire pointing down to the approaching sun. In sixteen hours it would be sunrise on the Cordillera Mountains. Three days after that the transit ship would be in orbit and it would be time to go.

"How's she doing?"

"The wound was very nasty. The bullet bent the cover plate of the CO_2 scrubber and pushed it into her back – without puncturing her suit, of course. Our doctor says she's going to have a very bad scar, but the kidney is safe after all. She's all right."

"Good. That's good. You know, did I tell you your English is really good?"

"Oh – it isn't really good. I don't think so. It's all right."

Morris Gates shrugged and turned away from the window. "It's good. How many Americans do you think there are can speak decent Russian?"

This American was a brooding man, his mood as dark as his skin color. For some idiotic reason, that had been a surprise. He'd taken over twenty minutes to find a channel to contact the man. It had taken the American forever to pick his way across the avalanche scree and then scale the impossible gully beside the bluff. By the time he got to the top he was already on his emergency life-support reserve. The umbilical on the rover was incómpatible with the American suit, of course. By the time Tsherbakov had driven them back to the lander the new passenger was starting to suffocate. He traveled all the way with his cracked visor lowered against the sun. When they had got the interior of the lander flooded with air and the spacesuit took hold of its own helmet, twisted it and lifted it off, for some reason he had been expecting a blond, square-jawed, thick-necked white Anglo-Saxon protestant. Mórris Gates had been a surprise. All our stereotypes always let us down. Reality is different.

Leonid edged around his desk and sat in the working chair. The American took the hint and settled in the one and only second seat between the narrow door and the end of the desk. An American in the base, and a negro – that was a novelty that still hadn't worn off after eleven days. Tsherbakov was quietly furious – the man was technically a prisoner, not a celebrity. He didn't behave like a celebrity. He behaved like a man waiting to escape from a crisis in his life.

"I'll tell you the secret of superpower politics. That's the right term, isn't it? I'll tell you the secret. Simple. All Americans are ugly and fat."

No real response from Morris Gates.

"Everyone knows it, all over the world. Your TV stars are beautiful and thin, but all real Americans are ugly and fat. Every Russian knows it. And do you know what, too? All Russians are ugly and have short necks. All over the world everyone knows that, too. Every American knows it. That's the secret of superpower politics. All Americans are ugly and fat, and all Russians are ugly and have short necks."

Still no response from the man.

"Of course it isn't true. It's true for the ugly and fat Americans and for the ugly Russians with short necks, but that's all. But if you know it's true? Now look at you. You aren't the stereotype, not a bit the stereotype. And me –

well, I've got a short neck but my wife doesn't think I'm too ugly. But so-what? All Russians are ugly and have short necks. I never realized before an American told me. He was in the Soviet Union. He had been seeing Russians, he was being surrounded by nothing but Russians for days already. But he still knew the truth, his eyes couldn't deceive him, facts were what he knew, not what he saw. So it's true about the Russians, it's true about the Americans. It's *all* true, all the awful things we know about each other. The facts of the real world don't have a chance. So we all know that every Russian sticks bayonets into babies and rapes every woman, and we all know that every American shoots babies and makes all women into prostitutes. Just communist cruelty and capitalist corruption. Simple."

"So?"

"So things happen. The things that have just happened. I shouldn't be upset, but I am. Why are you upset?"

"Wouldn't you be? With such a mess. Such a fucking mess."

"Look, you should come here again in a year – next time I'm back as commandant. We've already shown you our monorail and all our facilities. Well in a year we'll have ilmenite mining and processing at our outstation between the Cordillera and Rook Mountains. We'll have a monorail line going right the way to it, and we'll be manufacturing water, oxygen, lander fuel, and refining materials here on site. In five years you'll be able to ride on the monorail right over the Rook Mountains and into the middle of the Mare Orientale. Then I'll show you radio dishes in a huge interferometry array screened from Earth. We'll be mining ilmenite and other minerals, we'll have processing factories. We'll be making our own building materials, and so much fuel that we can refuel the transiter ships in orbit here and send them back to Earth full." Leonid stopped, and shook his head. "But your people – some of them – will still know that the monorail is really a disguised railgun. We'll always know from now on that you have missiles aimed at us, even if we can never prove it. Your facts don't interest us and our facts don't interest you. And the really tricky thing about it is, I can't know if our facts about you are true or not, and you can't know if your facts about us are true or not. Because when the truth is what you know, and what you know is always something that somebody else tells you, you never know if *their* truth is facts or just something that *they* know is true. Do you? You are honest and I am honest, and we like to think that the people who tell us things are honest, too. Who knows who's wrong about what and when? That's the secret of superpower politics. That's the way we run the world."

"I'm not sure anyone's honest. Not even me." Morris Gates shrugged his shoulders, a loose drooping gesture, the helplessness of someone caught in someone else's act. "Is there a decision yet on how I get handed over?"

"Yes. The handover in Earth orbit is off. It seems we can't get enough publicity out of it. We can have cameras everywhere, but it goes too quickly." Leonid let his face show a regretful smile. "Oh yes, we've learned a lot from you Americans. For the next few weeks you're going to be the most well-known face on TV in every country in the world. We're going to show you on the transiter ship. We're using the *Vladimir Komarov*, they tell me, although it shouldn't be scheduled for this trip – but it's the first transiter, a famous ship. I was mission pilot on board for our first landing here. We're going to show you on the space station, and we're going to show you to everyone in Moscow for days. I'm –" He spread his hands in a little gesture of powerlessness. "I'm really sorry about that."

"Huh, what the heck." The American hunched forward, elbows on his knees. "What wouldn't we do if we'd caught one of you people in the same situation?"

"Oh we haven't caught you. We've rescued you. At least, they tell me that's the game we're suggesting to Washington." Leonid smiled again, more happily. Politics might block off all true communication, but basic human sympathy could still get through undiluted. "After all, between you and me, that souvenir of yours isn't any use to our side as evidence. So our people are going to try a little practical give and take. You call it give and take?"

The American nodded, then lifted his head again to look straight across the desk at Leonid. "Look, this situation's no good. There's too much else going on in the background and we have to talk past each other the whole time. Can I get in touch with you? Keep contact somehow? I mean, you pulled me out of there at Schrödinger."

This time Leonid's smile was spontaneous. "Why not? We can try. Yes, that's a *good* idea. I'll give you my Moscow address for writing letters – you might have trouble with Star City. But I have to warn you, my written English is terrible."

"Well my Russian's non-existent. Da, nyet, and that's it."

"Perhaps next time we're on the Moon together we can talk, too. I don't think your bosses or my bosses are going to permit visits between bases for years. This isn't Antarctica, after all – it's strategically significant high ground. But now that everyone's been reminded that real accidents might also happen, there's an idea floating about that we should make a channel available over Selenos-10 between our base here and yours at Armstrong. NASA and Intercosmos like the idea, although our State Committee on Space Defense and your Space Force are very suspicious."

"When this is over I'm going to quit Space Force. Just hope I can switch to NASA and still get tours of duty on the Moon without being blocked as a security risk or something like that by the Defense Department. Maybe they'll be on a tighter leash for a while after this mess. But I want to get back here. You see, the Moon is – is –" The man shook his head. A light came back to his eyes. "I don't know how to say it. Splendid. Magnificent. The highest ground you can climb. But in some way – in some way. I don't know how to say it."

"The Moon is beautiful," Leonid said. "Very harsh but very beautiful. But beautiful in a way we don't have words for. Our languages are for the experiences of Earth, perhaps. The experience here is different."

"Maybe that's it. Just different." Morris Gates stared for a moment at the inaccessible reality on the other side of the opaque wall. "But it's wonderful. It gets to you."

Leonid Steffanovich Shalyapin nodded. "Yes." In his tiny office cabin inside the little base on a barren mountain range on the side of the Moon, three days up from Earth and on the edge of the rest of the Solar System, he nodded again, slowly. "It does. It really does."

Memorandum, November 10. Personal and confidential.
From: United States Ambassador, Moscow.
To: Secretary of State, State Department.
Subject: Summary to attached Report and Videotape (Gates/
Soviet State Committee on Space Defense).

In less oblique terms I would summarize our meeting with the
foreign secretary as follows.

We were shown orbital photographs of the Schrödinger site
taken before and after the incident of October 16. Clearly
indicated was a fresh and unusually formed (i.e. flat on the
slope) impact scar before the incident, and after the incident
a major ground collapse erasing the scar, together with the
identifiable wreckage of an ADV part way down the slope
between the first and second terraces. We were shown impeccable evidence on the impact dynamics and the rock type from
the impact at their base on the Cordillera Mountains that demonstrate a lunar origin for the rock and a launch point near enough
to Tsiolkovsky to fix Aldrin as the site. We were also shown
photographs of the modified 9mm Beretta taken from Gates
with a clearly recognizable USSF serial number, together with
a chemical analysis of the special lubricant it contained. We were
further shown photographs of the 9mm round dug out of the
personal life-support pack of the injured cosmonaut Alova. My
estimate is that the best we could get away with internationally
on that evidence is a hung jury except for our closest allies,
insofar as they can be relied upon.

The videotape is another matter. Major Gates gives a full
account of what happened on Clean Sweep and of the essentials
of Blue Bolt as far as he apparently knows them. As you will
agree upon viewing the copy, he is obviously neither drugged
nor suffering from any form of ill-treatment. I guess in defense

of Gates you might conclude he was acutely depressed at the nature and outcome of the operation, and probably in large measure embarrassed at being rescued by the people that primarily Blue Bolt, but also supportively Clean Sweep, were designed to kill. Possible disciplinary measures are an internal matter for Space Force. The videotape, however, will hang us in the international community at large.

I therefore strongly recommend acceptance of the deal they are offering. In return for not publishing their evidence of what the foreign secretary termed our acts of war perpetrated on the Moon, we should cease what they call our defamatory campaign concerning their use of space defense lasers against targets in South Africa, together with a stop on further public claims that they are constructing a laser or kinetic weapon for Earth interdiction at their lunar facility.

I know that one is going to be hard for certain people in other departments to swallow, and I know the White House will have to do a complete turnaround on a couple of points, but at least the president should see that they are making it easy for us by proposing to go along with a scientific accident story. To say it in plain terms, they have us over a barrel.

Frank Simons, Cape Town

Smoke hangs over Cape Town again. ANC forces are firing a continuous barrage of rockets against defensive positions established on Table Mountain. Many of the rockets fall short and explode in the city center or the suburbs of Woodstock, Observatory or Rondebosch. Already largely burned to the ground, Cape Town is beginning to resemble the field of ruins of a German city after the Second World War.

The evacuation is proceeding from the Atlantic shoreline protected by the shield of Table Mountain, Lion's Head and Signal Hill. The members of the Emergency Government have all gone. They are safe on board ships prepared to carry them to their next destinations in Europe or North and South America. Where the exiles will come to rest is still not clear, nor is it a matter of much concern here among those still remaining. Something like 5,000 troops and 20,000 destitute civilians are still camping in the city. The only way of escape for the civilians seems to be the helicopters which are ferrying a steady stream of refugees to the American warships cruising offshore. The alternative route, across the front line which is creeping hourly nearer through the rubble of the outer suburbs, is seen by most to be nothing short of madness.

The defending troops have no heavy equipment, and resupply is all but non-existent. Any military intervention by the USA that they might have hoped for has failed to materialize. The enemy is now overwhelming both in numbers and equipment, the rest of the world is not prepared to burn its hands in an attempt to rescue the defenders, and their government has fled the fortress it promised to build on the Cape. They have been sacrificed, and they know it. The eventual fate of these last abandoned loyalists will be decided within a very few days at the most. The time has come to write an epitaph for white South Africa.

The Pretoria regime has been described both as the West's most stalwart African ally, and as a grotesque and historically antiquated remnant of the self-satisfied belief that God created the world and the rest of its inhabitants for the exclusive pleasure of the white man. This war has been a second Vietnam, this time by proxy. It is a total defeat, a foreign policy debacle for the United States and a moral and political abdication by the governments of Western Europe. The apologist may take one of two possible standpoints: the West has done all it conceivably could to aid Pretoria in its struggle against communist aggression, but lost the war to communism just the same; alternatively, the West has made the terrible mistake of supporting an unsupportable dictatorship of one race over another, thus paving the way for an inevitable communist takeover. Both positions amount to the same thing – backing the wrong side from the very start. The lesson for the pragmatist is a simple one. Whoever oppresses members of another ethnic group by the imposition of measures backed up by naked force and terror, may indeed be a gross monster. But any minority that imposes its will in such a way upon a numerically vast majority is in the final analysis a band of utter fools.

Moral judgement, however, is not concerned with the practicalities of political games played across the face of the world, but with the motives, doings and fates of single human beings.

Morally, the evil of racism in South Africa has been a simple case, it seems to me. But a war is not the way to cleanse any land of its sins. Wars may produce a handful of heroes, but they produce far too many dead.

Excerpt of press briefing with Barbara-Ann Schwaetzer, White House spokeswoman, November 28th.

SCHWAETZER: Ladies and gentlemen, the statement concerns the events of October 16th as first reported here and in Moscow on November 12th, although of course the Soviet Government jumped the gun a little by announcing their rescue of Major Gates before the end of October. Well, I guess you can forgive them for seeking a little good publicity when you consider the kind of thing they're generally up to in this world. The statement is intended to clarify a couple of points on the degree of American-Soviet cooperation on the Moon, and the position of this newly re-elected Administration towards events up there during the course of this year. Okay, the statement is as follows.

This Administration wishes to emphasize its appreciation of the Soviet rescue of Major Morris Gates from otherwise certain death after the landslip on the north wall of Schrödinger on the Far Side of the Moon, on October 16th this year. The landslip led directly to the tragic death of Colonel Alan Browning, leader of the two-man expedition attempting to gather data on the nature and course of the meteorite which impacted at Schrödinger on June 27th this year. This meteorite is believed to have been associated with the one which struck the Soviet base on that day and led to the deaths of two cosmonauts. The purpose of the expedition was to seek further data on the two meteorites with a view to identifying the previously unknown parent cloud of meteoric debris orbiting the sun and crossing the path of the Earth. This effort has unfortunately failed, the landslip having erased all recoverable scientific data. Colonel Browning and Major Gates flew the mission to Schrödinger in preference to scientific astronauts in view of the extremely hazardous nature of the landing site, a hazard which unhappily has been confirmed. The coincidentally timed Soviet mission to the site was able to rescue Major Gates after the landslip had destroyed the Ascent-Descent Vehicle. Information and photographs supplied by Moscow confirm that no further mission to the Schrödinger site can usefully be undertaken, and that the location is no longer amenable to a landing. It therefore remains extremely doubtful whether at some future time an attempt can be made to recover the body of Colonel Browning. Three human beings have now died on the Moon, all victims of a freak cosmic accident. That such random forces can cause death on both sides of the great political divide which separates our peoples, and that scientific co-operation and the rescue of individuals can be undertaken despite our political differences, only serves to bring the two superpowers to a closer mutual understanding.

Well, that's the press statement. Now before we move on to questions on the issues of the day, I'd like to add one more point while we're still on this subject. I think we should emphasize one last time that the resignation of Secretary of Defense Mackover is in no way connected with the accident at Schrödinger. It's true that Secretary Mackover felt a personal shock at the death of Colonel Browning – he had after all approved the suggestion from Space Force that their people could attempt the mission – but such an undertaking is not his responsibility, nor would the outcome be in any way a reason to withdraw from public life. I'd like to reiterate that Secretary Mackover has resigned purely on grounds of ill health. He wished to do so for some little time, but chose to stay on the team until the president had been safely elected for a second term. I think that shows you the kind of man Willard Mackover really is.

Internal Memorandum USSF December 18.
From: Earth Interdiction Strategy Reassessment Group.
For: Chief of Staff Office, United States Space Force.
Subject: Program Suspension.

1 Extreme vulnerability to attack of any feasible lunar installation as demonstrated by the execution of Blue Bolt.

2 Relative ineffectiveness of an EIS-1 or EIS-2 system due

to the low density of targets in the Soviet strategic missile defense shield, plus ineffectiveness of an EIS-3 laser against terrestrial ground targets compared with existing near-Earth systems.

3 Apparent suspension of Soviet planned construction of an EIS installation at Mare Orientale effectively removes the imminent threat of Soviet supremacy in EIS systems.

4 Recent upward revision of cost estimates by a further 25% makes the entire concept of EIS systems less attractive as proposed.

5 Potential hostility in Congress to new-program funding, coupled with the risk of a re-discussion of Blue Bolt and Clean Sweep.

The conclusion of the Reassessment Group is that while the EIS concept remains valid and program leads should be conserved to allow a rapid restart should the USSR resume its drive to establish its own EIS system, further funding for EIS development should not be sought and the program should be shelved indefinitely.

Extract from interview with Dr Beverly Ryle, resident science director at Armstrong, by permission of Transworld-Telenews-2.

TTN-2: Coming back to the development of the entire complex here, would you say that the Blue Bolt affair had a positive or a negative effect on the way things have gone?

RYLE: Oh that old business again. Now you're not really going to ask me my opinion on that? The public discussion flared up years ago, and the thing itself actually happened two years further back than that.

TTN-2: But you were personally involved, and we're right here on the Moon, on the ground where it all happened. So I just wondered if Blue Bolt really hurt the Moon Program.

RYLE: I don't think it did. These kinds of issues are never that clear, but you might even say it helped. At least insofar as it shifted some of the emphasis away from military considerations and back to science and exploration and development. It was more or less as a direct result of Blue Bolt that the Earth interdiction strategy idea was canceled. Of course, all that came out a couple of years later.

TTN-2: Now that's a point I'd like to hear your views on. Ever since it came out, no one has been able to say who really blew the lid off the affair by first tipping off the media, although there has been a hardening of theories over the last twelve months. Who do you personally believe leaked it?

RYLE: You're angling for Joseph Hyland, I just know it.

TTN-2: Well quite a lot of people do seem to have concluded he was in the best position to know, and had the best reasons to want to embarrass the Administration at the time of his dismissal.

RYLE: You know, I think people have started to point the finger at Hyland just because he was killed in that car smash last year and can't defend himself, so it's convenient to try to pin it on him. Sure, he was instrumental at the time in ensuring the matter was opened up and properly investigated. He was the one who knew his way around well enough to put the right people in contact with each other to catalyze the investigation. But he really did arrange, you might say, for the whole thing to be handled strictly constitutionally *and* confidentially. Now he didn't have to do it that way, did he? One of the big liberal newspapers was just a telephone away. I feel sure the issue at the time for him was responsibility and political accountability, although I've never spoken with him over it.

TTN-2: And you really don't think Hyland leaked it later?

RYLE: I don't *know*, but I don't think so from the way he originally handled it. And just think how many people in and out of Congress and the relevant departments and agencies knew about it by then. All those people who were happy to take it up and make sure it all came out once the ball started rolling.

TTN-2: But if it wasn't Hyland, then who do you think it might have been?

RYLE: Well that I really don't know. I can tell you for certain some people it definitely wasn't. For a start, it wasn't Maclaughlin, even though she had quite a bit to say when she was asked. I mean, maybe you wouldn't lose your job as head of the Moon Program just for leaking something from the past, but you certainly *wouldn't* get the job of head of NASA if you'd been going around embarrassing people. Besides which, she told me years ago it wasn't her, and I believe her absolutely. It also wasn't me, and it wasn't Morris Gates. You can believe it, otherwise I wouldn't be sitting here and he wouldn't be Surface Flight Operations Manager. It's no secret that in the space business appointments are screened for basic security reliability and political acceptability, and NASA is inevitably right in the middle of that. We still work closely with the Defense Department on some things.

TTN-2: You don't have any suspects you privately prefer?

RYLE: I'd have to confess to a few. It would have to be someone who was right in the center at the time, had the chance to know exactly what happened and who did what. Someone in the Defense Department. Or at the White House, maybe. But I guess that's just something we'll never know.

TTN-2: You were caught right up in it at the time. In fact it was the way you were treated which set the original investigation in motion. What did it mean to you personally? Do you resent the way you were treated?

RYLE: You mean the CIA surveillance? I still resent that now, ten years on. When that's done to you and you realize it, well it really hurts and gets you wondering some about the values of the society you live in. But that's all over and done with, and the important thing for me is that it *didn't* damage my career after all. Wrecked my marriage, though. Well no – to be fair, the marriage was already heading for the rocks although I hadn't realized up to then. It just provided one more crisis than the thing could take. But all that's not important any more.

TTN-2: What's your personal assessment of the Blue Bolt operation?

RYLE: In just a few words? I think the world was a whole lot luckier than it realizes. It's nothing short of a miracle that only two people were killed at the Soviet base and that the entire place wasn't wiped out by a direct hit. Couple that with the fact that the Soviet Union had just landed a major success in southern Africa, and you probably have the reason why their reaction was so incredibly measured. Otherwise that might have been the one and only big bang. Instead it got the military braked enough to bring them back to being a more or less equal partner in space, which was more in line with the original idea of the highest ground.

TTN-2: Well that brings us right back to the motivations of Hyland and also of Maclaughlin.

RYLE: It was their creation in a sense, wasn't it? I mean the *label* on the concept that gave it enough focus to get up the political will to do it. Maclaughlin told me once about her first meeting with Hyland. That was way back in 1985. You know, he invited her to a meal just to talk over the notion of getting a major promotional drive together. The idea was to secure the commitment to space and see it through to the point where it would be respectable in the only way that really counts in any society, namely self-financing. Obviously the military angle was the lever to pull to get funding in the climate of the times and the years that followed, but what they were looking for was a concept to fit over individual programs so as to push manned spaceflight, exploration and science. People like that, even more than people like us, they're the real pioneers. They *believe* in the promise of space. Did you know, right at that first meeting, before the meal was even over, they had the highest ground already worked out as a name for it, although it didn't start into general use until years later?

TTN-2: And how has it worked out, the highest ground?

RYLE: Well, it got us to the Moon, didn't it? Here we are in a base with a permanent staff of over one hundred. A self-supporting and fuel and materials *exporting* science and manufacturing center on the Moon. This year Armstrong is actually *earning* money for the Government. Up here we're supporting all Earth-to-Moon transit traffic and already some

Earth-orbit traffic, we're supporting Aldrin over on Far Side, and we're the supply source for the establishing of Collins Base over in the Sea of Tranquility. We're building our first Clarke launcher to cut the cost of shipping products into lunar and Earth orbit, and definitely *not* any kind of railgun. In another five years maybe we'll *finally* catch up with the Russians at Mare Orientale. So I'd say – well I say it worked is all.

MAX MARLOW

HER NAME WILL BE FAITH

'National American Broadcasting Service. The latest report from the Hurricane Centre is that Hurricane Faith is still moving north-west at 20 knots.

'Reports from Crooked Point and Coney Island already indicate considerable flooding. Experts predict that if the tidal surge reaches 40 feet, New York could be threatened by the worst flooding known in recent years. 200 m.p.h. winds have already been recorded . . .'

Only NABS's new weatherman had warned that Faith's change of course was possible. Everyone, city authorities, police, station chiefs, had ignored him.

Until now when disaster was howling down on an unprepared city, built mostly less than 40 feet above sea level . . .

POST A LITTLE HAPPINESS

Post·A·Book

A Royal Mail service in association with the Book Marketing Council & The Booksellers Association
Post-A-Book is a Post Office trademark.

JAMES PATTERSON

BLACK MARKET

The threat was absolute:

At 5.05 pm Wall Street will be destroyed.

No demands, no ransom, no negotiations. A multiple firebombing would wipe out the financial heart of America. Stop the world's financial system dead.

There was just one extra point: a demonstration – just in case the threat wasn't taken seriously.

At 9.20 am Pier 33–34, once the docking point for the great trans-Atlantic liners, was destroyed. A sudden fire storm; flames rising four hundred feet over the Hudson River. Within minutes nothing left but a glowing red hot metal skeleton, cranes toppled, transit sheds gutted . . .

The threat was real. All emergency systems blared into life. The countdown to catastrophe had begun . . .

'*Black Market* thrills as you read and sticks. It's topical, terrifying and so totally believable'
    Anne Tolstoi Wallach, author of *Women's Work*

'A real nail biter'
    Douglas Terman, author of *First Strike*

'Every few years a really irresistible thriller comes along. *Black Market* was impossible to stop once I began. The first sixty pages mark the best opening to a thriller that I have ever read'
    Thomas T. Noguchi, author of *Coroner*

HODDER AND STOUGHTON PAPERBACKS

THOMAS BLOCK

SKYFALL

The in-flight movie was an old Robert Redford.

Enjoyable make-believe for the passengers on Trans Continental's Flight 42, outward bound from Los Angeles to Osaka, Japan.

At 2.30 am, 43,000 feet and nearly 600 mph over the darkened Pacific, the reading lights were flicking out as Flight Attendant Kathy Davis and her cabin crew padded the dimly lit aisles, settling their charges for the night. All was warm and lullingly calm.

Yet for Kathy, seeing among the passengers her former lover, ex-airline pilot Ron Jennings happily travelling with his wife and daughter, Flight 42 was already an unhappy, turbulent trip. A long painful night lay ahead . . .

Then, suddenly, everything changed.

The bomb had been carefully packed into the stainless steel washbasin of one of the First Class toilets. On the mirror behind it was a note:

This is a hijacking. Do not touch this radio-controlled bomb or it will explode. Several hijackers onboard with three more bombs. More information in one hour.

Enjoyable make-believe was about to turn into brutal, terrifying reality for everyone on Flight 42.

HODDER AND STOUGHTON PAPERBACKS

GORDON STEVENS

PEACE ON EARTH

Three photographs.

The first some thirty years old: a young couple, their children in their arms. The only known likeness of the Palestinian now known as Abu Nabil.

The second recent: a grainy newspaper shot of a Belfast street. Kneeling by the bomb-blasted child, a British soldier, an undercover SAS man caught and recorded by the chance of a free-lance's flash.

The last, a two-family snap outside a Moscow station. A farewell, tearful but hopeful: one family going at last to Israel, the other still condemned to wait.

Three photographs.

Still to come, the hijack, the sweating tension of the night-lit airport, the heart-rending glimpses of the hostages. The full terrible drama of a countdown to death.

HODDER AND STOUGHTON PAPERBACKS

MORE TITLES AVAILABLE FROM HODDER AND STOUGHTON PAPERBACKS

MAX MARLOW

☐ 50101 9   Her Name Will Be Faith   £4.50

JAMES PATTERSON

☐ 40226 6   Black Market   £2.95

THOMAS BLOCK

☐ 41555 4   Skyfall   £3.50

GORDON STEVENS

☐ 42211 4   Peace on Earth   £3.50

All these books are available at your local bookshop or newsagent, or can be ordered direct from the publisher. Just tick the titles you want and fill in the form below.

Prices and availability subject to change without notice.

HODDER AND STOUGHTON PAPERBACKS, P.O. Box 11, Falmouth, Cornwall.

Please send cheque or postal order, and allow the following for postage and packing:

U.K. – 55p for one book, plus 22p for the second book, and 14p for each additional book ordered up to a £1.75 maximum.

B.F.P.O. and EIRE – 55p for the first book, plus 22p for the second book, and 14p per copy for the next 7 books, 8p per book thereafter.

OTHER OVERSEAS CUSTOMERS – £1.00 for the first book, plus 25p per copy for each additional book.

Name ....

Address ....

....